SIREN SONG

CAT ADAMS

SIREN SONG

A Tom Doherty Associates Book New York

SIREN SONG

A Tor Book
Published by Tom Doherty Associates, LLC
175 Fifth Avenue
New York, NY 10010

www.tor-forge.com

Tor® is a registered trademark of Tom Doherty Associates, LLC.

ISBN 978-0-7653-2495-5

First Edition: October 2010

Printed in the United States of America

0 9 8 7 6 5 4 3 2 1

DEDICATION

As always, we would first like to dedicate this book to Cie's son, James, and Cathy's husband, Don, and to our families and friends. Special thanks to Merrilee Heifetz and the staff at Writers House, to our wonderful editor, Melissa, and all the other wonderful folks at Tor who have helped us so much. A special thank-you to my brother, Timothy Adams, to the folks at the Jim Butcher forums, and to K. Segovia, for assistance with research. Thank you so much. You're the best!

A NOTE TO READERS

In our opinion, for the most part, happy families do not make for interesting reading. We don't know why. They do, however, make for happy writers. But every time a writer creates a character with a particularly troubled background (or a kinky sexual bent) it seems that somebody in the "real world" assumes that the writer is working from personal experience. So allow us to state for the record that Celia Graves's background and troubles are all her own. They do not reflect any personal experience on the part of either of the authors.

Part of the fun of writing is research. In order to make the fantasy portions more believable, you have to be very careful to get the "real" portions right. Still, inevitably, some glitches slip in. The setting of this book is Southern California. We created a fictional city in Santa Maria de Luna and slapped it down on the coast between San Juan Capistrano and Oceanside, right on top of Camp Pendleton, which obviously doesn't exist in this reality (our apologies to the Marine Corps). Just as we created our own city, we came up with a university and rehab facility. We have used an Egyptian scrying system that is similar to a modern one but have given it its own name and made major changes to it. We have also deliberately taken liberty with dual citizenship and diplomatic immunity.

One or two scenes are set in actual locations. While those portions of the book were researched heavily, it is possible that errors slipped in. If so, please forgive us.

Cat Adams

Fan Information

Fans who wish to sign up for our newsletter can contact us at catadamsfans@gmail.com. Our website is located at http://www.catadams.net.

SIREN SONG

1

C**elia, everything's** going to be fine. You'll see."
Dr. Scott gazed at me earnestly in the back of the sleek
black limo, willing me with every fiber of his being to
believe the words.

Unfortunately, no matter how sincere the assurance of the
handsome, dark-skinned psychiatrist with slightly silvered hair
and a calming demeanor, we both knew he was lying. Nothing
was ever going to be *fine* again. A week ago I was an ordinary
human bodyguard, living a normal life in beautiful California.
Now I was part vampire, part siren, and struggling to maintain
not only my sense of self but also my sense of humor. He
wasn't helping either one with that line.

I raised my brows at him as I gave him the snort his words
deserved. My first meeting with him had resulted in my
stalking his secretary like a deer—complete with fangs bared
and red eyes glowing. I'd even chased the good doctor out of
the room in a panic. I hadn't been safe to talk to until after he
locked me inside his office with a full pitcher of barely cooked
beef juices, which in my sunset-induced predator mode I'd
happily sucked down like a strawberry milk shake.

I was still trying not to think about what I might have done without that pitcher of bloody juice. It had only been a few days ago and dawn was still hours away.

His expression changed as though he knew what I was thinking. I was aware that Dr. Scott was telepathic, but ethics and the law should prevent him from "peeking" outside of official therapy sessions. Still, he couldn't miss my physical reaction to his statement, and after a staring match where he blinked first, he finally had the decency to look chagrined.

The sound of the driver's door of the limo slamming shut shifted my attention away from Dr. Scott, giving him the opportunity to fiddle with the buttons on the side panel. Probably looking for another stiff drink to bolster him for the start of this adventure. We were on the way to Birchwoods, an ultraprivate psychiatric facility for the very rich and famous, where I was to be *evaluated* before I had to appear to defend myself against charges of mind manipulation.

While I'm neither rich nor famous, I'm not poor, either, and it was *so* worth the money to stay in a place that might someday release me. St. Mary's Detention Center was the only other choice outside of the state facility. But it's only licensed for short-term care, and with the looming legal problems caused by my newfound physical and psychic abilities I could be looking at a very long-term, even permanent, commitment.

My brow furrowed suddenly, because I felt . . . something. It was similar to the odd, pins-and-needles tingling sensation that I was beginning to associate with magical barriers. I'd never been able to get even a hint of the magical before the vampire bite. Now I'm aware of far too much. It was actually getting painful to walk around Los Angeles, since the city is the hotbed of magic you'd expect. The more power magic wielders use to guard mansions, protect movie stars, and banish evil forces from public buildings, the more intense it feels to me. This one *hurt*.

I sat bolt upright in my seat, actually flinching when I heard the automatic locks click with what felt like an ominous finality.

"What's wrong?" As a trained observer of human behavior, Dr. Scott didn't like the vibe I was giving off. He was suddenly very alert and looked completely businesslike.

"Maybe nothing," I answered. My voice stayed steady but sounded uneasy. It didn't feel like nothing. I could sense pressure building, making me want to wiggle my jaw like you do in an airplane to get your ears to pop. There are protective spells that can be used to keep moving objects, including vehicles, from damage. But they're hideously expensive, difficult to do, and create enough friction when a car is in motion to make any model a gas hog. A limo like this one was built like a tank. It shouldn't need that kind of a spell. But if it wasn't a protection spell, then what was it?

Maybe it was the liquor I'd just imbibed at the wake for my recently deceased best friend, Vicki, that had me feeling slow, but I couldn't think of a single reason for the powerful spell I'd sensed. Yes, I'd gone to college to get a preternatural degree. But at the time, I hadn't been able to *feel* magic. It's one thing to know that forces like gravity exist and relate the properties on a test paper. It's another entirely to feel the weight of it on your skin and know something's not right. Which made me suspicious. Well, more suspicious. I've been a bodyguard so long that I'm always a little bit paranoid. "Can you sense the driver?"

The car moved smoothly away from the curb, fitting nicely in between the pair of police cruisers I could see through the window . . . barely. Mostly I just saw my reflection on the inside of the glass. The woman I saw was attractive but cold, hard. It was my "business face." I use it a lot. So often that sometimes even I forget the softer me exists.

"That would be illegal." Dr. Scott didn't bother to hide the disapproval in his voice. It was combined with the stern look of an instructor.

I shook my head. "No, Doctor. Reading his mind is illegal. Just sensing to see if he's 'there' isn't." It was a fine distinction, but I was learning a lot about those as my attorney and I prepared for my upcoming trial. I had one of the best defense attorneys in the business. If he was successful, I would be a free, if considerably less wealthy, woman. I could live with that. If I stayed out of jail or a psychiatric facility, I could always earn more money.

I pretended not to notice Dr. Scott staring at me, concentrating instead on the scene outside the glass. We'd turned left. It wouldn't have been a big deal except for one little detail. We were supposed to be heading for Birchwoods, on Ocean View. The nearest exit to Ocean View was three blocks down and on the right.

Dr. Scott's eyes locked with mine in the glass. If he was checking my thoughts, I couldn't tell. At the moment I wouldn't even mind. Best for him to find out for himself that I wasn't joking. I was beginning to suspect we were in very real trouble. I watched his reflection as he pursed his lips thoughtfully. As he seemed to reach a decision, his face went distant and blank for a few seconds.

"That's odd. I can't sense him at all." He sounded puzzled and not altogether happy.

I turned to face him. "Null?" I made it a question. Psychic nulls were rare but not unheard of. I'd very briefly been assigned to a shrink who was a null. She was completely immune to magic and to psychic manipulation. Which would've made her the perfect doctor for someone like me if she hadn't also been one of the bad guys. As it was, her drugging me and setting me up for murder had started the chain of events leading up to my current legal woes—and did absolutely nothing for my trust issues with psychiatrists.

"No. It feels more as if I'm being blocked."

I wouldn't have thought I could tense any further, but I did as adrenaline pumped through my system. We'd just taken another left turn. While I couldn't be sure, yet, it appeared we were en route to the desert, where there was miles and miles of nothing . . . right up until you got to the state-run facility for "rogue" monsters and psychics.

"Doctor, are you lying to me?" There was a growling, hissing tone to my voice and my skin had started to glow, giving off a pale, gray-green light that filled the darkened passenger compartment like water in a pool. It was decidedly spooky. In just a few days I've grown to hate it, but right now it might prove useful in scaring the doctor. If he was scared maybe, just maybe, he'd be honest with me. Of course, getting angry was liable to push the limits of my control over the monster in me. But I needed the truth and I didn't have a lot of options as to how I was going to get it.

He shrugged but was more interested in concentrating on whatever was pushing him away. "Why would I lie?"

I waved my hand in front of his face to grab his attention and then pointed. "Look out the window."

He tried, even going so far as to press his nose to the glass. "I can barely see through the tinting. What am I looking for?"

No surprise there. I had the advantage of vampire-style vision. "Try looking out through the sunroof." I toned back on the spookometer. I wasn't scaring the doctor so much as pissing him off. I couldn't be positive, but I was beginning to think he didn't know any more about what was going on than I did, that maybe his choosing to ride in the limo with me had been an unexpected complication for whoever was running this little show.

He stood up, flattening his hand against the seat to steady himself from the vehicle's movement and the drinks he'd had earlier, at the wake. He'd been Vicki's doctor, too. He had to push into the invisible barrier surrounding the car and I felt an odd lurch in my stomach as it stretched to accommodate his movement. He noticed it, too, and pushed against it, smoothing his hands along to test the barrier like a mime on a street corner.

"We're going the wrong way. We're headed toward the desert." He sounded honestly shocked, afraid, and more than a little sick.

"Yes." My voice could've frosted the glass as I watched the lights of the city become swallowed up by the darkness.

I had to give the man credit. He had brains. "You think I set you up?" There was a hint of caution in his voice. Not fear.

He was too tough for that. But he was bright enough to not want to be locked alone in the back of a limo with an angry monster. Taking me to the state facility would most assuredly piss me off.

"The thought did occur to me," I admitted.

I watched as he waved his arm slowly.

"What are you doing?"

"We've got a police escort. I'm trying to get their attention. But they don't seem to see me."

I doubted that. More likely they thought he was being cute and drunk. Or they were just ignoring him. Whichever.

He lowered himself carefully onto the seat. Leaning back, he closed his eyes. "And I can assure you that if I'd intended to turn you over to the state, I would not be stupid enough to ride in the car with you. And as I told you before, I wouldn't consign a rabid dog to the state facilities."

I gave him a humorless smile. "I remember that."

"Oh good." His voice practically dripped sarcasm. "So now what?"

"Let me try your cell phone."

He blinked at me but reached inside his suit jacket to retrieve it. He was slower on the uptake than normal. The result of the liquor, no doubt, but not particularly helpful. My own inebriation was long gone. There are a few benefits to my partially undead body.

"If I'm just being paranoid, it should work just fine," I explained as he passed the top-of-the-line tech toy to me.

"And if it doesn't?"

I punched the number for Alex's cell phone. Vicki's former lover had been at the wake, so she should still be close by. She was also a cop. She could find out if this was legit. If it wasn't, she could get us help. Assuming I could get a call through.

He watched expectantly as I waited for the telltale ringing and instead heard only crackling static. *Damn.* I hit the "end" button and flipped the phone closed. The adrenaline that began to flow through my muscles was both invigorating and annoying. It wasn't just danger that was making my body tense. The abrupt rush of fear from Dr. Scott had me alert and watching his every movement. Yes, I'd had my requisite nutrition shakes and no, I wasn't hungry. But hunting is about more than just *feeding* and I was getting twitchy.

When I didn't answer, he repeated his question: "And if it doesn't?"

It wasn't an *if* anymore—just a statement of fact. "We're screwed."

2

So, calling for help didn't work. No surprise. I passed the phone back to him and he tucked it into the inner pocket of his suit jacket, his fingers trembling just the tiniest bit. I could hardly blame him, so I did my best to ignore it. Fortunately, now that I realized the situation, years of training and therapy kicked in and the dread of an unknown future faded into the background. "We need a plan." My voice was nicely calm. I doubted that the good doctor had any clue just how impressive that was.

He raised a single, eloquent eyebrow.

"Dr. Scott, have you ever been kidnapped?" My voice was as coldly polite as I could manage. I was not hysterical, though I deserved to be. But I've been in life-threatening crises before. While you never get used to it, you learn control, to cope. Either that or you lose your mind. So far I've hung on to my sanity. Barely.

"Of course not!" he snapped.

"Lucky you. I have." I forced myself not to shudder at memories I prefer to leave in the past. I'd been kidnapped as a child, by men who wanted my little sister to use her talent with the dead to find them treasure, like they'd read of a little boy doing in Florida. I had scars, physical and mental, but I'd gotten through it. She hadn't. My sister's ghost is a daily reminder of the experience. She'd attached to me after death and, much like Vicki—whose ghost had been the life of the party at her own wake—we weren't really certain what business she had yet to complete while she was tied to this realm.

Oh, and I'd also been drugged and set up for a murder charge just a few short days ago. "Trust me, this is the fun part. It only gets worse from here. If you're not going to help me, I suggest you stay the hell out of my way. Because I don't intend to go down quietly."

He took his time thinking about that. I knew he knew at least part of my history, medical and psychological. He was Vicki's doctor, after all, and she knew the whole story. He'd also personally assigned the doctor who betrayed me after I was bitten by a vampire. In my opinion, if he'd vetted her a bit more carefully, she wouldn't have been able to slip me a "roofie" and set me up for murder.

Bad things seem to follow me like a far-too-devoted puppy. I don't know why. But my past experiences give me a certain insight in situations like this.

He was obviously thinking hard. While he did, he reached over to the bar and began fixing us each a drink. Scotch, neat, poured into little plastic cups. Liquid courage. I sniffed to make sure it wasn't drugged. Still, I didn't take a drink until after he did with no ill effects.

"How do you propose to do anything with us trapped like this?"

I didn't answer him directly. Instead, I raised my face to the open sunroof. "Ivy. I need you." I was pretty sure she'd answer. Ivy is always with me. Of course, since she was only a child when she was murdered, her power and her perceptions are limited. But I'd sent Vicki away to rest after the party, so Ivy was all I had available.

The temperature in the limo dropped precipitously. Magical barriers have little effect on the dead unless they're intentionally set to keep them out. Dr. Scott started to shiver as frost began forming on the inside surface of the tinted windows. My sister was here. His eyes widened and I saw him withdraw a small spiral notebook and a pen from a jacket pocket. Yeah, in his position, this sort of thing was probably worth taking notes on.

I whispered quietly in case the backseat was bugged, "Can you blow a tire on the car for me? Maybe even pull the plug wires?" It was asking a lot. I knew that. But I knew she could do it . . . just. At least the tire. I wasn't positive she knew what plug wires looked like. She was only eight when she died, and so far it seemed to me that what she had when she died was all she got to keep as a ghost.

The overhead light blinked once. It was a standard code between the two of us: once for yes, twice for no.

"You actually think that is going to work?" Dr. Scott didn't bother to mask his incredulous expression.

"I wouldn't ask her to expend the energy if I didn't. That would be pointless and cruel. Beside, do you have a better idea?" I snapped out the words quietly but with whiplike precision. "I sure as hell don't want to get into the middle of nowhere with them. Look, Doc, first rule of survival—stay in public when you can. Anything they want to do to you where there are no witnesses you don't want to have happen."

"Oh." He took a long pull of his drink. It sloshed a little bit. His hand was shaking again—not much, and he was covering it well. But he was trembling with fear. I couldn't blame him. "By the way, call me Jeff." He gave me a sour smile, his voice thick with sarcasm and barely suppressed anger. "All my fellow kidnap victims do."

I couldn't deny we'd just stepped beyond the doctor-patient thing. "Okay . . . Jeff. Look, my hope is they'll have to drop the spell to get in the trunk to get the jack."

He glared at me over the rim of his second scotch. "And what if they use the jack and spare from one of the squad cars?"

I glared at him. Now he was just being difficult. "Then they'll have to drop the spell to take off the old tire." I paused and sighed. "Look, like I said. You don't *have* to help me." I turned my attention to the vehicles outside the window. "I wish I knew whether those are real cops out there. I don't want to go to the state facility. But I don't want to go up against the cops, either." It was a hint and he caught on at once.

"Nobody has told me about any change in the Court's order, and they would. But intruding on their thoughts is illegal." He was getting angry.

"So is kidnapping."

He didn't have a response to that. "If they're with the police, I'll be as guilty as you."

"If they're the cops, I'm Aunt Jemima." I pretended a certainty I didn't actually feel. Most cops are good people. But they're people. Which means there are always going to be a few bad apples. "Real cops would have stopped the car once we were out of a crowded area and told us they've received different orders. At the very least, they would have placed a uniform in the backseat. Right?"

He didn't deny it, but his body language was angry, his back stiff, as he pretended to stare out the window, refusing to look me in the eye. "It's wrong."

"Fine. Then don't do it. I'll just have to take my chances. But stay the hell out of the way. Because I'm not going along with whatever they have planned for me."

He didn't argue, probably because he didn't blame me. But his conscience wasn't the problem; fear was controlling him. I could even understand it. I'd seen him hold it together in life-threatening situations before. But that had been on his own turf, in the hospital, where he was prepared for just about anything natural or supernatural. This was different. He wasn't the one in control. And I've never met anybody who is really comfortable around ghosts.

"Are you ready?" I asked my sister's spirit.

The overhead light flickered once in response.

"Wait. Let me see if I can summon nine-one-one mentally." He set his drink into the little recess made for it. "Because if they really are police, you'll be resisting arrest and I'll be an accomplice. They'd have every right to shoot to kill. *Both* of us."

He wasn't telling me anything I didn't already know, so I didn't comment. I just waited and watched. There wasn't much to see. He leaned back in the cushions, closing his eyes, the very picture of relaxed concentration. That lasted all of thirty seconds or so, until he grabbed his head in both hands and screamed.

My adrenaline began racing anew as he doubled over and began throwing up everything he'd even thought of ingesting in the last twenty-four hours. That was the last straw. I spun in my seat and kicked the door with every ounce of strength, fully intending to pull the doctor out with me. The door mechanism gave way from sheer brute force, just as I expected, but I hadn't anticipated the strength of the magical barrier. Normally, magic only prevents magical creatures from passing through. But this kicked the door right back at me as if it had reached the end of a bungee cord. The door caught my legs so suddenly and painfully that I tumbled backward, winding up crumpled against the opposite door, just barely missing the growing pool of vomit.

The door was now hanging at a slight angle and wasn't latched. But it wasn't open.

Shit.

I ignored my throbbing calf muscles as I crawled back onto the seat. I used one of the bottled waters from the bar to wet some napkins and handed them to Jeff so he could wipe his face. There wasn't much we could do about the mess. It stank hideously to my newly supernatural nose and was generally disgusting to my still-human sensibilities. The wake had been at a Mexican restaurant known for spicy food and apparently he'd had copious amounts of tequila. Not pleasant. I scooted away as far as the seat would allow.

I heard the click and static of a speaker and a distorted male voice came over the intercom, just as the doctor screamed a second time. His face was contorted out of proportion, and this time even I could feel the psychic wave that invisibly assaulted him. "We've prepared for every eventuality, including your talents, Dr. Scott. Miss Graves, I'd suggest *you* not try any other foolish pranks or any mental manipulation—brain damage would be a very real possibility." The speaker clicked off.

Shit. These definitely weren't the cops.

Dr. Scott collapsed onto the cushions. His eyes were glazed and his breathing shallow and ragged. "Jeff? Are you all right?" Stupid question. Of course he wasn't. But it's what you say in situations like this.

It took him a minute to answer and when he did his voice was hoarse. "Do I *look* all right to you?" He glared up at me.

All I could do was shrug, embarrassed. He might not have gotten the second dose if I hadn't kicked the door. "Sorry."

"Give me a minute." He had another bout of dry heaves. They sounded painful enough to make me feel really bad for him. More than a little guilty, too. When he finally finished, he moved carefully to a spot as far from the vomit as he could get, sinking limply into the seat.

"Um . . . can you *see*?" I asked him.

"Yes. Why?"

"You've broken some blood vessels in your eyes." Actually, he'd broken most of them. His eyes didn't have whites. They had reds. That was going to hurt soon. Badly.

"Terrific." He sighed, closing his eyes. "At least I got a few things from his mind as he was attacking me."

Really? Wow. Tough guy, after all.

"They're not with the police. But they have someone on the inside, someone who gave them access to squad cars from the repair lot."

I opened my mouth to get Ivy started, but apparently he wasn't finished.

"Originally, they really were just going to deliver you to the state facility. Your future roommate has been paid to kill you. After I climbed in the car with you, they called the person in charge and there was a change of plans."

His voice was a whisper that I probably wouldn't have been able to pick up if I were still a vanilla human. There was a thread of rage running through it. They might have hurt him, but he wasn't out of the fight yet. Assuming he didn't go into psychic shock, which, looking at him, he just might. "Oh?"

"They're going to kill me and make it look like you did it, then claim they had to kill you in self-defense."

Great. Why wasn't I surprised? "You got all of that in a couple of seconds? I'm impressed." I meant it. The human brain is a maze. At any given time most people are thinking one primary thing, but there's all kinds of stuff going on in the background, autonomic physical functions, background sights and sounds that the conscious mind filters out but the subconscious records. It takes real skill and strong talent to pull out individual threads from the mess. Jeff had barely had any time to work with and had come up with the jackpot . . . while being tortured.

"Nice work."

He kept on talking, fast and low, like he had to get it all out in case they noticed his lips moving. He was probably right. "The guy I looked in on had just been talking to the boss, so it was at the front of his consciousness. I'd have gotten more if he hadn't caught me at it. That was probably why they attacked me the second time."

Maybe. But I figured I was sort of at fault, too. "You did good." Of course he knew that. "I'm sorry you got hurt."

"I'll live." He didn't really look like he believed it, but—

"Here's hoping we both will." I took a deep breath. "You ready?"

Jeff wedged himself into the corner, one arm pressed hard against the gray leather seat, trying to make it seem casual in case they were watching through the tinted glass. Then he pushed his other hand against the cabin wall. He still looked like hell. Pale, with beads of sweat on his forehead. But his expression was determined and he gave me a curt nod.

"Okay, Ivy, do it."

It took about a ten count before the car lurched left, hard enough to send me sliding across the slick leather. She'd chosen the tires. The force of the move to the side told me she'd gotten both on one side. I whispered to the cool breeze that flitted around, proud of herself, "Attagirl!" Our speed slowed and the driver moved over to the side of the road. Out of the corner of my eye, through the tinted partition, I saw the limo driver reach over to flick the intercom button.

"Don't try anything stupid." He turned to glare at us in the rearview mirror, then turned it down as he swept his jacket aside, giving me a good look at a very nice Glock.

I hoped he thought the flat tires were random chance, that they hadn't been listening in on my thoughts. I wanted the element of surprise if I could get it. Because while I'd tried to act confident for Jeff's benefit, the truth was that I could barely dignify this by calling it a plan. It was more the equivalent of a last-second Hail Mary pass.

"Too late for that," Jeff muttered, but without heat. Finding out that he was scheduled to die seemed to have given him a totally different outlook on making an escape attempt.

I leaned over and grabbed the champagne bottle and a glass. The glass was for show. The driver was watching through the glass as he dialed his cell phone. Let him think I needed another drink. I adjusted my position under the skylight as carefully as I could manage without being obvious. Tensing my muscles, I dropped the glass and started shaking the bottle vigorously. The driver had his back to us now, talking on his cell phone—which worked. Since I hadn't felt the magic go down, the front of the car wasn't covered by the spell. Which meant it was probably fifty-fifty odds whether the trunk and tires were. *Crap.* "Remember, as soon as the barrier goes down, try dialing nine-one-one." I sounded more confident than I felt. Not that that took much.

Jeff flicked a thumbs-up at me. He already had his cell phone out and I could see the numbers displayed prominently on the screen. All he had to do was press "send." I was gathering my strength, making sure of my placement. *I can do this.* I almost believed me, but it wouldn't be easy.

Keeping the driver in my peripheral vision, I strained the power that let me sense magic to the fullest. Luck was on our side. The second his hand touched the door handle I felt the barrier waver and fall. Still, I waited. I waited for that golden instant when he was outside the car and couldn't see. If I was lucky, it would be before the others got the door to our part of the limo open and their guns trained on us. They were bound to do it, but I was betting they were going to head for the damaged door.

Time slowed to a crawl. The driver climbed out of the car.

I slid from my seat into a crouch. As his door slammed shut I sprang upward, champagne bottle at the ready.

The windowsill scraped against my back as I passed through the sunroof, but didn't slow me down. In an instant that seemed to take forever, I soared nearly ten feet into the air. Thanks to adrenaline and vampire strength, I'd gotten a lot more loft than I'd expected. More than my captors had planned, too. The three cars had pulled onto the side of the road in a line, with the limo in the center. To my surprise there seemed to be only four men escorting us. Under the circumstances, I was thrilled.

The night was to my advantage. I could see the men as clearly as if it were daylight, despite the deep shadows that made the landscape disappear. Each man glowed and pulsed in time to the blood flowing beneath his paper-thin skin. I stayed in the air longer than should be realistically possible and it confused them.

The man in the front squad car was the smartest. He'd ignored the obvious exit of the door and already had his gun out, trained on the sunroof. The leap had startled him, but he was recovering, his weapon moving up to track my progress. So he got the prize. If it caught the guy with him so much the better. I flung the champagne bottle with all my strength to the ground at his feet. The shaken, pressurized alcohol exploded like a bomb, sending vicious shards of glass outward, shredding his face and legs as he screamed in agony.

The limo driver had been turned slightly to open the door to the passenger cabin, so he was a fraction too slow on the draw. By the time he had his gun out I'd landed on the roof. He looked at me squarely, confidence in his cold blue eyes.

So I hissed and bared fangs, my skin creating its own gray-green light. It startled him enough that he gasped and took a step back. That was what I'd hoped for. I had just enough time to send a spinning kick into his temple. I heard bone breaking and knew he was dead before he hit the ground.

Two down. But there was a luxury sedan racing toward us, black, with tinted windows. I didn't have time to do more than note it as a blur because the third man had me at a disadvantage and I'd lost sight of the fourth entirely. I was betting he'd slid underneath one of the cars.. The Jimmy Choo pumps Vicki had given me for my birthday weren't intended for the slick surface of the waxed roof. They put me off-balance and my counterpart was armed and ready. He braced his semiauto on the frame of the car door that was shielding his body and began firing. He was coming alarmingly close despite my speed. I couldn't take him. But I might not have to. Because the driver of the sedan was aiming it straight at the shooter while the wail of police cars in the distance grew louder with each second.

I did the only sensible thing I could think of. I jumped back down through the sunroof and hit the button for the door locks and roof, hoping to hide behind the nice, thick, bullet-proof glass until help arrived. I nearly landed on Dr. Scott. He was slumped on the floor, eyes rolled back in his head and breathing shallow. I didn't know if it was a delayed reaction to the earlier attack or if they'd gone after him again. All I could do was lift him onto the seat cushions and put cool, damp napkins on his forehead and the back of his neck while I waited for help to arrive.

––––––

Jeff was in psychic shock. The cops—the real cops—took him away in an ambulance, along with the limo's real driver, who'd been found drugged and unconscious in the trunk. They didn't take me. I asserted self-defense and asked for my attorney. So did Ivan.

Ivan Stefanovich had been driving the sedan and had opened the rear door to find me hovering over Jeff. I was honestly shocked to see him. A couple of weeks ago, during the fallout from my last job as a bodyguard, he'd been wounded badly enough that I hadn't expected him to make it. Then again, he was one tough bastard. Ivan served as the right-hand-man-cum-security-chief for King Dahlmar of Rusland. The same King Dahlmar whose son I'd helped rescue from a major demon. Rusland is not be a big country, only maybe the size of Ohio. It's tucked in between the Ukraine and Poland and touches on the Czech Republic as well.

Recently discovered reserves of natural gas made Rusland politically important. Ivan was an international headache for the cops—and he had diplomatic immunity. So we waited, with some seriously pissed-off cops. They wanted to hurt me. Hell, more than hurt me. I was a vampire and I'd been caught red-handed at a kill scene. I was toast—right up until they found out that the bodies on the ground had no bite marks and that I left no blood on the swab they ran around inside my cheeks. It didn't make them any happier to discover the men in the uniforms around the real squad cars weren't actually police. That pissed them off a *lot*. But at least they weren't pissed at me after that. So I got to wait for my attorney inside a spelled circle, in handcuffs, as they processed the crime scene, instead of being staked on the spot.

Ms. Graves, if you can hear me, nod your head. Ivan's voice came clearly inside my skull. He'd told the cops he was a registered mage. I'd forgotten he was a telepath. He'd only used that talent in front of me once—at the World Series game when we'd discovered one of King Dahlmar's sons was being kidnapped.

I gave a tiny nod. Nothing noticeable.

Good. I was afraid the spelled circle would interfere, as the barrier around the car did.

Since until recently I had no psychic talent, I'm not very good at talking mind-to-mind. I hoped my intense concentration wasn't showing on my face as I replied, *Not that I'm complaining, but how did you know to come riding up like the cavalry?*

I could almost hear the puzzlement in his thoughts. Either I sucked at thinking at him or the reference was too American for his English.

I was waiting outside the tribute to your deceased friend. I wished to speak with you. I saw them attack the driver. When the police guarding the doors did nothing, I decided to wait for a better opportunity.

Shit. The police outside the party had seen the switch? And didn't stop it? That was wrong. Really wrong. Thank God Ivan had been there. But why had he? And why had he come riding to the rescue? My past experiences with him hadn't shown him to be the most altruistic guy on the planet. In fact, he'd calmly left a man to die in order to follow his orders.

He answered my questions as if I'd voiced them aloud. I wasn't surprised he'd been listening to my thoughts. Not everybody has Jeff's ethics.

My king does not know I have come to you. But you may be our only hope.

What in the world could *I* do that a nation's king and all the money and favor of a hundred countries desperately trying to gain a strategic ally couldn't? *What do you want from me?*

"All right. That's enough, you two. I said no talking." Ivan's reply—if he had been going to make one—never came. The detective who'd set up the magic circle I was standing in straightened from where he'd been chatting with someone near the bodies. Whatever the guy had told him hadn't made him happy. He stalked over to where I stood, my hands securely cuffed behind my back. He bent down, pressed his finger to the edge of the circle, and began muttering a spell. Sound disappeared from the world and my vision sparkled like I'd been slammed face-first into a brick wall. I gasped in pain as the increased power burned across my skin. I didn't say anything, but he must've seen me flinch, because a look of satisfaction flickered across his face for just an instant. It was so quick, it could've been a trick of my imagination. But I knew it wasn't.

When they eventually released me to go to Birchwoods, Ivan was long gone. We never did get to talk. That worried me. Because once I got inside the facility, I probably wasn't going to be allowed calls or visitors for quite some time. There wasn't anything I could do about that, but it was a problem just the same. I pondered it on the long drive down Ocean View. This time I had a real police escort, and more. News crews had been minding their scanners and we wound up with *lots* of company. The more the merrier, as far as I was concerned. I wanted witnesses to this whole debacle. Something had gone horribly wrong within the police force to have this happen. There apparently hadn't been any sort of citywide all-points bulletin when I went missing, because that was one of the questions the nice reporters asked the incident commander. Keeping everything public and under the media microscope offered me the best possible protection. It'd be a damned nuisance. But I could live with that. Emphasis on the "live."

We made the drive in broad daylight because it had taken hours to deal with the fallout from the kidnapping attempt. I was glad for the press and for Roberto Santos. My attorney had rightfully insisted that I be moved out of the confining circle and behind tinted windows before the sun could crisp me.

I stared out the window at Birchwoods, wondering what it was that Ivan needed and wishing for about the millionth time that the damned bat had just bitten me and been done with it rather than trying to bring me over. He'd turned me into an abomination that was not vampire, human, or siren but some unholy mix of the three.

In the eyes of most of the cops I was a monster, one step below a dangerous animal, and now I'd publicly embarrassed the whole department. There were bodies on the ground and the police cars were real. Of course, the fourth suspect had gotten away. Maybe they'd catch him. Maybe not.

I had the sickening feeling this whole night was somehow going to wind up being my fault.

3

The covers went flying off the bed, but I grabbed an end and pulled the soft comforter back over me. Then the drapes opened abruptly to let in bright sunlight. I flipped the pillow so my head was underneath and returned to warm darkness.

"I don't *want* to go to therapy today. Go away." I heard a familiar squeak, like fingernails on chalkboard, and lifted up just enough of the pillow to peek out from underneath.

Have to.

The words were written in beautiful script on the dresser mirror, etched into the frost Vicki had formed on the surface. Technically, I wasn't allowed to have a "roommate," but there wasn't much the staff could do about it since she was a ghost and a former resident. I let out a little growl and dropped the pillow back over my face. Yeah, I knew she was right. If I didn't play by the rules now, they'd only get more restrictive and it would be a nurse or, worse, a mage attendant with compulsion magic who came to get me.

Another squeak and this time I smelled flowers. I lifted the pillow again and there was a single yellow daisy lying next to my face. The frost had formed a new word.

Please?

Well, hell. I couldn't help but let out a little laugh. Vicki always could cajole me into doing stuff. "Okay, okay. I'll get up." I spun my legs off the bed and walked to the dresser. "Let's see, let me choose from my expansive wardrobe."

I opened the first drawer to reveal gray T-shirts and sweatshirts. The second drawer held gray sweat*pants* and the third? Yep, gray undies. Everything gray except the bras. They were white. *Whoo.* All newbies to the Birchwoods program have their past stripped away so *the healing can begin.* Or so say the ads. Gray is the great equalizer among the classes. No amount of fame, money, or family title can stand against it. It's only later, further into the program, that personalities and preferences are allowed to reemerge, under strictly controlled circumstances. I took a quick shower, pulled on my graywear, and slathered on enough sunscreen to get me through the first part of the day. A baseball cap with the facility's logo would protect my scalp.

The windows were flung open and I got the day's first breath of salty sea air. The room was flooded with the sound of the ever-present gulls that were probably considered nuisances by the staff and other residents. What can I say? Gulls seem to be my thing lately. They've been flocking around me ever since I fought against my vampire sire by pulling on my siren talents. I have no idea why, or what to do about it, which is as frustrating to me as it probably is to the birds.

I looked out the window and tried to lighten my mood. It didn't take all that long. Birchwoods is a lovely compound, filled with flowers, stunning landscaping, and rolling, grassy hills. The view included the ever-present guards, who dress like tour guides but are actually tough and smart.

Security is tight, but that's as much for the protection of the guests as for the public. I looked over the campus: hospital, administration building, youth facility, main residential building. It's a good thing I'm not an autograph hound, because coming out of the youth facility at that moment was one of the biggest teen pop stars in the world. There were a lot more inside the building. The crème de la crème come here when they need to dry out or heal up and they don't want anyone to know about it, *ever*. The tabloids try desperately to get through security, knowing that if they did they'd get the scoop of the century. Thus far, they'd had no success.

More squeaking and I turned my head. *Hurry. Waffles today!*

It made me smile. It was so Vicki. We'd learned in the interval between her death and the wake that she could carry on a full conversation with only minimal responses. Whole sentences tired her quickly, but a few carefully chosen words were enough to interact.

For a moment I wondered how the investigation into her murder was going. Alex had specifically warned me to back off, to let the police do their job. God knew they were under enough pressure already with Vicki's parents in the mix.

Vicki's parents were Cassandra Meadows and Jason Cooper, *the* Hollywood power couple and an industry unto themselves. Jason wasn't such a bad guy, but Cassandra could be absolute hell on wheels. Not just a bitch, a *raging* bitch. I knew this from personal experience. The woman hates me with an unholy passion.

Another squeak underlined the *Hurry*. Vicki'd *loved* waffles in life—thick Belgian ones with malt in the batter. Coat them with fresh butter and real Vermont maple syrup and she could probably tie the Guinness record holder for number eaten in a sitting.

I let out a little chuckle as my shoes made a little hop across the floor toward me. "Okay, okay. I'm hurrying."

I shoved my foot into a pair of (you guessed it) gray slippers. I didn't like them much, no arch support and they were too loose to be completely comfortable, but nobody was allowed shoes with laces at Birchwoods. A precaution against suicides, no doubt, but annoying as hell.

You okay? screeched across the mirror in front of me and I smiled sadly.

"Think I'll ever make it out of here?" I paused as the frost began to form. "Truthfully?"

There was a pause on her side, too. Vicki had been a patient at Birchwoods for a long time. There was a good chance she really had been mentally unstable, but certain traumatic events pushed her over the edge. She came to Birchwoods looking for peace and for the most part had found it. But we weren't the same sort of people . . . our friendship was based on the "opposites attract" principle. While I like quiet, *peace* isn't really my thing. Otherwise, I wouldn't be a bodyguard for fun and profit.

Dunno . . . , was the reply, followed by a :-(

"C'mon," I said after a long silence that threatened to ruin what small amount of good mood I had. "Let's go do waffles." Even though I really don't like waffles all that much.

The frown was replaced by a :D

Text messaging from the beyond. My life is so weird.

Like most of Birchwoods, the cafeteria is bright, sunny, and clean. It looks more like the restaurant of a nice hotel than a cafeteria. Lots of plants and greenery, round wooden tables with matching chairs with a light oak finish. There are two separate sections, divided by a glass partition. Not smoking and non-smoking: suicidal and not. Those with any hint of suicidal tendencies get foods that don't require cutting and there's a much higher supervisor-to-patient ratio.

I have plenty of problems, but suicidal tendencies aren't among them. So I chose a corner table just outside the reach of the sunlight shining through the windows and sat at a place set with a real china plate and actual silverware. Not that I could use it. The changes to my body mean I don't get to eat actual solids. Not now. Maybe not ever.

Still, the waffles, even though in blended, liquid form, were actually *good*. Enough for seconds. My first gulp caused a surprised smile and Vicki showered me with flower petals right there in the cafeteria. Of course, having a four-star Michelin chef working the line probably helped. Money talks and what chef wouldn't love a truly captive audience to experiment with new textures and flavors? It was the ultimate test of his skill to make diners with weird-ass physical requirements happy.

I had just started a second helping when I saw Heather walk into the cafeteria. Heather was Dr. Scott's personal assistant. According to hospital gossip, she'd gotten the promotion thanks to her cool head in a crisis—helping Dr. Scott face down my bloodlust. She didn't like me much. No surprise there. But she was the only person here who might actually be able to tell me if Ivan had tried to reach me. Assuming Jeff let her. That was a coin toss.

I waved to her and waited for her reaction. She was too polite to grimace and it was too late to ignore me, so I got to watch her steel herself and bring her tray over to my table.

"Can I help you?" She smiled, showing lots of straight white teeth, but her eyes were wary, her body language nervous. I wasn't the only one who noticed. A couple of the nice attendants began moving closer, more or less discreetly.

I decided to cut to the chase. I figured she'd appreciate it. "The night I was picked up, a man from the Rusland Secret Service was there. He said it was urgent that he speak with me, but what with the kidnapping and all we didn't get to talk. Has he, by any chance, tried to get in touch? Left me a message or anything?"

She gave an unhappy sigh and looked put-upon, as if every patient in the facility was constantly trying to get messages in or out. Then again, they probably were. I tried a slightly different tack.

"Can you check with Dr. Scott to see if he'll let you look into it?"

"Fine. I'll check with Dr. Scott. *If* he says it's okay, I'll see what I can find out for you."

That was the best I was going to get and I knew it. So I smiled sweetly and said, "Thanks," and Heather hurried over to the table where a number of other staff members were eating. The attendants went back to their posts, back to scanning the room.

I left the cafeteria at 8:50, giving me plenty of time to make my way to Dr. Hubbard's office for my 9:00 individual therapy session. On the way I pondered whether or not I could stand living here long term. It wasn't a bad place. But I was already restless, after just a couple of weeks. And I couldn't stop thinking about things on the outside. I was seriously worried that I hadn't heard a peep from Ivan since the night of the attack. While I tried to tell myself that the situation, whatever it was, had probably blown over, I didn't believe that. I hoped Heather was being honest about going to Dr. Scott; I hoped that Dr. Scott would be willing to let her follow up. Neither seemed like a good bet. It made me feel helpless. I can't tell you how much I hate that.

"Good morning, Celia." Dr. Hubbard's greeting drew me out of this fairly unpleasant reverie. She greeted me with a warm smile that lit up a face that was otherwise plain. A woman of late middle age, she was attractive but not stunning, with ash-blond hair, minimal makeup, and a suit that was both businesslike and unremarkable. Then again, therapy is about the patient, not the therapist. The non-threatening, unnoticeable doctor might not bear a lot of resemblance to the woman I'd meet outside of work.

"Ann."

"So, what would you like to discuss today?"

This was how the sessions always started. She'd ask what I wanted to discuss, but in the end we'd wind up digging into all the stuff I really didn't want to talk about. Gotta love therapy.

An hour later, wrung out from crying, I was done with Dr. Hubbard for a few days. I'd recover just in time to go back and dredge more gunk out of my subconscious.

Usually I had group therapy at 10:30 A.M., but today I'd be

skipping it. I'd be meeting with my attorney instead. Doing witness prep and going over my testimony for my court hearing wasn't going to be fun, but I was tired of being the center of the group's attention. I mean the others had drug problems, depression, maybe out-of-control talent. Pretty run-of-the-mill stuff. My problems, on the other hand, were spectacularly weird. My fellow patients waited for each session like soap opera addicts. Which seriously creeped me out. The only upside I could think of was I was meeting a lot of high-end potential clients.

We were scheduled to meet in one of the small conference rooms in the administration building. I went there under escort. Patients don't get to leave the main building without. Because of the whole siren thing, I got to be escorted by a female guard. Greta was big, blond, Nordic, and no-nonsense. When she talked, which was seldom, she had a thick accent. Her uniform might look like that of a tour guide, but she herself looked like a prison guard.

I'd slathered myself with another layer of sunscreen, so I was able to walk down the sunlit sidewalk without singeing, but I was still glad to get back indoors. I was even more glad when Greta left me alone in the conference room, shutting the door behind her. No doubt she'd be waiting right outside when the meeting was over. But in the meantime, I wasn't sorry to see her go.

I settled into a comfortable leather chair at a small, round table and proceeded to wait. And wait. And wait. Since Roberto is normally excruciatingly prompt, I had to wonder what was wrong. But nobody came to tell me anything. So I sat at the little wood-laminate table and watched the hands on the wall clock move slowly around the dial. Forty minutes had crawled by when the door finally opened and my attorney came in, looking harried and worried.

"What's wrong?" Okay, maybe not the best conversational foray. I mean, usually I lead with "Hi," or "Hey, Roberto, good to see you'" But something was obviously amiss. It wasn't just that he was late. He was troubled and he wasn't bothering to try to hide it from me.

Shaking his head, he set a large briefcase onto the conference room table and took the seat across from me.

"Has anyone else been here to meet with you?"

That was an odd question, especially since Birchwoods' rules allowed me to meet with my attorney and no one else. I told him as much.

"I know." He took off his glasses and proceeded to clean the lenses with a snow-white handkerchief. It was a nervous gesture and so completely out of character it threw me. Roberto doesn't get nervous. He just doesn't. Which is why he's been lead counsel defending the famous and infamous, winning the unwinnable cases.

"Why do you ask?"

He met my gaze, dark eyes earnest. "I have messages for you from Bruno DeLuca, and the Landinghams—Warren, Emma, and Kevin. And I was contacted by a representative of King Dahlmar—"

"Ivan?" I leaned forward eagerly. "Did he get in touch with you? Tell you what it was he needed?"

Roberto nodded. "Ivan Stefanovich came to my office yesterday. He presented his identification and said that he had to see you as soon as possible. He indicated that it was a matter of national security. He asked that he be allowed to accompany me to this meeting. I was reluctant. But I called the embassy and checked on him and he voluntarily submitted to a truth spell. So I agreed to let him come in with me, pretending to be my co-counsel. He was going to say his piece, then leave, so that we could go over your case."

"Only he didn't show?"

"Exactly."

"That's bad. Really bad."

"I waited for a half hour, then called the number he gave me. It's not in service. When I called the embassy, this time they said he was out of the country. Do you have any idea what this is about?"

"No more than you do. He tried to talk to me the night of Vicki's wake, but the police separated us. He's a telepath. I half-figured he'd try to get in touch with me mind-to-mind, but I guess they have protections up against that here."

"Yes. They do."

"So what do we do?"

"I guess we just go forward with our trial prep. I'll try to find out more when we're done. Maybe whatever it was resolved itself. Or maybe he'll get back in touch with me. But for now, your hearing is the day after tomorrow and we've got to get ready for it."

So that was what we did. But in the back of my mind I couldn't help worrying, wondering what was going on out in the real world while I was tucked safely in the nuthouse.

4

I spent the rest of the day going through the motions, my mind caught up in worries about the court date, about whatever the hell was going on with Ivan, and, oddly, about Bruno.

Bruno DeLuca is the love of my life. I know, corny. But he is. We met in college. He'd come out west to study with Warren Landingham in one of the best Paranormal Studies departments in the world. *And* to put a little distance between him and his very large, very domineering Italian-American family.

We hit it off almost from the start. He's smart, fun, and sexy as hell. He also had enough of a sense of humor not to take himself (or much of anything else) too seriously. No situation was ever too dire for Bruno Deluca to crack wise about it.

We dated, fell in love, got engaged.

And then I met the family.

Oh boy. Wasn't that a load of fun. *Not.* His mother didn't just hate me. She *loathed* me. All of the other daughters-in-law hated me, too. And there are a lot of them. Uncle Sal was okay with me, so was cousin Joey. But that was it. Everybody else, no.

Then there were the arguments about where we were going

to live—East Coast vs. West. Children? Him: yes, lots. Me: uh, no. I like kids, but my life has been a series of dangerous disasters since I was little. I was not going to put an innocent child through that.

They say love conquers all. They lie. We loved each other desperately, but there were too many things pulling us apart. We broke up. And we stayed broken up for years. Right up until he reappeared in my life a few weeks ago.

God, I'd missed him. Miracle of miracles, he missed me, too. So, older, maybe a little wiser, we were giving it another shot.

In my mind I went over the messages he'd sent with Roberto, short verbal messages on a flash drive from the law firm's computer answering service. "The trip home to tell the family went pretty much the way I expected." That meant badly. "Job negotiations are going well. Uncle Sal went with me to meet with Creede and Miller." Oh, to be a fly on the wall for *that* meeting. "I love you. If you can get a day pass I'll show you just how much." Just thinking about that made my body react. Even when things hadn't been going well emotionally, sex with Bruno had been spectacular.

I had to get out of here. Soon. Which meant the hearing had to go well.

A long day bled into a sleepless night. After a few hours of tossing and turning I gave up on the idea of sleep altogether.

I showered and dressed, wondering what I was going to do to kill the hours until the cafeteria opened and the day actually started. I needn't have worried. I'd no more than pulled on my slippers when there was a tap at my door.

To my surprise a tall, slender woman stood in front of me, her long auburn hair pulled back to reveal a heart-shaped face with exotic features dominated by large eyes the rich blue-green color of the waters of the Mediterranean Sea. Her silk wrap dress was of the same shade and had been cut to make the most of a figure that was designed to turn men's heads. She was too perfect to be true. Still, I'd have sworn that every inch of her was absolutely natural. I certainly didn't feel any of the magic I'd come to associate with attractiveness charms and there were no obvious signs of cosmetic surgery. In fact, she didn't even appear to be wearing much in the way of makeup.

"Good morning, Celia." I got the full weight of those extraordinary eyes. And just like that I knew. She was a siren.

"Good morning."

"Dr. Scott was good enough to give me permission to see you."

Not by choice he didn't. I thought it to myself, but I was surprised when she answered.

No. Not by choice. She admitted it inside my skull. Eek. *There will be about forty-five minutes that he can't remember. He'll assume it's just one more sign of post-traumatic stress and schedule an appointment for an assessment.*

But it's not.

No, she admitted with a small smile. *I manipulated him. But he is having problems. He should make the appointment anyway. If this pushes him to get help sooner, is that such a bad thing?*

Probably not, but that didn't make me like it any better. Life had been a lot more comfortable for me before I realized just how easy it was for the psychically gifted to manipulate people. The more I found out, the more I could sympathize with the law's hard-line policy. If only it didn't apply to me. Damn the luck.

The big siren gift is to enthrall men to the point that they'd do whatever the siren needed even to the point of death. They betray their families, their countries, whatever, with a smile on their face and a song in their heart. It completely takes away their free will. Which is just wrong, on so many levels. I'm a big believer in free will.

"You're not what I expected." She tapped a manicured fingernail against her lip as she looked me up and down.

"Really? What *were* you expecting?"

"I didn't think you'd be so . . ." She hesitated and I saw in her mind what she was about to say, which was "pretty." She smiled and it was as beautiful as the first light of dawn after a long, cold night. I'm not gay, but I can appreciate gorgeous and this woman made the top-tier most beautiful in Hollywood look like day-old dog meat. I certainly wasn't in her league. Oh, I do all right, better than some. But there's a big step between playing in Little League and in the pros.

"Uh, right." I didn't believe her and it showed.

"I'm serious." Her expression sobered. "I expected you to look more human, or more vampire. But there's more than a trace of *us* in you. In fact, you bear more of a resemblance to Queen Lopaka than Adriana does. Except for the teeth, of course." She smirked and even that expression looked good on her. "Of course, Adriana takes after her father in *every* way."

I had no idea what that was supposed to mean, so I couldn't answer. Probably best that I stay quiet anyway.

She must have taken my silence to mean I was insulted. "I meant no offense. It's never a bad thing to have people underestimate you."

"Particularly my enemies." I kept my tone light, but I'll admit to being a teeny bit worried. My first encounter with my grandfather's relatives had been at Vicki's wake. While my current visitor actually spoke in American idiom and seemed friendly, it was entirely possible she was giving me a line of bull.

"You don't trust me."

"It's nothing personal." I gave her a polite smile. "I don't trust anybody."

That was the honest truth, put bluntly enough to make her blink and give me a long look through narrowed eyelids. "You mean that."

"I tend to say what I mean. It's easier." I gave her a grin that was only partly manufactured. "Of course I *can* lie, if the occasion calls for it."

"Of course. We all can." She walked over to the window, pulling aside the curtain with one hand and turning to watch the waves hitting the beach. "May I ask what arrangements you've made about your hearing?"

A siren had crashed Vicki's wake to tell me that I would have to attend a hearing on the siren island. They seem to think the vampire bite has made me a monster that may need to be put down. I'll have to go there and deal with it—assuming I get through the court hearing okay. "I haven't made any. Why?"

She whipped around so fast she pulled down the curtain, rod and all. She stared openmouthed at me, delicate peach-colored cotton in a death grip in her fist and puddled at her feet

I shrugged. "The other one . . . Adriana?" I made the name a question and she nodded. "Didn't tell me squat. She showed up, caused a scene, challenged me to a duel, said I'd be put up before the tribunal of Pacific lords. Then she left."

"A *duel*? The Pacific *lords*?"

"To the death. And yes."

She blinked a couple of times, batting lashes almost long enough to create a breeze. "Oh my. You certainly have managed to antagonize her."

"It wasn't hard." My tone was dry. "She was monumentally rude and looking to take offense."

My visitor threw back her head and let out a peal of honest laughter. "That would be Adriana all right."

"I don't suppose you're going to tell me where the 'Isle of Serenity' is and when I'm supposed to be there? Or are you the escort?"

The woman's head tipped down, her eyes narrowing dangerously. Her voice took on a dangerous purr. "She truly didn't tell you?"

"Nope. Got pissy, issued her challenge, and told me that since I wouldn't treat her like a proper princess she didn't feel compelled to tell me squat."

"*That* is also like Adriana and completely unacceptable." The woman smiled again, but this time it was more a baring of teeth. "As you guessed, I'm a siren; in fact, I'm as much a princess as Adriana and as *you*."

She sounded defiant about it, as if she expected me to argue with her, and I did, but obviously not in the way she expected. "I'm no princess. Not even a little."

"Oh, but you *are*." She shook her head, her blue-green eyes dancing with mischief. "You come from a royal line. Your great-grandfather was brother to the queen. In fact, you come from the Pacific royal line, just like Adriana. And she has pissed off so many of the other royals that having an alternative, even an unlettered heathen like you, will put her in a very precarious position indeed."

"Unlettered heathen?" I tried not to sound as hideously insulted as I felt but didn't quite manage it.

"You don't know the first thing about our culture, do you?" Her smile was poisonously sweet.

"Well, no. But *unlettered heathen*?" I repeated the words with some heat. "That has got to be an insult."

Her cheeks went a teeny bit pink. "I'm sorry. I'm just quoting some of the more vocal members of the family. Atrocious snobs for the most part." She paused. "Just so you know."

"I take it you're *not* from the Pacific line."

She blinked and blushed more furiously. "Oh dear. I really am handling this badly. How rude of me. I haven't introduced myself, have I?"

"Nope."

She curtsied. Actually pulled out her skirt and dipped a leg back before bowing her head for a split second. Then she stood. "I am Princess Eirene Medusi of the Aegean royal line, but you may call me Ren. I do beg your pardon. It was unbelievably gauche of me not to introduce myself the moment I walked in."

"It's no big deal." Right now, the lack of a proper introduction seemed like the least of my worries.

She gave me a long, measuring stare. "You actually mean that. You're not going to throw a fit or challenge me for the insult?"

I smiled. "Nope."

She grinned back at me, showing a set of fetching dimples. "How very refreshing. If we're not careful, I may actually come to *like* you." Her voice bubbled with amusement.

"Don't sound so shocked."

"Oh, but it *is* surprising. Your branch of the family and mine very politely *loathe* each other. Your side considers us upstarts because my mother broke off from the clan and formed her own hierarchy. We think they're a bunch of pompous . . . well, never mind. Let's just say that my motive here was to see if I could catch Adriana having done something embarrassing. And I *have*." Her delight was obvious. She gave me a conspiratorial wink. "Of course, the excuse we gave was something else entirely."

"Which was?"

"We're giving you a gift to welcome you to the family."

A gift? I tried to think positive and not conjure up mental images of big wooden horses. After all, my visitor could apparently get inside my skull.

"Adriana is going to *hate* having you actually show up for the hearing before the queens." Ren sounded positively gleeful. "You'll appear before the queens, not the lords. Entirely different areas of authority. The lords tribunal handles the laws of the sea. The queens deal with family matters. Oh, this is *delicious*! She would have had you at the wrong time and in the wrong place on the island. Queen Lopaka will be beside herself at the insult to her brother's great-grandchild."

"It's the same queen as when my *great*-grandfather was alive? Yikes. She must be a sturdy old girl. Then you're going to tell me where, when, and how?"

"Oh, better than that." She waved a hand, making the bracelet of seashells and tourmaline wound with gold wire she wore glitter in the sunlight. "If I can possibly manage it, I'm going to take you there myself. I can't wait to see Adriana's expression when you appear."

Ren's voice was delighted, but I could hear a deep bitterness in her words. She really did loathe the other princess. While I didn't have any reason to love Adriana, I'm not a fool. I was staying out of the middle of that catfight. "Um, I'm under house arrest."

She smiled. "You won't be. The official hearing before the queens isn't for a couple of days. By then all *sorts* of things will have changed."

"And you know this how?" I was really hoping she hadn't "arranged" it. Because as suspicious as the authorities were, they'd never believe I hadn't. And that would be *so* bad.

"We have our ways." Her eyes twinkled, then she started to pout at my lackluster reaction. "Oh, will you *please* relax. I haven't done a thing, nor have any of the other sirens. But the king you helped has and your government is *very* interested in your talents and abilities. Between one thing and another, you'd have to do something fairly heinous between now and then to be stuck here. And you don't strike me as the type for *heinous*."

She apparently didn't know me very well. Or she had a very

different definition of "heinous" than most. When I cause trouble it's seldom intentional, but I still wind up in hot water.

"Anyway." Ren waved her hand in a theatrical gesture and I felt a surge of power. With a shimmer of light, a small, elaborately carved box appeared in her hand. It was quite beautiful, elegant and detailed with Egyptian-style carvings of a snake having swallowed the sun. It was inlaid with lapis and moonstone and smelled ever so faintly of cedar. I couldn't say why, but it *felt* old. Old and powerful, in the way my favorite knives were powerful. Those knives, locked away in my safe, had taken Bruno *five years* of daily bloodletting to make. Which made me wonder what in the hell was in that box.

She reached out to give it to me and our hands brushed. The instant our skin touched I felt a jolt of power hard enough to rock me back a step. The box dropped onto the thick carpet, spilling out a small gold cup and a collection of brightly colored scarabs the size of my thumbnail. They scattered and I could see that symbols were carved into their flat bottoms.

Ren didn't fare nearly as well. The bolt knocked her onto her butt in the middle of the floor. I heard the roar of the ocean and outside a group of gulls began dive-bombing the windows, knocking themselves senseless trying to get in.

"Ow." I shook my hand, trying to make the odd pins-and-needles sensation that wasn't quite pain go away. There was a mark on my palm, about the size of an old-time silver dollar. Dark red, it was irregularly shaped, like a tentacled birthmark. It was seriously ugly and looked old, which made no sense at all, since it hadn't been there seconds before.

Ren stared up at me, her face drained of all color, her expression one of abject horror. "Let me see your palm." Her voice was shaky, but there was grim determination in her eyes.

"Why?"

She gave a hiss of displeasure. "Quickly, in case the mark fades! Let me see your palm!"

I held my hand, palm toward her, being very careful not to touch. After she had a good, long look she very carefully scooted backward and stood without my help. Using her hands to smooth her skirt, she bent carefully at the waist to study the spill of scarabs.

"I can see you've been given a death curse but not who did it or how. Perhaps the Wadjeti can tell us."

I watched as she very gingerly picked up the lid to the box, giving me my first glimpse of the exquisite scarab on the inside of the lid. One by one, she began gathering up the small bits of Egyptian pottery, looking carefully at the symbol on the bottom of each as she did.

"Cursed?" *Crap.* We studied curses back when I was in school. I even knew a guy who'd been on the receiving end of one. And while he'd been an absolute jerk who richly deserved it—still, *ouch.* I understand that surgery helped with part of the problem and he and his wife eventually were able to adopt. "Is it fixable?"

She didn't answer. Not good. I'd been hoping for a quick "yes."

She straightened up and I realized she had missed one. A single, red scarab had rolled beneath the edge of one of the chairs. Without thinking, I reached down and picked it up. It was warm and I felt a slow pulse of power flow through me. It didn't hurt. In fact, it felt really, really good. I was almost sorry to give it up, but I extended it to her, flat on my palm, carving side up.

I wouldn't have thought she could pale further, but she did. White showed around her entire iris as she took it from me. But she pulled herself together. With a shaking finger she pointed at the edge of one of the chairs. "Is that another one over there?"

I dropped onto my knees. Nope. Nothing. I rose in a smooth movement and turned to her.

"I need to talk to my mother." Almost slamming the lid shut, she shoved the box into my arms. "I realize it's probably useless to say this, but *try* to stay out of trouble."

And in less time than it took to blink, she was gone.

5

I **sat** in the visitor's chair in Dr. Scott's office. Not even 6:00 A.M., but I knew he was already on the grounds. I didn't technically have an appointment, but I'd at least called ahead. The night receptionist, Autumn, had reluctantly agreed to let me into his office. Mostly because I told her there'd been a major security breach and I needed to talk to him right away.

Dr. Scott's office takes up probably a fourth of the first floor of the administration building. It's on the same side of the building as the group therapy room, with a similar wall of glass facing the ocean. The decorator had done a great job echoing the golden tans of the sand and the blues and greens of sea and sky. Everything was beautiful, tasteful, expensive, and soothing.

I wasn't feeling particularly soothed. I'd found the visit from my "cousin" more than a touch disturbing on several levels. The curse mark remained fairly prominent. I kept glancing at it.

Curses, in general, are pretty variable. Say your coworker, sibling, mother-in-law, or whatever pisses you off. If you have any magical talent at all you can put a curse on them. How effective the curse is will depend on how much talent you've got. Someone like me, with no magic, equals no curse. Now someone like Bruno, who's got so much talent he practically glows in the freaking dark (now that I've got vampire powers to see it), well, there's not much he *couldn't* do, up to and including arranging for your enemy to die.

I felt a shiver run down my spine from a combination of fear and rage. Sitting there, holding my little wooden box, I wanted answers, about the curse, about the gift Ren had brought me.

I don't trust people. Never have. But I trust my instincts and my instincts were telling me that this "gift" was the magical equivalent of dynamite.

It wasn't exactly reassuring when Dr. Scott stormed into the room, his expression thunderous. He isn't that big a man, and normally he's reserved and elegant, someone you'd expect to see on the cover of *JET* magazine or one of the major psychiatric journals. He was wearing khakis and a polo shirt, but his attitude was anything but casual. "What the hell have you done now? Whatever you're holding was felt by most of the staff and woke half of the guests."

"What have *I* done? Oh no," I snapped back. "You need to have a chat with Security, because someone slipped through the cracks. I could have been killed. Like Vicki was killed, in case you've forgotten. I thought you'd *tightened* security around here."

He stopped in mid-stride, halfway around the desk. Taking a deep breath, he steadied himself, and I watched him very deliberately pull calm around him the way I'd seen a woman at my grandmother's church put on a familiar and comfortable shawl. He changed direction to sit in the guest chair next to mine. We were close enough that he could easily touch me if he wished, and it gave him an unobstructed view of what I was holding.

"I'm sorry, Celia. You're right." His voice was tightly controlled. I could tell he was still angry, but he wouldn't let the emotion control him. This was more like the Jeff Scott I knew. In fact, the fit of temper he'd shown coming in was so unlike him that I wondered if Ren wasn't right and he needed therapy.

"This wasn't your fault. May I?" He nodded toward the box.

"Are you sure you want to? Last time someone else touched it, it shocked the hell out of her."

A small frown crossed his face, but he was nothing if not determined. He set his jaw and reached out. "I'll take my chances."

I passed the box to him. He didn't flinch or hesitate and it moved into his grasp without event. I was glad. My hand was still tingling from earlier.

"What is it?" he asked, running his fingers carefully over the intricately carved wood. Lifting the lid, he set it on the desk beside him.

"It was a gift from my siren visitor. She called it a Wadjeti. It's used for some form of divination."

"Sirens." His expression soured. "I suppose that's how she affected me—made me do things without my remembering?" He shook his head and let out a low growl. "I wouldn't have believed it if my conversation with her hadn't been on one of the security tapes." His tone of voice made it clear how annoyed he was about this.

"Probably," I admitted with a shrug, "but don't ask me how it works. My gran said it's a form of psychic 'call,' but she didn't have much more information to give me than that." Actually, she'd told me quite a few things, but none of them applied here and I wasn't inclined to share them.

"The woman this morning manipulated me. She appeared in my home through a dozen magical barriers and I was compelled to bring her here and take her to your rooms. Then she sent me off, told me to get myself a cup of coffee. And I had to do it. *Wanted* to. Anything to please her." He shivered. "Birchwoods is supposedly secure against teleportation, but my home was not." He scowled. "I didn't think it was necessary. My home address is not common knowledge among the staff." He paused, his expression souring. "Of course, she could have *persuaded* someone to tell her."

There was a tension to his body that wasn't normally there. His gestures were too sharp, his voice just a couple of notes higher than normal. I might not have noticed had Ren not mentioned it, but Jeff didn't seem quite *right*. He was trying too hard. It was almost as if he was doing a really good impression of himself.

"It's possible, I suppose."

"Did she give you a reason for the visit?"

"She said she wanted to give me a gift." I indicated the Wadjeti.

"You don't believe her?" His face said he agreed, but he couldn't help but slip into doctor-patient mode every time he saw me now.

"Mostly I got the feeling she was trying to stir up trouble. Ren doesn't get along with Adriana and wants to make her look bad."

"Adriana being the siren from the wake?"

"Yes. The gift was just an excuse."

"Are you expecting any more visits?"

I shrugged. "No. But I wasn't expecting this one, either. You have to remember, until very recently I didn't know much more about sirens than that they existed. I still don't—and I need to. I'm caught up in the middle of some sort of political mess and I don't know what the hell is going on. I don't like it. And I really don't like that they can just come and go as they please."

He nodded. "Nor do I. Is there anyone you can discuss this with? Find out more of what's going on?"

"Not really. My grandfather might have known something. But he's been dead for years. Gran told me everything she knew. Maybe somebody at the university can help me. If nothing else, they probably have some information in the library. One way or another, I think I'm going to need a day pass."

He scowled. "You aren't *due* for a day pass. You certainly haven't earned one. More to the point, I'm not positive the courts would approve. Whatever it is can wait until tomorrow when you have your hearing."

"Can it?" It was a pointed question. "You're the one who was complaining about the magic that thing's giving off. I'd like to get it into the safe at my office. The layers of wards should be heavy enough to block whatever the Wadjeti is giving off."

If I did get a pass I was also going to find an expert to check out the death curse. But I didn't want to tell Jeff that unless I absolutely had to. It wasn't easy with him sitting so close to me, but I was doing my best to make sure that he didn't get a glimpse of that palm. Less easy but just as important, I was trying not to think about it so that he wouldn't "overhear."

Death curses are nasty, nasty business, dangerous to not only the victim but also those around them. My having one might get me kicked out of Birchwoods. I don't think Jeff wanted to see me in the state prison/asylum, but I absolutely believed he was anxious to get away from me. And if I got kicked out of here, there was a good chance no one else would take me—and that would mean the state facility, unless charges were dismissed at my hearing. I wouldn't need a death curse to get killed there.

"You're not telling me everything." Dr. Scott leaned back in his chair, steepling his fingers in front of his lips.

"Well . . . no," I admitted, "but I'm not lying. And you really don't *want* to know everything, do you?" That was a guess but a good one. The longer we talked, the more obvious his unease became.

He stared at me for a long moment in silence, his dark eyes burning with intensity. The tension built until he could stand it no longer. He spoke in a quiet voice, but his entire body was quivering, as if it was costing him everything he had to maintain control. "It doesn't bother you at all, does it? We were kidnapped . . . tortured. You *killed people*."

He sounded so damned judgmental. I felt sorry for him, but I was also angry. I'd saved his ass out there. They were going to kill us both. He knew it. He'd seen it in the driver's mind. "What the hell was I supposed to have done? It was a professional kidnapping. We could have died—*would have* if it hadn't been for Ivy's intervention and my fighting abilities. You want someone to blame? Fine. But it damned well better not be me, because it wasn't my fault." I met Jeff's gaze without backing down. I was *pissed*. How dare he sit there acting all high-and-mighty?

I continued. "Of course it bothers me. And it scares the hell out of me. Because they were pros—pros with *police connections*. But it wasn't your fault. It wasn't *mine*, either. And if it's a choice between me and them, I choose me. I made up my mind about that a long time ago."

"It's not that simple." He crumpled in the face of my anger. He was whispering and looking down at the palms of his hands in the classic "Lady Macbeth" pose. He was suffering, really suffering. He needed professional help.

"Yeah, it is." I spoke as gently as I could. "Ultimately, it really is that simple. You don't need to feel guilty. You didn't kill anybody. And I only killed those who would have seen us dead."

"That doesn't make it any better." He looked at me, his eyes haunted.

"It doesn't?"

"No. You can't imagine what it felt like to have him inside my mind—slicing, cutting just to hurt me. . . . It was—" He swallowed hard. "He laughed when I screamed and then did it again." Dear lord, they'd *raped* him, as surely as if it had been his body. He'd been tortured. Just like I'd been, with Ivy. "I can't even close my eyes at night without seeing flashes of raw magic."

Well, shit. Then I *really* didn't know how to help. I started to touch him and then realized it would be the wrong thing to do. Too personal. "Look, Jeff, you need to talk to somebody. You really do. Post-traumatic stress can do terrible things to a person if they don't get help. You know that better than anyone. I know it from firsthand experience. You've been tortured. Just because you don't have scars doesn't mean you don't have *scars*."

I watched him fight to pull himself back together, saw the pleasant mask slide into place. In a minute, two at the most, he looked like his old self. It was a good act. Anyone who hadn't seen him break down would never guess there was anything wrong.

"You can have the day pass. I'll take care of the paperwork. It'll be ready for you in a half hour." He stood, the usual signal that it was time to go. I rose but didn't move toward the door.

"I meant what I said. You need to get help. I know you don't want anyone here to know, but if you go somewhere else—"

"Word can still get around," he said sourly. "People talk. Oh, they don't use *names*. But it always gets around. It's too juicy not to."

"Not if you make them take binding oaths." My voice was cold, hard.

His eyebrows rose high enough to disappear beneath his hair. Obviously, I'd surprised him. Maybe it was that I cared enough to suggest it. Or maybe it was the whole "binding oath" thing. Most people aren't willing to take a true binding. It impinges too much on their free will. And it's not an easy thing to do. Only a top-flight magical practitioner or a true-believer cleric can pull it off. But if you can get it done, they are completely reliable.

"I'll think about it." I hoped he would. But I wasn't sure.

He gestured toward the door with one hand. I was being dismissed.

I felt bad, but I couldn't think of anything more I could do for him. So I left.

6

It took me an hour to leave Birchwoods. Thanks to Jeff's orders to the staff, I was able to get my keys, cell phone, and some of my personal belongings. I made a few calls, making arrangements, and decided to change into *real* clothes. I was almost deliriously happy not to be wearing gray. Stupid, I know, but still true.

Most important, I needed to eat—or, rather, drink. *Oooooh, baby.* I was overdue and it was starting to show. Thus far I've avoided actual uncooked blood, even animal. The longer I can keep it that way, the better, as far as I'm concerned. I mean, *ewwww.* And even if I eventually have to do the animal blood thing for nutritional reasons, that's as far as it will go. I am never going to taste human blood. Period. End of story.

Of course nobody else seems to believe that. They tell me that once I taste human blood, I'll turn into a full vampire. And everyone seems to believe that someday I'll "succumb." I refuse to. I am not a fucking bat and I have no intention of becoming one. Still, temptation is definitely something to be avoided.

On the plus side, the chef here has taught me that it's possible to have shakes that actually taste like what they were in the solid stage. I asked him to put together some recipes. It'll be worth the money. We've been experimenting with baby food in hopes that I can eventually work my way up to solids.

For the moment, I asked for a repeat of the waffle shake, with an additional protein component of some kind to get my day started on the right nutritional footing. They said it would take a few minutes to put together, so I took my time picking what I wanted to wear from among the extremely limited choices available to me at the moment. In the end I decided on my favorite pair of faded blue jeans and a polo in a shade of blue. My hair is naturally silver blond and while my eyes are gray rather than blue, the shirt was in one of the few colors that didn't look odd with my new complexion I decided to bring along a long-sleeved denim jacket and hat for practical reasons. Slathering on heavy-duty sunscreen works for a while, but when it wears off I can wind up with second- and third-degree burns in no time. They don't scar, but they're painful as hell. So like it or loathe it, I cover as much skin as I can during daylight hours.

I wished I had my weapons. Any weapons. But I hadn't brought any with me to the wake, so I didn't have any at Birchwoods. Unless Bruno had hidden a couple in my car when he'd brought it over, I was going to have to do without.

I took a couple extra minutes to do my makeup. My friend Dawna did some extensive online shopping in the short period between my being bitten and her becoming disabled trying to find colors that don't make me look like a clown. I ended up with a really minimalist palette that leans toward stark, cool colors. It's made me understand the whole "vampires in black" thing. There just aren't many colors that look good when you're undead.

By the time the food arrived I looked presentable. I even had a cute little purse to go with the outfit. When I'm working, I just slip my wallet and phone into the pockets of my jacket, but I was feeling girly today. Seeing Ren looking so flawless had pricked my vanity a little, much as I hated to admit it.

I wolfed down the warm, buttery, maple-flavored slushy, suddenly sorry I hadn't asked for two. It seemed hard to believe there was actually nutrition in it. Even better, the "meat protein" the chef had chosen was a maplewood beef sausage that went perfectly with my "waffle." It tasted like real food and I'd have paid money for it in any restaurant, even before the attack.

I was ready to dive out the door when a nurse stopped by with a syringe and a tray of tubes. "What's this for?"

"Your treating physician said we needed to test your blood to see if you were linked magically to anyone."

We'd talked about that in therapy. I was confident my vampire sire was dead. King Dahlmar had taken care of that as an advance payment for helping him with his son and the demon. I was grateful enough to have my sire dead that I'd wrapped my body around the unconscious prince to protect him while a seriously ticked-off demon sliced and diced me. But there were still questions about other vamps and sirens and heaven only knows what. Yeah, I wanted to know who I was "linked" to. "Oh, right. Can you make it quick? I need to get going."

"Do my best."

It probably only felt like he drew as much as the bloodmobile would. Still, I managed not to complain. I am trying very hard to be a cooperative patient . . . with limited success. But I am trying. Several tubes later I was able to grab the Wadjeti and dive out the door.

As the gate to the facility swung closed behind the back bumper of my Miata I felt a surge of pure joy. *Freedom!* There's nothing like it. I hate feeling trapped, and a gilded cage is still a cage. So while I might only be out for a mere twelve hours, I was going to make the most of it.

First stop—the university and a meeting with Warren Landingham. He was my favorite professor in college and had earned the affectionate nickname El Jefe. He's one of the top experts in the world on all things paranormal. And if he doesn't know the answers, he's bound to know someone who does. I couldn't wait to show him the Wadjeti and the curse mark and to find out what had been going on with my friends during my absence. As Kevin and Emma's father, he generally stays pretty well in the loop in our little circle of friends.

I turned onto Ocean View, windows down so that I could feel the early-morning breeze blow through, hear the sounds and smell the scents of the ocean.

It was going to be a busy day. There were a lot of things I needed to do and one or two others I wanted to. Top of the latter list was attending the reading of Vicki's Will. Jeff had actually suggested (strongly) I *not* go. If he'd had his normal presence of mind, he would have remembered that the reading was today. I felt a little bad about not reminding him. But only a little.

Vicki's mother is fairly ruthless and a little unscrupulous. I worried that if I didn't attend the reading, things could mysteriously . . . happen to the original Will. Yeah, it sucks to be that paranoid, but my own mom is no prize, so I have low expectations. Such were my none-too-pleasant musings when my cell phone rang. Swearing, I tried to keep my eyes on the road and the steering wheel steady with my left hand while I rummaged in my purse with my right.

I managed to get my hands on the phone without doing anything unfortunate and flicked it open, hitting the buttons to answer and put it on speaker. "Celia here."

"Oh good, I caught you."

I recognized Warren's voice immediately. He wasn't the first person I'd called about Ren's little gift. I'd tried to ring Bruno the moment I was outside the facility's cell phone–jamming range, but he didn't answer. I really hoped to get his take on it. Even more important, I had a couple of questions about the death curse and the mark on my palm. Like why hadn't anyone noticed it before this and, oh, I dunno, maybe, how the hell can we get rid of it? But with the time difference on the East Coast, he was probably already at work, doing something where he couldn't take calls. I'd left a voice mail. Even if he didn't get back to me today, I was pretty sure he'd be at my hearing tomorrow. Then I'd called Warren.

Now, I couldn't help but smile. "What's up?"

"I called a friend of mine over at UCLA. If you can put off your visit to the campus until four, I've arranged a videoconference call with her. She's very interested to see your Wadjeti. If it's as old and as powerful as you say, she'd like to arrange to come up and see it in person. She seemed astonished that you'd have such a thing."

"Why?"

"Apparently, while there are a number of imitation, mass-manufactured sets that have hit the market in the past few years, there are only two complete ancient Wadjeti on hand. One is on display in the Smithsonian. The other's in a museum in Cairo."

Wow. All right then. Just to make sure we were actually talking about the same thing I said, "Well, Ren called it a Wadjeti. Basically it's a carved box containing a bunch of thumb-sized scarabs of different colors with symbols carved onto the bottom of each."

"That's a Wadjeti all right. Used correctly they're extremely accurate tools for divination."

Which meant it would be pretty much useless to me. "As soon as your friend has had her look at it, I'm locking it up in the safe. It's got enough juice that my hand's still tingling and it knocked Ren flat on her ass." I continued, "Did you have any luck on the curse?"

"Possibly. Dr. Sloan agreed to come by the office and take a look at you while you're here. He seemed pretty skeptical. Said that if you'd had it long and the curse was that strong, one of us surely would've noticed it back when you were a student."

"Unless it got put on me after." I checked the mirror and changed lanes. If I wasn't going straight to the university, I might as well stop by the office before the Will reading. I wanted to check on Dawna, my secretary and friend, and there were no doubt plenty of messages and other things to take care of. I'd also be able to put Ren's gift behind wards until it was time to head for the university. Maybe I was being overly cautious, but better safe than sorry.

"Always a possibility." Warren agreed. "Aaron has class until four fifteen, but he said he'd stop by my office right after."

"I really appreciate all of this, Warren."

He laughed. "I don't mind. In fact, I'm rather looking forward to seeing the artifact. And curses are always fascinating."

"Particularly to the cursee." My voice practically dripped sarcasm.

Warren knows me too well to be offended. He laughed and said, "Just be careful. I don't want anything to happen to you before you can get here."

"Your lips to God's ear." I hit the end button on the phone.

I felt better. Oh, I was still worried, but Warren was on the job. If there was a way out from under this, he'd find it. In the meantime, it was a beautiful day in sunny Cali. I wasn't locked up. Things could definitely be worse.

Even thinking something like that is tempting fate. But hey, no risk, no gain.

After only a few minutes on the freeway I turned off and went tooling through the older section of the city. I felt the familiar sharp tingle as I passed over the wards around the parking lot of the building where I have my offices, pulled into my usual parking spot, and hopped out of the car.

My offices are on the third floor of an old Queen Anne–style Victorian mansion. It's a beautiful building, perfectly tended.

I took a deep breath, soaking in the scent of flowering shrubs and stately old palms. But I discovered the careful order was only surface deep. Because when I stepped through the door I learned a new definition of chaos.

Anyone who is used to having their office life organized by a really efficient secretary knows the kind of hell that breaks loose when said secretary is out.

It was instantly obvious to me that Dawna had not opened the office this morning—and that she probably hadn't been in for a couple of days at least. The phone was ringing off the hook, and as I raced to answer it I stumbled into a pile of UPS parcels behind the desk. The unmistakable smell of caramelized coffee was floating out of the kitchen, and somewhere in the middle distance I heard a cat yowling. A *cat*?

"What the *hell*?" Skirting the boxes, I managed to dive behind the desk. All four lines were ringing. I answered each and put them all on hold, then raced to the kitchen to take the coffeepot off the burner. I didn't feel like picking shards of glass out of my feet for a week if the carafe shattered from overcooking. With that crisis averted, I began wading through the rest of the mess. After about fifteen minutes and the third insulting and irate caller, I resolved that I never, ever, was going to be a secretary. I truly don't the temperament. Still, I managed to sort through things well enough that Ron, the attorney whose office is on the first floor, actually opened his door and looked out to see why the ruckus had stopped. Not that he had made any effort whatsoever to help stop the ruckus. But that was Ron, down to his probably pedicured toenails.

I'd noticed there were people in the waiting room, and

while my higher brain function recognized them, I didn't have time to deal with them until I could actually *breathe*.

When there was enough room to sit down behind the reception desk, I turned to face the visitors.

The man in the closest chair was John Creede. I was more than a little surprised to see him. He's one half of Miller & Creede, the largest security firm in the country, and Bruno's future boss. Creede might have enjoyed second billing, but I'd met both Miller and Creede and Creede was the one with real power magically. He'd been at Vicki's wake, guarding her mother, Cassandra. Who was she being guarded *from*? Why, yours truly, of course.

So why was he here—and without her?

Sitting across from him was a lovely older woman with a kind face and sparkling eyes. At her feet was a blue plastic box with a carrying handle and wire mesh door. A moment of pure panic coursed through me at the sight of her and the delicate *mew* that came from the carrier. *Oh, hell. I forgot. The cat. I agreed to take Dottie's cat. Shit.* But I'd told her at the wake that I couldn't take Minnie the Mouser until after I got out of Birchwoods. Had something changed?

"Sorry for the delay, folks. As you can see, it's been a little . . . busy."

"You're not that bad a receptionist." As Creede stood up and walked to the desk, I gave him the look that comment deserved and he laughed. He had a nice laugh, one that lit up his face. I couldn't remember ever seeing him laugh or even give more than a polite smile. Of course, I'd only seen him on duty. Bodyguarding is a very serious business.

Today he wasn't dressed for work. In fact, we looked almost

like twins. His jeans were a little more worn and his polo was a slightly darker blue, but other than that we matched.

He noticed me noticing and gave me a smile. It was a good smile, charming, showing straight white teeth in a face that was handsome but not excessively so. Like me, he hadn't won the genetic lotto, but he hadn't lost his shirt, either. He had a strong jaw and good cheekbones, but his nose was a little bit large and hooked, almost but not quite a beak. Eyes the color of honey met my gaze easily and today they held just a hint of warmth.

That made me immediately suspicious. What was he up to?

"So, John, what's up?" I kept my voice calm, but I knew it was tinged with frustration and wariness.

"I want to rent an office."

I blinked. Slowly. I don't doubt it made me look stupid, but I couldn't help it. I was struck positively dumb. I had to have misheard him. Miller & Creede owns two or three *buildings* in the greater California area. "Why would Miller and Creede open a branch office in our tiny little city? You've already got a huge office in L.A."

He gave me a look that held more anger than pain. "You might as well hear it from me first. Miller and Creede is becoming Miller Security. The news should hit the papers tomorrow."

"Crap! What the hell happened?" The words popped out. Probably not tactful of me. Then again, tact has never been my best thing. Another one of the big reasons why I work for myself rather than one of the big firms.

"The short version? My partner decided to fuck me and he didn't even kiss me first." John's voice was filled with a cold, hard rage that almost made me feel sorry for the other guy. He glanced at Dottie belatedly and had the decency to flush. "Pardon my French."

She waved it off. "I've heard worse, dear. Not much bothers me at my age."

Wow. Miller was an idiot. I mean, I'd only met him briefly and he hadn't struck me as particularly stupid, but you do not cross a man like Creede. He might not have as much raw magical *oomph* as Bruno, but Creede makes charms that has made him a major player, both respected and feared by the bad guys. No, you don't cross Jonathan Creede. Not if you want to stay healthy.

"I was also going to talk to you about going into business together."

Into business? Together? Me and one of the biggest names in the industry? My brain couldn't even wrap itself around that concept. But even as the ambitious part of my brain was screaming, *Do it! Do it!* I couldn't seem to be able to bring my lips to form words.

He shrugged and looked around. "But if you can't even afford a secretary—"

"I *have* a secretary. I don't know what happened to her. But unless somebody forgot to tell me something, I have one." That wasn't the complete truth. Dawna is more than my secretary; she's one of my best friends. And I was pretty sure I knew exactly what was wrong with her. Not long ago she had been mind-raped by a thousand-some-year-old vampire who'd been looking for me. It damaged her. She was supposedly getting help, but I'd been a little out of touch, what with being an inpatient at the mental facility and all. At a guess, judging by the office, she wasn't doing so hot. I tried to ignore the wave of guilt that washed over me and focused on the situation at hand.

"I think she quit." Bubba from Freedom Bail Bonds had come through the front door and immediately picked Creede as the man to keep his eye on. Bubba's a big ole southern man who looks and sometimes behaves like a stupid redneck, but it's a carefully constructed act. He doesn't belong to Mensa only because he doesn't like "clubs." He's originally from central Texas, keeps his head shaved and covered with worn ball caps. About six foot one, he's built like a linebacker or a small tank, with next to zero body fat. His nose has been broken at least once since I've known him, but I don't think it was ever actually straight. Today he was wearing a Lynyrd Skynyrd Free Bird T-shirt over black jeans and heavy black work boots. "She walked out early on Friday after throwing the phone across the room and saying she *couldn't take this anymore*. She hasn't called or shown up since. I got a temp in, but Ron pissed her off and she walked out after a couple of hours. I told Ron that this time *he* could take care of finding a replacement."

Which he hadn't, Ron being Ron and all. Bubba glanced coldly at Ron's closed office door and intentionally raised his voice to a low shout. "We're *supposed to be* taking turns answering the phones." The look he gave me said things that should never reach air. "Today was Ron's day."

Of course it was. *Asshole*. Never mind that every missed phone call was another potential client lost.

"All right." I took a deep, steadying breath and turned to Creede. "I *had* a secretary. I will either get her back or find us another one." Dawna was my friend. If I could save her job for her, I would. And I *so* did not want Ron in charge of hiring a replacement.

"There is an office available on the third floor." I pulled open the narrow center drawer of Dawna's desk and pulled out the master key she kept there. "Look for the doors without signs. Go see what you think."

Creede took the key. He was keeping a straight face, but his eyes were sparkling. Apparently he found the situation funny but was keeping his mouth shut. Wise man.

I just wish I could figure out why alarm bells were ringing up a storm in my head. I needed to get hold of Bruno right away, see if he'd heard anything about the Miller-Creede split and what it might mean for Creede and for *us*. Since Creede had been the headhunter for the firm, did that mean Bruno's new job was out the window?

"I'll take him up. Show him around," Bubba offered, his gaze very steady on Creede.

Perfect. "Go with Bubba." I made it a benediction as I gestured toward the staircase. They went, which left me with Dottie, her cat, and a stack of various-sized boxes.

Our eyes met and she smiled. In looks, Dottie reminds me of Betty White, but she has the disposition of Aunt Bea from Mayberry. Dottie's a savvy and talented level-seven or -eight clairvoyant. I'd met her when her ex-son-in-law, a detective for the local police force, had needed to get some answers about the night I was attacked. My memories had been blocked and she cleared them. Unfortunately, he had been very sick at the time. He probably would have been dead from his illness by now, but instead he'd managed to become a hero and die in uniform so his kids would get his pension. I think Dottie had seen his eventual death from the disease, because she wound up giving him the information to be at the right place and time to be killed in the line of duty. I liked her. Because I felt really bad about Karl's death I'd invited her to Vicki's wake and had agreed to take her cat, whom Dottie couldn't keep in her senior housing. Probably she'd seen that I was going to be in the office today and timed her visit for that.

She used her walker to carefully make her way up to the desk, schlepping the plastic pet carrier. I came around as quickly as I could and took the load from her. The carrier wasn't really heavy, but it was awkward, mainly because the occupant wasn't inclined to sit still. Every time she moved, the weight and balance of the thing shifted. I set the carrier on the countertop to take a look at the feline inside.

The cat was a tiny thing, orange and white, with huge green-gold eyes that seemed far too intelligent to belong to a supposedly dumb animal. I got the impression that she was sizing me up and wasn't really thrilled with the result.

"So, Dottie, good to see you. What's up?"

"You remember we talked about Minnie?"

I remembered.

"Well, I was afraid you'd changed your mind and hoping if you actually met her—"

"But Dottie—I'm still in Birchwoods and I'm not even sure I have a home to go to when I'm out."

She got a *look* in her eyes. Now, there are cold, hard-hearted, *sensible* people who can look deep into the watery eyes of little white-haired old ladies and tell them there is no way in hell they're taking care of a cat. Alas, I am not one of them.

Before I could stop myself, I sighed and "Oh, okay," popped out of my mouth. But I was at least able to mitigate the damage. "On one condition."

"What?" She looked at me with wide eyes. I suppose she was seeing her last hope for the cat disappearing.

"How good are you at answering phones? I've got kind of a crisis here."

She smiled and made a shooing motion with her hand. "Get out of the way and I'll show you how it's done."

I shifted out of the way. As she passed me, she gave me a beatific, if slightly smug, smile. "Minnie's litter box is in the backseat of my car. It's the white Oldsmobile. Do you mind?"

I wondered how many people wound up doing her bidding because of that walker and that smile. Another sigh. "Right."

I am such a sucker.

I reflected on that as I got the litter box. That and the presence of John Creede. *Damn.* I don't like the notion of working *for* anybody and I would never have fit in with Miller & Creede with their buttoned-down image and "team" attitudes.

But the thought of *partnering* with John Creede. Again, I say, *damn.* Of course it would piss off Miller to no end. But did I really care? The reputation would follow both men and Creede might bring along some of the talent. He could also cover for me with my own clients right now, while I was on my enforced leave of absence. Because if somebody didn't, those clients would go elsewhere. And if they wound up happy elsewhere, I'd lose them for good.

The empty litter pan and two bags of litter were right where Dottie had said they'd be, along with a box containing ceramic food and water dishes, hard and soft food, a cat bed, one of those carpet-covered cat condos, and a wider variety of cat toys than you'll find at your average discount store. Apparently Minnie the Mouser knew how to live.

I needed three trips to bring it all inside. As I brought in the last of it, I saw Dottie making desperate hand signals as she chatted on the phone. I dropped my burdens and walked over.

"No, dear. It's all right. Really. They haven't replaced you. I've just been hired as your *assistant*." Sweet little old lady she might be, but she lied like a trooper. "I really can't work full-time. If I do, it'll mess up my benefits. But I can cover for you for a day or so until you get back on your feet. You don't need to worry."

Dawna? I mouthed. Dottie nodded. *Is she okay?* She shook her head no, sadly. I winced.

"Here, why don't you talk to Celia, dear." She passed me the phone.

"Hey, Dawna. What's up?"

I spent the next half hour reassuring Dawna that I hadn't stabbed her in the back, she wasn't fired, and her job would be waiting for her when she got out of the hospital. She'd decided to check herself into St. Mary's for a one-week evaluation. Because if she didn't, she was going to kill herself. She didn't say that, but I could hear it in her voice. It broke my heart. It wasn't her fault. I'd met the vampire that "did" her. Nobody but nobody, could've faced Lilith down for long. I'd done it, but I'd had the help of a very holy man armed with the words of banishment and a cross shining with his faith . Dawna hadn't been so lucky. And she felt guilty because she'd given Lilith the address where I was staying.

As I was talking to Dawna, Dottie began, very slowly, putting things to rights. She opened the cat carrier to let Minnie roam around, gathered up the packages I'd dropped, and generally made herself useful. Bless her.

When I finally got through to Dawna that I wasn't angry, didn't blame her, and would visit her in person when I got out of Birchwoods for more than a day pass, she calmed down a bit. When I convinced her that her job was safe she took a shaky breath and said, "You hired me an assistant? And everyone agreed?"

There was an incredulity in her voice that I could fully understand. I interrupted her before she could get wound up again. "Dawna, I am not going to let anyone fire you just because you're having a reaction to being . . . injured. You need to go easy. So I hired you some help. If the group doesn't agree, it's on my dime. Dottie needed a way to pick up a little extra money that wouldn't be too physically strenuous, so I figured it might be the perfect fit." Okay, I was lying. But it was what Dawna needed to hear. Besides, it was a good idea. We'd needed a backup for vacations and sick time anyway, and most temps couldn't deal with Ron for very long. I had a feeling Dottie would be able to handle him. Minnie would be the bait; she could live at the office until I was out of Birchwoods.

It wasn't a bad plan really. Since many of our businesses run on twenty-four-hour workdays, there's nearly always at least one person in the building. Minnie could live in my office and Dottie could watch over her until I was released. Then we'd see how people had warmed to her. Maybe she could be a permanent office cat. I knew Bubba liked cats and

Ron . . . well, he doesn't like *anything*, so who cared what he thought?

"You're *sure* you're not giving away my job?"

"Nope. In fact, since you're going to be a supervisor now, I thought about giving you a raise." I winced the moment the words left my mouth. That really *was* a group decision. I hoped I could convince them it was overdue.

She perked up at that. "How much?"

Better judgment took over and I stalled. "We'll talk about it when you get back. I've gotta go." I handed Dottie the phone before I could get myself in any more trouble. If I wasn't very careful how I presented things at our next tenant meeting, I was liable to be stuck paying for Dottie's salary *and* Dawna's raise. And if anybody was allergic to cats— I shook my head. It would work out. It would. I was not going to think about it right now. Because I'd just glanced at the clock and somehow, during the course of things, it had become 10:00! I was already due to eat again and I hadn't even made it upstairs!

I was about to climb the first step when Dottie stopped me.

"Don't forget your Wadjeti." She gestured to where I'd left the box sitting next to the phone. "It feels quite powerful and looks as if it's very valuable. Such a shame it's missing the death scarab."

She could tell that without even opening the box? Impressive. Then it sank in. "It's missing a piece?" *Oh, crap.* I couldn't know for sure, but I was betting the sirens hadn't given me a defective gift. Which meant that there was probably a thumb-sized piece of ceramic somewhere on the floor at Birchwoods. Unless it had already been gotten rid of by Housekeeping. Which would be bad. Very bad. Nobody likes to think you are careless with their gifts. Of course, they might not ever find out. But, knowing my luck—

"Which one is the death scarab?"

"It's the red one."

That brought me up short. "There's only one red piece?"

She nodded. Well, now, wasn't that interesting? I distinctly remembered handing Ren the red piece. Of course she'd hustled off right after that. It might just have been an accident. Or not.

"You're sure? I mean, not too many people seem to know about these Wadjeti things."

Dottie smiled sweetly, but her voice had that same scolding tone you get when you put your elbows on the table at Grandma's house. "I *am* a clairvoyant, dear. It's a tool for divination. Karl was planning on giving me a set for my next birthday. He was hoping it'd be easier for me to use than my bowl. I found it and the card, when I was cleaning out his house after his funeral. It came with an instruction book. I read most of it in one sitting. It isn't hard to learn. I can bring the instructions in tomorrow if you'd like." She looked at me slyly. "Should I presume I'll *be* here tomorrow? Or was what you said to Dawna just to make her feel better?"

"You'd actually be willing?"

"Of course. And it will give me a chance to see Minnie regularly." She smiled sweetly.

"Cool." I was relieved. The temp situation was solved and, I hoped, the cat issues as well. "I won't be here tomorrow, so just leave a copy for me here at the front desk." I gave her my best smile and grabbed the Wadjeti box. "Now I have got to get upstairs, or I'm not going to get anything done. Are you sure you'll be all right?"

"I'll be fine." She winked at me. "We can talk about my salary later."

I just bet we would.

It was a relief to finally get out of the lobby and up the stairs. My office takes up a large portion of the third floor. There is no elevator, only a steep staircase. But if Dottie was going to work here . . . was there somewhere to put an elevator? Or maybe one of those electric stair lift things? It was a historic building. We technically didn't need to be ADA compliant. But still—

As I rounded the second-floor landing, passing the stained-glass window, I heard Creede chatting amiably with Bubba about boats and deep-sea fishing. Creede was admiring one of the photos of Bubba's boat displayed on the office wall. Technically, it's a good-sized yacht, and he bought it at a government auction. But he calls it a boat, because "I ain't that fancy."

As I came closer, the subject switched back to Creede's situation and what he was doing here. "I woulda thought you'd have had a binding oath set up to keep him from backstabbing you," Bubba chided.

Creede's small chuckle showed his dark side. There was evil under that laugh, mixed with the anger. "Oh, we did. He just decided that there'd be enough money left after the medical bills to make it worth it."

I shook my head. To my mind, Miller was stupid. That's all there was to it. Yeah, he'd get the money, but he'd made a bad enemy. Still, greed can make most people stupid.

"So, you gonna rent this place?" Bubba asked.

"I think so. Do you know if Celia had to get the floor reinforced to hold her safe? I'm going to want to put one in, too. Hers is just on the other side of this wall, right?"

"Yep. But you'll have to ask her, or the safe guy. He's due in a half hour. Comes in same time every week to reinforce the spells. If Celia's not here, Dawna lets him in."

A raw, jagged edge of paranoia rushed through me and I suddenly knew why Creede's being here had me on edge. Bubba was being *too* friendly. Creede now knew the layout of the office, knew how often my wards were reinforced and all the tenant names. Future tenant, or future *burglar*? I tried to think of some way to limit the damage in case this was all a very simple and therefore very elaborate trap. So obvious it was overlooked. I decided to make a blunt, direct accusation and see how he responded.

I hurried to the doorway into Bubba's office, just as he was saying, "We're a pretty boring bunch here. Same schedule every week."

"But, of course, that schedule will be changing . . . the moment you're out of earshot." They both turned and simultaneously gave me an odd look. My answering expression showed a lot of fang and as much distrust as was clawing at the pit of my stomach. "Tell me something, John."

I paused long enough that he frowned. It was a better look on him. He crossed his arms over his chest and said, "Maybe."

My nod was automatic. "Perfect. That's just the mind-set I'd like you in for this. Let's reverse our positions for a moment. You're a sole proprietor, in business for a handful of years, comfortable but not wildly successful. Clients are attracted to you because you have a slew of magical gadgets and the skill to use them. With me so far?"

He nodded but didn't comment.

"In walks *me*," I went on. "I'm a partner in a multinational company that is so far above your level I can't be considered competition. I only *personally* guard the most exclusive people, the richest of the rich."

His brow was furrowing even further, if that was possible. At this point, Bubba had also started to frown and his eyes kept flicking to Creede to watch his reaction.

"I made a deliberate point of coming to your office in the company of a client—a client who has a personal grudge against you. Yet now . . ." I held up my hands as though a revival preacher in front of the faithful. "I appear before you with the—you have to admit—slightly outlandish claim that I've broken up with my partner of more than a decade and want to partner with *you*. I inspect a vacant office which just happens to be *right next door* to where you keep your gadgets. I learn the schedule from the other tenants." I looked at him and smiled, showing as much fang as I could. "Tell me, John. What would you do, right this minute?"

His voice came out in a rumble that vibrated his arms on his chest while Bubba started muttering self-berations at himself. "Are you accusing me of *spying*?"

I shrugged, unwilling to react to his growl. "Spying, infiltrating . . . hell, maybe *hexing*. Or, you're completely innocent and I'm just paranoid. I ask again, what would *you*, a professional security consultant, do in my place?"

He glared. I just raised my brows. I could feel magic now, and while he wasn't casting anything, his emotional turmoil was causing energy to whip through the room like errant mosquitoes. You wanted to slap at them, but they were too quick and too small to be seen. Then the wheels started clicking. I watched as his eyes lowered to a place somewhere near but not quite on the floor. After a long moment, he let out a sound like a snort; his chest rose with the force of it. When he met my eyes again, he was actually blushing. "I'd put you in a full-body binding until I could call around to check out your story." He shrugged uncomfortably. "Either that, or I'd kick your butt to the curb and then"—now a smile appeared—"call my safe company and have all the combinations changed and add a few special hexes for anyone cutting through the adjoining wall or ceiling."

Actually, I hadn't thought of that and gave the idea the credit it deserved. "Good idea. I'll mention that. I'd only planned on waiting until you left, but then, I'm not a mage. I like the full-body binding, though. Do those come in a charm disk?"

He pursed his lips. "Dunno. I'd imagine I could come up with something." He grinned again. "But it'll cost you."

The muscles in my stomach were loosening a little as I let out a small chuckle. Either he was a consummate actor or his story was true. I was going with my gut. I hoped I wouldn't regret it. Bubba still looked embarrassed at being so effusive, but he was easing down a little, too. "Just make sure you're not the first person I'll have to use it on." Creede didn't respond, but his eyes were twinkling. "Obviously, I'll need to talk to the others and will have to find out from Dawna where she keeps the sample leases with the terms and house rules."

"Dawna's your secretary? I think I met her at the wake."

Bubba said, "Yeah, that's her," and shook his head. "Poor kid." Dawna wasn't exactly a kid, but his sympathy was well placed. He paused for a moment, then grinned and said, "My vote is to let him take it."

I gave Bubba a return smile. "I could use the rent to pay for Dottie's salary and Dawna's raise."

"You're givin' her a raise?" Bubba was obviously shocked. He'd probably expected me to vote for firing her for not showing up.

"Guilt money," I admitted. "The bat that got her was after me. I'd do more if she'd let me, but she's too damned proud."

Bubba nodded. He was a tenant in the building before any of the rest of us ever got here. He'd known Dawna a long time.

"That's *nice*." Creede sounded shocked and gave me a startled look.

"I can be nice," I answered, more than a little insulted by the implication.

He raised both hands in surrender and started to apologize. "Sorry. I'd just heard you were a stone-cold bitch. It's sort of one of the reasons I considered you for the business. I need someone tough."

I could just bet where he'd heard *that* from: Vicki's mom. *Damn it.*

"Celia's all right," Bubba rose to my defense. "She's only a bitch if you really deserve it. Act decent and she's cool. But don't make the mistake of thinking she can't be a bitch."

"I'll keep that in mind."

"Do." The growl that escaped me along with the word surprised us all. Apparently, Creede had dug deeper than I realized. I'd get over my annoyance faster if I wasn't in the same room with him, so I turned my back on them and walked to my office.

I unlocked the door and stepped over the threshold, feeling the buzz of power. Last time Bruno visited, he'd put a new set of wards on the doorway. He hadn't bothered to ask if I wanted them. He's sweet like that—he knows I'm *always* in favor of more security. But it was a damned good thing the vampire bite hadn't affected me to the point where I set them off. That would be so embarrassing. And painful. Judging from the amount of buzz I was getting, very painful.

I set the box with the Wadjeti on the desk and opened the safe. I got less of a buzz from it than from the doorway. Not because these wards were less powerful but because the safe had been made for me and was keyed to my DNA. I'd had to reset it postattack, but now that it "knew" the vampire and siren me, it was good. I was just hoping it wouldn't weird out again eight months from now. The safe thinks I'm *pregnant*. That's how we got it to accept my altered DNA.

I set the Wadjeti onto the shelf next to the box with my knives. They both started to glow, each reacting to the magic of the other. A soft, gentle hum filled the metal enclosure. I stared in pleased awe at the beautiful rainbow of colors—my own private aurora borealis that pulsed and danced inches away. *How pretty.*

That emotion lasted for about a second and a half before it occurred to me to shut the safe door in case I was in for more than a light show. Eek. I slammed it closed with a little more force than was probably necessary, just as I heard the gentle tap of knuckles against my office door.

"Yes?"

"It's John Creede. Can I come in?"

I didn't really want him to. But *if* he was going to be a tenant and on the same floor, I should probably be nice. "Sure."

He opened the door, then reached out a hand to touch the invisible line of power with a smile. He glanced over at me. "DeLuca?"

I nodded.

"He does damned fine work." Creede's expression darkened to a scowl as he visibly "swam" through the ward on the door. When he emerged inside the room, he rubbed his arms like they stung. "It just kills me that I may have recruited him to work for George."

"He hasn't said yes yet, has he?" I honestly didn't know, since I hadn't talked to him.

Creede sighed, as if I were being a fool and he was losing patience with it. "He might not have *signed* the contract yet, but you haven't seen the package we negotiated. For *some* reason he really wants to move to this coast, but he's a tough one to please." Creede said it drily and raised one brow. We both knew why Bruno wanted to move. I couldn't wait until he got out here and wished he'd call me back. I was going to be annoyed if he didn't get my message until after I was locked up again.

I wanted to hear his voice and definitely wanted to tell him about this situation. It was going to be damned awkward if I wound up partnering with Creede and Bruno was working for the competition. Because Bruno *is* the best. And the clients would know it.

"So, what just happened?" Creede asked. "I felt . . . *something* in this room, big enough to cause my hairs to stand up even through the wards."

"I put something new in the safe and the things I had in there already reacted," I explained.

"Reacted *how?*" He didn't bother to hide his concern. I couldn't blame him. Magic is dangerous and this was powerful stuff. I wasn't nearly as worried now that the safe door was closed and I had thick steel protecting me.

I shrugged, not to make light of it, but I was confident about the safe. Bruno did the original work, but I had a company that came in on a regular basis to recharge and layer the protections. "Put on a light show. Shot rainbows around the room, hummed a little bit."

"Did the things vibrate? Was the light red, green, what? Did the objects get hot or cold?" Creede fired the questions at me like bullets.

"No vibration, no temperature change, and literally *rainbows,*" I answered, "just colored light. It was really pretty. But I decided I'd better shut the safe door just in case."

"Rainbows." He shook his head and scowled. "*And* they reacted to each other. What the hell do you have in there and how did you get it?"

I liked Creede well enough. But I like my secrets, too. The knives Bruno made for me are valuable enough that there are people who would literally kill to get their hands on them. Even people I've known for years have no idea they exist. And if what El Jefe said about the Wadjeti was true, it was basically priceless. So I just smiled sweetly and said, "Gifts from friends."

"You must have some powerful friends."

I thought about the demon that almost killed me and the woman who set him onto me. He was banished, but you can't kill a greater demon, and she got away. I was pretty sure Kevin was hunting her, but she was definitely going to be a hard target. Was that what Ivan had been contacting me about? I wished I knew. "I'm just hoping they're as powerful as my enemies."

Creede didn't have an answer to that, so he changed the subject. "Look, I'd like to apologize to you for what I said earlier."

"It's all right." Actually, it wasn't. It still stung. I tell myself I don't care what people think, that the tough-girl image is part and parcel of the whole bodyguard thing. But it's more a suit, a persona I put on in the morning. It's not the *real* me and I do care. It's stupid, I know. But I do. And I'm not a bitch. I know plenty of them and they don't want me in the club.

He shook his head firmly, which did more to make amends than the apology. "No. It's not all right. I know better than to believe gossip. But if it helps any, I'm about to get my share of karmic repentance in the press." He gave me a chagrined look. He was right, too. The tabloids were going to have him for lunch once they learned of the split. The spin-off partner can easily become a public pariah in any business. Magic just makes it worse. It wouldn't be hard for the press to find present and former M&C employees who would demonize John, off and on the record. After a second of me *not* assuring him it'd all be okay, he sighed. "Let me make it up to you by buying you a meal. We can talk business, so your boyfriend won't get jealous."

"Bruno doesn't get jealous."

"Bullshit." Creede's grin lit up his face and he went from good-looking to handsome in an instant. "You forget, I saw you together at the wake." He laughed. "And I've met 'Uncle

Sal.'" He made little quotes in the air when he said the name. "Trust me, I'll behave. There are some people that even magic won't save you from."

I believed that. You did not cross Uncle Sal. But I kept my tone casual. "I'll have to take a rain check, I'm afraid. I have an appointment downtown in a few minutes. I hadn't planned on staying here this long as it is. But yeah, I'll want to sit down and have a heart-to-heart talk with you before I let you actually sign."

Another small, amused curl of his lips. "You still don't trust me."

I just shrugged and returned the smile. Hell, I barely trust *myself*.

I arrived at the offices of Pratt, Arons, Ziegler, Santos, and Cortez a few minutes after the Will reading was supposed to start. Mostly it was due to traffic, but I also didn't want to have a scene in front of the office staff when Vicki's parents saw me. Sadly, the receptionist recognized me and smiled. I say "sadly" because I've spent a lot of time and a truckload of money here lately because of my upcoming hearing.

"Morning, Tabitha. Where are they holding Vicki's Will reading?"

"Good morning, Miss Graves." Tabitha's voice was painfully polite. She didn't like me. It was all over her body language. But I was a paying client, so she'd play nice. "We weren't expecting you." I knew I was on the list of attendees, but I'd also been in the room when Dr. Scott had called to tell Barney Arons I wouldn't be attending.

I didn't reply, just raised one brow. She nodded and picked up the phone, dialing three numbers before moving her gaze to the desk in front of her. I've noticed most receptionists do that when they take a call, as though it creates an invisible wall between them and the person standing at the desk. "Yes, sir. Celia Graves is here?" She made it a question and I knew why. Would Arons tell me to take a hike? He had every right.

I could hear the reply with my shiny new vampire ears. "Tell her to come up, please. We haven't started yet."

"Of course. Thank you." She put down the receiver. "They're in conference room B-nine." She turned and pointed to the stairs. "Next floor up, take a right at the top of the stairs, go all the way to the end, turn left, and it's the third door on the left."

"Up, right, left, left. Got it. Thanks."

"Have a nice day." She tried to make it sound sincere and failed. Whatever. I turned right, as instructed, and started walking. I knew from previous visits that this entire floor was devoted to conference rooms, which I thought was a really nifty idea and very smart planning. Cozy little enclaves held just two or three people—I'd often met Roberto in those (usually when his office was too trashed to dig out a chair)—while other, massive rooms could seat forty or fifty people around a single, unhexable table. All the tables were various shades of marble or slate, which made me wonder aloud to Roberto once about the logistics of hauling the solid stone slabs up. He'd replied with a snort, "Cranes, scaffolds, reinforcing floors, removing windows . . . you don't want to *know* the headaches." And he was probably right.

The reading was apparently in one of the big rooms, because

it took a while to get to "third door on the left." At least I had time to admire the stunning abstract paintings on the walls and feel the soft cushion of high-dollar carpeting underfoot. It was utterly silent in the bright hallway. Every room was soundproofed for confidentiality and I could feel the press of avoidance spells that forced me not to stop at certain rooms — probably where other meetings were taking place.

In the end, it wasn't hard to spot the proper room: It was the one with armed guards standing on either side of the door. Both men were big and wore crisply starched brown uniforms that looked almost like those of a state trooper. They were armed and each wore a holy item on a silver chain around his neck. I wondered if they were here to keep the parties inside safe or to keep the rest of the office safe *from* the parties inside.

They didn't seem surprised at my appearance, which meant someone had warned them to expect the fangs. I was glad. I was already tired of the commotion my new teeth could bring about.

One guard made me show him my driver's license, which made good sense. Then, after checking my name off a list on his PDA, he opened the door, then carefully closed it behind me. I paused just inside to scan the room and its occupants.

Barney Arons sat in the center of the room, on the far side of the table. The others faced him, along with a large video screen that covered one window. They'd turned their heads as I entered.

"Hey, Celia. Great to see you!" David greeted me warmly, and he and Inez both smiled as I slid into a chair. David and Inez ran the mansion Vicki had lived in when she wasn't at

Birchwoods. David kept the grounds in enviable condition and Inez did the same with the interior . . . including the guesthouse I called home. I wasn't surprised to see them here. Vicki had always said she'd take care of them if anything happened.

I sat near the door in case Cassandra launched herself at me. She looked like she might. Her beautiful face had moved from neutral and sad when I'd first stepped inside to livid hatred. "What are *you* doing here?"

Vicki's father, the legendary actor Jason Cooper, nudged his wife with more force than was probably necessary. He hissed, "Let it go, Cass," and gave her a look. She returned the look with force and he raised his brows. "I mean it. Drop it now. This isn't the time *or* the place."

Instead of relaxing, she pushed back her chair. I tensed. Sure, I could handle her, but I really didn't want to hurt her. She was my best friend's mother. Vicki would be hurt beyond belief if I harmed Cassandra. The worst part was that I hadn't done anything wrong. I'd loved Vicki like a sister. It made me sad how much Cassandra hated me. But she didn't turn my way. Instead, she moved to the far end of the room and sat down in the chair opposite me. Then she proceeded to ignore me completely. She pulled a nail file from her purse and began shaping her already perfect nails.

Sheesh, all that trouble, just so I'd *know* she was ignoring me. I shook my head and leaned back. So she was going to be dramatic instead of physical. Worked for me.

Alex was also there. She gave me a sad smile. Her eyes were red—she'd been crying again. Detective Heather Alexander had been Vicki's lover. They were as close as a honeymoon couple and had one day hoped to marry. While we aren't close, Alex and I get along well enough to get by.

It was disturbing to see the person next to Alex face-to-face. Sybil Jones was the woman Cassandra had selected to be Vicki's double. Hired when Vicki was just a teenager, Sybil was the public face of Victoria Cooper, the darling of the social set in Monte Carlo and the Hamptons. Personally, I never thought Sybil looked all that much like Vicki. She had a different facial shape—oval to Vicki's heart—and her nose wasn't the same at all. She'd cut her hair into the latest bob, which would have looked ridiculous on Vicki but dramatically altered Sybil's overall appearance. I might not have been so uncomfortable with her if I hadn't known that her very existence had been a source of never-ending hurt to Vicki— not just that her parents wouldn't acknowledge who she really was but also that they were *embarrassed* by her.

The press had finally gotten wind of the deception. Vicki had commented more than once that she actually felt sorry for Sybil. Yes, she was given a life of privilege, with jewelry, trips, and fame. But now what? What did the future hold for a woman who had lived most of her life as a lie? She'd betrayed every relationship she might have made—*had to*, to keep the secret. I'd imagine it was like being a spy, a James Bond. Frankly, I couldn't do it. It would ruin me emotionally.

She glanced at me blankly. We'd met just once, so I wasn't surprised she didn't remember. It had been . . . awkward. Like Alex, Sybil had been crying. For the loss of a woman she never knew, or the end of her life of privilege?

We sat in silence for several minutes. Arons continued to

make notes on a yellow legal pad. After checking her watch for the fifth time, Cassandra finally spoke: "Are we going to get *on* with this? We only planned for this to take an hour. We have a flight at three and still have other errands."

Arons looked up and blinked at her from behind thick horn-rimmed glasses. "We're still waiting for five interested parties. According to Ms. Cooper's written instructions, I'm not to read the Will until everyone is present." He went back to writing notes, flipping pages in a thick manila folder with the other hand.

"But we have a *flight*."

The attorney sighed and put down his fat Waterman pen. He took off his glasses and began to polish the lenses with a handkerchief. "Ms. Meadows, I can't imagine what gave you the impression this entire event would take only an hour. Your daughter had an extensive estate, owing to both the inheritance from your parents and her own investment skill. Vicki crafted a very creative and carefully thought out Will. She chose not only to have her wishes memorialized in a standard legal document but also to create a video so there was no question of her intent. Being a highly attuned clairvoyant, she set up a precise timetable for this event. We have another"—he glanced at a gold watch that I was betting was a Rolex—"eight and a half minutes before we begin. Everyone should have arrived by then. If you wish to use the time to good effect . . ." Arons carefully put his glasses back on and cocked his head just a bit. He concluded, "You might want to make a call and change your flight."

I stifled a smirk, but Alex laughed out loud and Cassandra's pale face reddened.

There was a knock on the door. The attorney looked up, glanced at his watch, nodded, and wrote a checkmark on the top sheet of his pad. "Yes?" he called out softly.

The door opened and it was my turn to be surprised and a little angry. John Creede walked in the door and started visibly when he saw me.

I didn't mirror Cassandra's outburst from my arrival, but I did raise an eyebrow and he could probably feel the anger that made my muscles clench. How *dare* he play me, pretend to want . . . well, *what*? Honestly, I couldn't decide why I was angry, but I was. "There wouldn't have been much time for lunch, would there?"

"Celia, I—"

Arons interrupted whatever lame apology Creede had been about to offer. "Thank you for coming on such short notice, Mr. Creede. I was unaware of the change in your office administration. Once I was informed you hadn't received our messages I obtained the number for your cell phone from Mr. Cooper."

"Well, I didn't have anything else scheduled, so I was able to come right over."

John sat down right next to me with barely a glance at Jason and Cassandra; this gesture and his stony facial expression told me that he wanted nothing to do with his former clients. I couldn't bring myself to look up to see the reaction of the Coopers.

Barney Arons clucked his tongue in disapproval. "The receptionist at your former firm should have advised us you were no longer working with them." He sighed. "No harm done, I suppose."

There was another knock on the door, another "Yes?" from Arons.

When the door opened this time, my jaw dropped. A dozen emotions swam through my stomach as my gran stepped in, wearing her best Sunday dress and clutching the little golden purse Vicki had given her one Christmas. Her smile when she saw me lit up the room and she raced over to embrace me in a hug. "Oh, sweetheart. I'm so glad you made it. I've missed you."

I returned the hug with gusto. I'd missed her, too.

Dr. Scott walked through the door at Gran's heels. He took in the occupants with a glance and then his gaze fell on me. His voice was a threatening rumble. "Celia, I am *beyond* angry with you. I believe I made it clear that you were *not* to come to this meeting." He took a single step toward me and Creede stood in a flash, blocking his path. Power began to bleed off them both, filling the room with enough energy that even the protection spell couldn't completely dampen it. John held his hands in classic mage mode, hip level, fingers spread and cupped—ready to throw a fireball if needed. The doctor's brow had furrowed and he'd adjusted his stance so all his weight was on the balls of his feet. I wasn't sure what the *classic* position of a psi-warrior was just before battle, but I was pretty sure I was seeing it.

While I didn't think the doctor would hurt me, I didn't really like the look in his eye. All the little stresses were piling up on him, straining his composure to the breaking point.

Gran likewise turned, putting herself squarely in front of me. But I don't need a bodyguard, much less two. I *am* a bodyguard. I stepped out from around Gran and said, "Guys, let's all calm down, okay? Doctor, I didn't trick you. But as long as I was out for the day I decided I should be here. I may be a patient at your facility, but I make my own decisions. You are not my treating doctor and Dr. Hubbard never saw any problem with my attending. Yes, I'm under court order for treatment but—"

All of a sudden, I started to feel shaky and realized breakfast was wearing off quickly. I was staring at the doctor's neck and the fast-pulsing vein just under the skin. . . . I could feel the drool pooling in my mouth. It wasn't just the good doctor who needed to calm down. I hissed. Everybody stepped away from me as the world slipped into hyperfocus. My hands rose, glowing green fingers curled into claws. Calf muscles twinged as I sank into a crouch, the better to spring at and land on my prey.

Crap. No, not now! Not with Gran in the room!

A cold wind abruptly blew my hair back, probably slapping it against John's face. The temperature in the room dropped hard and fast and my breath began to come out as steam. Writing appeared on the frost-covered glass over an ocean scene. *Knock it off!*

I heard the furnace kick on and warm air began to flow up around my feet and down on the top of my head. The cold had pushed away the hunger and I could think again. Before it could return, I retreated from the situation. I slid my chair away from the table, into the farthest corner of the room, and curled up in the chair, legs against my chest as I struggled to get control of my breathing and my predator's response. The others sat down as well but scooted just a bit farther from me. Even Gran watched me with a new nervousness that I didn't like. But she'd only seen the vampire peek out once and never like this, so I could hardly blame her. I could only hope it didn't affect our relationship.

"Thank you, Vicki." Arons's voice was calm but leaked a bit of nervousness that said that this might not have been on *the schedule*. After taking a deep breath, letting it out slow, and then wiping the fog that had appeared on his glasses, he picked up the phone receiver. "Becky? The confrontation phase is concluded. Please bring in our next guest and the refreshment for Ms. Graves."

Wow. So Vicki had foreseen even this? Damn, she was good. But who was *the next guest*? I didn't even expect half the people already here.

The door at the far end of the room opened and a slightly disheveled brunette woman stepped in the door. I'd seen her around the office before, so I presumed she was Becky. She held open the door and waved someone inside, then brought me a large thermal mug filled with what smelled like French onion soup.

The young man she'd ushered in had skin that was pale, and freckles stood out in sharp relief under a shock of carrot orange hair. Mr. Arons stood and held out his hand across the table. "Mr. Murphy? Barney Arons. We spoke on the phone last month. Thank you for coming. I hope you had a comfortable trip. Is your hotel satisfactory?"

I'd never seen him before in my life and apparently nobody else in the room had, either. Jason and Cassandra were exchanging confused glances, as were Alex and Sybil.

"Yessir. I've never flown in a private jet before and Molly and the girls are loving the hotel room. But you really didn't have to put us up in a *suite*. A regular room would have been just fine." He had a light southern drawl but with a sophisticated edge. I couldn't quite place the location.

"Not at all. Ms. Cooper was very clear in her wishes for your stay here. You were to have the best of everything, with no expenses spared. So, please . . . enjoy it." He waved toward a seat between Cassandra and Jason. "If you'd have a seat? We're ready to start."

Mr. Murphy stopped in his tracks, jaw dropping when he actually got a look at the people he would be sitting next to. I watched him swallow hard and pull himself together enough that he wouldn't act starstruck and embarrass himself in front of everyone.

Arons had said *five* new people. So, Creede, Gran, Dr. Scott, and Mr. Murphy. Was Vicki the fifth, or was there someone yet to arrive? I put down my soup to ask, "Didn't you say *five* people, Mr. Arons?"

He nodded. "Vicki was the fifth. Oh, that reminds me—" He turned to Mr. Murphy. "Mr. Murphy, do you have any problem with ghosts? Or vampires, mages, or psychics?"

Yeah, that was probably a good thing to find out. We had sort of a weird bunch here today.

"Well . . . I've got a cousin who's a mage and my grandma stayed in the house for a bit after she died, until we found her Will. But I'm not a fan of bats, and psychics sort of creep me out. Why?"

"Ah. I see. Let me make formal introductions, for those who don't know each other." Arons took a moment to identify each person gathered at the table and ended with, "Finally, if you'll direct your attention to the ceiling, you'll see a sparkling formation." We all dutifully looked up. The gaseous cloud that was Vicki's normal state in this realm sparkled in the remaining cool air. "The deceased has elected to attend this reading. I hope that doesn't bother anyone."

Mr. Murphy eyed the cloud with an odd look but finally shrugged. "I suppose there's not much to be done about that, is there? Ghosts do what they will. But if she starts throwin' stuff, you'll find me somewhere between here and the hotel. Try to keep up if you want to talk."

Laughter erupted from nearly everyone. It was just what we needed.

Arons checked his watch again. "Excellent. We're right on schedule. Let's begin." He picked up a remote control and pointed it toward the wall. The lights dimmed and the blinds turned to block out the sunlight.

With a press of a key on his laptop, the big screen in front of the windows flickered to life. I couldn't help but smile as Vicki looked out at us. She was sitting in a comfortable-looking chair in front of a bookcase filled with legal volumes, so probably she'd taped this somewhere in these offices. She looked directly at me and smiled, as though she knew right where I was sitting. Then she turned her gaze to each person in turn, ending on Alex, with a wink and a blown kiss. Alex burst into tears anew.

Seeing the screen was a little tricky, so I moved my chair until I had a clearer view.

"My family, friends, and guests," Vicki began. "Thank you all for coming. And thank *you*, Barney, for going to all the trouble to gather everyone together. I know it wasn't easy in some cases."

Arons looked up at the ceiling rather than the screen. "That's our job. We're here to serve."

The Vicki on the screen smiled. "Yes, but you *do* go above and beyond the call. Thank you."

Whoa. That sounded like a *direct* response to what he said. The revelation caused me to lean forward so I could see the screen more closely. Vampire vision was good for a few things, and seeing in the dark was one. Yep, just as I suspected, Vicki's eyes were glazed over slightly. She had been having a vision during the filming. She really was seeing us here, in this time, and was going to actually "talk" to us. Just to clue in the rest of the confused-looking people, I asked, "You're really here right now, aren't you, Vick? You're seeing all of us, in the future, while you tape this?"

Her head turned and she looked at me—not where I had been sitting a minute earlier, but where I was now. "You always were one of the smartest people I knew, Celia. Yes, I'm here but in the past. If you look at the file for this recording, you'll see it was taped at least a year ago. I say 'at least' because I'm not really sure what year I die. That's the trick with this gift. You don't always see your own life with any clarity. But I can *see* each of you sitting in front of me." She sighed. "I'm really sorry that Dawna couldn't be here. But it's more important she get well." She turned her head again, looking past Alex. "I like what you've done with your hair, Sybil. It's a good look on you."

My friend's former body double gasped and put a hand up to her hair. "Um . . . thank you?"

Vicki's eyes sparkled. The cameraperson must have thought she was nuts. Or not, since it was no secret that Vicki was clairvoyant. "Now, Barney has the full document each of you will be given a copy of. But I wanted to tell you the terms in my own way." She turned to face David and Inez. "I don't know if you two knew how special you were to me. Even after I moved to Birchwoods, you kept my house feeling like a *home* whenever I was there. I could think of only one way to express my appreciation for your years of hard work."

"Pshaw," David said under his breath. "We'd have done it for free . . . it's a beautiful place."

"I know you would have," she interrupted, causing him to stare at the screen openmouthed. "And that's exactly what you're going to get to do for as long as you want to. David. Inez. Cooper Manor is yours. Take care of it. And yes, Inez, your mother is welcome. Please bring her home to live with you. I know you've been worried about her."

Now it was Inez who burst into tears. She stared up at the screen with shining eyes that probably only I could see. "Miss Vicki, no. We can't. It's too much. That house . . . it's so expensive."

Vicki snorted and rolled her eyes to the ceiling. "And it does me what good now? I can float on the ceiling almost anywhere. Inez, please . . . accept this small token. Really, it *is* small in the scheme of things. And just so you know, I'm also leaving you enough money to take care of the taxes and such for as long as you live there."

"This is ridiculous!" Cassandra apparently had had enough. She stood up and slammed a fist down on the table. "I will *not* watch my daughter leave a multimillion dollar home to a *servant.*"

"Mother, *shut up.*" Vicki's voice was cutting as she half-stood from her seat. "It is not my fault that you could never make amends with Grandma, nor is it my fault that her estate was left to me. You've made your own way and I'm very proud of you and Daddy. But this is my money and my property and I will damned well leave it to whomever I choose. I already know you're going to challenge this Will and have made appropriate arrangements to defend it. Just so you know, I win. Now . . . *sit down!*"

I couldn't help but smirk. Vicki was finally able to do in death what she'd always wanted to do in life. "You go, girl," I whispered. Gran elbowed me in the arm. But Cassandra wouldn't be able to see my smile in the dark.

"Ms. Meadows," said Arons, "you really do need to sit down."

With a light growl, she threw herself back into her chair so hard the springs squeaked.

"Thank you." Vicki sat back down and returned to looking at Inez and David. "Now, no more arguments. Plan for the house to be yours. Until the lawsuit is over, you'll be renting it from the estate. Barney has papers for you to sign before you leave. It'll cost you a dollar a year. No telling how long the suit will last, but the lease is ironclad, so don't have any fear you'll have to leave. Oh," she continued, and pointed to me. "There's one exception. I've asked Barney to hire a surveyor. The guesthouse is going to be split off from the main house into a separate parcel. That property will be yours, Celia. That's surprise number one."

Holy crap! She was giving me the guesthouse? "Um, wow. Thanks, Vick."

"You need to live near the ocean. You just do. So the beach

is going to go with the guesthouse. I hope you don't mind, David."

He shrugged and looked my way. "Nah. Never did go there anyway. I've got the pool if I want to swim."

"Now, as for the rest of my real estate . . . Celia, did you know that I own a holding company called C and S Enterprises?" She stared at me, smiling, waiting for me to get whatever I was supposed to get. It rang a bell, but I couldn't place the name. I shrugged helplessly and she finally sighed. "Okay, I'll give you a hint. One of the properties is an old Victorian with a big old palm tree out front."

The penny dropped with a bang. "You own my office?"

Vicki threw up her hands in joy. "Yay! You got it in one. Surprise! The office is also yours. You're the new landlord. Promise me I get to be there, at least in spirit, when you tell Ron."

I laughed out loud. I couldn't help it. God, he was going to *hate* that. "What does 'C and S' stand for, anyway?"

She grinned and tipped her head. " 'Chips and Salsa.' In honor of all those late nights at La Cocina with you, Emma, and Dawna. I'm also giving Emma's apartment building to her. But I knew she wouldn't be able to be here today, so Barney will send her a letter to let her in on the secret. Now, don't spoil my surprise and tell her early. She won't believe it without the official letterhead. Dawna's getting a surprise, too, but I'm not telling you what, so don't ask." She winked at me.

How well she knew us. She was absolutely right about Emma Landingham. Everything had to be by the book with her. And wow . . . I knew how much our nights at the cantina meant to me. Apparently they'd been just as important to Vicki. "You are . . . *were* an amazing woman, Victoria Cooper."

She gave a little bow at the waist. "Yes. Yes, I was."

I heard Jason chuckle. His face was entranced at seeing his daughter like this, so animated and happy. Maybe he'd never really known what an awesome person she was. He hadn't spent much time around her. More's the pity.

"So, that's all my real estate. Now comes what Barney calls the *residue*. I've split my estate into four parts . . . well, technically, *five*. Sadly, it's going to take a fifth of my total estate to fight my mother's lawsuit. Pity. But there's no helping it. I know you won't be able to step back from this and let it go, Mom, so, I've planned for it."

"I cannot believe you think so little of me." There was no hurt in Cassandra's voice, only rage.

"I don't think little of you, Mom. I actually think quite highly of you. You're a shrewd businesswoman and a talented actress. But today, here, anything you show us is just that—an act. You can't help it and I can't blame you for it. I pray you'll stop before you completely drive Daddy away, but that future is unclear even to me. It's all about choices. Celia was right. If you can just see past your anger and your hurt, you'll know that what Grandma did she did for you. Denying you the inheritance money forced you to go out and earn it. She knew it would spur you on. She might not have been a clairvoyant, but she was smarter than you and me put together. And she knew that my talent had helped her earn a good part of her fortune, as much as you hate to admit it."

I wished Vicki hadn't invoked my name, because it turned Cassandra's attention back to me. "I knew it! I knew you were the one who poisoned my daughter against me. You influenced her, manipulated her. *Bitch*, I swear you won't see a dime of the money."

Why wasn't I surprised?

Vicki interrupted. "Celia had nothing to do with my decisions, Mom. This is all me. Just me, and if you'd only listened when I tried to tell you, Celia . . ." She paused and looked my way and panic was suddenly etched in her voice. "*No!* Celia! John, do something!"

I turned to Creede and saw a bright flash of red light. Creede flung one arm toward me and I flew across the room, hit the wall, and slid down to the floor. His other hand was thrust in the opposite direction. I heard glass breaking and the sound of a rifle shot far in the distance.

The lights came up abruptly and hanging in the air where I had been sitting was a copper-jacketed bullet, a Glaser round that expanded on impact. They're used by the police when they don't want stray bullets going through walls to kill innocents in the next room and by bodyguards everywhere who want to make sure that a shot into a bad guy doesn't kill their client. Vicki's ghost zoomed down from the ceiling to hover around me protectively. I wasn't sure cold gas could do much, but it was a nice thought. Gran was likewise by my side in seconds.

I could feel the pulse of incredibly powerful magic sealing the entire length of the windows. The second and third bullets never made it through, just hovered in the air, not quite touching the glass, outside the window. The magic raised the hairs on my skin, more a caress than a sting. The sensation was soft and electric, close to erotic, and pulled at parts of my body that shouldn't be excited by a near assassination. I really didn't want my body equating nearly dying with sex, so I refused to look at Creede to see if it was intentional or not.

I didn't know many mages who could pull off a shield this powerful just with raw power and no prior spell. Even Bruno might struggle with that. There was a box of tissues sitting on the table; Creede took one and used it to keep his fingerprints off the bullet as he plucked the bullet out of the air. "The police will want this." He looked up at the screen. "Any idea where it came from?"

Vicki shook her head, looking actually shaken from the experience. "No idea. Sorry. I only saw the red light. It looked like a laser sight on a gun. Apparently, this is why I invite you to the party. I'll definitely have to spend some time to figure out how to get you here, since you're working for my parents right about now. Hmmm—"

She dropped into her own thoughts while everybody watched me struggle to my feet. The slam against the wall hadn't done my back any good, for which Creede at least seemed a little embarrassed. But I waved off the apology that was about to escape from his mouth, even though I still couldn't look him full in the face while my body struggled to shake off the effects of his magic. "No apologies. I'll be fine in a few minutes. Great thing, vampire metabolism. And nice job with the window. Can you keep that up for the rest of this, or should we get the heck out of here until they find the shooter?"

Barney Arons was busy typing on his laptop while Vicki mulled on the screen. "No, we'll stay here. I've just activated the emergency shields for this floor and have e-mailed Becky to call the police. Nothing, not even a bullet or a bomb, can get in or out of this room for the next hour. So please sit down. I'd frankly forgotten about this part of the event after a year or I would have put up better shields. I should have watched the tape before the appointment."

"And yet, Vicki *knew* you wouldn't. So she made alternate plans."

"An amazing woman." He shook his head in renewed awe. "Mr. Creede, you may release your shields whenever you feel appropriate."

"I'll leave them up until someone flies up to collect the bullets. I wouldn't want them disappearing."

"Again I thank you for the compliment." Vicki was back with us. "Now, this reminds me. Celia, I know you distrust most people. Sadly, you have reason. But let me assure you now that John Creede, even if he can be an ass occasionally, is being honest with you. About what, I don't know. But you can trust him. Trust *me*. You'll need him soon, so please know you can rely on his skill and his courage."

This time, it was John who let out a snort. "Even if I can be an ass occasionally. There's a ringing endorsement."

I couldn't help but smile as I picked up the chair, righted it, and settled painfully down. "That's about the best you'll get from Vicki. She was nothing if not a realist."

"Now," she said, right on cue, "let's finish up quickly before anything else happens. Sybil, I'm leaving you my clothes, jewelry, furs, and Cadillac convertible. I'm sorry you got sucked into the middle of my life. It was bad enough for *one* of us to live it. At least you can sell the furs and buy some new clothes." She turned her head. "I mean, really, Mom. Her *clothes*? You took back her clothes? For what? What could possibly be the purpose in that?"

My jaw dropped. I knew Cassandra Meadows could be a bitch, but that was ridiculous! I agreed with Vicki.

"They weren't *hers*. I bought them. I paid for them. They were just a uniform and I had every right to take them back when the job ended."

"Whoa, whoa, whoa." The outraged voice belonged to Jason. "Cass, when you said you'd retrieved 'our belongings' from Ms. Jones, you didn't say anything about clothing. Good god, hon. That makes no sense."

Cassandra's mouth was tight-lipped, so it was Sybil who spoke up. "The people who showed up at the door were from one of the local charities. They were very nice about it and I probably wouldn't have minded much if I'd had warning. But it *was* a surprise."

Oh, for heaven's sake. Jason let out an exasperated breath. "Of course, we'll have your clothing returned to you, Sybil. And if that's not possible, I'll *personally* replace it. Please pardon my wife. Apparently, grief has made her . . . well, anyway, we'll get your things back to you. It's the least we can do."

"Thank you, Daddy," said Vicki from the screen. She took a deep breath and let it out slow. "The residue of my estate, other than a few minor bequests and what I've given to you already, less what will be expended in the Will contest suit, will be divided as follows. One-quarter goes to Heather Alexander, the love of my life. It's not enough to show you how much you meant to me, but money's all I have to give now."

Alex's lip was trembling and Sybil reached out to touch her hand gently. "Next, a quarter will be donated to the Birchwoods Therapy Center for the sole purpose of creating a new building. The *Ivy Graves Center for Gifted Children* will be built and fully funded for the next ten years through investments and bonds. Dr. Scott, I leave it to you to handle the details. You know my wishes after all those weeks coming up with a curriculum and program, for both inpatient and outpatient care. Emily, I wanted you and Celia to both be here to hear the news. Celia, of course you will have a quarter of my income, even though I know you'll probably give it to the Center. But do try to keep a little for yourself. You really do deserve it."

Jeff Scott bowed his head gently and then looked up at the ceiling to where Vicki's ghost had returned after the threat to me was gone. "I know your wishes and I'll take care of it."

Gran let out a sob that could be either joy or sorrow and I couldn't deny that I was getting choked up. It was more than I'd ever dreamed Vicki would do and I honestly didn't know how to respond. She was right, though. If it was between me and a center for other messed-up magical kids, the kids would win. I'd just sign over the check wholesale when I got it. I could still make my own money. I didn't need hers.

Creede handed me the box of tissues as Vicki spoke again. "If such a center had existed when you were young, maybe Ivy could have learned to use her gifts to protect herself before . . . well, before. And maybe if I'd had early training, I wouldn't have wound up in a nuthouse for most of my life."

The room erupted in explosions of sound, as everyone who knew Vicki rejected that statement. But she held up a hand. "Nope. Folks, I appreciate the support, but I am very nearly nuts. I tried my damnedest to have a normal relationship with each of you, but it was hard. So very hard. Just ask Dr. Scott.

Every visit from you, no matter how much appreciated, came at a price. I hid it well, but the stress has been getting to me for some time. I'm making this tape now because I'm still fully in my right mind, competent by both legal and medical standards to dispose of my estate. That's why you'll lose your suit, Mom."

Cassandra let out a very unladylike snort.

The ghost floated down from the ceiling and hovered right in front of her mother's face. Then it drifted down the table until it was in front of Sybil. The apparition vanished and Sybil's head dropped face-first to the stone table with a crunch that made me wince. After a moment, she sat back up, but Sybil wasn't home anymore. The woman sitting next to Alex was Vicki Cooper. I could see it in her eyes, in the way she held her body. Alex flinched and swallowed hard but didn't move away. I was proud of her for that. No matter how much she loved Vicki, sitting next to a possessed person had to be unnerving.

Vicki/Sybil turned and faced the attorney. "Mr. Arons, would you please begin recording?" The screen split, with old Vicki on one side and new Vicki on the other. "Mother, I wanted to make something very clear. *Crystal* clear. I was not manipulated or influenced in life. And while I might have been frustrated, hurt, and angry during life, in death there can be no deception or influence. Ghosts can't lie, Mom. It's impossible. Ask any postdeath therapist. So I say to you all, on tape, that my Will is true and correct and was made of my own free will and not under duress. Those are the right words, right, Barney?"

Arons nodded and she continued. Even the inflection of her voice had changed from the way Sybil talked to the true

Vicki. It was, frankly, weird. I'd seen it once before, right after
she was killed, but that didn't stop the tiny hairs on the back of
my neck from rising. "I say this because I'm intentionally,
and with full knowledge, leaving my parents out of my Will.
Not because I bear them any grudge. I love them very much.
But they have their own money. They don't need mine. My
final bequest will raise eyebrows all around the room, but I
believe with all my heart and with all the skill I possess as a
level-nine clairvoyant, that it's necessary." She motioned toward the one person not yet mentioned.

"I'm sure you're all wondering about the redheaded gentle-
man next to Dad. Frankly, I've wondered about him myself.
I've had visions of him and his family for some time, but I
don't know why. I only knew it was imperative . . . *critical* that
he be here today and that I make this bequest. I've learned to
trust my instincts, even if they don't make sense at the time.
Since I see him here, I know that you found him, Barney.
Thank you. I know it was a royal pain, what with the police
sketch artist and the private investigator. Unfortunately, sir, I
don't know your name as I'm taping this and I assume you
don't know me."

Murphy shook his head. "You seem like a nice lady, but
I've never seen you before in my life."

Vicki turned to me. "Celia, I'd like you and John Creede to
take the time and spend whatever money from my estate that
you have to, to find out why this man is at this reading. I'm of-
ficially hiring you both. What ties him to me? Why is it important for me to do what I'm about to do—because frankly, it's
making me nervous as hell."

She turned Sybil's body in her seat and faced him. "Sir, I'm pleased to inform you that you and your family will inherit a quarter of my estate. At the time I made this Will, that came to about twenty-four million dollars . . . after taxes."

"Holy Mother of God!" Mr. Murphy exclaimed. I was pretty surprised myself. *She gave him twenty-four million dollars? She gave me twenty-four million dollars? Plus the house and the office? Damn.*

"Naturally," Vicki continued, "like everyone else, you'll have to wait until the end of the suit for the cash, but I did set up a special life insurance policy using this law firm's escrow account as the beneficiary. Mr. Arons will give you that money now. It's not much, just a hundred thousand, but it'll make your life better." She sighed. I could tell that she was getting tired.

Murphy turned to Barney Arons. "Are you sure this isn't some sort of joke? Is someone from *Punk'd* or *Candid Camera* going to jump through the door now?"

Arons shook his head, with the tiniest of smiles, just as Sybil went face-first on the stone. Ouch again. She sat up moments later, nursing a bleeding nose and looking confused.

Vicki was gone. Arons turned off the tape. Maybe he'd show it to Sybil later.

The reading didn't last much longer. People crowded around Arons, trying to dig out more information. Even Gran wanted to find out more about the details. I didn't really care. I felt exhausted. Maybe Jeff had been right and it had been a bad thing for me to have come. But I'd had to do it. Sometimes all you can do is make your choices and accept your punishment. Right now, my punishment was to partially collapse against the table as I tried to stand.

"Ready to eat now?" John grabbed my elbow to keep me standing. "Looks like you could use some protein." Maybe it was my imagination, but the sensation that crawled up my arm when he touched me felt a lot like his magic had and it made me gasp and pull away even as warmth spread through my body.

I wasn't going to refuse a meal and I really needed to get out of the room. But touching seemed like a bad idea. "You have no idea. But how will we get through the shield? The hour's not up yet."

"You forget who you're talking to," he whispered with a small, secret smile and a wink. "Who do you think *crafted* the shield? This firm is one of M and C's biggest clients. Haven't you ever heard of a coder's back door? Besides, you need someone to protect you until they catch the shooter."

I couldn't deny that. I was having a hard time concentrating, or that little red light would never have made it to my forehead. He took my arm and tucked it through his and then, I kid you not, as my body tingled disturbingly, we walked right *through* the closed door, without a single person noticing we'd left.

I had to give him points for style.

We went to lunch in his Ferrari 599 GTB. Let me say for the record that it is one helluva car. I mean, I love my Miata but *damn*! Low-slung, sleek, and a vibrant red, it had a V12 engine that could roar like a lion or purr like a kitten, depending on the driver's mood. The interior was real leather; the dash was polished wood and it had seats more comfortable than most of the beds I've slept in. It could go from zero to outta here in 3.2 seconds or less. It made me glad I chose La Cocina y Cantina on the other side of town just so I could ride in it a little bit longer.

La Cocina is a tiny family-run restaurant tucked up against the college campus. It's kind of a dive, really—tiny and old. Most of the tables are for two, with gleaming white tablecloths and red bowl candles that give the place an intimate feel. People joke that it's kept dark to hide the dirt, but in reality the place is spotlessly clean and the food is absolutely amazing. They have an open patio with an awning, but we'd taken a table inside, next to a "stage" the size of a postage stamp where they have karaoke on Friday nights. Where we'd had karaoke the night of Vicki's wake.

I hadn't been here since that night. Of course, I hadn't been anywhere else, either. Coming back now, things felt different. I didn't know if I'd ever feel the same, if I could ever walk in the doors without feeling sad.

"Celia! Oh my heavens, you poor thing!" Barbara grabbed me in a bear hug before I could protest. Thankfully, I managed to fight back my hunger, which had been growing steadily since we'd left the lawyer's office. She leaned back from the hug and gently lifted my upper lip. I knew her concern was genuine, so I took no offense. "I couldn't believe it the other night. I thought I must have been drunk. But look at those teeth." She made tsking noises as she pulled me nearly off my feet toward a table, leaving Creede following in our wake with a look of amusement. "Now you just sit down. Pablo has made it his mission to make you good food. We've been reading up on your condition, so you can keep coming here."

"Really? Wow, thanks!" I meant it. I *loved* Pablo's food. My mild success at Birchwoods had me hopeful that there might be a time when I could go back to a nearly normal diet.

Creede excused himself to make a few calls in private after setting up a shield of protection around me. I took the opportunity to grab my cell phone and speed-dial Bruno.

"Hullo?" He answered on the first ring, but rather than feeling warm and fuzzy at the sound of his voice, I felt . . . strange. He sounded tense and I felt more than a little guilty about being here with Creede. But I figured I could fix that by just being honest.

"Hey, you. How's it going?"

"Celia, oh, hey, it's going pretty well. How'd you get to a phone?" There was a flat, distracted tone to his words, like I'd interrupted something that was requiring his attention.

"Day pass. I take it you didn't get my message?" I pressed the key to increase the volume to high.

"No. Sorry. Things have been a little hectic."

"Oh, well, there's stuff you need to know. Is this a good time?" Maybe he could hear the deeper question, because he immediately came back to full focus. It made me feel better and the fluttering things clawing at my insides calmed down.

"Absolutely. What's up?"

I told him about the Will reading, the shooter, and the breakup of Miller & Creede. "Is that going to change your plans? I don't have any idea whether they're still going to honor your deal. Creede said it's up to Miller."

"Well, crap!" Apparently, he hadn't known. "Goddamn it! You'd think that would come up in conversation. I just talked to Miller this morning and he didn't say a thing. I was joining because John Creede asked me, not because of Miller. He's a horse's ass and doesn't have as much talent in his whole body as Creede has in his little finger."

"Thank him for saying so." John was standing next to the table, a pleased smile on his face. "I'd suggest he call his attorney. Since it's still in the verbal stage, there might be a chance to get out of the deal now. I'd enjoy forming a company with him as part of it."

"Really?" Now Bruno's voice sounded more than a little excited. "Hey, tell him —"

I shook my head, amused. "Why don't *you* tell him? I need to use the bathroom." I handed Creede my phone and they started talking terms. Worked for me. I'd be happy to have them team up. Bruno working in *my* building. That would be amazing.

By the time I got back, the phone was closed and waiting for me on the table and there was a combination plate in front of John. He lowered the fork that was halfway to his mouth and said, "Hope you don't mind. I'm starving."

"Me, too. Go ahead." I sat down and picked up the old-fashioned malted glass that was obviously waiting for me. The contents were warm and smelled wonderful. But scent isn't everything, sadly. There was an odd, metallic tinge to the smoothie and the cheese was stringy and lumpy enough to nearly make me gag.

Barbara came to the table, looking like an eager puppy, watching for my reaction. Should I lie to save her ego, or tell the truth and give them the chance to try again? I went for analytical. "Spices are about right, not too much garlic or onion. But there's an odd metallic aftertaste. And maybe a different kind of cheese? This didn't melt fully and I can't do solids. At all." Okay, good. She was taking notes and didn't look at all offended. I breathed a sigh of relief. "But a great first attempt! Really."

She picked up the glass even though I'd taken only a few sips. "Okay, let us give it one more go before we give up today. Just take a second."

It was a torturous few minutes. I could smell John's plate and watch him chew it with obvious delight, and my hunger was getting hard to resist. He wasn't quite done with his plate before Barbara was back. "Try that," she said with pride.

I took a tentative sip. And then another. *Yum!* "Wow! Not bad, Barbara! Not bad at all. I can live with this. What did you do different the second time?"

I was sipping as she spoke and nearly spit it out when I heard, "We cooked the cow blood just a little bit, to get rid of the metallic taste, and I switched to Velveeta instead of regular cheese. I don't use it much, but it does blend better."

"Cow blood?" I asked as my tongue conflicted with my brain and good sense.

She looked at me as though I were nuts. "Well, of *course* cow blood. Girl, you got to have plasma protein and there's none better than cow. Just short of human for taste. Pig is a little better for nutrition, but there's all those diseases they carry and you are still part human."

It was like finding out I was eating worms and *liking* them. John didn't say a word. He made a little smirk that he covered with a coffee cup. But I knew he thought it was funny. That's okay. I had plenty of time and many ways to get him back.

I forced myself to drink the smoothie because logically she

was right. But it still disturbed me to realize how good it tasted. Almost immediately, I started to feel better. I even felt my hands warming up, although I hadn't realized they were cold until they heated. Reluctantly, I stopped myself before I licked the glass down more than a few inches.

Then Creede and I talked business, including discussing who the shooter might have been. After a little hesitation, I unbent enough to show him the curse mark and tell him what had happened . . . jeez, was it only this morning?

"And you're sure there was no sign of the mark before then?"

"Nope." He was holding my hand in his, palm up, running an index finger over the ugly discoloration of the mark. His touch wasn't in the least erotic this time and I was grateful. Because if there was any chance we were going to be working together I did not need that kind of distraction.

"About the only thing that can create and hold that level of illusion for any period of time is demonic energy."

Oh, crap. Demons. Again. I shuddered at the memory of facing off against a demon in the parking lot of Anaheim Stadium. It had been one of the most awe-inspiring and terrifying experiences of my life. I did not, ever, want to encounter the demonic again.

"I can feel a hint of it still. But that was just the masking. The curse itself isn't demonic at all. In fact, I can't really tell what kind of energy is behind it. But whoever or whatever cursed you was damned powerful and the curse feels *old*." He shook his head and gave me a wry grin. "You do lead the most interesting life."

"Tell me about it."

Juan, the oldest son of the owner, was waiting tables today. I've known him since he was too young to carry a fully laden tray. Bright and handsome, he was wearing a starched white shirt and crisp black trousers. I smiled in greeting as he brought my third margarita to the table. Creede had excused himself to use the restroom, so Juan and I spent a couple of minutes chatting, catching up on family gossip.

I hate having my back to the door. But I didn't have much choice when we'd arrived. When I saw Juan stiffen and heard a commotion by the door I had to turn sharply in my seat and look over my shoulder to see what had drawn everyone's attention.

Three imposing men in hand-tailored suits had come through the front door and were peering through the gloom, obviously looking for someone in particular. As soon as I got a good look I knew they wanted either me or Creede. The man in front was George Miller. How the hell did he know we were here? Sure, Creede's car is pretty unique, but La Cocina isn't in a common area of town and I don't think George had ever been here before the wake.

Juan made a noise in the back of his throat, clearly unhappy. I couldn't blame him. You could tell from their body language that they were looking for trouble.

Miller looked angry but also like death and not even warmed over. It was obvious even in the dim lighting of the restaurant. The last time I'd seen him he'd been strikingly handsome thanks to a combination of good genetics and better plastic surgery. He kept fit, dressed in the very best hand-tailored suits, and was more fussy about his appearance than any woman I knew. Not today. Today his wide face was gray and coated with a faint sheen of sweat and there was a fine tremor to his body. His left arm hung absolutely limp at his side. When one of the servers accidentally bumped it Miller's knees buckled beneath him. Only the lightning-quick reflexes of his men kept him from collapsing to the floor in a heap. From the corner of my eye I saw Barbara scurrying to assist, but he waved her away.

"What's the matter with *him*?" Juan had paled to a shade almost as white as the tablecloth.

"Binding oaths are a bitch."

"He broke a magic oath? Is he *insane*?"

"Yes. And possibly." I took a long pull of my drink. I'd probably need it and I was glad for the restorative powers of Pablo's mexi-shake. But unless and until they came up to the table, I was going to pretend this was just a coincidence and assume that George brought his well-coutured ass down to this neck of the woods all the time. No doubt for the huevos.

"You know about this?" I looked up and realized that Juan didn't look like a kid anymore. He was all grown-up and ready to play bouncer if need be. I hoped he wouldn't have to. He's a tough kid, but I'd feel guilty as hell if anything happened to him and the M&C boys are professionals.

"A little," I admitted. "John Creede, the man with me? Likely he's the one who cast the oath on Miller."

Juan started to swear, softly, under his breath. I almost couldn't hear him and I was sitting right there, so the rest of the diners were spared. Kind of a shame. They might have learned something. He was doing a *very* thorough job of it. When he'd gone through his repertoire he took a deep breath. Looking me straight in the eye, he said, "I have your back. But you're paying for any damages."

I nodded and shifted in my seat, unfastening my denim jacket. I'd taken some of my usual armament from my car before we left the attorney's. I always feel naked without a few weapons.

Juan stepped away from the table but didn't go far, just a few steps away, behind the bar. He stayed there, puttering around in the general vicinity of where I knew the shotgun was kept. I don't know what signal passed between them, but while he didn't say a word, I noticed that Lola, his sister, had stepped out from behind the maître d' stand and pulled on a server's apron.

"Ms. Graves." George Miller had come up to my table. I'd thought he looked bad from a distance—up close it was much, much worse. And the smell. Eww. Maybe it was my enhanced vampire senses, but he smelled like meat left in the sun to rot. My stomach roiled in protest even though I was holding my drink close to my nose to try to mask the stench. I moved the salsa bowl so that it sat on the table right in front of me. Pablo's homemade salsa is really spicy. I figured the pepper smell might help. It's strong and I don't like it much, but it was better than the alternative.

"Mr. Miller." I gave him a pleasant expression, empty of any emotion. I was not going to gag. I wasn't. Mind over matter.

There are a number of different binding oaths available. All of them are pretty hideous. My guess was that they'd used the necrosis variation. If they had, then his arm was literally rotting off. And unless he (a) made complete recompense; (b) had the arm amputated before the rot spread; or (c) killed Creede, Miller might lose more than just an arm.

"I'm sorry to intrude. But I wanted to take this opportunity to warn you about my former partner."

I looked up but didn't say anything. If I opened my mouth, I would retch. I really would.

"You can smell what he did to me. Can't you?"

I fought down bile and managed to answer him through gritted teeth. "The way he tells it, you did it to yourself."

"And you believe him?" Miller's tone made it clear he thought I was a fool.

I set down my drink and picked up the salsa bowl; bringing it up to my face, I took a long whiff. It worked: peppers, onion, and spices drove off less palatable scents. After just a few seconds, I was able to talk almost normally. "It's easy enough to check out. Written notice of any binding oaths would have to be filed with the state with your corporate documents. And you don't strike me as the type to skimp on the paperwork."

His face flushed, bringing the first bit of color to his cheeks. Scowling fiercely, he told me, "John used black magic to avoid the effects of *my* oath on him."

I shook my head. "Not possible. The magic used in binding oaths is a neutral force. It doesn't care who, or what, the oath takers are. In fact, the man's a mage. His own power would probably turn on him if he broke the oath."

"You know that for a fact?" Miller was so bitter. The words dripped venom like acid. I felt as if my ears should actually be burning.

"I graduated with a degree in Paranormal Studies and was

engaged to a powerful mage." I met the heat of Miller's gaze without flinching. "So, yeah, I do."

He was visibly shaking now, but whether it was from rage or exhaustion I couldn't tell. Maybe both. Because he was furious. His eyes were dark, his square jaw set tight enough that I could hear his teeth grinding. Still, he mastered himself enough to speak civilly. "If you partner with John Creede, Ms. Graves, you will regret it."

"Is that a threat?" I kept my voice sweet and utterly bland, but my eyes were on his hands, making sure he wasn't about to go for a weapon. It would be a crazy thing for him to do, but I'd pretty much decided the man was nuts. However, I was curious. How did he know about mine and Creede's discussions? Had he been to the office, or was one or both of us bugged?

"A promise," Miller growled. With his message delivered, he turned on his heel. At his curt nod, his companions fell in behind him. They were just leaving the restaurant when John stepped out of the restroom. The whole encounter had only taken a couple of minutes. But that didn't make it any less disturbing.

John stopped, stared after them for a long moment, his features hard and distant as a granite cliff. Then he strode stiffly over to the table, not bothering to sit down.

"What were George, Bobby, and Ian doing here?" His voice was flat, inflectionless.

"Miller wanted to warn me not to go into business with you." I gave him innocent eyes before grabbing my margarita glass and taking a long pull of lime-flavored frozen goodness.

"And?" Standing there, glowering, he reminded me a little of Miller, only without the BO. They were quite a lot alike: hard, dangerous men who could be equally charming and deadly. Good friends/bad enemies.

"He was trying to intimidate me if he could." The drink was perfect. As always. And with the kick of a mule. With any luck it would help me relax. Unlikely under the circumstances, but certainly worth a try.

"Did he?"

Juan was coming up behind him with another margarita for me and a fresh basket of tortilla chips. He gave an expressive snort as he reached around the other man to set the fresh drink in front of me before waving a container of cinnamon incense around the area to get rid of the smell. "This one is on me."

I thanked Juan, then answered Creede. "I'm not easily intimidated. I'm just glad they didn't cause trouble in the restaurant." I paused for effect. "Are you going to sit down, or are you planning on standing there all day?"

He glared. I didn't wilt. So, eventually, he sat. He even unbent enough to grab a chip. I passed him the bowl of salsa I'd hijacked. We sat in silence as he munched and I drank. I would've liked to join him. I miss munching. But the combination of salt, lime, and kick-ass tequila was taking the edge off my disappointment. In fact, it was taking the edge off of pretty much everything. I'd probably better slow down a bit.

"So now what?" he finally asked.

"Well, first I think it would be a good idea to find out how Miller discovered we were here and how he knew you'd offered to partner with me. I'm still not sure about whether we'd work as business partners. But I do *not* like being threatened and I really don't like being bugged."

"I can't believe he actually had the balls to threaten you—and in the middle of a public restaurant." A slow flush was spreading up Creede's neck and his voice was low and growling. "Has he lost his fucking mind?"

"Ah, wait." I raised a finger. "It was not a threat. It was a *promise*." I rolled my eyes. "Relax, John. I'm a big girl. I don't terrify easily." I watched as he forced himself to calm down. It took a few minutes. He was not taking this situation well. Then again, who would? "Seriously, until you get your legal issues dealt with and I get *my* legal issues dealt with, we may not want to even try. Because if he can make trouble, he will. He has the connections to do it and apparently he has the technology. You'll want to do a full scan of your car for trackers and maybe even take it to a priest. Oh, and throw away your clothes."

"I *know* how to search for bugs, Celia. I've been doing this longer than you." His growl was growing, but I wasn't done. Because it needed to be said.

"And yet, they were here and overheard our conversation somehow. I'm pretty sure you'd be chiding me under the same circumstances. Because he's not going to stop. You know it. Not until he finds some way to get to you—assuming he lives that long."

Creede's head jerked and his eyes widened with shock. I could tell he was jumping to conclusions from the look on his face, and it irritated the hell out of me.

"Oh, for heaven's sake," I snapped, "I'm not going to do anything. But I don't need to. That must have been one powerful oath you set up, because he was barely able to walk on his own and I'm pretty sure his arm is literally rotting meat."

Creede looked from me to Juan, who nodded his agreement.

He started drumming his fingers on the table, his eyes going distant. I could tell he was going over the oath in his mind, checking to see if it was more powerful than he'd imagined. He shook his head. "That doesn't make sense. It shouldn't be that bad. Don't get me wrong. If he's not careful, he'll lose the arm. But that should be the extent of it."

"You didn't smell him. The man is dying."

Creede leaned back at an angle, his fingers drumming an irritable rhythm against the tablecloth. "The only way it would be that bad is if the oath is still active. So long as he's still screwing me over, the oath is going to eat at him."

Ah, I got it. It was a vicious cycle. "He blames you and is bitter, so he keeps trying to get even. And every time he does, the oath gets worse."

"He can't be that stupid." Creede shook his head. He was still angry but there was sadness mixed in with it. I wasn't surprised. They'd been friends and business partners for a long time.

I snorted. "He's obsessed. Besides, you know as well as I do that people delude themselves all the time. Given enough time, he'll have the whole thing being your fault. Probably even sue your ass." There was a little lisp at the end of that. I've been having some trouble adapting to talking with the fangs. However, I will say it was harder than it should have been to put the glass down straight on the table.

"How many of those have you had?"

I sighed. "Not that many. Don't worry. Vampire metabolism. I'll be dead sober in no time." I hadn't meant the pun but recognized it when I saw his lips twitch. He had good lips. Very kissable. Not that I was ever going to, even though I could feel the brush of magic, just at the edge of my skin. Bruno was moving back soon. Just the thought made me smile, but that didn't mean I was blind. I could look. I just wouldn't do anything about it.

Right?

Creede scolded me, "You can't eat anything solid. Drinks are going to hit you harder and faster than they did when you were human. Even if they do wear off quicker." Shaking his head, "I'll drive you back to Birchwoods."

"Nope. I'm not leaving my car in town." I shook my head firmly. Well, sort of firmly. Maybe the margaritas had gotten to me a little more than I'd thought. "And besides, I've got things to do."

"You're not driving like this."

"Of course not. I'll take a cab." Actually, by the time we got back to the attorney's office I'd be fine to drive. Definitely. Well, at least probably.

"Don't lie to me, Graves."

"Who's lying?" I batted my eyes at him in a deliberately exaggerated gesture and ran a fingernail down his hand. I wasn't using full siren magic on him, just flirting a little, but he pulled his hand away like it was burned. He was affected. I could tell. I could sense he wanted to help. Wanted to . . . but he fought it off with a shake of his head.

"Fine. You have things to do. I get that. But you nearly had your head blown off earlier today and you just got threatened because of me. So I'm sticking with you until the alcohol wears off and you have a better chance of defending yourself."

"Whether I like it or not?"

"Is being driven around by me really such a terrible fate?" He gave me that charming, handsome smile that he seemed to be able to turn on and off at will. It was nice, but I liked the real one better. Shame he didn't get much chance to use it.

7

had John drive me to Isaac and Gilda Levy's shop. They'd
redone the place and I would've loved to spend some
serious shopping time there—as would Creede, judging by
the way he was eyeing Gilda's new stock of magical artifacts—
but the day was getting away from me. I still had a lot to do
before I met with El Jefe at the university and I really needed
a little time on my own, to think. So after only a couple of
minutes of good-natured fussing from Gilda, I was able to
leave with my new jacket—outfitted with receptacles for my
favorite weapons—and a promise that she'd have Isaac "age" a
replacement death stone for my Wadjeti. She swore they could
have it to me within the hour, so I could wait, or they'd deliver
it to my office.

I didn't have the time to wait, so delivery it was. By the time
we were finished at the shop I was stone-cold sober and Creede
agreed to take me back to my car. Before he left he insisted on
putting a protective spell on me, strong enough to protect me
from bullets. He swore it would last through the day—long
enough to get me back to the protective confines of Birchwoods.

When I walked in the front door of my office at around three, the reception area was clean, quiet, and smelled of lemon furniture polish. *Thank God. Well, actually, thank Dottie. Maybe both.* Whatever, I was grateful. I snagged a large stack of messages from my slot on the front desk before pounding up the stairs.

One call from Dawna. Three from reporters who wanted my take on the statement Cassandra Meadows had made to the press after the Will reading. Since I didn't know what she'd said, I couldn't comment. But I wouldn't anyway. In a mudslinging contest, everybody gets dirty.

I unlocked my office door, tossed my purse and keys onto the desk, and sat. No messages from Ivan. I debated calling the embassy. He'd made it sound so urgent, but I'd managed to see a piece of the continuous news feed shown on the television in La Cocina's bar and nothing big appeared to be going on in Rusland. The king was attending a financial conference in Greece, and since Ivan was his head of security, he was probably there as well.

My attorney had called. Seeing the message reminded me forcibly of the hearing I'd been trying very hard not to think about. Roberto didn't expect the trial to last more than a couple of hours. By this time tomorrow afternoon I'd know whether I'd be spending the rest of my life in a cage. My stomach did a little flip-flop from nerves and I tried to tell myself that it was going to be fine.

I didn't believe me.

"The hearing will end in your favor." Dottie stood in my doorway, leaning heavily on her walker. How she'd made it up all of those stairs I had no clue. Grown men have been known to quail at the sight of them. They're steep and the treads are narrow, having been made in a time when people had smaller feet. "I . . . *peeked.*" She moved slowly across the threshold, a small package rattling on the tray she'd attached to the front of her walker.

"Dottie. You should've called. I'd have come down."

She sighed and lowered herself halfway into one of the pair of wing-backed visitor's chairs across the desk from me, then fell the last few inches onto the seat. "Next time I'll do that. But I wanted a little privacy to talk with you and Ron is a terrible snoop."

She'd figured him out quicker than most. Then again, Dottie's bright. It's one of the many things I like about her.

"What do you want to talk about?"

She reached over to retrieve the little jewelry box from the tray. Opening it, I saw that Isaac had delivered the Wadjeti stone. *Damn, that was quick.* I walked over to take it from her. I rolled it over, on my palm, examining it closely. When I'd seen the stone in the Levys' shop, it had been red, and it still was. But now the shade seemed both richer and more faded and there were little scratches and scuffs on the finish that made it look . . . ancient.

"Wow. Go, Isaac."

"I take it this isn't the original stone?"

"Nope. But it sure looks like it." I turned it over in my hand. It was perfect. How the hell had he managed that? And so *fast*? Trade secret from a misspent youth?

Dottie paused, licking her lips nervously. "Celia, would

you indulge me in something? Please?" She wasn't quite wringing her hands, but she was getting close and she was pale and a little bit shaky.

"Why don't I get you a glass of water?"

"No, thank you, I'm fine. But would you let me do a reading for you? I don't have my bowl, but now that you have a full set I can use the Wadjeti, I'm sure of it."

"Is that a good idea?" I didn't say she looked like hell. But she did.

"Please, Celia. I have to try. I *have* to." She was shaking in earnest now.

"Sure. I suppose˙ . . . but . . . do you know how?"

"I told you, I read the instructions," she said without heat. "I'm pretty sure I remember enough. And . . ." She paused, licking her lips again. "I need to do this. I've only had a compulsion like this a few times, but it's always been important. Please?"

I turned around and went through the rigamarole of opening the safe. By the time it was finished she was practically jumping out of her skin. "You're sure you want to do this?"

She nodded. "Positive."

Okay, I could get that. Vicki had once told me about something similar happening to her. She'd also called it a compulsion. I might not understand, but I could accept it. That compulsion had caused her to have Bruno make the knives that had probably saved my life.

I pulled the box from the safe and started to hand it to Dottie, but she shook her head. "You need to take all of the stones and drop them one at a time into the cup. I can't touch them. I only touch the cup."

"All right." It sounded a little odd, but magic is one of those things that frequently defy explanation. The rules may not make logical sense, but they're the rules . . . and if you don't follow them, the magic doesn't work.

I took the cup from the box and set the box on the desk. The cup was small and, compared to the box, quite simple. It was made of beaten gold set alternately with lapis and moonstone. I set it on the desktop and began dropping the scarabs in, starting with the one Isaac had aged for me. Each stone landed with a soft click. With each, I could feel the power build, drop by drop, until the air actually felt thick with it. I felt heat radiating upward and when the last stone fell into the cup shafts of brilliant white light beamed out through the moonstones, practically blinding me with their brilliance.

"Hand me the cup."

I picked it up. It was warm to the touch and surprisingly heavy. I passed it to Dottie carefully and she used both hands to take it from me. "We need to do three throws to get guidance for each of the three levels of your present existence: the first is for the physical; the second, the intellectual; and the third, finally, for the spiritual and emotional."

"If you say so."

She gave me a sad little smile. "I do." She shook the cup and scattered the stones across the top of my desk. They glowed, each stone shining with its own light. They scurried like the beetles they resembled to form two precise groupings.

Dottie gave a soft gasp. I didn't blame her. It was one hell of a show: both startling and surprisingly beautiful.

She began pointing to the arrangements. "The group over there represents your past. There was danger, suffering, and death, but it served to make you stronger."

I couldn't argue with that and I didn't want to break her concentration. Her voice had taken on a singsong quality that I recognized as indicating the beginning of a trance. If I interrupted her now she'd lose her train of thought and the reading would be ruined.

"The right grouping is your present. You notice the death stone in the center halfway between the two groups? It has a double meaning. First, the death of your old self and your rebirth with new powers and abilities."

That didn't sound so bad. I'd been afraid it meant something more . . . well, sniper bullet–ish.

"But it also represents real danger. You must be very careful. There are traps and betrayals ahead, people plotting your death."

Sniper. Bullet. That pretty well says it all.

"Your survival may depend on your acceptance of your changed existence."

She looked up at me; her expression was serene and her eyes were shining, but Dottie, the Dottie I knew, wasn't "home." I wondered if she'd even remember the things she was saying to me when this was done. Probably not.

"Fill the cup."

I did, again feeling the power build, and she repeated the throw. This time, though, the beams of light shone through the lapis, the shafts of intense blue looking like nothing so much as Luke's lightsaber slicing across the room.

This time the scarabs formed a single picture, again with the death stone in the center.

"You are clever. But so is your enemy. Life and death balance on a knife's edge with deception determining the winner. You must be brave, but more, you must be *intelligent* if you are to save yourself and those under your protection. You cannot let emotions cloud your judgment. You *must* remain clearheaded." She gestured imperiously at the cup. "Once more."

I dropped the scarabs into the cup with increasing dread. I'd had enough experience with clairvoyants that I had never before been bothered all that much by the process. But while I might not admit it out loud, this frightened me. There was so much *power* to it. So deep, so elemental, that I felt as if we were channeling the energy of an earthquake, the tides, or the sun itself. My mouth was dry as I picked up the last stone, the death stone. It felt warm, almost alive in my hand, and the mark of my curse began to burn where it touched. Hissing with pain, I threw it away, into the cup. It hit with an explosion of light and a roar of sound that left me deaf and blind for a full minute. My eyes were watering so hard I was practically weeping and I groped through my tears for the box of tissues I kept on the corner of my desk. I wiped my eyes and handed Dottie the cup.

She spilled the scarabs onto the desk. Several scurried across my hand, sharp pinpricks like tiny claws on my skin. Shuddering, I pulled back, and they moved to form a picture.

Dottie waited until I'd recovered before continuing, her voice both sad and thoughtful. "There is deception here and a deep, crippling loss. Endings and beginnings, if you are willing to be open to them. Lies and pain. But hope. You must be strong and not lose faith in yourself. Do not let the inevitable betrayals keep you from trusting those worthy of trust, but beware the smile that hides the viper's fangs."

She fell silent, her head drooping onto her chest. I rushed

around the desk to check her. Her pulse was fine, her breathing steady, but her skin had taken on a grayish tinge. I turned to call for help and saw Ron and Bubba standing awestruck in the doorway. Apparently they'd seen the light show and wanted to know what was going on. Following their gaze, I watched as the scarabs scurried back into the carved wooden box. Well, that was more than a little disturbing.

Bubba took Dottie to the ER to be checked out. I couldn't go. Hospitals are a bad place for people who crave blood. So far, lunch was holding, but I couldn't guarantee it beyond a few hours. She was awake and acerbic, swearing she was fine, just tired, but we all wanted to make sure she was all right. I made Bubba promise they'd call me to let me know what the doctors said.

Dottie's vision had given me a lot to think about and the light and bug show made me want to lock the Wadjeti back in the safe and never take it out again. Definitely creepy.

Still, a promise is a promise and El Jefe had gone to a lot of trouble to get the expert from UCLA. So I slathered on more sunscreen, pulled on my new jacket and black straw fedora, armed myself to the teeth, and drove off to meet some of the world's leading experts on the preternatural. Here's hoping they didn't give me *more* bad news.

8

You should be dead. It is that simple. Based on what I'm looking at, this mark has been here since you were a very small child. There is no possible way you could have survived through puberty." Dr. Sloan was a dessicated little man with freckled brown skin. What hair he had stuck out in a wiry white ring around his age-spotted scalp and his heavy graying brows bristled over the top of Coke-bottle glasses that made his watery eyes seem too large for his face. He was holding my hand, palm up, staring at it with absolute absorption through a jeweler's loupe. The rest of us might as well not have even been in the room—assuming, of course, I left my palm behind.

The three of us were crowded into Warren's office. Despite his status within the university and the field, El Jefe had a very small and ordinary office space. Warren had chosen the L-shaped workstation with a round table and four chairs in the far corner from the university's catalog. He'd added bookshelves along two walls, filled partially with research books but partially with odd collectibles such as an actual shrunken head and a voodoo doll that (thank heavens) didn't resemble anyone I knew. Hanging above his desk were framed original movie posters of *The Birds*, *Raiders of the Lost Ark*, and *The Curse of the Werewolf*. The ugly eggplant-colored industrial-grade carpet had been covered by a Persian rug thick enough to sink into. It picked up the colors of the stained-glass window hanging from a pair of chains in front of the ordinary window. The decorating scheme was certainly eclectic, but somehow it worked. And it was very definitely Warren.

El Jefe is one of my favorite people in the world. He's got that rare combination of brains, common sense, and a terrific sense of humor. The package is nicely rounded out with better-than-average looks. All of which he'd passed on to Kevin and Emma.

"It makes no *sense*." Sloan's words brought my attention back to the matter at hand. He ran his finger lightly over the mark and I felt a warm, tingling sensation. "This mark was made by a semidivine creature. Leaving aside the fact that there simply aren't that many of those, the divine just don't *do* curses like this, certainly not on a child. That's more the style of the nefarious. There's a trace of demon signature, but it appears to be the remnants of a covering illusion. But the curse itself? A demon might do it, if it thought delaying a death would cause more damage, or even if it just found it amusing." I felt a little surge of magic as he tested the mark. "No. Definitely divine." He shook his head as if to clear it, then looked up at me, the liquid brown eyes behind the thick glasses wistful. "I don't suppose you'd let me—"

"Study it further?" I ended the sentence for him. It wasn't hard. He was an academic, and to him my curse was the opportunity of a lifetime. He might have sympathy for me but only in the abstract. What was real for him, right now, was the thrill of discovery and the potential for publishable papers. "Publish or perish," as the saying goes. Sure, he was being insensitive, but social skills aren't the forte of a lot of professors. I knew it wasn't personal, but that didn't make me feel all that much better. "Not today. Maybe sometime in the future."

He gave me a pointed look that somehow managed to contain both wheedling greed and, finally, a little real sympathy. "You may not *have* a future. This is a very potent piece of magic."

"And yet I'm here. You just said that it was put on me in childhood."

"I know." He sounded exasperated. "It obviously was. I can tell by the way it's affected your life line." He turned my palm so that I could see it and started pointing at places where the mark intersected the lines palmistry buffs use to analyze your life. "And it has completely altered your career path." He frowned, his eyebrows wiggling like caterpillars above the glasses. "Did your family ever take you to the Vatican? Get you blessed by the Pope?"

"No. Why?"

"Well, a major blessing could mitigate the curse."

"My gran's a true believer," I suggested.

He made a harrumphing noise. "Shouldn't be enough. I really need more time—"

"What kind of creature are we talking about?" Warren interrupted. I noticed that he'd opened the laptop on his desk and was discreetly taking notes.

Sloan didn't look up from my palm. "Well, there are angels, of course, and demigods from some of the more ancient religions."

"Egyptian?" I made it a question.

"Why do you ask?" Sloan's voice was sharp and he met my eyes.

"The mark was invisible until I touched the Wadjeti this morning."

He mulled that over for a moment, then shook his head no. "I suppose it's possible, the Egyptians were known for their curses, but I don't think so. Wadjet was an Egyptian deity, the patron of lower Egypt—there's some debate as to whether she precedes Isis or is simply another incarnation. But this really isn't her type of thing. What do you think, Warren?"

"I think it would be beneficial to look into what creatures are *capable* of this type of curse. Then perhaps we can find a way to break it."

"Oh no! You can't do that!" Dr. Sloan paled and dropped my hand as if burned.

I blinked a few times at his vehemence. "Why the hell not?" I asked.

He shook his head firmly. "The curse has been a part of you for too long. I can't imagine how you've survived, but you have, and your body and psyche have incorporated the curse into your development, your very being. To simply break the curse now would destroy you." I could tell he meant it.

Well, crap. "Then how do I get rid of it?"

He thought about that for a long moment. "Your best bet would be to get the person who cursed you to withdraw the curse."

Like that was likely. Anybody who was willing to put a death curse on a little kid wasn't likely to be the merciful sort. If they'd admit to it in the first place. After all, death curses are a felony—attempted murder.

"What if the person dies?"

He gave me a penetrating look that was fraught with disapproval. "Ms. Graves—"

"I'm not going to do anything," I assured him. What was it with people today? Did I *look* like a murderer? *Wait, I had fangs and glowed in the dark, so I probably did. Hell.*

I hurried to reassure him, "The kind of person who uses death curses doesn't usually live a nice, quiet life in the country, Dr. Sloan. If whoever cursed me dies, do I? Or does the curse unravel after their death?"

He tapped his lip thoughtfully with his index finger. "You're assuming whatever being cursed you can die. Most divine and semidivine beings are immortal or the next thing to it. Still, I would guess it would unravel. Most curses do." He turned to Warren. "I don't suppose you have a digital camera? I would love to take a photograph of this, see if I can find anything out about its origins."

Warren shook his head no. "Sorry."

"Not even on your cell phone?"

"Nope."

"I have one in my office." Sloan looked at me. "Do you mind? You'll wait here?"

"I'll wait." He scurried out, moving with remarkable speed for such an old guy. Then again, he was probably more excited than he'd been in over a decade. For an academic like him, this was big stuff. As soon as he was out of hearing range,

Warren rose and shut the door. He turned to me. "Not exactly the essence of tact, is he?"

I laughed. "No. Not really. He doesn't seem to get that while this is just a mental exercise for him, it's life or death to me."

Warren's eyes darkened, his expression sobering. "He's one of the best in the country, maybe even the world." Warren settled back in his chair. "And he's tenacious. Once he goes after this, he'll keep after it. If there's any kind of solution, he'll find it."

"So I just have to stay alive."

"That would be preferable," he said drily.

I laughed. "I know it sounds weird, but talking to him actually made me feel better."

Warren leaned forward so fast his chair made a thunking noise.

I hurried to explain. "Seriously. I've always wondered, 'Why me?' How could all this shit keep happening to one person? Now I know. It may not change anything that's happened, but at least I know it's not my fault."

"No one ever thought it was."

It was a nice thing for him to say. It was not, however, precisely true. Get a few drinks in people and they'd let all sorts of things slip out. As my dear gran always says, "A drunk man says what a sober man thinks." More than once I'd been accused of "manufacturing crises" so that I could be the center of attention, as if I'm some sort of desperate drama queen. No. So no. I don't even like being the center of attention.

I must have let the silence drag on too long. Warren said, "All right, no one sane ever did."

I laughed again, my mind going back to identify the particular folks he was insulting. Still, it was probably time for a change of subject. "So, when is your lady friend going to conference in?"

"She should have logged in by now." He glanced at the time indicator on his computer screen, his brows furrowing with worry. "If it's all right with you, I'd like to give her a call. She planned to drive to her office to call and probably just got caught in traffic, but—"

"Go for it. Do you want me to step down the hall so you have some privacy?"

"Do you mind?"

I rose from my chair. "Of course not. In fact, I think I'll go grab a can of pop. Would you like one?"

"No, thanks."

I closed the door behind me and started walking down the hall. I hadn't quite reached the vending machine area when I heard Dr. Sloan call out, "Celia, wait. You're not leaving, are you?"

I stopped and turned around, letting him catch up with me. "No. Warren's making a call. I figured I'd get myself a drink."

"Ah." He offered me the book in his hands. "I found this on my shelves and thought it might interest you."

I took the white leather volume. It was quite slender, probably not more than a couple hundred pages. Most texts have a lot more heft. The title appeared in silver foil letters on both the spine and cover: *Man's Experience of the Divine*.

"There's a chart in the first chapter of the various divine and semidivine beings, demigods and so forth, that might be useful for you. You can keep the book if you like. Consider it a thank-you for bringing me in on this and an apology for my being . . . insensitive." He gave me an earnest look. "I realize this is your life, but this curse is simply extraordinary. The first one of its kind I've seen on a person. A *live* one, anyway."

I gave him a wry look. "That's one way to put it."

He gave a sheepish laugh. "I did it again, didn't I?"

"It's all right." I meant that. He really was trying to help, and I needed all the help I could get.

"Thank you for being so gracious. Now, if you'll hold your hand still, palm out, I'll take a few pictures." He held out a camera phone. "With your permission, I'm going to share them with some of my colleagues. If there's a cure for this, one of them should know of it."

"That's very kind of you."

"Yes and no." He gave me a conspiratorial smile. "Posting these *may* help you, but it'll definitely give me bragging rights. You have no idea how jealous some of my colleagues are going to be."

I switched the book to my other hand and moved to a spot where the light was better. Holding my hand palm up, I let him take half a dozen photographs. When he'd finished, he tucked the phone back in his pocket. "There's one more thing I think you should know." He looked uncomfortable and I just knew I was getting bad news.

"What?" I tried to sound casual and failed.

"Until yesterday the mark was invisible, correct?"

"Yes."

"You encountered something magical that changed that and was powerful enough to injure both you and the other woman?"

"Yes."

He sighed. "Then I'm sorry to say, there's a very good chance that whatever happened affected the curse. It *could* mean that you encounter problems less frequently or that the threats are less intense."

Sounded good to me.

"Or it could be the exact opposite."

No shit.

"Given what you've said about your past, I greatly fear that you're going to be facing more and greater dangers now. I'm very sorry." He was all earnest now, no longer just a scholar with an interesting puzzle to work on. It's never fun to be the bearer of bad tidings.

"It's all right. Thanks for telling me. I'll just have to be very careful."

"Please do. I'd hate to see anything happen to you. Now, I have to go. But I promise I'll look into the matter thoroughly and I'll contact you through Warren as soon as I find out anything that might help."

"I appreciate that. Thank you for meeting with me." He waved and hurried off. I pulled out my cell phone and dialed Bubba's number from memory. Yeah, he'd said he'd call, but I was getting impatient. Dottie'd talked a good game going out the door, but she hadn't looked good. Pinning the cell phone between my shoulder and ear, I dug in my pockets for a bill that was crisp enough to feed into the pop machine. He answered just as my can of "pure liquid refreshment" dropped into the dispensing bin.

"Hey, Celia. The doctors say she's fine. Said she should get some extra rest over the next couple days, but no harm done.

I did make her promise she wouldn't be taking those stairs anymore. They're too damned steep for a woman her age, particularly with a walker!"

"Amen to that." I let out a silent sigh of relief. I'd tried not to worry, but I couldn't help it. Then there was the guilt. I mean, I was absolute hell on secretaries lately. What was worse was that the death curse meant I would continue to be a danger to the people around me. I didn't want to live in a cloister, but . . . oh, hell.

"Anyway," Bubba continued, "she insists she is *not* quitting. And she told me to tell you that you'd better not fire her just because she wore herself out. You need her. She'll just be more careful from now on. She does want to be around Minnie, and Dawna does need the help."

He was quoting Dottie. I knew because I could hear her in the background, sounding waspish as an angry schoolmarm.

I shouldn't agree. I knew I shouldn't. But I also saw a lot of me in her. I knew instinctively that Dottie needed something more in her life than soap operas and cleaning her apartment. Karl had brought that to her, bringing her people to do readings for, giving her a way to use her gift and help others. Now that he was dead, she'd been set adrift.

I understood, but I was not going to push it. "Only if she promises not to overdo. She's not going to do anyone any good if she winds up dead or in the hospital."

He repeated what I'd said and Dottie agreed. I could hear the relief in her voice even over the phone.

She'd be careful. So would I. Until I dealt with the whole curse thing, I'd spend as much time as I could away from the office.

One step at a time, Graves. You found out about the curse. Now you find the caster and get the damned thing removed. Then you won't have to worry so much about Dottie, Dawna, or anyone else.

9

I could've gone to dinner with El Jefe. But I was exhausted. It had been a long, tiring day. Besides, neither of us was very good company. He was worried about his friend from UCLA. He'd made calls and learned there'd been no sign of her since she'd left Los Angeles a few hours before. It might be nothing—traffic, car trouble. But she should have called. There aren't a lot of cellular dead zones between L.A. and Santa Maria de Luna. Of course her phone battery could've gone dead. Or she could've forgotten it. Or any of a million other things. But it wasn't like her. So he worried. I was concerned, too, and asked that he call and let me know as soon as he found out anything. I wanted to eat something quick and get the Wadjeti back under wards and behind cold steel. Then I wanted to go back to Birchwoods before John's spell wore off and go to bed.

One good thing about keeping busy—I hadn't had time to fret about my upcoming court date. I kept telling myself that Roberto was the best. We had witnesses, including a slew of holy men who'd come at my psychic call to banish the demon. I reminded myself that Ren had sworn I'd get off; and that

King Dahlmar, whose son I'd saved, would do everything in his considerable power to help me. All of this was true. Even so, I was scared. On the long drive from my office to Birchwoods I went over my testimony and my attorney's plan of attack in my head.

I've been a witness before, plenty of times, mostly in paparazzi stalking cases, defending myself against assault charges from people who tried to get through me to the people I was guarding. But this was different. This was a paranormal manipulation charge. And I was now considered a monster. Both of which meant that I was considerably less likely to get a fair trial. My attorney was sure that, worst-case, I'd be confined to an institution of my choice. I hoped he was right.

The spectre of a state-run facility had been haunting my nightmares even before the attack on the limo. Now, knowing that someone there had already been paid to murder me . . . I shuddered. Were the same people behind the shooting at the Will reading, or was that something else entirely? I wasn't sure I had the energy right now to track down more than one threat.

The closer I got to my destination, the worse I felt. By the time I slid my ID card into the slot of the security machine for the outer gate I was well and truly depressed. A full-body shudder hit me as the heavy metal grill rolled closed with a clang behind my car. Would this be the rest of my life? Locked away to protect the world from me — or worse, to protect me from the world?

The night guard at the second gate was a new guy, but apparently he'd been briefed about me, because the fangs didn't panic him. We went through the expected routine with holy water and silver; then he opened the gate and I drove through.

I parked under one of the lamps, locked my weapons in the car trunk, and, feeling vulnerable and naked, made my way through the open parking lot to the administration building and the night-check-in desk. A very nice, very professional nurse took my shoes, my cell phone, and my name before sending me off to my quarters.

A message had been written on a slip of paper and slipped beneath my door. I picked it up and read: *We must talk. It is urgent. I will contact you tomorrow.* It was signed: *Ivan.*

Oh, freakin' goodie. Just what I needed. More trouble.

I dropped the note onto the nearest flat surface and shambled off to bed.

I wish I could say I slept well. I didn't. My dreams were weird and haunted, my sleep fraught with tossing and turning.

So, after a long, restless night, I rose and got ready to face the music. Since this hearing was an "official" event, I was escorted to the courthouse by the police—and not in my own car. At least I wasn't under arrest, so I didn't have to arrive in handcuffs. But the police insisted I eat two jars of beef and vegetable baby food in the back of the squad car before we set off. Logical, but yuck!

The Santa Maria de Luna Justice Center is a big four-story box of a building, built of stucco painted brilliant white with brick red trim. Red tile steps lead up to the four front entrance doors, each of which is manned by men and machines whose job it is to make sure nothing dangerous makes it into the building. I'd been through those doors many times. To-day, however, I was taken in the back to avoid the hordes of press staked out front waiting for pictures of the vampire who could attend day court.

Roberto met me at the back door. He checked my appear-ance carefully, to make sure I would make a good impression. I was dressed for success in a conservative navy suit with a red silk blouse. It felt absolutely bizarre to be wearing one of Isaac's signature jackets and not be carrying any weapons. Roberto had insisted on panty hose and heels. I hate panty hose. Who-ever invented them was a sadist. They are hot in summer and never fit quite right, even if you don't get them on crooked, which I usually do.

The goal was for me to, in Roberto's words, "channel Laura Bush." So the skirt hit me well below the knee and the pumps were low heeled and plain. I was supposed to be dignified, se-date, conservative, and still look good. I had no idea whether or not I was succeeding at it.

My escort stayed close as we went up the stairs and through the hall leading to the courtroom. The place was full of spec-tators. The most obvious glares were the ones I was getting from Gerry, one of the head guards at Birchwood, and a group of five police officers, all in their very best finery and seated to-gether in the gallery. Gerry and I had been friendly once — before he saw me go all spooky. It scared the crap out of him. Now he was making it his personal mission to see me put away. I think he honestly believes it is the right thing to do. Of course that doesn't make it any better for me.

I recognized one or two of the police officers. They'd been among the people I'd used my siren abilities on. If I hadn't, a greater demon would've wreaked havoc at that World Series game in Anaheim a few weeks back. I had witnesses willing to testify to that.

But the prosecution had witnesses, too. According to the list they provided to Roberto, they were even bringing in Dr. Greene from the state pen. Greene was a null and a shrink. She was also the woman who'd drugged me and set me up for the murder of a minister. Compulsion spells might make her tell the truth and nothing but the truth. But I wasn't sure the *whole* truth was what I wanted the jury to hear.

Shit.

My stomach tightened into knots. If I were still able to eat solids I'd probably have tossed my cookies by now. As it was, I tasted bile in the back of my throat, despite the claim that baby food is a low-acid concoction.

"Celia, you need to calm down." Roberto murmured the words softly enough that they barely carried to my ears. "You're starting to glow."

I looked down and felt my stomach try to do a backflip. Oh, that was so not good. Glowing is not human. It is not normal. It was not going to reassure the prosecutor, judge, and jury that little ole me was no threat to anybody.

I closed my eyes and took deep, cleansing breaths, forcing myself to think about the rocky stretch of beach where I go to be alone when the stress of life gets to me. I was starting to feel better—until I heard somebody say "Do you smell salt water?"

But I wasn't glowing anymore and Roberto hustled me to the front of the courtroom without further incident.

"In front of the bar" has real meaning in a courtroom and only those who are on the daily docket can get through the magic barriers that separate the "working" area from the main gallery. Roberto went through first and I saw a flash of silver light as he passed through the scanner and heavy-duty wards. Then it was my turn.

I stepped in, closed my eyes, and stood perfectly still so that the scanner could do its thing. I saw a flash of red through my closed eyelids, felt the hot rush of magic across my skin, and it was over. I was cleared.

I tried not to show how relieved I was. I tried to act normal, but I'd left normal so far behind at that point that I was definitely faking it. Still, I meekly followed my high-priced attorney to the small table assigned to the defense and took my seat. I glanced around the courtroom, hoping someone I knew was there to cheer me on. In the corner I saw my gran, sitting with El Jefe and Emma. And toward the back on the right side I spotted Dr. Hubbard and Dr. Scott. But no Bruno. I felt my heart sink. I'd hoped . . .

I tried not to fidget as I watched Roberto pull folder after folder from his big, boxy trial briefcase. The prosecutor came over to shake Roberto's hand. His name was Jose Rodriguez and he looked to be about thirty-five, or maybe a young-looking forty. Tall and slender, he was very handsome, with wavy black hair with just a touch of silver and eyes the color of dark chocolate. He had a winning smile and his navy suit looked nice and expensive until I compared it to Roberto's.

"Bob. Good to see you again."

"Joe." They shook hands, "Here to give me a last-minute offer?"

Joe stepped back, his eyes widening. "You don't know? Seriously?"

"Know what?"

The prosecutor looked at me and his expression darkened. There was a slight edge to his voice when he replied, "This hearing is just a formality. It isn't going to last five minutes. Your client has some *very* powerful friends."

Roberto looked at me over his shoulder. I shrugged to let him know I didn't have a clue.

Rodriguez's eyebrows rose until they almost disappeared beneath his hair, his expression conveying not just surprise but more than a bit of disbelief.

"Care to enlighten us?" Roberto's smile didn't quite reach his eyes. Until that moment, they'd seemed like friends who happened to be on opposite sides of a case. Now Roberto had shifted gears and shown he was all business.

The prosecutor turned to his associate, who handed him a thin stack of papers. Turning back to us, Rodriguez began laying the sheets on the table one at a time, like playing cards, indicating what each was as he did.

"A certificate of dual citizenship with Rusland. The official letter and certificate announcing Ms. Graves's appointment as Official Security Liaison, with full diplomatic status, signed by King Dahlmar himself, including the royal seal. A letter of pardon signed by the governor to be used in the event of your conviction. A letter of pardon signed by the president of the United States, to be used in the event of your conviction. And we received a visit from some of the boys over at the State Department, suggesting that, all things considered and since you were acting in defense of others, we should save the state the money it would take to prosecute."

"You've got a letter from the *president*? Seriously?" I just about choked on the words. "The *president of the United States* wrote a pardon for me? Holy crap. Ho"—I took a breath between syllables—"ly *crap*."

Rodriguez smiled. It made him look younger, less cynical. "Yes. And I've got to tell you, the politicos don't *do* that. Not in advance. It's too likely to blow up in their faces."

"I'm not surprised." Roberto smiled benignly, leaning back and folding his hands across his waist. "Ms. Graves's actions saved the lives of King Dahlmar and his son Prince Rezza and unmasked a political plot that would've destabilized their nation. She also assisted in the banishment of a major demon who had been summoned to wreak havoc at one of the largest public sporting events on the calendar. Who knows how many lives might have been lost if Ms. Graves hadn't done as she did? King Dahlmar previously indicated to me his intent to do everything he could to keep her from being imprisoned as a result of her actions."

"Well, he's a man of his word." Joe gathered up the pages, stacking them neatly.

"So, are you going to prosecute?" I asked. I couldn't help myself.

Rodriguez shook his head. "Why bother? It'd be an open-and-shut case and a complete waste of the taxpayers' money."

"And the other matter?" Roberto's voice was silken.

Rodriguez's expression darkened, all the humor draining out of it in a rush, his features seeming to harden into stone. "It was self-defense. She and the doctor were kidnapped." He turned to me, his eyes capturing mine, his gaze intense. "But know this. If you ever again set so much as a toe out of line, we will prosecute. We might not be able to put you away. But if you show you are a threat to our citizens, we will find some way of getting rid of you, even if we have to deport you to do it."

I didn't doubt that he meant it. I really hoped it never came to that. It bothered me deeply that I wasn't considered one of "our citizens" anymore and somehow I just knew it wasn't because of my new diplomatic status.

We were spared further conversation as the bailiff came in and announced the judge. The prosecutor stepped back behind his table as we all rose for the Honorable Sarah Jacobsen to take the bench.

Once she took her seat, the prosecutor made his announcement about dropping the charges. Judge Jacobsen immediately asked the attorneys to approach the bench, and it didn't take vampire hearing to catch the gist of the conversation. She didn't like this. She didn't like it one bit. Governor, president, king, or no, she wanted me locked up somewhere far, far away from vulnerable humans and she did not appreciate the fact that people higher up the food chain were usurping her judicial authority.

She motioned the men back to their seats and stared at me for a long moment. Finally, she spoke. "Ms. Graves. The prosecutor has asked to dismiss the charges against you based on what, in my opinion, are political threats from people who have no business interfering in this case."

Shouts and swearing erupted from the gallery behind me and I was suddenly very glad no weapons or magic was allowed in the room.

"While I might not have the power to change the prosecutor's mind and press this case forward, I most certainly *can* take testimony from the experts already identified by both parties to satisfy myself that you are not a danger to yourself or others."

Shit. This had taken a rather nasty turn. I might not go to jail, but there was suddenly the very real possibility I could still be committed and I might not be in a position to choose to return to Birchwoods.

"I will allow prosecution and defense ten minutes to confer with your experts. The question is whether Ms. Graves, in her current condition, can be a productive member of society without endangering the citizenry." She banged a gavel on the bench while glaring daggers at me. "Court is recessed until ten thirty."

Roberto leaned over and whispered next to my ear as the rest of the room erupted in chaos, "She's already prejudiced against you. It'll be easy to overturn it on appeal, no matter what she rules."

My jaw dropped and my skin started glowing again. "And what am I supposed to do until then, Roberto? Sit in the cage like a good dog, hoping someone will spring me before they bring in the needle?"

He looked at me seriously, his eyes filled with pain. "I'll do the best I can, Celia. You know that. Can we count on Dr. Scott's testimony on your behalf? I know he isn't your treating psychiatrist, but he has credentials Dr. Hubbard doesn't, and from what I saw during depositions Ann Hubbard will make a terrible witness. You told me therapy has been going well."

I bit at my lower lip, puncturing it with a fang and making myself wince. "I think you should call Dr. Hubbard anyway. Dr. Scott isn't . . . happy with me right now."

My apologetic look didn't help much. Roberto sighed. "No. Never mind . We'll go with Professor Sloan."

Ten minutes goes really fast when you're listening to people deciding your fate. Before I knew it, the gavel was banging again. I let out a little yelp, but I don't think anyone other than Roberto noticed. "Mr. Rodriguez, you have ten minutes to make your case."

A slender woman, dressed in an electric blue skirt set, approached the bench. She was not channeling Ms. Bush. Her heels were at least three inches high and the skirt length wouldn't have been acceptable by my high school dress code. The witness bench hid most of the show, so all she offered the audience was a tasteful electric blue jacket and white shirt, with pearls, beneath shining auburn hair. Nifty.

Rodriguez apparently didn't like being timed, because his words came out less smooth and polished than I expected. "Could you state your name for the record?"

"Jessica Marloe."

"And what is your occupation, Ms. Marloe?"

"It's *Dr.* Marloe. I'm a protective therapist at the California State Paranormal Treatment Facility."

She was one of the guards at the state facility!

"Do you have any experience with vampires, Dr. Marloe?"

"I have studied vampires extensively and in a previous position worked on research into reversing the vampiric process."

"Could you please tell the Court what success you had with that?"

"We had no success, unfortunately. Once a person is turned, the process always leads to loss of higher brain function and increasing violence until we're forced to take measures to protect our other patients." Meaning, they're put down. I hadn't been kidding with my comment about a cage and needle.

The testimony went no better for the remainder of the ten minutes and concluded with Dr. Marloe's conviction that I was a ticking time bomb. I was sure I was done for. But I'd underestimated Roberto. He'd been taking notes the whole time Marloe was talking and stood smoothly when it was time for cross-examination.

"Dr. Marloe, have you ever treated a siren in your facility?"

She looked at him like he was an annoying fly. "No, of course not. There are very few sirens in existence."

Now it was Roberto who raised his brows. "But surely you've read about other cases of sirens in state treatment facilities? Yes?"

She shook her head. "No. There's never been a siren in a treatment facility."

He leaned on the edge of the box. "Really? *Never?* Nowhere in the world? That seems odd, even considering the small population of full- and partial-blooded sirens. Why do you suppose that is?"

She turned on the icy glare. "I have no idea."

"Could it possibly be because sirens are unique in their mental *stability?* After all, in order to manipulate a person's mind, wouldn't they have to have a great deal of mental *strength* and intelligence?"

"I . . ." She paused. "I can't say one way or the other."

He nodded and looked expressively at the judge before turning his attention to the doctor again. "In the course of your education, you've studied most manners of preternatural . . . creatures?"

"Of course."

"Then are you willing to certify to this court that you've studied the physiology and psychology of sirens, even if you've never actually treated one or read about the treatment of one?"

Marloe made an odd face. "Well, I know as much as *can* be known. They're a highly secretive society and international law prohibits infringement on their territory."

"Because they can manipulate people's minds, right? That is, after all, what this case is about."

I bit at my lip again and let out a muttered swear when I tasted blood. *Damn fangs.* Where was he going with this?

"Yes, that's correct."

She was glaring at me as though daggers were going to shoot out of her eyes. Roberto noticed. "You don't like my client much, do you, Doctor?"

Her chin went high and haughty. "I don't even know her."

"But you think the world would be safer if she was behind bars. Yes?"

Um . . . Roberto? You're on my side, right? I struggled with everything I had not to move or show my panic.

"I do."

He scratched the side of his nose lightly. "Doctor, isn't it true that most fertile women who meet sirens hate them? Want them put behind bars or sent away?"

"Well, it's not the way you say it—"

He pounced like a cat on a mouse, putting his face inches from hers in classic Perry Mason style. "Really? Because I could have *sworn* that my preternatural expert told me that sirens can't influence postmenopausal women, or prepubescent children, or gay men, and that fertile women find them to be a threat. It's an involuntary emotional reaction that causes the woman to work against the siren. Is that correct?'

Marloe looked at the prosecutor, the judge, the spectators, Roberto—everywhere but at me. Roberto prompted her, "Please remember you're under oath, Doctor."

She let out a frustrated breath. "Well, of course, there are exceptions to a siren's influence. The siren's psychic call primarily appeals to a certain demographic—"

Roberto kept talking, right over her. "Exceptions like men over sixty and men with vasectomies and even ordinary men who wear magically created charms that prevent them from being affected by that influence. Is *that* correct?"

She shrugged and shifted in her chair. Her fingers were nibbling at her skirt now and she was having trouble meeting his eyes. Her voice went soft. "Yes, I suppose."

He stood up to his full height, turned toward the gallery, and spoke without looking at her. He ticked his points off on his fingers as he went. Marloe couldn't see, but the judge could. "So, what you're *really* saying is that Celia cannot affect all senior citizens, all young children, all gay men, all sterilized men, and around half of the women in this great big world. The remaining men *might* be affected by the Defendant, provided they don't have a charm to prevent it, and the remaining women will actively work against her rather than do her bidding. Is that what you're saying?"

"Yes." Her voice was a whisper now, her eyes firmly on the floor in front her. I stole a glance at the prosecutor. His jaw muscle was bulging from clenching his teeth so tight.

The judge squirmed, clearly affected by Roberto's argument. "The prosecution's ten minutes are up. As are defense's."

"Your Honor . . . ," Roberto began to protest. We hadn't had a chance to put on our witness after all. But the judge cut him off with a glare. She stood up and picked up a thick file. "The witness will step down. Court will recess for thirty minutes while I consider the evidence."

For the next half hour, I sat on my uncomfortable wooden chair trying to look inoffensive and harmless while conversations buzzed all around me. People were flat out calling one side or the other idiots. To add to the confusion, a flock of gulls had lined the window ledges outside the courtroom. They were just sitting, staring in at us . . . like tiny, white-winged vultures.

Finally the bailiff announced Jacobson's return and we all stood.

She sat, we sat, and I waited, the bats in my stomach rising anew.

"The Defendant will rise." Roberto nudged me and I stood as ordered. I did my best to hide my fangs under my lips and gave the judge my full attention, even though I was shaking more than a little. *Please don't send me away.* Would tears help or hurt? It hardly mattered, because I was already crying.

"Ms. Graves. Your attorney gave a masterful performance here, clearly intending to sway me into allowing a known vampire, an admitted psychic manipulator, to go back into open society." I was clutching the table so hard I was pretty sure my nails would leave marks. The baby food was inching its way back up my throat and the birds began to take flight, hovering outside the courtroom.

"And he managed it." I let out a breath I hadn't realized I was holding. I felt my body partially collapse against the table. "While I'm still concerned about your . . . abilities, there's a sizable portion of the human population you cannot affect. You're not fully vampire, or human, or siren. Yet you currently have command enough of your body and mind to appear here, in full daylight, and at least *look* repentant. To commit you against your will would be the equivalent of locking up a clairvoyant who chose to reveal the future to people, or a mage who performs magic for pay.

"As much as I may loathe the result, your ability is bio-logical and you quite literally"—she motioned toward the birds thumping against the bulletproof glass—"can't help it. I find it rather disturbing just how very distasteful I find you, even though you've done nothing to deserve that reaction while in my court. Therefore, I have no choice but to believe that I'm biologically prejudiced against you, and will rule based only on the written record and testimony given today. I will recuse myself from any further proceedings involving you."

She paused for a long moment, anger etching deep lines in her face. "However, know that this court will be watching you carefully. If you start to run amok or appear to be a threat to the general population, I *promise* you that you will be put away without a second thought. Is that clear?"

I nodded, feeling suddenly light-headed. "Crystal."

And just that quick, the whole thing was over. On to the next case. A witch, I think. I didn't stick around long enough to find out. I wanted out of there, and the sooner the better. I wanted to find some fresh sea air and an empty beach so that

I could calm my frazzled nerves. Unfortunately, there was a wide band of unhappy uniformed cops between me and the exit.

"Excuse us, Officers." Roberto moved ahead of me, using his body as a shield between me and the angry men. He looked up at the lead officer, meeting his gaze without flinching.

The cop was a big man, six three or four, with the kind of build that you can only get with the benefit of serious weight lifting. He stood there, a solid wall of silent, blue-clad muscle. It was his partner, a smaller, blond man with harsh features and icy blue eyes, who spoke, addressing his words to me rather than Roberto.

"Graves, don't think you got away with anything. It isn't over. We'll be watching you. You'll screw up eventually. When you do, we'll have you."

Roberto's smile was as warm and friendly as a hungry shark. "I must have misunderstood you, Officer"—he glanced at the man's name pin—"Clarke. What you just said sounded suspiciously like a threat. You wouldn't be planning to harass my client, would you?"

The crowded courtroom fell so silent you could hear Clarke's harsh breathing. He said nothing, but his expression was answer enough. He looked murderous, his jaw clenched so tight I could hear his teeth grinding.

Roberto continued, "Understand, Officer, if you and your men harass my client, we will have you up on charges."

No one answered. There was another long, tense moment of silence. A standoff. Neither side willing to back down. It was the judge who broke the stalemate. With a gesture, she stopped the witch hearing and signaled for the bailiff, who headed in our direction. As if that were a signal, the cops turned as a unit and filed out of the room. As the last man passed through the door, the courtroom erupted into noise and chaos.

"Sorry about that," Roberto said softly enough that only the bailiff and I could hear.

"Not your fault." I forced myself to give him a smile. "Nothing we can do about it, either."

"We can if they harass you."

I sighed. "Only if we can prove it. And honestly, how far do you really think we'd get?" I felt and sounded tired and more than a little bit bitter. Roberto might have kept me out of captivity—for now—but there was no way I was out of danger.

The bailiff had moved off and the judge was pounding her gavel. Time for me to get out of here.

"I have another case," Roberto said. He reached his hand out for me to shake. I shook it, told him "thanks" one more time. "If you need me, you've got my number." He walked away briskly, heading for his next client. I hurried into the hallway myself, hoping to join my friends and family.

I am a big, bad-assed bodyguard, with vampire fangs and siren abilities. Is it wussy of me to admit that I wanted to be held? Because I did. I wanted Bruno, needed to feel his arms around me, to hear him to say it was going to be all right. I knew, logically, that everything had changed, that I could never get my old life back. But I wanted it just the same.

The door was still swinging shut behind me when my gran pulled me close, hugging me as tight as she could. "Oh, Celie, thank God! When I saw it was a woman judge I was so scared! But my prayers were answered. It turned out all right."

She squeezed me tight enough to cut off my breath. For such a tiny woman, she's *strong*, in every way. My eyes stung, but I promised myself I wouldn't cry. I held her close.

"They caught the shooter from the Will reading," Gran said.

My eyes widened. "No! Who was it?"

"They don't know yet, but he's in custody and they're bringing in mages to interrogate him."

It was great news. Warren and Emma both hugged me, then Warren excused himself explaining that he'd promised to let Kevin know how things turned out. Since no cell phone use was allowed in the courthouse, Warren wanted to immediately head outside and call his son.

It would have been nice if Kevin had come to the hearing, but I understood why he couldn't.

I half-listened as Em and Gran started talking about taking me to dinner. I was looking for Bruno. He was here. I knew it—I could sense his magic. It slid over my skin like liquid silk, making all the little hairs stand up.

But where was he? Turning slowly, I began searching in earnest, finally finding him standing next to his brother Matteo, the priest. I smiled at them and started to hurry over, my steps faltering when I saw the expressions on their faces.

Matty came forward first. He pulled me into a fierce hug. I barely had time to hear his whispered, "I'm sorry, Celia. I really am," before he let me go and strode toward the exit at a speed that was just short of a run.

"Matty?" I looked after him for an instant, then turned to Bruno, who had sat down on a bench in a shadowed alcove not too far away. He didn't look up, just sat there, head in his hands. "Bruno . . . what's wrong? We won."

I stopped about eighteen inches away, afraid to come closer. Why didn't he say anything? Why wasn't he looking at me?

He looked up just then and my heart fell to my feet. His expression was so lost, pain etched deep in his features.

"What's wrong?" I came closer but didn't touch him, knowing somehow that I shouldn't.

There were voices behind me. The others were coming. I could hear them.

Bruno gently took my hand and led me into a small meeting room usually used by attorneys to meet with their clients. He pulled a ceramic disk the size of a quarter out of a pant pocket. Setting it on the floor at the doorway, he muttered a soft incantation under his breath. A wave of blue-white light spread out in a perfect circle with us at the center. I could feel the power of it like pressure in the air and I found myself working my jaw, trying to get my ears to pop. All of the ambient noise in the hall was just gone, as if I'd stepped into a soundproof booth.

Maybe I had.

"Bruno?"

He still wouldn't meet my eyes. Instead he sank into a chair and gestured for me to sit opposite from him.

My throat was tight. I barely dared to breathe. I sat.

"I love you, Celie. I always have. I always will." His voice cracked. Tears filled my eyes and the world grew blurry.

"You're everything to me. You always have been . . . since the day we met." He meant it. I could feel the intensity of it.

He looked at me then. There were tears rolling down his cheeks. Big, tough Jersey Italians aren't supposed to cry, but he was crying and his voice was a hoarse croak.

"I went back to Jersey, to tell Irene it was over, that I was taking a new job and moving to L.A. to be with you."

I couldn't speak. I hadn't known there was someone else, that he'd had to make a choice between me and anyone. My chest was heaving as if I couldn't get enough air, my heart pounding as though it would explode. No. Not explode. Break. My heart was breaking. He'd never mentioned another woman. You'd think she would have come up in conversation.

"She's pregnant."

I didn't hear much after that. He kept talking, explaining. He loved me. But he'd grown up without a dad. He couldn't do that to a child of his. He had to be there. And it wasn't fair to her to have to raise a kid alone. From the first sentence, it was a foregone conclusion. It was over. He was leaving me. The reason why didn't really matter.

I couldn't believe it. Couldn't bear it.

We sat there, crying and not touching, for long minutes. Eventually he stood. "I'm sorry. The shield will stay in place as long as you want it to. You can leave whenever you're ready." His voice was hollow, as if crying had emptied him of everything. He walked away. I didn't watch him go. I was too angry, too hurt. I sat there alone for a long time and cried tears that were tinged red.

I didn't want to face anyone. I wanted to be alone. But Gran was out there and Emma. They were probably worried. And hiding wouldn't change anything. He was gone. Again. It felt like my soul had been ripped from my body, but life went on. I needed to face that, sooner rather than later. But right now, oh, God, it *hurt*.

I felt the magic of the shield disintegrate as I stepped across the barrier and found Emma standing outside the room, waiting.

"Your gran saw you go off with Bruno, so she figured it was okay to go tell your mom the good news. I ran into Bruno's brother outside. He told me what happened. So I came back to wait for you."

She stared at me in silence for a long moment, taking in the pile of used tissues I was stuffing back in my purse. Though I'd cried myself out, my nose wasn't chapped. Nor were my eyes red. Vampire metabolism strikes again. So other than the fact that most of my makeup was gone, I probably didn't look too bad. Emma asked, "Are you all right?"

I gave her the look that question deserved, then shook my head with a shrug.

"All right. Stupid question." She sat together on the same little bench Bruno had sat on just minutes earlier. "Breaking up sucks, and I'm sorry." She took a deep breath. "I know we've never been as close as you were with Vicki and are with Dawna—"

I started to say something, but she cut me off with a gesture. "It's all right, Celia. I'm pretty sure it was the siren thing."

"Was?"

She rolled her eyes, knowing that I was trying to change the subject. I was. But I was also curious. So she indulged me and explained, "I don't want kids. I had a voluntary tubal last week. No longer fertile. No more siren problem."

"Oh." I wasn't sure what to say. "Um . . . congratulations?" I wanted to ask why she hadn't told me, but the answers seemed obvious—I was stuck at Birchwoods, prepping for my hearing, and, oh yes, the "siren problem."

She gave a weak chuckle. "Whatever. We can talk about everything over dinner. You've been here quite a while and you've got to eat something soon, before your hunger gets out of hand."

I had never felt less hungry in my life. But wandering the streets filled with bloodlust wasn't appealing, either. The cops would be watching me. I absolutely believed that. I might feel like hell, but I was free. It would be a shame to get locked up again the same day.

I stood. Taking a deep, shuddering breath, I struggled to pull myself together. "Right, food. Preferably something quick."

"New China's only a couple of blocks from here. They've got a buffet. You can probably handle egg drop soup."

"Do they have a bar?" My voice sounded as lifeless as I felt. I'm not a big fan of Chinese food, but I probably wouldn't taste it anyway.

"I think so."

"Good. I need a drink. Maybe several."

"Celia—" She started to say something but stopped, thinking better of it after seeing my expression. "Never mind. Let's get some food before things get ugly."

Talk about prophetic. Then again, she is a clairvoyant.

10

was not myself. That's the only excuse I can give. I tried to be decent company and failed, miserably. Emma understood, trying valiantly to carry the conversational ball single-handedly—telling me about the job she'd landed in New York with Seacrest Artifacts. I tried to listen, but Emma's voice was just white noise in the background. It was as if there was a vast distance between me and the real world. So while I heard her talking about how her father didn't approve, that he thought she should finish her degree, I didn't really take it in. I drank my drink and listened to her rattling on and tried to make interested noises at the right intervals.

She told that it was a great job, working as personal assistant to Irene Seacrest herself. The last person had walked out, so Irene needed Emma to start as soon as possible. She'd be flying out first-class day after tomorrow and staying in one of the corporate-owned apartments until she could find a place of her own. She was really excited. When she paused for a breath, I manage to ask how she'd found the job.

Bruno had recommended her for it. And while she didn't say it, Emma's sudden horror and rapid retreat to the bathroom let me put two and two together. Irene. He'd said her name was Irene. Emma was going to be working with Bruno's baby momma.

I sat at the table, numb. I didn't know what to think. I'd built a perfectly good life after Bruno and I broke up the first time. I could do it again. Of course I could. But right now, at this moment, I felt as if something essential had broken inside me.

I took another long swig of the salty-sweet frozen concoction in my glass, emptying it. I refilled the glass from the pitcher on the table. Now that was empty, too. Had we been here that long? A glance at my wrist made me do a double take. Not even an hour? Was that right?

I'd get past Bruno's loss. I knew I would. Why did it hurt so much? He'd only been back in my life for a few weeks. Logically, it shouldn't hurt this much. Of course emotions aren't logical. Still, I didn't have a choice. He was gone. I had to move on. The only way to do that was to keep moving. Winston Churchill had said it best, I suppose: "If you are going through hell, *keep going.*" I took a deep, steadying breath, letting it out slowly. I could do this. I would do this. Reaching beneath the table, I retrieved my purse from the floor.

Judging from her red-eyed, flying exit, Emma was likely to be gone awhile. If I didn't distract myself, I'd think. Thinking would lead to feeling. Feeling was a bad idea right now. So I dug through the used tissues and detritus in my purse until I laid my hands on my cell phone.

With the simple push of a couple buttons I was listening to my voice mails. There were a lot. The first was from Kevin, congratulating me on my win.

The next message made me pick up my drink again and

slug it down, then start looking for the waitstaff. It was Gran, telling me Mom was in jail again, picked up for driving without a license and insurance. I shook my head with annoyance. "Terrific. Just what Gran doesn't need." It would be Mom's third strike. I doubted they'd offer bail this time, but if they did, even Bubba wouldn't take her on. She was a flight risk. She was probably going to be spending some time behind bars. I'd need to call Gran back, see if she could come see me during Birchwoods' visiting hours tomorrow.

There were lots of other messages, none of them urgent. Congratulations on the win. One or two reporters fishing for a story. The last call was from Creede and was less than fifteen minutes old. Stupid cell phone. I hate it when it doesn't ring.

"Graves . . . Creede. You need to get back to me right away. I'm at the office. We have a situation." He recited a cell number that matched the phone's caller ID.

A *situation*. In my line of work, that phrase never means anything good.

The lump that had settled in my chest eased for a moment as the weight of a looming crisis started my brain clicking. Hallelujah for that. It was probably stupid to be grateful for someone else's emergency, but I hit the button for callback with something close to eagerness.

"Creede."

"Graves here. What's wrong?"

"You have an important client with a situation. You need to get your game face on. I explained your circumstances, offered to take the job. But he swears nobody else can handle this for him except you."

"Who's the client?"

"No."

Okay. Cell lines aren't secure, but it usually isn't an issue. If it was now, then there was a serious problem. *Great.*

My eagerness went away. The last time I'd been in a situation where names weren't revealed, I'd earned my fangs. Bile rose into my throat and I struggled to swallow it back down. I reached for the pitcher again, trying to drain the few drops left in the bottom. The remaining chips of ice tinked against the glass from how hard my hand was shaking.

Crap. This shouldn't be bothering me this much. I'd handled a hundred cases before the one that went bad and I'd fully planned to handle a hundred more after. But what if I couldn't?

I stole Emma's remaining drink, chasing the acid back down to my stomach where it belonged. The trouble was, it wasn't just *me*. I was used to the threat of death. Been playing that game since I was a kid. No, it was the other people who were pulling out my insides right now. The Ivys and Bob Johnsons of the world who were sacrificed.

For nothing. There wasn't a single good reason why they died, and it tore out little bits of my soul every time I thought about it. I'd failed to protect them. I was supposed to guard them, even though I knew they would say it hadn't been my job. But they hadn't had to be the ones *left*. The ones to stare into glazed, still eyes that would never see again, or cradle bodies that cooled to the touch the longer you held on and cried.

A big part of me wanted to say "screw it," to hang up the phone and go curl up in a ball in some dark corner of the world with nothing for company but a bottle of something that would make the pain go away.

Just like my mother had.

Shit.

I couldn't do that. I *wouldn't* do it. How many would be hurt, how many would die, if I just gave up? Yes, it would be easy, too easy, to walk away. But people need bodyguards and I do know my stuff. Plus, now I had better hearing, better sight, and quicker reflexes. It should be a cakewalk to do personally what I'd often had to rely on gadgets for in the past.

Once I made that decision, the rest was easy. If I was going to keep going, keep living, I might as well start with this difficult case.

Looking on the bright side, someone else's crisis might take my mind off my own. But even if it didn't, life goes on. Whether you want it to or not.

"Where are you?" Creede asked.

"Just finishing dinner." My voice sounded remarkably calm. "I can be at the office in ten or fifteen minutes." I raised my hand, signaling to the waiter for the check as I spoke.

"Don't bother. Give me the name of the restaurant. We'll come to you."

"Emma Landingham is with me."

I heard muttering in the background but couldn't make out the words.

"Get rid of her. We'll be there in five minutes." The phone clicked off.

Get rid of her. Gee, how charming. Even worse, having experienced the way Creede drove, I knew they'd be here in four. The waiter I'd flagged approached the table as Emma emerged from the restroom. "Ms. Landingham is leaving, but I have other friends coming. Could you please bring me the bill and a large soda?" Time to get off the sauce. Yeah, it might not affect me like it did my mother, but that could change in an instant. I didn't want to be hooked if it did.

"Certainly, ma'am." He turned and hurried off.

"I'm leaving?" Emma gave me a look of alarm. It took me a second to realize she probably thought I was upset about her job.

"It's not about you working for Seacrest." I tried to force myself to smile. It felt like my face was breaking and probably looked like a grimace, but it was the best I could do. This wasn't about Emma. It wasn't. "I'm glad you found a great job. I know you'll be good at it." I blinked back tears and swallowed hard against the lump in my throat. *Damn it!* I'd been doing so good just a second ago. "Keep in touch. You can always e-mail or text me. I want to know everything. Honest. This won't change a thing between us."

"Celia—"

I shook my head mutely, fighting for control. "Really, this isn't about you. I've got to get my shit together, Em. I've got a situation at work."

She paled a little. Hanging around with her older brother had taught her enough "tough-guy speak" to know just how bad a "situation" could be.

"Are you up for that? I mean—," she stammered, afraid of having misspoken yet again.

I gave her a wry smile. "Doesn't matter if I am; I don't have a lot of choice. Creede will be here with the client in just a couple of minutes." I tried to make light of it. "Nothing like a little panic to take your mind off a breakup. Nine out of ten dentists surveyed said so."

"Celia—" She stared at me, her mouth moving with no sound coming out, not knowing what to do or say. She knew I was messed up. She'd been around since Bruno and I were together the first time and had watched when I dissolved into Jell-O when he left. That was the thing. It wasn't that he left me. It was that he left me twice. Both times without even giving me a chance. I could tell that she felt helpless. Emma was my friend. Maybe not my best friend, but dammit, she was trying; I loved her for it.

"I'll be fine, Emma." I stood up and gave her a hug. Honesty compelled me to add, "It just may take a while."

She sighed and gathered up her things. "Fine. I'll go. But be careful. And I'll be watching the mirror for you."

Ah, the mirror. After Vicki's death, Dr. Scott had given me back a magically crafted mirror that had been my final birthday gift to her. It was a very powerful focus. Since I'm no clairvoyant, it was useless to me, so I passed it on to the person I thought Vicki would want to have it. Emma might only be a level four, but with a focus that powerful she'd probably be able to keep an eye on me.

I made a little face. I didn't want to offend her, but that wasn't a good idea. "I'd rather you didn't. I don't want any client confidentiality issues."

Her eyes rolled expressively. "I know how to keep a secret."

"Please?"

She gave me a long look but didn't answer, just sighed and left. Whether that meant she would or wouldn't keep tabs on me I had no clue. I trusted her, but there are legal and ethical considerations.

More important, I'd never forgive myself if I dragged her

into the middle of another one of my problems. She's an adult, but to me she's always been Warren's baby girl and Kevin's little sister. *They'd* never forgive me if anything happened to her. Whether the constant crises in my life were generated by the death curse, my career, or just bad luck didn't really matter as far as this went. My life was dangerous. I didn't want her getting hurt.

I hadn't been able to protect my sister, and I might never know for certain whether or not Vicki's death was a direct result of the mess that had ended with the demon being vanquished in Anaheim. But they were both dead, and I didn't want to lose Emma. So I'd be careful. Of course Emma would probably like that about as much as I would.

Ah well. She's been mad at me before. Would be again. It's that kind of relationship.

I didn't have long to think about it because just then three very familiar men walked into the restaurant. The minute I saw them, I knew I was in trouble.

King Dahlmar of Rusland is an attractive man. Not young, but holding up well, with dark good looks and more than his share of charisma. All of the other times I'd seen him he'd been expensively dressed, impeccably well groomed, and surrounded by the extremely big, threatening men who are the royal equivalent of the Secret Service. Tonight he was incognito, wearing a pair of cheap jeans of such a rich indigo blue that they almost glowed. Vertical and horizontal creases screamed "fresh off the shelf." A bright red Mickey Mouse Disneyland T-shirt, sneakers, and the sort of cheap sunglasses made famous by ZZ Top made him look like a tourist who'd lost his luggage. He also looked as if he hadn't slept in far too long—his face was pale and haggard. But the oddly cheerful clothes and his poor physical condition couldn't hide the rage in his every move. At his side was the retainer who'd saved my butt a few weeks ago and who'd been trying to reach me ever since: Ivan. He was injured. I could tell because he was moving oddly from pain and trying not to show it. Been there, done that.

Pain or no, he was all business. He scanned the room, looking for threats, keeping his body between Dahlmar and the restaurant patrons until he was reasonably sure they were safe. Creede did the same on the king's other side.

Looking at them, I knew that this was real, serious trouble: trouble I was probably not equipped to handle. For all of ten seconds I thought about leaving, saying no and walking away.

But King Dahlmar's intervention was probably the only thing that had kept me from being locked away for the rest of my life. I owed him. And everything I'd seen, everything I'd read about him, had told me he was a good man and a great king for his people.

"Ms. Graves." Dahlmar slid into the booth across from me and finally took off his sunglasses, revealing dark circles under his eyes that made him look like he'd been beaten.

Creede took the next table over, far enough away that I couldn't feel his magic but close enough that I couldn't help but smell his cologne. The last thing I wanted to do was enjoy the scent, but my nose wouldn't cooperate with my injured heart. He just flat smelled good. It actually started to piss me off.

I shook my head to clear it and saw Ivan move to stand at the pay phone near the bathrooms, where he could discreetly cover most of the room. It's exactly what I would have done and it eased my anger, leaving my head sort of empty. Numb was a good place. I decide to ride it for as long as I could.

"Your Majesty." I forced myself to smile. "May I recommend the egg drop soup or the kung pao chicken? They're quite tasty. You look like you haven't eaten for a while."

He grimaced. "No. I haven't."

"Well, the food here is quite good. And you need to keep your strength up to deal with whatever is going on. I'm guessing it's your sons?"

He sighed heavily, absently tapping his knuckles against the table. "My son Kristoff has staged a coup d'état. I escaped with my life, thanks to a core group of my men. Rezza did not." There was a pained pause. Rezza was . . . *had been* the crown prince. Kristoff was the younger son. While Rezza had been more hard-core religious than his father, they both shared a deep love of their people and truly believed they knew the best way to lead the country into the future. Kristoff didn't have a deep love for anything except himself. More to the point, he was stupid. Even his father admitted it. Stupid people make bad rulers.

I opened my mouth to voice my condolences, but he waved me to silence. When he spoke again, his voice was flat, inflectionless. Just the facts. "Thus far, no word has leaked out and Kristoff has been using demon spawn as impostors to maintain an appearance of normalcy. As he is neither cunning nor strong enough to manage something like this on his own, there must be someone else behind this."

I knew all about demon spawn. The products of humans breeding with demons, they were born without souls and with the magical abilities of their demon parents. A spawn could change into an exact replica of anyone, right down to the cellular level. My last job—the one that left me with fangs—had been to guard Prince Rezza. Only it wasn't Rezza but a demon spawn. I'd been really angry when I'd talked about this in group. I'd guarded a *demon spawn* . . . how laughable! Guarded it against *what*? An angel? That was about the only thing that could hurt them.

I shook my head with both weariness and frustration. Kristoff didn't realize what kind of dynamite he was playing with. He might think he was in control, but it was an illusion. A demon spawn will turn on you in a red-hot minute. "So they've taken your country from you and you don't even know who the villain is."

"Yes. But our advantage is that they must kill me and make it look like an accident. I don't plan to give them that opportunity."

"Why do they have to kill you? They've got the country. You're on the run and powerless. Rezza's dead. Why not just announce that Kristoff's in charge? There wouldn't be much you could do about it."

The waiter started toward our table, carrying a water glass and a menu for my companion. As he came near, Dahlmar's expression changed, as if a switch had been hit. One minute angry, deposed monarch; the next, pleasant dinner companion. While a part of me had always known a ruler needed to be a good actor, it was disconcerting as hell to watch.

King Dahlmar listened to the list of daily specials with apparent cheerfulness before ordering exactly what I'd suggested when he arrived.

The instant the waiter left, Dahlmar's smile disappeared. His expression was grim. "You don't understand politics, Ms. Graves. I've gained enough international favor that he doesn't dare simply exile me. My allies will intervene. For example, my iron ore contract with France depends on reserves that only *I* know the location of. No, he needs the respectability of a seemingly honest inheritance."

"Again, why?" I took a sip of my water. He didn't touch his. "It would be just as easy to claim to the world that you'd snapped and he had to take the throne."

He thought carefully before answering. Until that moment I don't think he'd slowed down enough to just think things through. He'd been on the run, desperate, with too much happening. In those circumstances you react. He'd done well thus far. He was still alive. But if he seriously wanted to get his throne back, he needed to stop reacting and start thinking. Even then the odds against him succeeding were ridiculously long—and probably getting longer by the minute as Kristoff settled in.

After a long pause, the king nodded. "First, my people wouldn't believe it, even if the leaders of other countries did or pretended to for their own purposes. Kristoff is disliked by the upper class. Also, I am a popular ruler and many of the more moderate clerics would not condone patricide and fratricide. And we have many opportunities now, with the wealth from the natural gas reserves. We even have a vote on the UN Security Council."

"So, you go to the U.S. government, ask for asylum, make them go public."

He shook his head sadly. "It is not so simple. It may be that your government will feel that Kristoff would be an easier monarch to deal with. He is a simple soul, much like his mother. Wave shining objects in his face and he will follow blindly."

I gave the King a dark look. I like to think that, regardless of which party is in power, my country wouldn't buy a despot like a new handbag.

Yeah, yeah. Don't quote history to me. Let me have my delusions of honesty and fair play. He raised his hands in mock surrender. "Perhaps I am wrong. But there are things your government does not know about . . . weapons that I would prefer not to divulge and that I do not want to fall into the hands of the unscrupulous."

His face was studiously impassive. "Are we talking about the kinds of weapons I *think* we're talking about?" As in the Russian nukes that had gone mysteriously missing last fall or maybe some of the very specialized biological curses I'd heard of that didn't even bear thinking about.

"Let us say that should Kristoff's backers discover the location of and gain access to the weaponry that was at my disposal, there is the definite possibility of a third world war."

Oh, fuck a duck . . . twice.

I'd been right. This was out of my league. Way, *way* out of my league. "Why come to me?"

"I believe you may be the only person I know who has the appropriate contacts to handle the situation."

If he thought that would enlighten me, he was wrong. I don't have government connections. I don't even *want* government connections, despite what Ren had intimated earlier.

Seeing my lack of understanding, Dahlmar continued. "My son is being controlled by a woman. I believe her to be a siren."

Oh, shit. Well, that certainly explained why me. He probably *didn't* have any other siren contacts. They're notoriously reclusive. I might be his only option, but he had a right to know the truth—that I wasn't a good option. "I may have siren abilities, but I don't really know any sirens. And those I do know have made it clear I'm not their favorite person. In fact, they're going to have a hearing to determine whether or not they'll let me live or destroy me as an abomination."

He gave a fierce smile, baring his teeth. "Perfect."

I raised an eyebrow at him in inquiry because, for the life of me I couldn't see an upside.

"Ivan is a mage. Before the coup, he had his suspicions about this woman. She was too secretive, too careful to make sure none of my people saw her. It sent up a"—he searched for the right phrase—"red flag. He managed to obtain a few of her hairs and used them to create a protective charm that enabled him to escape her influence. With a simple spell, it can be used to identify her if we are in her presence." Dahlmar didn't explain how he'd escaped being influenced. I was betting the omission was intentional. And boy, did that make me curious.

Using the amulet to track the culprit might work. But somehow I didn't think the sirens would be wild about my bringing Dahlmar and Ivan to their island to track down and kill one of their own. Assuming, of course, I could even find it, or that I was willing to let the king use me that way.

"If she's not there?"

"Oh, but she will be." His smile was predatory and quite chilling. "There are not very many sirens in existence to begin with. Your siren ancestry being activated by a vampire is something so strange and so dangerous that I've no doubt every one of your kin will be called to this hearing. She will be there. And so will we." His voice was compelling, and despite his weariness and the silly clothes, I could feel the power and force of his personality. I honestly didn't think it occurred to him that I might, say, refuse him. It was both a strength and a weakness, this royal arrogance. I'd seen this in him before. But even as we'd spoken, even though he seemed to be *him*, I needed to be sure. I needed to be careful. Because I have been fooled before. See the previous notes on spawn.

"How do I know you're you?"

He blinked at me, completely dumbfounded.

"I've dealt with spawn who wanted to take your crown before. Who's to say you aren't another one? After all, King Dahlmar is at a very public finance conference."

"He is the impostor. I am not demon spawn." He puffed up, taking offense.

"Yes, well, obviously you would *say* that." I didn't add the "duh" because it was just too insulting. "So here's what we're going to do. I'm going to leave this restaurant and in exactly twenty-four hours I will meet you at the place where you and your men delivered my sire's head to me. If you're you, you're bound to remember that. When you get there, you'll have to cross the line of protection *and* I'll be dousing all three of you with holy water. You pass the test, we'll talk."

He looked irate and opened his mouth to argue, but I didn't let him.

"Look. You need food and rest and more of a plan than just 'find the siren and kill the bitch.' I've got things to do, too. So . . . twenty-four hours. Nothing critical is likely to happen in your country before tomorrow, and Creede will keep you safe until then." The waiter came up with Dahlmar's food. I'd timed it perfectly. I rose as the waiter began setting dishes on the table in front of the king. Ivan was glowering at me from his spot in the telephone nook. Creede was looking very thoughtful. They were probably them. Probably. I'd find out tomorrow.

11

I'd had one of the most physically and emotionally draining days of my life. I was freaking exhausted. I did not have the energy to go back to Birchwoods. I just didn't. So I called, left a message at the night desk, and crashed on the floor of my office, using a cushion from one of the chairs as a pillow. I often have recurring nightmares when I'm stressed, but if I dreamed that night, I didn't remember it.

I woke to the sound of purring and the feel of sharp little claws pricking my thigh. It didn't hurt, exactly, but it wasn't something I could ignore. I cracked open my eyes. Bright sunshine had filled most of the room. A few more minutes and my arm would've been burning.

I started to roll over and Minnie the Mouser leapt to safety. "How in the hell did you get in here?" She hadn't come in with me last night, that was for sure.

She moved to sit by the door, her expression and posture saying as plainly as words that she wanted out. Now. I got up, stretched, and obliged her. As I did I noticed a couple of significant things. First, on my desk were a huge carafe of coffee, an empty mug, and an ice bucket holding ice and two of the canned diet shakes that I use for food in a pinch. Second, my gym bag was sitting on the floor next to my desk. Third, it was 3:00.

P.M.

Holy crap. I'd slept most of the day away. No wonder my mouth felt like something the cat had dragged in to die. But I was more than a little alarmed that people had been able to come and go in my office without my knowing it.

As long as I was up, I grabbed the gym bag and went down the hall to the bathroom and set about doing those things one does to get the day started on the right foot. The third-floor bathroom isn't large, but it's not tiny, either. Modest by current standards, it would've been considered positively luxurious back when the house was built. In those days, not everybody had indoor plumbing and the standard was one bath for an entire house. But this building had been a mansion. Along with real parquet floors and a stained-glass window on the landing between the first and second floors, it had a bathroom on every floor. The original tub had probably been a big, claw-footed monstrosity, but that had gone the way of the dodo during a sixties rehab.

Now we had a shower and a matching oversized tub in flamingo pink. They exactly matched the pedestal sink and toilet. The wallpaper was candy-cane striped in pink, silver, black, and white. It was loud but undeniably eye-catching. It occurred to me that I could now afford to change it if I wanted. The thought was startling. I looked around again. If the design magazines I'd seen in the rec room at Birchwoods were any indication, this look was coming back in vogue. And I had to admit I really did like the candy-striped paper. The air felt lighter suddenly, as though the room itself had breathed a sigh of relief. I smiled and started to dig through the cupboards.

I keep travel sizes of my toiletries at the office. My hours are so weird that it just makes sense for me, so I was able to get cleaned up and dressed in something more comfortable and less wrinkled than the skirt and top I'd slept in.

Zipping open the gym bag, I found the lavender and white tracksuit my gran had bought me for my last birthday. Thinking of Gran made me sad. She was probably having a really hard time. God knows Mom has her flaws, but my gran loves her as only a mother can. Getting picked up again meant serious jail time. The good news, Mom might dry out, get into AA. But I'd gotten my siren blood through her. If Dr. Marloe was correct—and I was pretty sure she was—sirens do not get on well with other women. Locking my mother in jail with hundreds of other women would be a recipe for disaster, no matter how richly she might deserve it. I wondered if we could use the Americans with Disabilities Act to mitigate her sentence. I didn't know, but I could at least mention it to my mother's attorney. Once she had one.

Once I was presentable, I went into the office and ate. I was just finishing when I heard the gentle double whump of a walker on stairs. *Damn it, Dottie!*

"That had better not be Dawna's new assistant coming up those steps. We have an agreement. No stairs," I called out.

There was a pause and I was almost sure I heard soft laughter. "I'm going slow."

I growled with the last bit of chocolate mocha in my mouth. "I'll come down."

Jumping out of my chair, I hurried out the door and down the hall. Dottie had stopped at the second-floor landing. Her walker could be used as sort of a chair when turned backward, and she was sitting comfortably, the light from the stained-glass window painting her with a vibrant rainbow of colors.

I sat on one of the steps facing her. "You *said* no more stairs."

"No." She smiled beatifically. "*You* said no more stairs. I simply didn't argue."

That wasn't how I remembered it, but she might be right. Even if she was wrong, I knew she'd just blame the faulty memory of old age and do what she wanted. I was beginning to realize just how hardheaded she could be and wondered if hiring her had been the best idea after all.

"I'm the boss," I reminded her.

"Yes, dear, you are," she said in a tone that clearly said I wasn't—or that even if I was, it really didn't matter.

"I suppose you've already made this trip once, bringing up my breakfast?" I gave her a stern look.

"No, that was Bubba. He insisted that if he did it, nobody would notice. If Mr. Creede had known you were right next door, asleep on the floor—well, you know he's quite taken with you."

"John was here?" It was a stupid question. But I'd only just had my coffee. I didn't know what to think about the rest of her comment. But it did make me think well of Bubba that he hadn't said anything.

She nodded. "Along with the client and his bodyguard. They spent the night. Ron seemed to recognize the man with Mr. Creede. Bubba said he was gushing over the man, which I got the impression was unusual."

I found myself chuckling. I couldn't help it. I probably should've guessed that John would bring Ivan and the king back here. The wards are excellent. I make sure of that. If King Dahlmar had enough money for a decent hotel, he wouldn't be running around in a souvenir T-shirt and a cheap pair of no-name-brand jeans. That this hadn't occurred to me before meant that I'd been further off my game than I'd thought. I'd needed a good night's sleep.

"You needed your rest. Are you feeling better? I'm so sorry about your beau, dear. I didn't mean to snoop, but I did want to know how the court case was going—"

She looked like a softer version of Gran. I couldn't help but offer her a sad smile. "That's all right. I know you meant well." Clairvoyants. You can't stop 'em looking. At least with most of them there was a chance they'd be wrong. But in Dottie's case, like Vicki's, it was a damned small chance.

"Thank you for understanding." She sighed. "So few people really do." Her expression grew even sadder than mine. It made me wonder about her family. Were they dead, or did they just never get around to seeing her, like Vicki's parents?

"I saw something just a few minutes ago, too." She sounded mournful.

"Yes?"

"I'm not certain. It's just an impression. But . . . I really think you need to check on your grandmother."

My stomach tightened, but I kept my voice calm. "I'll do that." I rose to my feet. "Anything else?"

"Not right now."

"All right. But Dottie, I mean it. *No more stairs.* Promise me, right here and now."

She gave me an impatient look. "If you don't want me taking the stairs, you're going to need to move down to the first floor." She stood, flipping up the little seat and turning the walker around. "There are too many secrets in your life and Ronald is *far* too interested in things that are none of his concern."

I watched her go down the stairs. It was a slow, painful process, but she made it safely. Once I knew she was all right, I dashed up the stairs to my office to give my gran a call.

She didn't answer on the house phone.

It could mean nothing at all. But I just couldn't get over Dottie's expression, the tone of her voice. I set the phone down, debated with myself what I should do. I was probably already in deep, deep trouble with Jeff for not being back at Birchwoods. But I had to know that Gran was all right.

Screw it. If he gets pissed, I'll have to live with it.

I grabbed my purse, slipped on the jacket to the tracksuit. It was broad daylight and nowhere near the full moon, so I shouldn't need weapons from my werewolf or vampire kits. But I slapped on some sunscreen and strapped on my knife sheath and the knives Bruno had given me. Just in case.

I didn't speed on the way to Gran's. I wanted to. But a cop car pulled behind me about a block away from my office and stayed there, obviously following me, all the way across town. When I pulled into Gran's driveway, the cruiser drove off but not before I got a glimpse of the driver: Officer Clarke. Oh joy.

Gran's house is a small two bedroom, painted gray with white trim. An old-fashioned wire mesh fence surrounded a pair of flower beds on either side of the steps leading up to the front porch. California poppies and Shasta daisies exploded from the beds and filled my nose with flowery goodness. Gran lives in a working-class neighborhood that's not as good as it used to be when she and Grandpa first bought the place fifty or sixty years ago but is still not bad. The neighborhood population is aging because back then people bought houses with the intention of staying in them until they retired or died, whichever came first.

My gran was sitting on the front porch in the same old metal rocking chair she'd cradled me in through skinned knees and childhood heartbreaks. She didn't rise when I drove up, didn't call out a greeting, or react at all. Just stared into space. It reminded me forcibly of my own actions yesterday. As I climbed from the car I saw the track of tears on her cheeks.

"Gran." I opened the gate and hurried up the walk to the house.

She looked up. "Hello, Celia." She didn't smile.

"Gran, what's wrong?" I knelt down in front of her chair. "What's the matter?"

"I met with your mother's lawyer this morning."

Oh, crap. "Gran—," I started to say something, anything.

"You were right. All those times when you told me not to let her drive. You were right. They have pictures, taken by cameras at intersections for months. Even though they didn't pull her over right then, they're going to show them to the judge. The attorney said there's no chance we can say this time was a mistake."

I touched her shoulder, but even then she didn't react. "Gran, it's not your fault."

"If I hadn't let her use the car—" The tears were flowing hard now and she reached into the pocket of her sweater to pull out a damp clump of tissues.

Sometimes the truth, although harsh, can be comforting. I'm hoping she took it that way. "If you hadn't let Mom use the car, she would've taken it anyway. You know that. I'll bet she had her own secret set of keys made." I gave her a wry smile. "Nothing ever stops Mom."

Gran laughed, but it was more of a croak and it died as quickly as it had come. "He says she'll go to prison. My poor baby . . . my Lana, in *prison*."

I didn't say a word. Any time my mother served would be richly deserved. She'd driven drunk and without a license or insurance more times than I could count. She'd wrecked cars, and while she swore to us that nobody had ever been hurt, she'd endangered herself and everybody else on the road. But my gran wouldn't believe that and didn't need to hear it. She needed comfort. Unfortunately, I had very little to give.

"Does she have a public defender?"

Gran squirmed in her chair and wouldn't meet my eyes. I just knew what that meant. I sighed. "You hired an attorney."

"I had to." A little bit of her old ferocity returned. "I've heard terrible things about public defenders. They're in all the papers and you know it. It's my money. If I want to—"

Throw it away, I thought, but I bit my tongue. Instead, I said, "It's your money and your choice, Gran." I spoke softly. "But I had an idea last night and I want to call her attorney and see what he thinks of it. How do I get hold of him?"

She blushed and wouldn't answer me. That was never a good sign. When she doesn't want to tell me something, the news is always bad. Seeing the flush of embarrassment, the stubborn set of her chin, gave me an idea, a really, hideously, awful idea.

"Gran, you didn't hire *my* attorney, did you?"

"Why not? He got you off—do you think he's too good for your mother?" Her eyes flashed with renewed anger.

"Of course not," I lied. My mom's case was open-and-shut, no, not shut—*slam* the jailhouse door. Hiring Roberto would cost everything Gran had and the case was unwinnable. She might as well just flush the money down the toilet. "But Gran, you can't afford him. It took all of my savings for me to afford him. *All* of my savings."

She turned to me then and looked me straight in the eyes, her expression determined. "I told him I'd sell the house."

It took me more than a few seconds to process the words and even then I couldn't believe it. The meaning caught me in the chest like a baseball thrown by a star pitcher. I struggled not to gasp, but the great, heaving weight of it made my heart tight and painful. I know I clutched her shoulder tighter and she finally reacted . . . staring up at me with pain-filled eyes. "Oh, *Gran*." She could wind up homeless. Broke and homeless, with no place to call her own. It was the ultimate sacrifice for a woman of her generation. She had always told me how proud she was that she and Granddad had owned, even during the war. She wasn't like Dottie, who could work within the government system.

Any more than Mom was.

We spent the next few hours talking out the details. It became clear early on that I wasn't going to be able to talk her out of this last-ditch effort to save my mom. Gran knows my mom better than anyone alive. She knows what makes her tick, knows that jail would quite literally destroy her. I now learned that Gran had been working with Mom, trying to dry her out ever since the vampire had claimed her mind a few weeks ago. That had really scared Mom, to have no control over her actions. It had caused an epiphany that Gran had been trying to build on.

Crap and double crap.

I tried to salvage what I could of the situation by calling the attorney handling the probate of Vicki's will to see if I'd missed anything after the reading was finished and what, if anything, I needed to do to work on getting hold of the money Vicki had left for me. Then I got transferred to Roberto's assistant to make my suggestion about using a psychological or an ADA defense for Mom because of her siren blood.

Finally, I called my banker to see whether I might be able to get a mortgage to buy my grandmother's house. It's not easy for someone self-employed to qualify. Not every year's income resulted in profit. All a small-business owner can do is save when the money's good so you can spend when the money's bad. But banks want to be paid *every* month. Still, with the inheritance I had coming, I thought I might be able to swing it.

She suggested I fill out the online application and they'd let me know.

At about that point I realized that I was enabling my grandmother to enable my mother. The circle of dysfunctional life. I could almost hear Elton John singing in the background.

By the time I left, Gran had at least stopped crying and was looking a little more hopeful. She really hadn't wanted to give up the house. She'd have done it. But she didn't want to.

The sun was setting as I pulled out of the driveway. Almost immediately I picked up a fresh tail. A police cruiser that trailed two cars behind, all along the route from Gran's to my office. Not Clarke this time; not that it mattered. It pissed me off, but that didn't matter, either. They would do what they were going to do. I couldn't stop them. Reacting too strongly would imply guilt where there was none and give them an excuse to dig even deeper. So I counted to a hundred and tried to ignore the cop, with minimal success.

I had about an hour before I was supposed to go to Phar-Mart and meet Creede and the others. I wanted my weapons. Now. I know hand-to-hand. It works well on humans. But there's nothing like advanced weaponry when you go up against the monsters.

And we were going up against someone willing to traffic with the demonic.

The militant ministries have the best record fighting the demonic. True believers do well, too. I'm not either. I'd just have to make up for it with knowledge, planning, and excellent armament.

I felt the surge of magic as the car crossed the magical perimeter that guards the office and parking lot. It wasn't as painful as it should have been, which meant the wards needed refreshing. I promised myself I'd write Dottie a note to make the arrangements as soon as I got inside.

I caught the cat before she could slip out the door and was rewarded with a deep scratch on the wrist. She hissed. I hissed right back. It startled her, but she didn't look particularly intimidated. With a flip of her tail, she pranced off in the general direction of Ron's office. I hoped she'd leave him a particularly stinky present.

There were messages in my slot and the UPS boxes were still stacked in the reception area. Grumbling, I took a look at the label on the top box. Yup, they were for me. The return address was for the ex-wife of Bob Johnson, a friend of mine who'd gotten killed in the same ambush where I'd been bitten. Vanessa was as nasty and bitter a piece of work as I've ever run across, screaming at me and blaming me for his death when I'd called to offer condolences. God alone knew what she'd mailed to me. I decided I didn't *want* to know. At least not tonight. Time was a-wastin' and I had things to do.

I grabbed the message slips and started pounding my way up the stairs. I hadn't gone far when Bubba's voice called down to me, shouting to be heard over the blaring volume of one of those reality singing competitions. It must have been one of the early rounds, because the singer was really, seriously bad. I could do better . . . and you do *not* want to hear me sing.

"Hey, Graves, that you?"

"Yeah. It's me."

"Dr. Scott called after Dottie left for the day. Said you needed to get back to him right away."

"Thanks. I'll give him a buzz," I called out, and kept climbing, going two stairs at a time without feeling breathless.

Bubba's office is just down the hall from mine on the third floor. As I walked past, the competition's judges were eviscerating the poor kid verbally. Why anyone considered that entertainment I'd never know, but Bubba seemed to love it. I hurried to unlock my office door. If I was lucky the heavy wooden door would cut down on the sound. Situations like this made me truly hate having vampire-enhanced hearing.

I stepped over the threshold, feeling the familiar buzz of the wards reacting to me. If I'd looked, I might have caught a glimpse of the silver sigils Bruno had used to create the protections. Thinking about him, his smile, his voice, the touch of his lips . . . hurt enough to incapacitate me if I let it. But I wasn't going to let it. I'd had my own epiphany in the restaurant.

One of the things Gran told me was that part of what went wrong with my mother was that my father left her. That men simply aren't supposed to be *able* to leave sirens. His going broke something inside her. I hadn't really thought about things from a biological perspective before. Bruno shouldn't have been able to leave me. Maybe he could because I wasn't fully siren, or because we met before my powers were activated by the vampire bite, or because he's such a strong mage. Whatever the reason, he had left, and it was hitting me much harder than it should, given that we'd only just gotten back together.

I'm not my mother. I was not going to crawl into a bottle. No matter how much it hurt right now, I *would* get past this. What had worked best for me last time was keeping busy, working hard. Fate was certainly giving me the opportunity to do just that. Life was apparently going to be interesting, in that ancient curse sort of way.

Which brought me back to curses. Setting my purse on the desk, I dropped into my office chair. Dialing the phone with one hand, I stared at the mark on my palm. It was faint but still clear. I didn't know a lot about palmistry, but now that I knew what to look for I could see that it did, indeed, mingle with both my life and career lines. *Crap.*

Apparently Dr. Scott had given me his direct number, because he answered on the first ring.

"Hello, Celia." His voice was flat, without inflection, and it unnerved me.

"Hey, Jeff, what's up?" I made my voice as cheerful as possible. I intended to say I'd been going to call him anyway, but he spoke before I had the chance.

"Your aunt's personal assistant was here."

"My *aunt*? I don't have any aunts."

"A very *regal* woman. She bedazzled the guards without any effort at all and just walked right through all of our security."

Oh, crap. A siren.

Judging from Jeff's tone of voice, whoever the siren was, she'd gotten to him I heard his anger, but underneath it there was a hint of hysteria.

"Look—" I started to speak, but he kept talking. With every word he seemed to grow more confident and more pissed. Which was probably good for him. Not so much for me.

"She was quite upset to find you gone. Apparently, your aunt, the sovereign of the sirens, Queen Lopaka, has been trying to reach you. She's quite insulted and offended that you haven't returned her messages."

"I can imagine she was upset." Because queens don't like to be insulted. Except that nobody had tried to contact me that I know of, other than Ren's visit. "But since I had no idea she's been trying to reach me, I'm not sure what to do about it. Has she been trying to reach me, Jeff? Has your staff withheld messages from me?"

"Nobody has contacted our facility until today, I promise you. It's not the sort of thing we'd keep from you. We would discuss it in therapy at the very least. I've sent you an e-mail with the details of her visit, along with the results of your most recent blood work and . . ." He paused for a long moment and I could hear him breathing as though summoning his courage. "I've also sent you an agreement to sign, terminating your stay here and releasing us of all responsibility. Once you fax it back to us, we'll refund all your money."

"B-but—," I stammered, trying to wrap my head around what he was saying. He was kicking me out? Could he do that?

"I'm sorry, Celia, but the fact is that you're simply too much of a security risk. I can't have people wandering in and out of our facility at will, manipulating the patients and staff. It's dangerous. I know you're not responsible for it, but the fact of the matter is that they are coming here because of you."

I wanted to argue, but I couldn't. He was right. I might not want to be a patient at Birchwoods and might not think I deserved to be there, but I sure as hell didn't want it to get out that I'd been *evicted*. If word got out, I'd never get another facility to take me if things went south. Of course, the state would still be more than happy to let me in and then throw away the key. I wasn't going there. I'd rather die.

"Tomorrow, movers will pack your possessions and deliver them to your office. We'll cover the cost." His voice was still cold, flat. He was doing his very best to be businesslike and make it absolutely clear that this was non-negotiable. *Damn it! Dammit, dammit, dammit.*

"Is there anything else?" I sounded a lot calmer than I felt. Shock maybe. Possibly fatalism. There's only so much the mind can take in a short period of time. At some point, if you have enough disasters hit close enough together, you just get shell-shocked. I had not only reached that point, I'd also sailed right past it. All I could do now was just keep putting one foot in front of the other.

He kept talking, a little too clipped and high-pitched to sound normal. "Your therapist has indicated she is willing to continue seeing you privately, off-site. Dr. Talbert has also indicated her desire to work with you in the future. I took the liberty of giving them both your e-mail so that you can work that out between you."

Did I want more therapy? I wasn't really sure. While a part of me was thrilled that I could go home and didn't have to be locked behind gates and wards anymore, I also felt . . . sort of weird. Now I understood what Vicki had meant when she said that the outside seemed too *open*. But there was nothing more to be said, at least not to Dr. Scott. "Wow. Well, I guess that's it, then."

"Yes, it is." Long seconds of silence ticked by. Finally, I couldn't stand it anymore.

"Good-bye, Jeff."

"Good luck, Celia."

He hung up. For a long moment I just sat there, holding the receiver. I was stunned. As of this moment I was probably the only homeless multimillionaire in the country. I had inherited the guest cottage and part of the beach from Vicki. But that was still in probate and I hadn't signed the lease papers before Creede spirited me out of there. No doubt Cassandra would even contest *that*. Everything was going to be tied up in legal limbo for God alone knew how long. I hadn't worried too much about it until now, because I'd been scheduled to be at Birchwoods for weeks.

Where the hell was I going to stay? Even if I bought Gran's house, it would still be her house. And if Mom didn't go to jail, she'd probably live with Gran. I couldn't live there, too, and I couldn't afford to buy another place and pay two mortgages if I bought another place. I make a good living but not that good.

I set the phone back in its cradle and put my head in my hands. Dammit, I didn't need this shit. I'd had enough. More than enough.

There was a tap on the door. "You okay? You don't look so good."

I looked up to see Bubba leaning against the door frame. He was holding a pair of beers from the mini-fridge in his office. I appreciated the gesture, but no alcohol. Not right now. Every day, every negative event was becoming a new temptation to drink. I didn't need crutches, I needed solutions. The hard part was, there weren't any to be found.

"You ever just want to say 'screw it all' and walk away?"

He grinned, giving me a glimpse of a chipped tooth that hadn't been there the last time I'd seen him. Ah, the joys of being a bail bondsman. "All the time, babe, *all* the time." He twisted the cap off one of the bottles and tossed it into the trash with a deft flick of his wrist. He offered the second bottle to me, but I shook my head no. "But what else am I gonna do? And you know it wouldn't be any better anyplace else."

I gave a gusty sigh. "You're probably right."

"You know it." He set the unopened bottle on my desk in case I changed my mind, and sprawled into one of the guest chairs. Raising the bottle in salute, he said, "Screw the bastards," before taking a long pull of beer.

"Screw the bastards," I agreed.

"So, what can I be doing to help you?" Bubba asked. "'Cause I know you're needing help." He looked me up and down and my eyes followed his gaze, trying to see if I had shit on my clothes.

"I don't look that bad."

"Nope. Worse." He smiled to soften the words.

Ouch. Well, that was not particularly flattering but probably honest. We sat in silence for a moment, and in that moment of peace and quiet something occurred to me for the first time. One of the biggest problems I'd been having was that too many things were happening to me, so many that I didn't have time to do more than react to them. I got bit, I reacted. I got charged, I reacted. I was put in Birchwoods, I reacted. We were kidnapped, I reacted. Over and over again until I was exhausted and looking for escape.

If that went on, the pressure would break me, and soon.

It was time to break the cycle, to start forcing people to react to me. I raised my eyes to Bubba's. I smiled, showing my fangs. *Screw the bastards, indeed.* "You still have that GPS navigation unit?"

"Yeah. It's down in my truck."

"Any chance I could borrow it for a couple days?"

"Sure. Why?"

"I have to find an island." Specifically, I needed to find the Isle of Serenity. If the queen was annoyed I hadn't dropped by . . . it was time to go find out who didn't want me to meet her.

He didn't seem bothered by my request. Then again, Bubba liked to deep-sea fish. Every time he could manage to wrangle a couple of days off he was out on the water in his boat, *Mona's Rival*, so named because she was the only thing that came close to his wife in his affections. She was a good-sized vessel, too, big enough to hold five in reasonable comfort. That was convenient, since that's exactly how many I needed to bring along. I didn't know what Bubba would charge me, but it had to be less than one of the commercial rentals. Despite what I'd told Gran, I wasn't broke yet, but I was going through capital at a truly alarming rate. That refund from Birchwoods couldn't come too soon.

"I'll go get it." Bubba rose with a lazy grace and meandered downstairs.

I closed my office door and locked it. I stripped down to my undies, changing out of the comfy-but-not-practical-for-business workout clothes and into the things I'd picked up from my old bedroom at my gran's. I hadn't had a lot to choose from and most of it had been black—from back in my "I'm cool, I'm goth" teenage period. I pulled on black low-rise jeans and was pleased to discover that they still fit perfectly. Yay. Let's hear it for the all-liquid diet . . . at least until the next time I craved a pizza.

The cropped black tee with the motto *Don't get even . . . get odd* was a little tight across the bust but not enough to be uncomfortable. The blazer I'd bought from Isaac was black, so it would match well enough and cover enough that I wouldn't look slutty in the tight top. Which left me with a choice of shoes. I could go with the white sneakers: practical but not terribly stylish; the lace-up, heavy-duty, steel-toed Frankenstein's work boots, which would certainly make a fashion statement but were a little extreme; or the dress pumps I'd worn to court. Not the pumps. There may be people who can run and fight in heels, but I'm not one of them. The Frankenboots were fun but heavy. So I went with the sneakers.

Once I was decent, I opened the door. Bubba would be back in a minute. Then, taking the jacket off the hanger, I spread it out flat on the desktop and opened my safe. First, before I forgot, my passport. We were going to a foreign country, after all. Then I began arming up again. I was strapping on the shoulder rig for my Colt when I heard Bubba's tread on the stairs. I checked the gun, going with silver-jacketed loads. Not cheap and not necessary for dealing with ordinary baddies, but damned near essential if you want to do more than annoy the monsters. In my case, better safe than sorry.

I put a pair of One Shot water pistols, filled with holy water, in the snap loops Isaac had sewn into the jacket lining to hold them, then strapped on an ankle holster with my backup Derringer. When Bubba reached my doorway I was staring at the safe, wondering what else I should take. I have quite a few preset spells, little ceramic disks like the one Bruno had used at the courthouse. You don't have to be a mage to use them. You just break the disk to release the magic. It would be very cool if Creede really could put a full binding spell in a disk. Not knowing what I'd be up against, I couldn't know what spells I might need.

"Damn, woman, you're arming for bear." Bubba set the GPS unit on the desk and picked up the beer bottle he'd set there earlier.

"I'm in the middle of a situation."

"This is about what Dottie saw in those bugs, isn't it?" Bubba opened the beer and took a seat, leaning forward, elbows on his knees.

I sighed and glanced at the Wadjeti, visible on the shelf of my open safe. "I think so." I decided to grab a handful of boomers—tiny things, the size of a quarter, that were spelled to emit a flash of light and a deafening sound when broken. They're useful in any number of situations. I popped a few in each of the front jacket pockets.

"You're going to need backup." Bubba's voice was flat. When I turned to look at him, his expression had hardened, his pale blue eyes narrowing to slits. "And you'll need a boat to get to that island."

I really wanted him to take me, but I didn't want to lie about what we might be facing. Not that I knew much about the details. "Yeah, but I'm pretty sure it's going to get ugly."

He smiled and the chipped tooth was proof of his next words. "I can do ugly."

He probably could. He was definitely a tough ole boy. He stood up, grabbing the beer. "Give me a couple minutes. I need to let Mona know and call Stew."

12

Stew is Bubba's brother-in-law. He has the same dark good looks as Bubba's wife, Mona, but none of her fire. Mona's ambitious, driven in both her career and her home life. Stew, on the other hand, is a handsome, charming, cad. He has a bail bondsman's license, but the only time he uses it is when he's covering for Bubba. Mostly he pays bass in a band, making just enough money to pay for a cheap apartment and his booze. Food he cadges off of the most recent in a successive line of sweet young things who think that his being in a band makes him cool.

He arrived promptly, a sure indication that he was broke. While he half-listened to Bubba, enough to parrot the appropriate answers, the focus of his attention was my T-shirt. Apparently the jacket wasn't doing as good a job of concealing things as I'd hoped. *Terrific.*

"You've got my cell number. Call me if anything comes up. If you can't get me, call Mona." Bubba was repeating himself, but it was probably a good idea. Sometimes you have to use a sledgehammer to drive a point home to Stewie.

"I got it already." Stew wrenched his gaze away from my

boobs long enough to glare at his brother-in-law. "It's not like it's the first time and it's not like it's rocket science. Give me some credit."

I went downstairs to write Dottie a note about the wards before I could say anything unfortunate. Bubba followed a few minutes later.

We drove to the PharMart in Bubba's behemoth of a four-wheel-drive truck. It's an older model but tricked out with every conceivable luxury, including the requisite chromed mud flaps with a naked woman and a bumper sticker proclaiming him a "PROUD REDNECK." He calls the truck Baby. His vanity plates say: *BADA55*. How he got that past the censors at the DMV I'll never know.

PharMart is one of the bigger pharmacy chains. The stores are all pretty much identical: big tan brick boxes with windows all along the front. Their product selection is good and they're not terribly overpriced. This particular store is the one where I usually get my prescriptions filled. It was also the site where Bruno, Matteo, and I had set the trap for Lilith that had gone so terribly wrong.

More important, that was where Dahlmar had given me my sire's head.

Better than roses, in my opinion.

I felt the power of the PharMart's wards buzz across my senses as Bubba steered the truck into the parking lot. It didn't occur to me until we were pulling up next to the Ferrari to wonder how Creede had managed to drive three large men in that tiny two-seater. Had the king ridden in his bodyguard's lap? Creede was leaning against the building, smoking a cigarette, looking perfectly comfortable and casual. I assumed

Dahlmar was in the car, hidden behind the tinted windows. Ivan wasn't visible, but I was betting he wasn't in the car. Probably out of sight somewhere, keeping an eye on things.

They had passed test one. The real Dahlmar and Ivan would know about PharMart. Fakes wouldn't. Of course I'd still spray them all down. In this game, safe was definitely better than sorry.

"So what's the game plan?" Bubba asked. I'd filled him in on some of what was going on. Not all. I hadn't had a chance to ask King Dahlmar if I could reveal his identity, so I hadn't given Bubba any names.

"You stay here. I get out and make sure they're what and who they're supposed to be. If they are, we head out for your boat."

"It's going to be a little crowded if we're all going."

"Yeah," I agreed. "But I'm hoping that getting out on the water will make it harder for people to use mundane magic to track us." I unfastened my seat belt and turned to open the truck door.

"Mundane magic?"

I sighed. I probably shouldn't have worded it that way. "As opposed to siren magic. Sirens are water creatures. The ocean's their thing."

"You're a siren now," he pointed out.

"Yeah, but I don't have magic." I sounded grumpy. Then again, I felt grumpy. Funny, when I was growing up, I'd wanted desperately to have some sort of paranormal talent. I'd failed the tests so miserably that they'd checked to make sure I wasn't a null. I wasn't. But back then, I hadn't been a siren, either.

But so far, other than the illegal psychic manipulation and

the ability to drive seagulls insane, I haven't discovered any magical ability.

It was ironic. All of the kids I went to school with had some sort of talent. I'd wanted one so bad, just so I could fit in. Now that I did have paranormal abilities, I desperately wished I was rid of them. Some people are just never satisfied.

Bubba turned, unfastening his seat belt.

"I thought you were staying here."

"Groceries." He pulled out his wallet to check the contents. "More people, more supplies. We'll need a few things. I won't be long."

I couldn't argue. It was a sensible thing to do. We were going to be out on the boat several hours at least. At least. Bubba swore he knew where the Isle of Serenity was. But the wards around the island had pushed his boat away. He'd tried, but he couldn't even swim underneath with the poles.

I wasn't kidding about Bubba being a fisherman. The fish near the sirens' island stay inside the magic circle. Bubba could see them, but he couldn't cast to them. It's enough to drive any boat captain to drink—or to try to swim through the barrier. With his fishing pole in his mouth.

Speaking of drinking, I'd probably have to go inside and stock up on the ever-handy but God-am-I-sick-of-them diet shakes and some baby food. I swear, if the vamp that tried to sire me wasn't already dead I'd hunt him down and kill him—as painfully as possible.

Get your mind in the game, Celia, I scolded myself. Right now I needed to chat with my client and let Creede know the plan. Then I could do the shopping and move on to the next thing.

I am not a particularly small woman, but there's a certain knack to getting in and out of a vehicle that big. By the time I'd finished climbing down from Das Truck, Bubba was already inside the PharMart. Creede had crushed out his cigarette and the passenger window of the Ferrari had lowered to reveal Dahlmar's profile.

I pulled out one of my little squirt guns. "Who wants to go first?" Creede rolled his eyes but extended his hand. I squeezed the gun's trigger, just enough to lay a couple of drops of holy water onto his palm. The problem with *one-shot* water guns is that they hold just that . . . one shot. Pull the trigger and you might as well throw the thing away until you refill.

No reaction. Creede was Creede. Actually, I'd known that from the scent and the effect his magic had on my skin. If he noticed that all the hairs on my arms were standing at attention, he didn't mention it.

The success with Creede didn't keep me from repeating the process with King Dahlmar. When Ivan showed up, I'd do him, too. In the meantime, just to make sure they were comfy with me, I sprayed my own palm.

"Who was that man?" King Dahlmar snarled. Apparently "we" were still miffed about having to sleep in an office and wait twenty-four hours for a meeting. I was kind of surprised he hadn't met Bubba during his sleepover, but there you go.

"That's Bubba. He is a friend and he owns the boat that is going to take me to where we think the Isle of Serenity is."

"You've arranged the meeting? Good." Either he missed the "me" and the fact that I wasn't actually sure where I was going or he was ignoring it. I was betting on the latter. "This Bubba—do you vouch for him?"

"I do."

"I do not like it." Ivan's voice shattered the illusion that had made him appear to be a newspaper vending machine. It startled me enough that I let out one of those girly little yelps. Creede snickered; Ivan looked smug. I couldn't really blame him. I'd only ever seen one other mage do that. A few weeks ago, Bruno had done an impersonation of a rubber tree so he could sit in on a meeting where he wasn't wanted. It hadn't been easy for him and he is one hell of a mage. That Ivan could do the same thing raised my estimation of his skill level considerably. His lips stretched into what could only loosely be termed a smile, but he held out his palm for the requisite test. He passed.

"You arranged a meeting with the sirens?" Creede was scornful. That pissed me off. Who the hell did he think he was dealing with? But I bit back the first response that came to mind and answered him politely.

"Supposedly, the queen has been wanting to see me for a while now." I didn't mention the fact that they were already pissed in front of the client. That was something better shared privately, when we were doing our planning, if at all.

"How'd they contact you?" he snapped.

I tried not to be too obvious about glaring at him. He was questioning my abilities, my authority, and my judgment. If this was how he thought our partnership was going to work, he was sorely mistaken.

He didn't wilt at the look, but I hadn't really expected him to. He's used to running things, being the big dog. I'm used to being my own woman. If we really were going to make a business relationship work, we needed to iron out the kinks. But, again, not in front of the client.

"They left word for me at Birchwoods."

"I do not like this," Ivan repeated. "It could be a setup."

"I'm with you, big guy," Creede agreed.

"That's all right. The three of you won't be going to the island with me, so even if it is a setup, it doesn't matter. You'll stay on the boat with Bubba."

"And how am I supposed to work my magic from the boat?" Creede asked.

"You won't be doing any magic until I've cleared it with their queen."

Dahlmar scowled. "I do not wish to proceed in this manner. I will meet the queen."

Creede stared at me thoughtfully and finally nodded. "Celia's right. She needs to lay a foundation. It makes sense to let her do the preliminary groundwork. The only way this is going to work is with the queen's support."

Well, hallefrickinlujah. Apparently he wasn't going to argue every decision I made, just the ones he didn't like. I took a deep breath and tried to look professional. I didn't feel professional. I was angry. I didn't need the men questioning my every move. If I'd thought it was sexism, I would've been even more pissed, but my gut instinct said that this was just good-old-fashioned paranoia.

Ivan didn't argue, but I could tell from his expression that he was annoyed.

"Fine." Dahlmar's voice was cutting, making it clear that

he didn't like being on the sidelines and hinting that there would be nasty repercussions if things went south.

Ivan still didn't say a word. He just looked at me, and I knew if this went badly, if anything happened to his king, he would make sure he lived long enough to kill me himself, as slowly and painfully as possible.

Peachy. Just . . . peachy.

Bubba came out of the store, laden with groceries. He loaded them into the truck bed, then strolled over to join us.

I turned to introduce him to everyone. "Bubba, you know John. This is—"

"Robert." Ivan extended his hand. Okay, secrecy was fine from the bad guys, but for God's sake . . . Bubba might look like a hick. He sometimes acts like a redneck. But he is well-read and he's nobody's fool. He knew from the international newspapers who King Dahlmar was. But Bubba shook Ivan's hand without a word. "And this"—I gestured toward Dahlmar—"is—"

"Michael." Dahlmar extended his hand out the open window. "But you may call me Mike."

Bubba smiled and made nice. When the formalities were finished, he turned to me.

"What's the plan?"

"I've got to get some holy water, to refill the gun I just used, and some liquid food. After that we go to the marina, get on your boat, and go to the island."

"Are we expecting trouble while we're on land?"

"I hope not. But it's a possibility."

"Fair 'nuff." He nodded. "Let's do it."

I gave him a sunny smile. He'd earned it. Because while everybody else was being macho, arguing with me, and being general all-round pains in my ass, Bubba just trusted me to know what I was doing. How refreshing.

"Who's with me?" Bubba asked.

"Robert and I will ride with you in the truck," Dahlmar said. "No insult to you, Mr. Creede, but your vehicle is not meant for three." He climbed out of the car and stretched. I heard a couple of the joints in his back pop.

"Fine. Bubba, give Creede directions while I go do my shopping. I won't be long." I walked toward the store entrance, half-listening to Bubba telling Creede where they would be heading next. I saw movement from the corner of my eye just as I reached the door and my heart skipped a beat. It was a bat, swooping under the light—but it was just the furry mammal sort, not the evil, undead sort.

I stepped inside the brightly lit store, trying to get my emotions and my blood pressure under control. I didn't want to think about Bruno, but being here brought back the memory of that horrible night, of Matty hurt and bitten and Bruno holding his broken body. It had worked out all right in the end, but it had been touch-and-go. The events of that night were part of what had drawn Bruno and me back together.

I shook my head. I needed to stop thinking about him. If I kept this up, my emotions would get the best of me and I wouldn't be able to think clearly enough to do the job.

Have you ever tried to *not* think of something? The problem, is if you're thinking about not thinking about something, it's already on your mind.

It didn't take me long to go through the aisles and get what

I needed. I was trying to decide which baby food I was least sick of when one of the clerks came up to me.

"Hi."

I looked up at the same kid who'd waited on me right after I was attacked—who was, not so coincidentally, the selfsame kid we'd later saved from Lilith and her companion.

"Hey." I smiled at him. "I'm a little surprised you're still willing to work nights."

He grimaced. He was a bright kid, smart enough to know just how close a call he'd had. It didn't make much sense for him to be here. "My dad lost his job. Right now I'm the only one bringing money into the house."

Ouch. Didn't that just suck. But it explained him being willing to take the risk. Still, I noticed he was wearing a very conspicuous cross around his neck.

"Well, be careful, okay?"

"Oh, I'm being careful all right. And the store's doing their part, too. The manager's arranged for the wards to get recharged every week now."

"Good."

He shuffled his feet. I didn't blame him for feeling awkward. I did, too. "Look, I didn't get the chance to thank you."

"It's okay, really."

"I mean, I know your friend got hurt real bad and all. And I'm really grateful, so, thanks." He smiled again. It was a nice smile. He was a good kid. Seeing him here, alive and well, made me feel good, like I'd done at least one thing right.

He changed the subject. "So, baby food and liquid protein shakes. Doesn't look particularly appetizing."

"It's not," I admitted, "but it's what I'm stuck with, at least for now." I pushed the cart up to the cash register with him at my side. He introduced me to the girl behind the counter as the woman who had rescued him. He made me sound really impressive. It improved my mood when I'd thought nothing could. In fact, I was actually feeling pretty good as I paid my bill and took my bags. The good feeling lasted right up until the automatic doors whooshed open.

The parking lot looked empty.

It wasn't.

I could smell them. There were three of them. One wore cheap aftershave and I tried to remember who I knew who favored that scent. It mingled with the smells of gun oil, fresh shoe polish, and stale beer. There were other smells, too, but those were the most prevalent . . . until a man stumbled out of the shadows, covered in blood.

My pulse pounded. My vision shifted into hyperfocus; I could see every pore of his skin, that there were no actual injuries under the shredded T-shirt, that the mouthwatering blood he wore was not his. It was the blond cop from court . . . Officer Clarke. I felt a growl escape from between my lips. He would be easy prey. He believed he had the upper hand here and his fear when he realized he didn't would make his blood taste all that much sweeter.

I looked around for Creede and the others. No surprise Bubba's truck was gone, but where had Creede got to?

I forced myself to turn back into the store, shouting at the girl at the nearest cash register, "There's an injured man in the parking lot. You need to go help him." The clerk I knew started to run past me, but I grabbed him by the arm. I whispered urgently in his ear, "It's a setup. Someone's trying to frame me for this. I need to get out of here. Back door?"

His eyes widened, then narrowed in anger. He pointed toward the swinging doors at the back of the store, then dashed out the front after his coworker. I didn't waste any time, racing toward the back, plastic bags of groceries banging against my leg as I ran. Yeah, I should have dropped them, but what good is surviving if I'm still hungry when I get to safety? That really would endanger the client.

I have to admit I was proud of myself for thinking of that while running for my life.

I burst out of the back door onto the loading dock, moving at vampire speed. All of my senses were ramped up—which was a good thing, because they'd thought to put reinforcements on the back exit. Gerry, nice guy Gerry, who now apparently thought I should be put down like a dog, shouted something to the other two as he reached under his jacket for his gun. I didn't dare hit him—they wanted me to fight, wanted the excuse to execute me. I wasn't going to give them the satisfaction. But the monster within me was very close to the surface now that I'd smelled fresh blood. So I gave Gerry a gentle shove, intending to throw him off balance, keep him from clearing his weapon. But adrenaline and vampire strength gave more oomph to the move than I intended. He went flying, body slamming against the building with a sickening thud and a crunch that I hoped wasn't his spine breaking.

I didn't slow, just kept running, leaping right off the edge of the dock between two trucks. There were gunshots and I felt a sharp stinging in my legs. But it didn't hurt enough to be a gunshot wound, so I kept going. I spun, making a sharp right, putting a parked car between me and the shooter. Seconds later I heard more shots and the explosion of car glass shattering.

A hard left took me up a driveway and into the welcome embrace of the shadowed alley between a pair of boxy warehouse-style buildings. I passed a vampire feeding on some hapless drunk. I only caught a glimpse of his shocked expression before I was out the other end of the alley, pelting down Ocean View.

I glanced backward as a squeal of tires and the roar of a high-performance engine raced past me in a blur of red and the scent of gasoline. A familiar Ferrari pulled to the curb just ahead of me, the passenger door swinging open before it was even stopped. I caught a whiff of Creede's distinctive cologne and felt his magic rake over my skin. I hurled myself into the car, slamming the door shut. As we peeled away from the curb, I caught sight of four armed men converging on the spot where I'd just been.

13

I **didn't** get a good look at the boat as we went on board, what with trying to keep the scent of my own blood from making me leap on Creede and suck on that amazing-smelling neck. I'd taken a previous fishing trip with Bubba and knew that *Mona's Rival* was a really nice boat. Bubba was telling King Dahlmar all about her.

"She's a 1986 Chris-Craft Catalina, but I put in a custom hardtop and upgraded the motor and dinghy. My wife decorated the mess and the stateroom."

I was lying on my stomach, facedown on the pillows in said stateroom, trying not to scream or break something as Creede used a sterilized knife and tweezers to pull fragments of baby food jar and shake-can shrapnel from my calf. That's what the pain had been. A shotgun blast had shattered the jars and exploded the cans, which had sliced right through my jeans and embedded in my leg.

He had to reopen the wounds over and over again to dig out the bits because my skin kept healing over. I was watching television and trying to pretend that he didn't have his hands all over my bare legs. Because it felt really, incredibly good. Until it hurt, that is. But then it went back to feeling good.

No, he probably didn't *have* to keep putting his hand on the back of my thigh for balance, but . . . some of the glass had gone that deep, and it didn't want to come out with the tools in the rinky-dink first-aid kit on the boat.

"Okay, hold still. This is the curved one I've been avoiding." I braced myself and stared at the cartoons on the screen—a DVD of *SpongeBob SquarePants*. Bubba's a huge fan, for some reason. The sound was off, but at least there was motion and bright colors to distract me. Still, when Creede dug out that last shard I screamed and it was all I could do not to break something.

There was an abrupt moment of silence topside, where Bubba, Ivan, and Dahlmar were enjoying a perfect night under glittering stars as the boat skimmed toward the Isle of Serenity.

Creede said, "Look, lighten up a little. You're alive. We lost them for the moment. We're on a boat over moving water, so they can't track you. And on the ocean you have the advantage."

"They're cops, Creede, and they're hunting me. 'Splain to me how this can possibly end well." I didn't mention that I wasn't sure what advantages the ocean gave me.

He didn't like the sound of that at all. I didn't blame him. "You're sure they're cops?"

I nodded. "They were at my court hearing. They were supposed to be witnesses for the prosecution. They were seriously pissed when I got off, swore they'd get me."

He swore a little under his breath and I felt a tug as he

pulled another shard from my skin. A soft clink as he dropped it onto the growing pile and he was back to digging. "Missed one. I'll try for the big one again now."

I grunted a little from the pain as he cut open my skin once more. "I'm guessing it was bad enough when they thought I'd be locked up in a ritzy mental health spa like Birchwoods instead of being put down or locked up by the state."

He finished the thought for me. "But you didn't even get that."

"Right. So the best they can probably hope for is to get me deported, or 'catch me in the act' and be forced to kill me in 'self defense.'"

"Good cops don't pull vigilante bullshit." He sounded disgusted. His next cut was deep enough that I let out a hiss. I couldn't blame him. Cops are supposed to be the good guys, protecting the innocent and upholding the law. Vigilantes make their own law and they're considerably less fussy in the application.

"So they're not such good cops." Of course they probably thought they were. To serve and protect. Protect the *humans*. I was getting a little bit bitter about that. After all, I hadn't chosen to get turned, hadn't wanted this life. I'd accepted the risk of injury as part of the trade. Bodyguarding is a rough business. People get hurt, disabled, sometimes even killed. But they do not generally get turned into one of the monsters. I suppose I should be grateful. But for a freak of genetics and the intervention of Kevin and Emma I'd be dead. Looked at that way, I'd been unbelievably fortunate. But I didn't feel lucky in the least.

We were silent for a minute or two. When Creede spoke

again, his voice was flat and unhappy. "They got a good look at my car. All they'll have to do is run the plates to know it's me."

"Sorry." I really was sorry. The men stalking me were assholes with power. They could, and probably would, make his life hard. They wouldn't be able to arrest him—this little escapade was completely off-the-books. That wouldn't keep them from harassing him, pushing and prodding, trying to find something they could use against him. Of course that would be against the rules. But I'd noticed that they'd already shown a certain . . . cavalier attitude about that sort of thing.

"Shit," he growled. He dug a little more forcefully after a curved shard and I yelled again before I could stop myself.

"Sorry. Sorry." His voice was apologetic as he was using a cloth soaked in rubbing alcohol to disinfect the most recent cut. He was going through a lot of alcohol because he had to keep resterilizing his tools and reopening the cuts. He started to rub my thigh in a very comforting way. I didn't stop him, which surprised me. Yeah, I didn't know if I could get an infection, but having food- or crud-encrusted stuff embedded in your body can't be good for you. So, if I had to put up with a little more pain to be on the safe side, that was fine. But the parts of my body that were tightening from his magic and his touch didn't seem to care that I had just been dumped.

Apparently, he hadn't even realized he was rubbing my leg, because when he *did* finally notice the slow, smooth back-and-forth motion of his hand from the back of my knee nearly up to my panty line he pulled back his hand as if he'd been caressing a hot stove.

For the next few minutes, I felt nothing but pain as the curved shard of baby food jar inched its way out of my leg. I did my best not to kick or scream, though I pounded a fist against the wall once or twice. When the glass shard was finally out, he spoke. He sounded tired, which might be the reason he was letting down his guard. "I know it's not your fault, but I really don't need any more trouble than I've already got at the moment."

Was he still talking about the cops? I didn't ask. "Yeah, you and me both."

He gave a wry laugh. "We're quite the pair." With brisk efficiency, he gathered the mess into a neat bundle and walked toward the door. "I'll take these up top. Bubba has a grill we can use to burn off the blood before we put it in the trash."

"Thanks." Leave it to a mage to take care of the magical details. My blood could be used against me magically in all sorts of nasty ways I didn't even want to think about. Oh, it usually isn't. Blood goes bad pretty quickly. But under the circumstances I was inclined to be cautious.

"I'll be up in a minute."

"Don't bother," Creede suggested. "We're going to be on the water for hours and you need to get some rest."

"So do you and the others."

"Yeah, well there's a bench in the mess that looks fairly comfy and a couple of decent chairs. We'll make do. You take the bed."

"Because I'm a girl?" I asked with a smirk.

He snorted and somehow that restored us to the way we usually behaved toward each other. At least it made the tension in *me* ease. "Hell no. Because you're injured."

I wouldn't be injured long. But I was exhausted. And *somebody* was going to get the bed. I closed my eyes and slept.

"Yo, Graves. We're almost there."

Bubba's voice boomed down the staircase. I blinked a few times, trying to wake up, remember where I was, and get oriented. Bright sunlight filled the stateroom and I was glad for the air-conditioning that kept the room comfortably cool and doubly glad for the sheet I'd pulled over myself. Otherwise I'd have been crisped. One good thing about boats, they're small enough that you can find things fairly quickly. Things like the bathroom . . . I mean, the head. I threw back the sheet and stumbled over to avail myself of the facilities and wash up.

My legs looked fine. Not a scratch, and the only scars were the old ones from back when I was full human. I'd been afraid that the cuts would screw up the ivy tattoo I had climbing up one leg, but it had come through it just fine. I'd spent a fortune getting it done, in honor of my baby sister. Thinking of my sister usually brought me a sense of her spirit presence. Not today. I didn't know if she couldn't follow me onto the boat or just hadn't, but neither she nor Vicki was here. Of course, they weren't always near. They came and went as they wished. Ivy usually came if I called her—but not always. Unlike my sister, I've never had actual power over the dead. Thank God. Just thinking about the horrors Ivy's uncontrolled talent had visited on our family in my childhood gave me chills. She'd been so young and so powerful it had been really hard on all of us.

I shook my head to clear it. I needed to eat and get topside. It was only a couple of steps from the door of the stateroom into the kitchen and dining area. The tiny, galley-style kitchen was well organized and spotlessly clean. The microwave and dorm-size refrigerator were built-in, and everything else was designed to keep things from moving around in rough weather.

Opening the fridge, I grabbed one of the three cans of diet shake that had made it through last night's adventure, flipped the top, and drained it as fast as I could. I'd been getting increasingly tired of them. The Creamy Chocolate Mocha didn't taste too bad, but I seriously regretted the loss of the toothpaste and toothbrush I'd had in the bag that got shot. And I definitely needed a hairbrush and . . . aw, crap, *sunscreen*. I'd completely forgotten to buy any.

"Bubba, do you have any sunscreen?" I shouted. I really hoped he did.

"I think Mona's got some stashed in a cabinet in the bedroom. Help yourself. But hurry up. You gotta see this."

He sounded both awed and amused. Curious, I hurried past Dahlmar and Ivan as they came down the stairs from the deck. Based on their expressions and the tones of their voices, they seemed to be arguing, but they were doing it in a language I don't understand, so I didn't worry too much about it. Either I'd find out about it later or I wouldn't.

I grabbed the sunscreen and stepped out onto the deck while slathering it on, momentarily blinded by mid-morning sunshine. I could still hear and I heard boats: lots of them; and the raucous call of gulls. Lots and *lots* of gulls.

Holding up a hand to shield my watering eyes, I looked to the west. A group of perhaps a dozen boats of various sizes and styles was coming up fast, moving in perfect arrowhead formation. Above them, the sky was dark with seabirds, also in formation.

Wow.

"See what I mean?" Bubba lowered his camera to grin at me. "Told ya I knew where the island was. Pretty cool, huh?"

It was cool, assuming they didn't mean any trouble. Twelve to one would be rotten odds if things went south.

Creede grinned at me. He looked a little rough around the edges. There was stubble on his cheeks, but the look suited him, gave him kind of a rakish charm. Today he smelled of salt air, fish, and charcoal in addition to the cologne. Very outdoorsy and nice. "Your relatives know how to make an impression."

Eleven of the boats stopped about five hundred yards away. The lead boat continued moving closer. I could see a bearded man in jeans and a T-shirt standing at the prow, a loudspeaker in his grasp.

"*Ahoy, captain of* Mona's Rival. *Is Celia Kalino Graves on board?*"

Bubba set down the camera and headed behind the wheel. A moment later his voice boomed across the water, only slightly distorted by the megaphone in his hand, "*She is.*"

"*Stand by for her escort,*" was the prompt answer.

"Your escort?" Creede turned to me.

I shrugged. "How the hell would I know? I didn't even know they were expecting me. I thought I was going to surprise them."

We didn't have much time to wonder about it. The words were barely out of my mouth when Ren stepped out of thin air and onto the deck of *Mona's Rival*, accompanied by a stunning woman of about twenty or so with Hawaiian features and a dark braid twined with flowers. They each wore the colorful lavalava common in Polynesian cultures and they looked damned good doing it. Ren's hands were empty, but her companion carried a paper-wrapped package.

"What the—" Creede doesn't like being surprised, and admittedly he should have felt magic being crafted nearby. He stepped back, reaching his hands out in the same stance he'd had during the Will reading. He froze in mid-motion at a signal from me. I didn't think they meant trouble and I'd learned from experience that sirens are a touchy lot.

"Celia." Ren dipped her head, more an acknowledgment of my existence than any show of respect.

"Ren." I gave her the same in return.

Even her hand wave was as graceful as flowing water. I hated her. Well, okay, not *hated*—not the way Cassandra thought of me, more in the California sense. She was just so much better at the elegant stuff than me. "This is Hiwahiwa. She is Queen Lopaka's foremost aide. Hiwahiwa, this is Princess Celia Kalino."

Creede's eyebrows just about climbed off his face at the title, but he kept silent. Probably just as well. The sirens were pretty much ignoring everybody but me.

Hiwahiwa bowed, her braid swinging forward to brush the ground. "It is an honor, Highness."

"The pleasure's mine," I answered. Only then did she straighten up.

"Her Majesty assumed that since you were coming on such short notice you wouldn't have time to pack." *How the hell had they even known I was coming? Sigh.* I did not need to be messing with sirens who were also clairvoyant. "She asked that I bring you something appropriate to wear."

They were dressing me for a meeting I hadn't even known I was having. *Great. Just great.* I smiled and took the package she held out. Turning, I made introductions, then excused myself to go change.

I went down to the stateroom, carrying my package. The Rusland contingent was in the mess/kitchen area. They'd quit arguing in favor of glowering silently at each other. I should probably find out what was going on, but I figured it could wait until I got changed.

The queen had sent me a lavalava. I'd never worn one before, so it took me a few minutes to get the knack of tying the skirt. Both the sleeveless top and the ankle-length skirt were a vibrant red that I expected to look hideous on me but just didn't. The fabric wasn't cotton. In fact, I couldn't identify what it was. But it was natural and it breathed beautifully. Much better than the jacket I slipped on over my new outfit. If anyone complained about the jacket, I'd explain about the sun sensitivity. If they complained about the weapons, I'd remind them about my upcoming duel. But I was wearing it and I was going armed. Both Ren and Hiwahiwa had been barefoot. I didn't do barefoot much. I hoped there were no rocks. Because sneakers would be . . . gauche.

When I finished dressing I stepped once again into the tiny space that served as the ship's head. I was delighted to find toothpaste and a couple of unopened toothbrush boxes in the cabinet above the minuscule sink, along with a hairbrush. I wished for makeup, but that was too much to ask. Still, in just a few minutes, I was dressed and presentable.

When I opened the door, Dahlmar was standing outside. His hands were clenched into fists, but his voice was calm.

Almost serene, in fact, which made the fists all the more noticeable.

"Ivan has reminded me that my first duty as king is to remain alive. He also pointed out that I have no immunity to the siren glamour. Thus, we are staying hidden downstairs."

Ah, so *that* was what the argument was about. Couldn't say as I blamed Ivan. But it does take balls to stand up to a king like that. Then again, Ivan had brains and power and had somehow managed to get his king to safety in the middle of a coup. A sure sign that Ivan had great big polished brass ones.

King Dahlmar brought my attention back to the matter at hand. "It is traditional in this situation to present a gift to a monarch . . . something of significance to you personally or of great value. It would be a grave insult not to do so. Do you have such a gift? We had little time to plan this trip."

No, I didn't. I could probably come up with something. Maybe. "Do you have something that would work?"

His expression grew rueful. He made a gesture to include his Disneyland getup. "If I did, would I be dressed like this? I just felt I should warn you. But she anticipated your need for clothing, so perhaps she will understand—" But he sounded doubtful.

"Don't worry about it," I told him. "I'll think of something."

He opened his mouth to say something, but I didn't let him. "I said, don't worry about it." I'd had a thought. Not a welcome or happy thought, but there you go. I had something that would work as a gift. It was magical. It was valuable. And I really, really, didn't want to part with it. That should make it perfect.

I pushed past him, moving quickly up the stairs. I was tired. Tired of not being able to eat, of having to slather myself with sunscreen; tired of political bullshit, constant near-death experiences, and narrow-minded assholes stalking me. I hated it all. My life was completely out of control. I was still reacting because everybody else kept anticipating my plans. Worse, there wasn't any guarantee that any of this was going to change, no matter how much I wanted it to, tried to, change it. And today I was going to have to part with one of my most treasured possessions because of some political bullshit no-body'd bothered to warn me about, and then defend my right to exist.

Sucks to be me.

I stepped onto the deck; the ladies were waiting patiently. Bubba raised a brow at the lavalava, which admittedly hugged every curve. Creede didn't take his eyes off the women who'd managed to surprise him. I didn't blame him at all.

"Let's do this."

14

A four-seat motorboat was sent to fetch us. Ren explained with some embarrassment that she could only teleport herself and one other person. I pointed out that this was exactly two more people than I could manage. It made her laugh. Even Hiwahiwa managed a smile, though she tried to hide it. The sailor driving the dinghy didn't bother. He was grinning ear-to-ear.

I returned Bubba's wave as we drove off. He actually seemed happy to be staying behind with Dahlmar and Ivan. Creede wasn't happy at all.

I didn't blame him. I was nervous as hell, bordering on frightened. Would I make it back? Maybe, maybe not. I might be able to talk my way out of this, assuming the queen would listen. But I was already at a disadvantage because she thought I'd insulted her deliberately. I doubted I'd get a chance to explain. Even if I did, Adriana and Ren were both princesses. I was betting their word would carry more weight than mine.

Then, if I made it past the hearing, there was the duel. But that didn't bother me as much. A straight-up fight I could handle. Until I'd been locked away, I'd trained nearly every day. I'm familiar with most weapons and have made a serious study of a couple of different disciplines of unarmed combat. And when it comes to experience in flat-out dirty street fighting, well, I've got plenty of that.

So I just had to get past the talking—which I wasn't good at—and on to the fighting, which I was. *Piece of cake. Yeah, right.*

The dinghy pulled up to the mother ship. She was huge and gorgeous. I don't know enough about boats to describe the ship with any degree of accuracy, but suffice it to say that I imagined her featuring prominently in Bubba's wet dreams. Strong arms helped me up the ladder and onto the deck, releasing me as soon as I was standing safe on my own two feet. As soon as we were all on board, the fleet began to move away from *Mona's Rival.*

You seem worried. Are you well?

I didn't recognize the voice in my head, so it wasn't Ren. Since the crew all appeared to be male, I looked to Hiwahiwa by process of elimination. She smiled.

"I'm fine, thanks. Just a little nervous about meeting your queen."

Queens. You'll be presenting yourself to the high queen, yes, but to the others as well.

Okay, so Ren hadn't been messing with me and neither had Jeff. Multiple queens with one *high* queen. And Hiwahiwa was thinking at me, which meant I probably was supposed to communicate telepathically as well. One problem: I hadn't been able to do that before the bite and I hadn't actually learned how since. Still, the basics had been covered way back in grade school when they were testing all of us for the talent, and there was no time like the present to learn new party tricks.

I concentrated, forming the words in my mind while I pictured her face. *How many queens are there?*

Again she smiled, apparently pleased I'd responded in kind. *Currently five. The Pacific line is home to High Queen Lopaka; the lesser queens are from the Aegean, the Baltic, the Sea of Japan, and the Indian Ocean.*

None from the Atlantic?

Not since the end of the first age.

The end of the first age had been quite a while ago, B.C. According to the legends, which were really all that was left, the first age had ended with the destruction of Atlantis.

One of the sailors came up with a message for Hiwahiwa. She excused herself, leaving me alone looking out to sea with plenty to think about. I wasn't sure where Ren had gone off to or if she was even on the boat. Hard to keep track of someone who can teleport. I didn't mind. It was kind of nice, feeling the breeze against my skin. I had a few more minutes before the sunscreen gave out. Judging from how quickly we appeared to be approaching land, I could stay right here until we arrived without risking skin damage.

I did turn to look back, see if I could catch a glimpse of Bubba's yacht. I could see *Mona's Rival*, but she was a goodly ways out on the horizon. Hard to judge the exact distance, particularly with the visible haze caused by the magical barrier that separated us, but too far to swim for sure. I was betting she would be invisible from the island. Nor were they being guarded. Not a single ship had been left behind. Was that a good or bad thing?

I watched the seabirds swirl and swoop in what truly appeared to be organized chaos, a sort of dance that seemed to be for the sole purpose of my personal entertainment. They scattered once we reached the inlet, and then I watched the sailors go about their duties. Hiwahiwa didn't return until the boat was fully at rest, at which point she approached, smiling broadly.

"I'm sorry we weren't able to talk more. Having so many royals on the island is making my job a bit more complex than it normally would be."

"It's all right. I was enjoying the trip."

"You like the ocean?"

I didn't answer right away. I wasn't sure how to put what I felt into words without sounding like an idiot. Then the words formed in my mind like magic. *I love the ocean. It's where I go to find peace and calm when life's storms are too much for me, the one place where I can truly relax and clear my head. Its beauty restores me, its majesty awes me. I need it like I need the air I breathe and the food I eat.*

Another smile, one that lit up her whole face. *I understand. It's like that for us all. And your affinity with the birds shows that you are truly one of our own. You belong here.*

I wasn't sure how to respond to that. I've never *belonged* anywhere.

The captain approached. "Ladies. If you are ready." He gestured toward the gangplank.

Hiwahiwa led me down onto docks that were absolutely ordinary, perfectly modern, and, I guessed, well designed. Stepping out of the harbor area, however, was like taking a step out of time. A perfectly tended path wound through lush greenery, past tiny waterfalls and other natural wonders. Overhead rang the raucous calls of birds and small mammals. A heady perfume of tropical flowers and rich, damp volcanic earth filled my nostrils. Higher in the sky, the gulls soared ahead of us as though announcing our arrival.

The trail wound slowly upward. My companion and I rounded one last bend and stepped into a secluded glade ringed with brightly colored hibiscus.

As we passed into the clearing, musicians began pounding a compelling rhythm on skin drums. We moved forward, along ground that rose in ripples that looked as if they had been formed by the downward movement of an ancient lava flow. The rising ground made for a natural dais at the far end of the clearing, perhaps a hundred yards to the right of a steep waterfall that splashed noisily into a wide pool of water so clear and pure I could clearly see every stone and swimming fish.

I didn't waste much time looking at it or any of the other natural wonders surrounding me. Because we had come into the presence of royalty, judging by the arrangement of six thrones carved from the native stone, in graduating sizes and complexity leading to the massive center chair.

The thrones were occupied, each chair seating a siren of imperious beauty. While I couldn't be sure, I could almost guess which woman represented which ocean based on their appearance. Each was completely unique in her appeal, coloring, and dress. One throne was empty. I presumed it was for the Atlantic queen who no longer existed.

They were dark skinned and light, Asian and Caucasian. One woman bore a particularly striking resemblance to Ren — presumably her mother, queen of the Mediterranean branch.

A tiny woman with Japanese features was, I assumed, the ruler of the Sea of Japan.

On the center and largest throne sat a tall blond woman who looked remarkably like me, only better. A *lot* better. Her blond hair was loose, flowing unhindered to the waist of a crimson lavalava hemmed in glittering gold. Her skin was too fair to actually tan, but it had the hint of a warm glow. All of her features were beautiful, but her eyes . . . her eyes were unforgettable. Because while she had the body of a youth, one look in those storm gray depths and you knew she was ancient. There was both wisdom and cold, implacable pragmatism in her gaze. I knew I should look at each of the queens, take their measure. But I couldn't seem to look away from Queen Lopaka.

Even without the benefit of my vampire talents I would've felt the power in that clearing. It was thick, thrumming, almost a separate, living presence that grew with each passing moment.

Ren appeared beside Hiwahiwa and the two of them led me forward until I stood directly in front of the row of thrones. The drumming continued, growing in intensity as more women, sirens all, filed into the clearing, sitting on the ground in groups of four or five on either side of the main path.

At a tiny gesture from Lopaka, the noise of the drums and the murmurs of the crowd stopped in an instant. The rushing splash of water was deafening in the sudden silence.

Hiwahiwa bent almost double before her queen, her long hair brushing the ground at her feet. "Your Majesties. I present to you the abomination, Celia Kalino Graves."

Abomination. Great. Just great. Although I suppose it was better to find out right at the beginning where I stood.

*She means no insult. It is simply a label for what you are:
not human, not siren, not even vampire.*

The voice in my head was calm and melodic, as if it was set
to music I couldn't quite hear, a song so heartbreakingly pure
that I'd never forget it if I did.

I shook my head, trying to break the spell. It didn't help
much. But that was all right. The warmth of the unheard
music clashed in harsh counterpoint against the harsh words
of the tiny Japanese queen. She rose from her throne next to
Lopaka. Glaring at me with cold, dark eyes, her beautiful
features twisted into an expression of disgust.

Again the words formed inside my skull. *This creature,
this . . . thing . . . has no place among us. Siren blood may be
in her veins, but it is blood corrupted. She was summoned to appear before us weeks ago. Where has she been? She hasn't even
the decency to show respect by bringing a gift for the queen of
her line.*

There was no sound, but I could feel the stirring of their
minds against mine. Psychics. They were all psychics. Well,
I'd guessed as much and Hiwahiwa's actions on the way here
had warned me. Had she done it deliberately? I was grateful
either way.

Each voice in my head had its own melody. Some beautiful,
some harsh. It wasn't music, precisely, unless they chose to focus it that way. It was a psychic call. Until now I hadn't understood what my gran meant when she'd tried to explain it to
me. Hell, maybe *she* hadn't understood it, either.

I took a single, small step, putting myself a fraction ahead
of Ren and Hiwahiwa. Bowing at the waist, I tried to focus
my thoughts and project them, the same way I'd done with

Hiwahiwa on the boat. I knew I was bad at it, clumsy. Several of the faces surrounding me were openly sneering. But I kept trying. Because if I couldn't use telepathy, they'd hold it against me and claim that I wasn't siren enough to live.

I am here. And I have a gift. My thought wasn't musical. It was harsh as the caw of a gull. But I heard it. And so did they. For just an instant, I saw a hint of a smile twitch at the corner of Lopaka's perfect lips.

By all means, bring it forward. Her voice was calm, but I would swear I felt a hint of amused approval.

I reached into my jacket while I was still obviously outside striking distance and drew one of the pair of knives Bruno had made for me. Designed to slay monsters, it was a powerful tool. As I laid the weapon across my palm, hilt toward her, my vision misted. The knife was the perfect gift. It was the undamaged one of a formerly matched pair. The other still worked, still held its magic, but slaying a thousand-year-old übervamp had changed it. Instead of silver, it was black, and no amount of polishing would restore it. On the other hand, this knife was perfect. Magically powerful, it was beautiful and practically priceless. Bruno's feelings for me and mine for him were bound up in that blade as surely as the magic was. It killed a part of me to offer it. But it was the part of me already injured by his leaving and this was the only thing I had that was worthy of her. I would keep the other knife, use it, and remember him. But this one . . . this one would be my gift to the queen of all the sirens.

I extended the weapon to her, keeping my eyes down, not so much from respect but to keep my tears from showing. I was crying. I couldn't help it. Never mind that this was the worst possible time and place for it, the pain was suddenly there, as fresh and intense as that moment in the courthouse when he told me he was leaving.

Lopaka stood. Her hands deliberately clasped mine for a long moment before she took the knife. The gesture was warm and curiously gentle. I glanced up. Our eyes met and I realized she knew, could *feel* exactly what giving this knife away cost me—what Bruno meant to me.

When she held the knife aloft, rainbows shot from its surface, just like in the safe when the magic of the Wadjeti had touched it. A single note sounded, pure and clear, echoing through the clearing like a crystal chime.

Wow. Even after she brought it down to look at the blade more closely, I could feel that tone in my chest lingering softly as a dream.

A most *worthy gift. Crafted in love and pain, as is most that is powerful and lasting. I accept it from you with great thanks, daughter of my line.*

There was an actual, audible gasp at that and the other queen—

Chiyoko, her name is Chiyoko.

Chiyoko staggered as if struck. She half-collapsed onto her throne, her face angry and confused. *You cannot mean to*—

Lopaka twisted her head fast as a snake and *looked* at Chiyoko. If thoughts passed between them, I wasn't allowed to hear them. But while the small Japanese queen paled, she did not back down, in fact she rose to her feet, her expression defiant.

Celia Kalino Graves is a child of my blood, if not of my body. I accept her as I accepted her ancestor, my brother Kalino. Lopaka's voice was utterly calm.

No! A raven-haired beauty rose from the throne two seats down from Chiyoko, her blue-green eyes flashing. *She is* not *a royal. Where is her prophet? Her warrior guard?*

She has them. Adriana's voice was unmistakable in my mind. Clear as a bell and just as clearly unhappy. *When her previous prophet was murdered, within a day another appeared. And the warrior wolf followed her to the alley where she was attacked and killed the monsters that harmed her. She even has two attendant spirits . . . one the spirit of her former prophet. Even after death, her guards are faithful to her.*

"*I cannot believe you would support your mother in elevating a rival to the line of succession!*" Chiyoko was so shocked she spoke the words aloud as well as inside my head.

Truth is truth. Adriana was calm.

It was hard to get a mental word in edgewise when I had to struggle so much to even get a word to appear in my own mind. *I'm not a rival for anyone's throne.*

Well, *that* certainly got everyone's attention. Everyone but Lopaka was staring at me, most literally openmouthed with shock. Lopaka's gray eyes were sparkling merrily and those perfect lips twitched just a little, as if she was having a difficult time keeping a serious expression.

You would refuse the throne? Chiyoko's voice was barely a whisper in my head.

I couldn't help but laugh. It startled a parrot in the tree overhead. I spoke out loud simply because my brain was starting to hurt from all the thinking. "I'm no ruler. I'd only be kidding myself to think I was. I've always been human. I don't know your people or your customs. So, yes, if someone was actually foolish enough to offer, I'd refuse the throne. But it shouldn't come up. You have other options." I gestured toward Adriana and Ren. They were the only ones I knew. There might be others. But I figured either of them would be a better choice for queen than me. They'd almost have to be. Hell, Bruno or Creede would be a better queen than me. They had the magic and the telepathy. I had fangs and gulls.

"You have heard it from her own lips," Lopaka said smugly, also out loud, which caused more than a few shocked glances between the others. "She has shown wisdom and prudence and has honored our customs to the best of our ability." She held up the knife. "She came here as soon as she was made aware I was trying to reach her." The looks she gave her daughter and Ren said that people would be paying dearly for that particular oversight. Lopaka finished by speaking into my mind. She stepped down from the dais, put a hand on my shoulder, and turned back toward the other queens. Her hand was warm and gentle and felt remarkably like Gran's. *I say that she has earned the right to live. Do any dare gainsay it?*

There were some grim looks from the women seated on the other thrones. Chiyoko looked positively murderous. Still, she gathered her skirts around her and sat fussily back onto her seat. The dark-haired beauty moved more slowly. But eventually she, too, sat down.

Very well. Lopaka gestured to Hiwahiwa. *Have the servants prepared the feast?*

Yes, Your Majesty.

Excuse me, Mother. With all respect. Adriana bowed very, very low. I guessed she knew that Lopaka wasn't going to be happy to hear about the duel. Especially not right after she'd given me the siren equivalent of the Good Housekeeping Seal of Approval.

What is it . . . dear? Just the slightest emphasis on the last word, the tiniest hint of annoyance.

Princess Celia and I have a matter of honor to attend to.

Nothing serious, I hope. Lopaka's tone said that it had better not be.

Adriana straightened, her eyes flashing a little in defiance. *We had a . . . contretemps . . . the night we met. We have agreed to a duel. Since she is apparently a siren, it cannot be to the death.* Adriana didn't bother to hide her disappointment about that. I'd thought her quarrel with me might be resolved by the whole refusing-the-throne thing. Apparently I'd been wrong. Maybe she just flat disliked me. *Someone who dislikes me? Surely not.*

You are a princess, Adriana. Queen Lopaka's voice was stern. *Princesses do not duel to the death, regardless of whether both combatants are sirens.*

I have no prophet. I have no guard. I will never rule. My title is an empty one. The bitterness in Adriana's voice cut like shards of glass.

Shit. Well, didn't that just suck. For her. But for me, too. Through no fault of my own, I had what she didn't. To someone as proud as she was, that was just unforgivable.

Empty or not, you are not allowed a duel to the death. To clear victory or first blood only. Lopaka gave me a look that let me know as clearly as any words that I'd better watch myself. If I hurt her baby, all those warm fuzzies from a few minutes ago would evaporate into thin air.

Great. Didn't this just suck moss-covered pond rocks.

To clear victory then. Adriana turned to me. *Agreed?*

Like I had a lot of choice. And like I knew what that even meant in this culture. *Fine with me. Do we get to use weapons, or is this hand-to-hand?*

Hand-to-hand would be better. Less chance of accidentally going too far. Although even that would be tricky. I have vampire speed and increased strength. I hadn't worked out hard or tried to spar since the bite, so I wasn't exactly sure how careful I'd need to be. Sirens are immortal beings, but you can hurt them. Amputated limbs don't grow back and brain damage and severed spines don't heal any better than they would for a human. Then again, I'd never actually seen a siren fight. It might be that I was outclassed. I could be in for a serious butt whipping.

Adriana's one big advantage was jealousy. Dr. Marloe had said that jealousy works like a magical poison. I wasn't jealous of Adriana. Yeah, she was prettier and a princess, but she was *so* screwed up. I mean, Lord knows I have issues with *my* mother, but Adriana didn't seem to be doing all that much better with the queen. Adriana envied me for some bizarre reason. Envy is a form of jealousy. Knowing my luck, her weapons would be poisoned for me.

Hand-to-hand. Adriana paused. *I wouldn't want to be on the wrong end of the weapon that matches the one you gave my mother.* Now how had she'd known about that? Telepathy, I suppose. *One scratch might kill me. Or not. I can't be sure.*

I was a little surprised. A moment ago she'd been more than ready to risk dying. Now she wasn't? Not that I was sorry, but what the hell?

You are not who and what I thought you were. Adriana's

voice held clear puzzlement. *Honor must be served, but I am no longer certain your death would be a good thing for me or my family.*

Ah, so she'd been that sure of winning. She must be very good to be that cocky. *Cool.* Since this was the equivalent of a sparring match, it could be fun. I do love a challenge.

In front of the dais, people rearranged themselves into a loose circle about twenty feet in diameter. The queens remained on their thrones. Since the thrones were on a higher level than that of the fighting area, they'd be able to see well enough.

I stripped off my jacket, wondering what I should do with it. I didn't want to leave it lying around where anybody could get at it. Most people are honest. But it only takes one who isn't. I already suspected that Ren had sticky fingers. I didn't want to lose either my weapons or the jacket itself.

I was saved by Queen Lopaka yet again. At her gesture, Hiwahiwa stepped forward, taking my jacket and then standing before me, waiting expectantly.

For what? I looked around and saw Adriana standing nude in the center of the fighting ring.

Oh no. I'm not good at casual nudity. I looked at Queen Lopaka. "Is there some big ceremonial reason we have to fight nude? I mean—" I pointed at the rock-strewn sand. "There are places I really don't want to get sand embedded."

She fought not to laugh. The machinations a person's face goes through when trying to stifle an involuntary reflex are actually pretty interesting to watch. Finally she spoke and her words held all the laughter her well-schooled features didn't.

"Nudity guarantees there are no weapons or charms secreted that could injure the other or protect one from the other. We have fought nude for millennia. However, I can accept this is a different age and that you are not familiar with our customs. I will permit enough clothing for modesty, but no more."

So, while everybody watched, I stripped down to my undies. I'd sort of cheated when I put on the lavalava to begin with; I'd just tucked down the straps of my bra. Fine. I'm a prude. But even though I was wearing my panties and bra, I was seriously uncomfortable. Adriana being nude was going to change my fighting style. There was something about throwing a punch at a breast that wasn't the same as punching a shirt. Weird but true.

Pretending a poise I didn't actually feel, I made myself walk casually through the path the crowd made for me until I reached the center of the ring.

I don't know what I expected: maybe one of those formal bows that start a martial-arts match, maybe somebody shouting, "Go!" I *wasn't* expecting Adriana to launch a high kick at my face with no warning whatsoever.

She was good and she was *fast*. Whoever had trained her knew what they were doing. I hadn't realized that sirens were on par in speed with vampires. If I'd still been a vanilla human, that kick would have laid me out flat, maybe even broken my neck.

But I'm not fully human, not anymore. I saw the blow coming and was able to duck, twist, and grab her ankle. Using her foot as a handle, I continued my turn, pulling her off her anchoring foot and flinging her to the rocky ground with a heavy thud. It had to hurt. Hell, it was painful to *hear*. But she rolled and stood, blood oozing from scrapes where her skin had been torn off by the coarse rock. *Ouch*.

But it didn't even slow her down. Before I could even step backward, she was flying at me. She grabbed my arm and tossed me probably a dozen feet. The circle of people parted to let me fly past. On landing, I shook my head and tried to clear the fuzz from my brain. As I stood up, the calf that had been injured the night before informed me there was still glass somewhere in my muscles. The pain was sharp and immediate as I frantically moved left to avoid a kick square in the face. I leapt to my feet from my knees like I was an extra in a Jackie Chan movie and we were off again.

We circled, eyeing each other, looking for telltale movements. Blows flew and were blocked. Feints succeeded or failed.

Soon, the scent of blood filled the air, adding copper to the salt filling my nose. I figured out pretty quickly that "first blood" wasn't actual first blood. I paused briefly when that happened, but nobody stopped the fight, so oh, well. I'd keep going until someone yelled, "Stop!"

My vision was flowing in and out of hyperfocus, making it hard to think. Fortunately, there wasn't really time to think, so it didn't much matter.

The two of us were well matched. She had me in reach. I had better strength, though not by as much as I would've expected. We both were well trained. We would've been equal if I'd neglected my weight work. This could wind up being a long, painful ordeal with the winner determined by willpower and stamina. Fortunately, I have quite a lot of both.

She moved to sweep my legs, putting all her weight on her left leg. Timing my jump with exquisite care, I went for a flying kick. She turned, taking the blow on her shoulder rather than giving me her back and risking a spinal injury.

The impact staggered her, threw her off balance. It was the break I'd hoped for. I dived at her in a flying tackle, the pair of us hitting the ground with a jarring impact.

I thought I had her, but she managed to pull herself out of my grip and roll away before I could pin her.

I scuttled back, trying to gain my feet, but she was quicker— quick enough to kick me in the ribs as I rose. That hurt. I came to my feet hissing with pain and annoyance, blood gleaming like neon on the surface of glowing skin.

She was on her feet as well. Her expression flickered from startled to grim determination and she moved in to attack.

My eyes shifted into full vampiric hyperfocus. Everything was suddenly so *clear*. I could see each grain of sand, the pores and flaws in each stone. Adriana's tiniest muscle movements were grossly exaggerated. I knew what she was going to do almost before she did.

She shifted, throwing a hard punch toward my solar plexus, but I wasn't there. I'd dropped down and was sweeping her legs out from under her. She went down hard. Her head slammed against the same rock hard enough this time to stun her for a second. In that second I was on her, pinning her body with mine. She started to struggle, turning her head back and forth as she searched for some way of escape. I hissed again, but this time it wasn't a sound of pain. It wasn't a human sound at all.

My eyes focused on her neck and the pulse that beat so rapidly, so close to the skin. My sense of self began to fade as the world narrowed to that tiny fragment of flesh. I needed to taste the blood underneath . . . more than I'd ever had to do anything before in my life. I couldn't breathe, couldn't think. My mouth opened. Adriana's eyes went wide and she struggled anew, but the sinews in my arms had turned to iron straps and she couldn't get away.

The vampire within me started to lunge forward to feed and the siren in me was going to let it happen. *Clear victory* would allow a taste of flesh. But at that last moment, my human conscience forbade it.

People are not food!

Throwing back my head, I howled in hunger that was so strong it was an actual pain. It ripped through every nerve in my body like an electric shock. Pain. So much pain.

But I had to be human enough to say no: human enough not to do this even though another part of myself demanded it. I might be part vampire and part siren. But I was born human and I never intended to lose that part of myself.

I crawled off of Adriana awkwardly, moving painfully to the opposite side of the ring from where she lay. I had beaten my hunger, but I was going to pay dearly for that victory. Rising to my feet, I shoved through the eerily silent crowd to where Hiwahiwa stood beside Ren. I grabbed my clothing without ceremony and turned to Ren. "Get me the hell out of here. Now." I spoke aloud. I needed food, now, or someone was going to die.

"But—" She glanced over to Queen Lopaka. The queen was still nodding her assent when I felt the world lurch and I was back on the *Mona's Rival*—and in the middle of a battle.

15

We materialized into chaos. My eyes burned from smoke and the deck shifted beneath me as an explosion of magic erupted from the door of the front cabin. I watched as a half-charred man flew backward over the rail to slam into the side wall of the cabin of a boat that was tied to our railing.

I felt, rather than saw, Ren vanish. Whether she'd gone for help or just gone was anyone's guess, but I didn't have time to worry about it. I ducked down, my world still slowed by vampire vision and the need for blood. But my effort at stealth was spoiled when the billowing smoke made me cough. The nearer of the two invaders turned, startled by my sudden appearance and state of undress. Surprise only slowed him for an instant. Still, that instant was enough for me to find my jacket in the pile of clothes and pull out the first weapon that came to hand. I threw the boomer hard, not at him but at the floor by his feet. Covering my eyes, I was rewarded by a flash of heat and light I could feel through my upraised arm and a roar of sound meant to temporarily deafen anyone in range.

I managed to get my gun pulled and safety off quickly

enough to step out of the way of the man charging blindly toward me. He might not be able to see now, but he'd glimpsed me before the light show and was attacking based on that knowledge. Not a stupid move in close quarters like these. There wasn't a lot of room between me and the railing and he was bigger than me.

Still, I had the advantage. I could see. Rather than waste a bullet I might need later, I stepped aside, ducking beneath his outstretched arms. Coming up behind him, I leveled my hardest punch at his right kidney. His knees folded. He probably screamed, but I couldn't hear it. My ears were still ringing from the boomer.

Hitting the safety, I pistol-whipped him, and he went down. As I shoved him under the railing into the welcoming ocean, I realized that I'd seen him before. At La Cocina. He'd been with George Miller.

What the hell?

It didn't matter. Well, it did, intellectually. But it didn't in reality. Because the second man had positioned himself, legs spread and braced between the railing and the cabin wall. Blindly but methodically, he was firing off shots, holding his weapon at waist level. Shoot, adjust an inch to the left, shoot again. Smart. Because if I was blinded, too, he'd get me eventually, based on the limited space. I dropped to my stomach, braced my elbows, and flipped off the safety. Then, just as methodically, I shot him. The bullet took him between the eyes. Gruesome but effective. I was on my knees, getting ready to rise, when a man came around the front of the cabin, apparently checking to see what had happened.

I fired at him, but I was in an awkward position and he was

damned quick. I missed. Swearing, he ducked back behind the cabin wall. I had to scramble to get out of his line of fire. The bullet missed me but embedded itself in the wall, sending fiberglass chips and wood splinters into my naked flesh. *Damn it. Ow.* I was backing up when I saw the shadows shift on the wall beside me. Instinct made me whirl and I fired into the chest of a monster.

It was tall and oddly shaped, with a long, eyeless head. Its russet body was scaled, naked, and hugely male. Its body was oddly shaped, with knees that bent the wrong direction. Half a dozen curved bone horns surrounded its head where the brow line should be and wicked brass-colored claws sprang from the ends of its hands and feet.

An imp. A lesser demon. A *demon.*

Oh, shit, oh, shit, oh, shit.

It turned toward me, its mouth opening to show wicked fangs that dripped venom. A long black tongue flicked out in a gesture reminiscent of a snake scenting the air.

I scrambled backward, tripping over my empty holster in my haste to make sure I was out of the reach of that *thing.* I fell on my ass, hard, dropping my gun, which skittered across the deck to fall into the ocean. The impact made me bite the inside of my cheek. Blood filled my mouth and I spit it out. The creature turned, tongue flicking faster at the smell of fresh blood. It and me, quite a pair.

I reached down to the deck and began rummaging through the pile of clothing, digging for the one thing that might help me against the monster I was facing. I managed to get my right hand wrapped around the plastic handle and was about to pull the little squirt gun free when I heard movement behind me. Heard it—which meant my hearing was coming back.

"Well, if it isn't Ms. Graves." Miller's silken voice was condescending as hell. Of course, considering the advantage he had over me, he had reason to be. "I did warn you not to cross me."

The demon leaned forward, reaching toward me with its claws. "Halt!" Miller's command was sharp and the creature jerked back as if it were at the end of a leash. Throwing back its head, it screamed, a harsh, hateful sound with all the musicality of nails on a blackboard or static feedback.

"It's a little extreme, isn't it, dealing with the devil just to get back at your ex-partner?"

He shrugged, albeit mostly with one shoulder. The other wasn't working so well. "In for a penny, in for a pound. I'm damned in either case. And the only way I can put off my eternal unrest for even a little longer is by killing Creede. So, where is he?"

"Haven't got a clue." Absolute truth. He could be anywhere. He was probably on the boat. But I sure as hell hadn't seen him. For all I knew, he was already dead.

"Don't make me do something you're going to regret, Ms. Graves."

The imp strained against its invisible tether and he let it come just a fraction closer. I could smell its breath and a tiny drop of spittle splattered against my leg, burning it like acid.

I screamed. The pain was incredible. Just that one drop had burned through my flesh nearly to the bone.

"Where *is* he?" Miller's voice was right behind and above me now. I turned my head, craning my neck upward, and was rewarded with a close-up view of his suit trousers: lightweight wool, gray, with a light pinstripe. But past him I saw something that heartened me. The other bad guy stood silent, empty hands at his sides, Bubba's .38 tucked firmly under his chin. Creede stood behind Miller, gun at the ready.

"I'm right here."

Miller actually jumped a little. With his loss of concentration, the imp lunged forward, but not at me—at him. I pulled the One Shot, rolling out of the way of a clawed foot, shooting holy water into the demon's open mouth.

I was too late. The creature's clawed arm swung forward, punching completely through Miller just below his breastbone. He screamed, though his lungs had to have been damaged, his left hand clawing weakly at the pocket of his jacket.

The demon was screaming, too. Each, painful, earsplitting shriek was accompanied by a belch of flame as the holy water burned it from the inside out. Throwing Miller aside with a vicious swing of its arm, it turned. Without eyes, I wouldn't have thought it could find me. But it knew precisely where I was and that I was the one who'd injured it.

It stalked forward, claws extended, following me as I backed away. I was in trouble. The man who had summoned it was dead or dying. There were no priests here to banish it and my little shot of holy water had injured the monster just enough to really piss it off. If that wasn't enough, even if by some miracle Ren popped in and saved my butt, it could follow me. Anywhere, anytime, with just a taste of my blood, or a hair from my head.

Exactly the way it had been used to trail Creede.

I was on the far side of the boat now, and even using vampire speed I was barely keeping ahead of those swinging claws. Every time it missed, the imp became more enraged. And while its bellows no longer belched flame, they did send ichor spraying. It burned through whatever it touched, be it fiber-glass, metal, wood, or skin.

I was on the farthest side of the boat, my path blocked by rubble and fallen bodies. I could dive into the water, but then everybody else on board would be toast. There was no way I was strong enough to beat it hand-to-hand, and I didn't dare risk closing with it enough to try out my fangs. It stalked to-ward me and I had nowhere to go.

The gulls wheeled and dived overhead, drawn by the scent of blood on the wind. They squawked and squalled above me. I screamed up at them, "If you want to do something useful, attack that damned demon!" I pointed at the imp and, I shit you not, they actually *did it.* The imp screamed as a hundred talons grabbed at it. Birds were thrown to the side, hopefully not wounded beyond repair. But they were actually beating the demon back.

Holy shit.

Creede's voice shouted something incomprehensible and a whirlwind formed around him. Magic flared so hard it made my skin hurt. There was something amazing about seeing Creede on the deck of the boat, arms outstretched, eyes glow-ing with fire, wind whipping at his clothes, looking for all the world like a pirate mage from a history book. All he needed was a red cape and sword to complete the image.

He advanced, words spewing from his mouth in a jumble of incomprehensible syllables. Though *I* didn't understand the sounds, the demon did. It froze in its tracks, howling in frustrated fury as the birds continued to tear at it. Again Creede called out and this time I felt a wave of magic accompany the words. The beast shuddered and seemed to waver, as if it were a heat shimmer or a mirage. A third call and with it the crack of ceramic breaking. The air pressure changed as our dimension opened just enough. The birds scattered frantically and I grabbed onto a railing as my feet rose into the air as a sudden vacuum tore at me. Though it fought and clawed with every ounce of its being, the imp was sucked back into hell.

I collapsed onto the deck, my heart pounding so loud that I couldn't hear anything else.

16

I was going to have to buy Bubba new sheets for this bed.
Oh, hell, who was I kidding? I was going to have to buy
him a new boat.

Mona's Rival was still afloat—just. But the deck and cabin
were riddled with bullet holes and demon claw marks. And
one of the magical explosions had taken out a wall.

Of course, this fight had really been because of Creede.
But Bubba would blame me.

Speaking of the attack, who were we supposed to report it
to? Did Serenity count as a country? They did have their own
law enforcement. But were they internationally recognized? If
the siren government couldn't, or wouldn't, handle the whole
thing aboveboard, Bubba couldn't claim on his insurance.
And Miller and the others would simply disappear, which
wasn't really fair to their families, if they had them.

As I was thinking all of this, I lay on the sheets in intense
pain. I'd been too busy to notice what was happening, what
with avoiding the imp and all, but the battle had taken place
in full daylight. I had been nearly butt naked and hadn't sun-
screened anything other than my face. Between the fight with

Adriana and the one with the demon, I had second-degree burns over most of my body. Third-degree burns where the acid had splattered. I had all kinds of nasty little injuries and there was that remaining embedded piece of baby food jar that needed to be dug out. So to try to distract myself from the pain, which wasn't being eased all that much by the wimpy little aspirin tablets that were all Bubba had on board, I was trying to think of anything and everything else. One thing was certain. If I was going to keep running into the demonic, I was going to need to take precautions.

A light tap on the door distracted me. I pulled the lightweight cotton sheet over me for modesty's sake. A little late for it, all things considered. But hey, we were just going to pretend I hadn't flashed Creede, Dahlmar, and the entire siren navy as they'd come to the rescue. Apparently, I'd leapt right out of my bra when I went over the demon. Creede swears he didn't notice.

Not even when he was handing me a towel to cover myself with.

"Come in."

I rolled over to see who it was and immediately wished that I hadn't. The burns were healing. But it was slow going. I'd had the last two shakes, to take the edge off of my hunger and make sure the humans didn't look tasty, but my body apparently needed more. Less food, slower healing. But there wasn't anything else on the boat I could digest unless I decided to go fully vampire. So until they finished hauling the boat into the harbor and found something I could drink, I was pretty much screwed.

"How are you doing?" Queen Lopaka stuck her head

through the doorway. She wasn't wearing anything ceremonial, just a pair of faded jeans and a white cotton button-down shirt with the sleeves rolled up. She wore boat shoes, probably a good thing considering the splinters and worse that littered the deck.

"Been better," I admitted. I probably still looked like one of the lower rungs of hell. When I'd gone into the bathroom to take the aspirin I'd scared myself. Second-degree burns on the face were *not* pretty. I was just glad I hadn't burned my eyeballs. I didn't even want to think how much that would have hurt. "Be sure to thank Ren for me. I appreciate her calling in the cavalry."

Lopaka smiled and I swear it lit up the room. Straight white teeth and dimples to die for. "Yes, well, better late than never. You apparently did well enough all on your own. Although at some cost." She sighed and lowered herself onto the edge of the bed. "You must be in pain. And my condolences on the loss of—"

I dipped my head and sighed. "Ivan. He was King Dahlmar's bodyguard." The king was beside himself, though he wasn't showing it much. There's a point at which a bodyguard becomes a member of the family.

"And he died in the line of duty." She sighed again. "How do you want to handle this?"

"I don't know," I admitted. "It's a complete clusterfu—" I stopped in mid-syllable, horrified at myself. You don't use language like that in front of a queen, no matter how appropriate or how casual the situation.

She laughed, hard enough to shake the bed. Wiping a tear from the corner of her eye, she said, "Yes, it is." She looked thoughtful for a moment. "All right. If you don't mind, I'll have my people handle the questioning of the remaining pirate. I'm also going to have them investigate King Dahlmar's allegations of political tampering in Rusland. We have very stringent laws forbidding political machinations of that type. If indeed that is what's happening."

"You don't think it is?"

She gave me a long look. "It's a landlocked country."

I put two and two together. Sirens need oceans. Need them. But just because they couldn't live in Rusland, that didn't mean they wouldn't want to control the power and the gas. I started to open my mouth to say as much, but I didn't have to. She'd been listening to my thoughts. Which I hated. I tried to stifle that thought before it got me in trouble.

"We have hospital facilities on the island. Your injuries can be tended there."

I shook my head no. Hospitals had bleeding people. The smell of blood could make me very dangerous—particularly when I was hungry and injured. "I appreciate the offer, but I can't." I didn't explain further, but I didn't have to. Either she was still eavesdropping on my thoughts or she was bright enough to figure it out on her own. She reached the right conclusion and quickly.

She gave me a horrified look. "It really is that much of a problem? I saw you looking at Adriana's neck and you left so swiftly, but—"

"Oh, it's a problem. So far, I've been able to deal with it. It's better, easier, if I have some broth or baby food with meat. Or something with protein that's run through the blender. But no hospital. That would just be a bad idea right now."

"I understand." She gave me a speculative look. "I can arrange for the food. And if you'll let me, I can help with the pain and let you rest until it's ready."

"That would be lovely."

She reached forward, touching me on the forehead. I heard her voice inside my head. *Sleep.*

I slept.

I woke to the smell of food: beef broth, French onion soup, and other, more exotic things that I couldn't name but that smelled of tropical fruits and banana. Opening my eyes, I discovered it was night. I rolled over . . . and it didn't hurt. For just a moment I reveled in the fact that I didn't *hurt*. The absence of pain was absolutely glorious.

The boat wasn't moving. Well, it was rocking gently, but not like it was out on the ocean. We'd apparently made harbor. Which explained why somebody'd felt secure enough to leave several open food containers on the nightstand next to my bed.

Vampires have terrific night vision. I didn't even need to turn on the light. I sat up in bed and begin tearing into the food. I was ravenous and most of it tasted wonderful. I skipped the fruit drink, though. I loathe bananas. I was just finishing the last drop of soup when I noticed a slip of folded note paper that had been tucked under one of the bowls.

I unfolded it, to find a note.

> *We need to talk, but Queen L. said not to wake you.*
> *We're staying in her guesthouse. See you there.*
>
> *Creede*

I was glad they'd let me sleep. Now that I'd healed up and eaten, I was much safer to be around. But I wanted to clean up before I went out in public. The shower in the head on the boat was tiny but in working order. I dug up some toiletries and made myself presentable. Thankfully, some kind soul had brought my things down from the deck. It would've been nice to have some fresh clothes, but unless I wanted to swipe something from Bubba, I'd have to make do. Since the lavalava didn't have any blood- or food stains, that was what I put on, covering it once more with my jacket to protect my still red and somewhat tender skin.

I sighed as I laid the empty holster on top of the bed. No point in putting it on. The gun was gone. That sucked. One of my knives was gone. That was even worse. But I was alive. Bubba, Creede, and Dahlmar were all injured, but they had made it, too. I was sorry about Ivan. But considering what we were up against, it was practically miraculous we'd only had one casualty.

I glanced at the clock built into the wall. One A.M. Most likely everybody else was in bed by now, but maybe not. Besides, having rested and fed, I was wide awake. So I picked my way through the disaster area where the mess used to be and made my way to the stairs and up top.

It was a beautiful night. Not too hot, with just enough of a breeze to flap the sails on the boats that had them and rustle the leaves of the palm trees on the shore. Water lapped gently against the hull of the boat, and the clear white moonlight made it easy to see but also made the shadows seem that much darker.

As I stepped from the cabin doorway, I saw one of those

shadows move ever so slightly. Someone was trying very hard to remain unseen.

I pulled my knife and charged, using vampire strength and speed. Before my opponent knew what was coming, I was on her and she was down, pinned to the deck with the edge of my knife at her throat.

I felt magic building and I pressed down on the knife so that the tip dimpled her skin without drawing blood. "Don't even think about it." I hissed and bared my teeth to make the . . . point perfectly clear.

Then my vampire sight kicked in and I suddenly realized she was just a kid. She couldn't be more than fifteen or sixteen. When I'd hissed at her, she'd let go of her power and lay still, her eyes wide as dinner plates. Her entire body quivered with fear. I could hear her heart pounding like a trip-hammer, her breath rasping. She was obviously terrified. But I didn't move the knife.

I heard running footsteps and a voice called out from the dock, "Princess, is something wrong?"

"I have company."

There was swearing and pounding feet. Three armed guards swarmed on board, shining flashlights like spotlights onto us. The kid beneath me started to cry. She was pretty, with exotic features—dark brown skin and hair that would've been kinky-curly if it hadn't been kept cropped close to her skull. She was wearing a black sports bra and matching jeans. A gold belly button ring twinkled in the harsh light.

She looked up and around at the people behind the spotlights and whimpered, "My mom is going to kill me."

"Only if I don't do it first." I smiled, deliberately letting her get another good look at the fangs.

She swallowed hard and tears filled her eyes. "Please don't kill me, Princess," she whispered.

"Give me one good reason not to."

The nearest guard was a tall woman. Her hair was cropped short in a buzz cut that should have been very masculine. But it looked good with her chiseled features and the seriously buff body encased in camo pants and an olive tank top. The loaded weapons belts were the perfect accessories. A small, embroidered name tag was affixed to the shirt. Marks on the tag probably signified rank. Her name was Baker.

"Okalani, what are you doing here?" she snapped.

The kid didn't answer. Tears were trailing from the corners of her eyes.

"How did you get past the guards?" I added.

"Oh, I know how she got past us," Baker snarled. "And her mother is going to hear about it." Baker gestured to an underling. "Go to the kid's house and tell Laka what happened. Bring her back here with you. And send Martin to notify the palace. We don't need this to go over the airwaves."

The second guard took off at a trot. I still hadn't let the kid up. The knife was still at her throat. I didn't figure she was out to kill me. She probably wasn't a threat. But I'm not inclined to take chances, and she needed to be taught a lesson.

Baker gestured and the rest of the guards left the boat, probably going to resume their positions. "Why are you here, Okalani?" she asked.

The kid blinked and snuffled. Tears were running freely

now, but she didn't dare move to wipe them away. "I wanted to talk to the princess. I want to know about the mainland."

The guard shook her head. "You had to know how dangerous it was. Word of what happened to this boat is all over the island. The queen provided the princess with guards for a reason."

The girl tensed beneath me and even through her tears I got a sense of stubborn anger. She was determined. She had balls, too. More balls than brains, actually. Pinned to the ground, knife at her neck, and she was still going to argue. "I want to meet my father." There was pain in that simple statement, so much pain that I cringed. Because I have my own daddy issues. I still have nightmares about him turning his back on me.

"Not going to happen," Baker said. Her voice was a little more kindly. Well, not kind, exactly, but less hostile. "You know that."

The kid turned her head, not wanting to meet Baker's eyes, and I had to pull the knife back a little or she would've cut herself.

"Why not?" I asked as I climbed off of the kid and put the knife back in its sheath.

"Mom sent him away with my baby brother. I'd be with them, but my mother thinks the mainland is too dangerous." The kid snuffled again as she scooted herself into a sitting position and started digging in her pockets. She pulled out a tissue that looked a little worse for wear and began blowing her nose noisily.

Baker squatted down so that she was eye-to-eye with the kid. I took a few steps back, giving them room. It was obvious the guard knew the family. Maybe she could talk some sense into this Okalani. Probably not. It was painfully obvious that the kid was stubborn and headstrong. But it was worth a try and Baker was making the effort. "She's not wrong, you know. If the princess was a full vampire, you'd have been dead before we could get to the boat."

"There aren't any vampires on the island."

"True," Baker admitted. "No werewolves, either. But there are on the mainland."

"I wouldn't be out after dark on the mainland," the kid countered, her jaw jutting out aggressively. "I'm not stupid."

"And yet you're here." I flashed the fangs again.

My sarcasm was not well received. Well, not by the kid. Baker gave a snort of amusement.

"I don't *belong* here." Wow, the despair those four words could hold. I felt her pain in my own chest.

Baker shook her head. "I get that. I do. Once you're an adult you can do what you want. But you're not old enough. Not yet. It may seem like forever, but it's only a couple more years."

"My mother doesn't want me to leave at all," Okalani said resentfully.

Baker gave a snort that might have been laughter. "Of course not. She's your mother. Once you're of age, she can't stop you. Until then . . ."

"I'm trapped."

God, she sounded bitter. Baker had been trying to be nice, but her patience was limited. I watched as her expression hardened, her gray eyes darkening to the color of storm clouds. "Yes. You are."

I turned away from the two of them, my attention attracted by movement on the island. There was a lit path into the woods—probably the same one I'd walked earlier today—and someone was coming our way. I concentrated, deliberately getting my eyes to do the vampire hyperfocus. It took a few seconds, but I finally got it to happen. A guard was approaching, accompanied by a woman who bore a strong resemblance to Okalani. She had that scared-frustrated-angry look on her face that you see so often on the mothers of teenagers.

The guard on the path gave a call sign. One of the two on the dock answered. Once they'd been given the all clear, the mother and her escort stepped onto the dock.

I'd moved away to stand at the railing and was only half-listening to Baker explain that I'd thought I was being attacked. She told the siren that I'd had a knife at her daughter's throat when the guards came on board and that because Okalani had broken the law by boarding the boat she was liable to be facing legal charges.

"She's very lucky to be alive," Baker finished.

Okalani's mother tried to hide it, but I saw her give a tiny, full-body shudder at what might have happened. Still, her voice was cold and controlled when she spoke to her daughter. "You should apologize to the princess."

"Yes, ma'am." Okalani stood. I watched her take a deep breath. Gathering her courage, she walked past her mother, toward me. I turned and waited.

"I'm sorry. I wanted—" She stopped, swallowing hard. The tears were perilously close to returning, but she fought them back. "I wanted to talk to you and I knew they wouldn't let me see you. But I shouldn't have done it. I'm sorry."

"I forgive you. But you need to be more careful. People have been trying to kill me. I thought you were one of them. Normally I don't hesitate when I'm defending myself. You were really, *really* lucky tonight."

She shivered. I hoped she was remembering the cold, razor-edged blade against her throat, the fangs, or both.

It was important she remember. But it was also important that she get a chance to talk to someone about the mainland. Because if she didn't, she was liable to do something even more stupid than sneaking onto Bubba's boat. She was desperate. I understood because I'd felt exactly the same way when I was only a little younger than she was now. I'd gone looking for my father. I'd found him with his new family. He'd turned his back on me. I hadn't believed that was possible. I'd believed that he loved me enough . . . and he hadn't. You can't protect kids from everything. But I'd spare anyone that kind of pain if I could. "Look, I don't know how long I'm going to be here or what my schedule is going to be like. But if it's okay with your mother and we can work it out, I'm willing to sit down with you and have a talk."

Her face lit up like a Christmas tree. "You are?"

"If it's okay with your mom."

She turned to her mother, her expression pleading.

Her mother's face was impassive. "We'll see." She turned to Baker. "Can we go?"

Baker nodded. "Yes. If the princess isn't going to press charges, you can take Okalani home."

She turned to her daughter. "Go home. Get in bed and *stay there*. We're going to have a talk when I get home."

The way she said the word "talk" made it very clear who

would be talking and who would be listening. But the kid was smart enough not to argue this time.

"Yes, ma'am." She ducked her head, gathered her power, and vanished.

The instant she was gone, her mother closed her eyes and shuddered. It took her a moment to pull herself together. When she managed it, she turned to Baker. "If you'd be so kind, I'd like to speak to the princess privately."

Baker gave me an inquiring look. Apparently I was in charge. I guess it came with the title. "Sure. No problem."

She waited until Baker was on the dock before coming to stand beside me at the railing. Still, at least two of the guards were in earshot. So it didn't surprise me when she decided to talk to me mind-to-mind.

Thank you for not killing my daughter.

I try not to kill people unless it's really necessary. It still wasn't easy for me to communicate this way, but I was willing to work at it. Because this was obviously important to her. *But it really was a close call.*

I noticed that. She shivered. Hugging herself tight, she turned, looking out to the ocean in the distance. I didn't say anything, just waited as she searched for the right words. *I love her so much, but I'm not sure what to do with her. I hate admitting that. But . . . her talent is so strong. The queen suggested that she might join the guards. She could be useful moving troops on a moment's notice, without a trace. But she hates it here. The other children pick on her so cruelly.*

Why?

She stared out at everything and nothing. *I forget, you don't know about us.* She turned around, resting her back against the railing, her eyes meeting mine. *The siren talent does not coexist well with other magical abilities. So those with siren talent do not manifest strong magical or psychic talents. They rarely even have another minor ability.* She paused for a moment, then went on. *There are not many children among our people. If one of them shows a magical ability, particularly a strong one . . .*

She's not going to be able to do the siren thing.

No.

Ren can teleport, I observed.

The other woman nodded. *Yes, but only herself and one other.*

I stared into the distance, instead of staring at her and making it obvious we were talking. Heaven only knew who could overhear. *And her siren abilities?*

Weak. Very weak. She can influence, *but only temporarily, and the very strong willed may be able to resist her.*

Not such a good thing for a princess. *Adriana?* I asked, because I had to.

Clairvoyant. She does not have a prophet because she is a prophet.

So, neither was going to be considered suitable to rule. Which explained the bitterness. With her talent, Adriana probably could see who would get the throne. Fate can be so cruel.

My daughter can teleport a dozen easily, possibly even two dozen with effort. But she hasn't even enough siren abilities to talk mind-to-mind.

And the other kids give her shit for it.

Oh yes.

Poor kid. I could relate. I'd caught all kinds of hell, growing up—until the day I beat the crap out of the biggest, baddest kid on the playground. They stopped tormenting me then. The other kids still didn't like me and it didn't stop the whispers, but for the most part, everybody left me alone.

Poor Okalani. *Teleportation is a very rare talent. She might do well on the mainland when the time comes.*

Yes, she might. But she needs to be an adult. Her father has made it very clear that he won't help. He is most bitter at having been sent away. He has a new wife and a new life. She has adopted our son as her own but has "no interest" in our daughter. I could force him, if he hadn't taken steps.

Steps?

He wears a charm similar to the ones your client and Mr. Creede wear. She gave me a sour look. *I believe his new wife bought it for him. He could not have afforded such a thing on his own.*

Ouch. But it was interesting that Creede had one. I hadn't known that. *I'm sorry.* I thought about it for a moment. *You haven't told Okalani about her father's new family, have you?*

That he rejected her? No. It seemed unnecessarily cruel.

Maybe she was right. But the kid was going to find out eventually.

Maybe so. She'd read my thoughts. I'd have to be careful of that. *But I'd like to spare her that particular pain as long as I can.* She uncrossed her arms and straightened. Speaking out loud for the first time, she said, "I must go and try to talk sense to my daughter."

"Good luck with that." My tone was dry, but I meant it. She'd need every bit of luck she could scrounge up to get through Okalani's thick teenage skull.

"Thank you for not killing her and for agreeing to speak with her. Maybe you can get through to her."

"I'll do my best."

She gave me a sad smile, followed by a very low bow, and left.

I watched her walk along the path until she disappeared into the night. It was time to find Creede and Dahlmar. I hoped the guesthouse had Internet access. I wanted to check my e-mail. I was worried about El Jefe's friend from UCLA and hoped that Em had written about her first day at work. I should also have word from the bank and from Roberto about my mom's case. Real life, such as it was, was still moving right along, whether or not I was home to participate.

I walked over to the ladder and climbed down to the dock. I didn't look back at the wreck of the *Mona*. It'd just make me sad.

Baker came up to greet me almost immediately. "Is there something we can do for you, Highness?"

"Creede left me a note that they were going to the guest-house?"

"Ah." Raising fingers to her lips, she gave a ear-piercing whis-tle. Almost immediately I heard the soft purr of an electric mo-tor. In an instant, a golf cart driven by a uniformed guard pulled up. Two others jogged along beside.

A golf cart? I must've looked as surprised as I felt, because Baker was smiling. "No automobiles are allowed on the east half of the island, where the royal compound is. West Island is as modern as you could want. There's even an international airport. East Island has the compound, the queen's private docks, and the nature preserve."

All right then. "Are they going to—"

"Jog alongside the vehicle all the way to the guesthouse?" She grinned. "Yes. We are." She winked at me. "Fortunately, it's only about a mile. It's been a long day."

At her gesture, I climbed in. I'd barely gotten my seat belt fastened before we were zipping along a narrow strip of pavement, heading steeply uphill. Baker and her guards kept pace. I jog nearly every day, but I wouldn't have wanted to run that hill in full gear and honest-to-God army boots. Still, they might be sweating, but they didn't seem to be struggling. Maybe I needed to up my regimen.

She hadn't misled me. It wasn't far and like the clearing where the ceremony had been held, it wasn't obviously visible until you were very nearly upon it. When we got within a couple hundred yards, motion sensors at the edge of the trail brought fairy lights to life. Perimeter lights came on when the vehicle pulled to a stop in the wider section of pavement used for parking.

I don't know architecture. I don't know what style goes by what name, and periods are something women have once a month. But I dated an architect for a few months a while back. He was a nice guy but boring. His absolute hero, the man he bored me to tears about, was Frank Lloyd Wright. He spent hours poring over everything ever written about Fallingwater.

That's what this looked like, right down to the waterfall, though the stones were darker. *Wow.* And this was just the guesthouse. Apparently Queen Lopaka knew how to live.

I climbed out and started walking. Baker fell in beside me. The other guards moved, dark and silent as my very own shadow, directly behind us.

Another pair of guards appeared at the doorway. Passwords were exchanged, holy water was sprayed by both sides. I approved. Since we'd had a verified imp encounter on the boat Queen Lopaka's people weren't taking any chances. Very professional. I *like* professional.

One of the guards pressed a series of buttons on the keypad next to the front door. A light flashed green, the door opened, and I stepped over a threshold with enough buzzing power to take my breath away.

Baker noticed my wince and where I was rubbing my already sore arms. "Sorry, Princess. But we upped the wards and also spelled the building so nobody can to teleport in or out."

Actually, that was nice to know. "Thank you."

"It's my job. So long as you're on the island, my team is charged with your personal security."

I had my own secret service detail? Seriously. Oh, that was just wrong on more levels than I could count.

"I'd appreciate it if you could give us a couple minutes' notice before you leave the building."

I could understand that, having worked the other side of the equation. "I'll do that. I'm probably in for the night, though."

"Thanks." She smiled. "Explore the building all you want. Your suite is the top floor and has a balcony with an ocean view. It's a sheer drop, so there's no good spot for a sniper, and the space has been spelled. No chance of getting pushed off, either."

She was giving me more detail than I expected, and I appreciated it. Then again, she'd probably been briefed that I worked in security and was making sure I knew they had all the bases covered.

"Thank you."

"Again, it's my job. But you're welcome." She bowed and let herself out.

There was a lot to explore, all of it gorgeous and still comfortable enough to make you feel like you could put up your feet and unwind. I found Bubba in the TV room doing just that, watching football highlights on the big screen. Beside him were half a dozen empty beer bottles and a big bowl of buttered popcorn.

"Yo, Graves." His greeting lacked its usual warmth.

"Yo, Bubba." I walked behind the wet bar and opened the fridge. It was fully stocked with several different varieties of beer, juices for mixing drinks, and a few cans of soda. I grabbed one of the latter, flipped open the top, and went to make myself comfortable on one of the bar stools.

He didn't say anything, keeping his eyes glued on the game. *Shit*. Well, I could either sit here and let him give me the cold shoulder or grab the bull by the horns.

"Bubba, I'm really sorry about the *Mona*. I told you I was into something bad, but I didn't expect it to be *that* bad."

"It's not the boat." He dropped his feet to the floor, rose, and went behind the bar to get another beer. Twisting the cap off, he tossed it toward the waste can . . . and missed. He never misses. He was drunk. *Holy crap*. Bubba can hold his alcohol. He must've had a lot of beer—more than the empties indicated. Still, his feet were absolutely steady as he came around the bar and took the stool next to mine.

"How many years have we known each other, Celia?"

He was using my first name. Not good.

"A few."

"You've been to my kid's birthday parties, helped me pick out Mona's anniversary gifts."

This was going nowhere good. "Yeah."

"And you never told me you're a princess? That you have your own freaking *secret service detail*?"

I interrupted him before he could get any more outraged. I needed to nip this in the bud. I'd thought he was pissed about the boat. This was worse. He thought our entire friendship had been based on a lie. "I know. How weird is that?" I shook my head in disbelief. "I'm a bodyguard and they give me bodyguards?"

He opened his mouth, but I waved him to silence.

"Bubba, you've met my gran. You're my mom's bail bondsman, for Christ's sake. You've seen the house where I grew up. I didn't hide anything from you. Until Vicki's wake, I had no idea any of this shit existed. I swear it to you."

"But—"

"I didn't even know I had siren blood until after the vampire bite. If the bat hadn't tried to bring me over, the talents wouldn't have manifested and none of this would've happened. To be honest, I didn't really believe the woman when she told me I was siren royalty. I mean seriously, that is so . . . *Disney*."

Surprised, he choked a little on his beer but managed to swallow it. "Oh, God, I'm picturing you starring in that movie—the one Sherry likes so much."

Sherry was his daughter, eight years old and every inch the little princess down to her rhinestone tiara and pink tulle bedroom. She had her daddy wrapped around her little finger and had made him watch *The Princess Diaries* with her over and over again.

I rolled my eyes, but it was mostly for effect. He was grinning like an idiot. *Thank God.*

"Can it, Bubba."

He started humming. I didn't know the theme song for the movie, but I'd be willing to bet that was what it was.

I grabbed the first thing I could reach on the bar—one of those little foil bags of roasted nuts—and flung it at him. He caught it in midair, giggling like a lunatic. He ripped it open, still chortling. It took him a minute or two to settle down. I didn't mind waiting. We were going to be all right. I was glad. I don't have enough friends to be willing to lose one over something stupid.

He ate a few nuts with a chaser of beer. I sipped my soda.

"I called Mona, told her what happened."

Oh, shit. Mona was gonna kill me. "Maybe it's a good thing I've got those secret service types."

He choked again and this time he wound up coughing. I patted him on the back. A useless gesture, but I was pretty sure he didn't need the Heimlich.

Tears were flowing from his eyes. "Oh, God, Graves, don't *do* that to me."

"Sorry," I apologized meekly.

He shook his head. "I told her about the imp. How you stood toe-to-toe with it, damn near bare-ass naked, and fired a One Shot of holy water down its gullet."

He sounded awed and it made me blush. It sounded a lot more impressive than it was. Honest truth, I hadn't had a lot of choice. I mean, it was a frickin' *boat.* It wasn't like I'd had anywhere to go.

"You know what the wife said?" He was chortling now, his big body shaking with mirth.

"What?"

He imitated his wife's voice as best he could: " 'Very impressive. But tell me something, Bubba. Why was Celia running around your boat naked?' "

"Oh dear."

17

I could so get used to this. The bed was heavenly, with the perfect soft-to-firm ratio and sheets with a thread count so high they ought to cost as much as my car.

My suite was elegant and gorgeous, and since the security was so good, I'd felt perfectly fine leaving the French doors to the balcony open so that I could listen to the waves and smell the ocean breeze.

I woke to a light tap on the bedroom door. "Who is it?"

"Creede. You decent?"

"Hang on a second." I jumped from the bed and pulled on one of those ultra-thick terry-cloth robes you can only find in the really high-end hotels. Belting it tight around me, I called out, "Okay, come on in."

The door opened and Creede stepped inside. Once again, everything that was *him* preceded ahead of his body and I fought not to shiver. He took a long look around, taking in the solid oak cabinets, dresser, and built-in desk equipped with a top-of-the-line computer. The curtains were dark gold, the color a perfect match for the carpet, which had also been color-coordinated with the cream-, gold-, and brown-checked comforter. There were half a dozen throw pillows in brown and gold, although at the moment most of them were piled in the far corner of the room rather than on the bed.

A conversational group was arranged at the other end of the room, all of the furniture expensive, comfortable, and color coordinated. The final touch was a beautiful abstract oil painting that used all of the colors in the room. It was huge, taking up most of one wall. It was gorgeous, the kind of thing I could stare at for hours, noticing more and different details. It probably cost more than the house I was buying from my gran.

Creede did a slow turn, taking in the sights. "Nice."

"It is, isn't it? Yours?"

"Oh, it's not bad. But it's not like this or Dahlmar's. Then again, I'm not royalty."

He was trying to sound casual, but he was tense. I could see it in the tightness of his shoulders, the way he kept flexing his hands. He looked a little worse for wear. There was a big bandage on his cheek. His jeans were gone, replaced by a pair of drawstring sweatpants, his nice blue polo shirt by one of Bubba's T-shirts. It was black and showed a slavering bulldog with the caption *Who's the bad dawg?* So very Bubba.

He gave me a long, appraising look. "You have clothes?"

"I sure as hell hope someone's going to find me some. The lavalava's nice, but you can only wear something like that so long." I gestured toward his ensemble, "And somehow I don't think Bubba's loaners would fit me."

Creede wandered over to take a seat on the couch. I took the love seat directly across from him, curling my legs up onto the seat beside me. It was worth it to me to stare him square in the eyes. "Thanks for banishing the imp yesterday."

He scowled. He was a tough guy and I'd just broken rule one of the *Certified Tough Guy Manual*. I'd said "thanks." You don't do that.

He cleared his throat uncomfortably and I wasn't sure if it was just because I'd said "thanks." "Seemed the least I could do under the circumstances." Which was the acceptable way of saying "thanks" to me for my part in the rescue.

"So, what have I missed?"

"Quite a lot really. I'm not even sure where to start."

He shifted his weight and there was a tension to his posture I didn't like. Something had gone wrong. I didn't know what. I wasn't sure whether it was important. But something had definitely gone wrong. I raised my brows, encouraging him to spill. He did, sort of.

"Queen Lopaka met with King Dahlmar. Privately."

I wasn't certain why that was bad. But it did seem a good time to bait John about the charm I'd learned he made. "I'm surprised he'd be willing to talk to her without a protection charm. I wouldn't have thought he'd trust her not to screw with his mind."

Creede smiled, a swift baring of white teeth. "He didn't." But he didn't seem inclined to elaborate and I didn't feel like pushing. Not when he was in this mood. "And while they were doing détente, the sirens interrogated Bobby."

Bobby must have been the only surviving attacker. Talking about him, Creede's voice was too flat, too matter-of-fact. We'd finally hit the sticking point. *Thank God.* The suspense had been killing me. I tried to think what the problem was and it occurred to me. Bobby was the name of one of the guys who'd come with Miller to the restaurant. It had to bother

Creede that someone he knew, had worked with, had tried to murder him. But I was betting that wasn't all of it. I tried to meet his eyes, but he wasn't looking at me. He gazed out the French doors, as if the sky and sea were utterly fascinating.

"A woman, probably a siren, was manipulating Miller magically. It's tied back to Dahlmar and his problems. Apparently she figured with you in the hospital and out of the way, he'd come to us for protection. So she screwed with Miller's head, turned him against me."

Whoa. So Miller's rage-filled betrayal was against his will? That moved the whole issue from simply sad to criminal. "Did they find out who it was?"

Creede looked at me then, his eyes as cold and hard as Arctic ice. "No. He told them everything else. No problem. But when they tried for that, they hit a block."

I cringed at the razor-sharp edge in his voice. I've heard of psychic blocks. They were never good. "What happened?"

"It broke his mind. Left him a drooling idiot."

I didn't say anything. There wasn't anything to say. I mean, yeah, he'd been trying to kill us. But there are worse things than death and I'd count what happened to him as one of them—and I hadn't known the guy. Creede had.

"Why didn't she just influence you both not to take the case? That would've been easier."

He gave me a haunted look. Reaching beneath the neck of his shirt, he pulled out an amulet—a feather tied to a small sack with silver wire and what looked like a suspiciously familiar long blond hair. "She couldn't."

"So you *did* come to visit me just so you could hijack my DNA, didn't you—you bastard."

He shrugged, not admitting but, more important, not denying. "Ivan had one like this. They're hard as hell to make and it's a constant drain on my power." He gave me a fierce look, filled with pride. "I may not be Bruno DeLuca, but I managed it. I managed to repower Ivan's so Dahlmar could have his little chat with Queen Lopaka safely."

I didn't say anything. I didn't like that they'd taken the charm from Ivan's dead body, but I also didn't like Creede making one from my hair. But it wasn't my call. All's fair in the bodyguard game. I'd have done the same in reverse. Ultimately, it was practical. King Dahlmar needed protection from the sirens. Ivan didn't. Not anymore. But I didn't like it.

"I first guessed what you were when we were guarding Cassandra. Her reaction wasn't normal, even for her. So I stole some of your hair from your hairbrush in the bathroom at your office. Made myself one of these as insurance for whenever you were around—just in case you were more than you appeared to be."

I didn't like that. But it was also my own fault. I'd been careless, leaving things out in the open. Yes, it was my office. But if Creede could get bio samples, so could other, less savory types. Note to self: start locking the hairbrush and toothbrush in the safe.

"I don't know how the siren knew she couldn't manipulate me, but she did."

"Could she have come by the office? Sensed it on you then?"

"Maybe," he admitted, "but I think I'd have noticed."

I shook my head. "Not necessarily. It's a big building, with a lot going on. Miller might not have felt the need to tell you about the meeting. Hell, she might have forced him not to."

"Maybe," he repeated. Silence stretched between us for what seemed like an eternity. Finally, he spoke again, his voice harsh, angry. "I was going to use magic to trace the hair in the amulet Ivan made for Dahlmar to find which siren is behind all this."

"And?"

"The spell didn't work."

"Maybe she wasn't in range."

He shook his head. "I don't think so. From what they tell me, anybody who's anybody was here for the hearing."

"But that doesn't mean they stayed after the ceremony was over. I know a couple of them can teleport and there's an airport on the west half of the island. If I was working security, I'd have gotten everybody important off-site as fast as I could once the demon showed."

"Maybe you're right." He leaned back into the couch, looking tired and more than a little depressed.

"Speaking of Dahlmar, where is he?"

"He's sleeping in and Bubba's on the door." Creede's face darkened, his disapproval patently obvious. *Well, yeah.* Bubba was probably still drunk, but it wasn't like the king was a . . . *wait a minute.* I abruptly realized what the problem probably was. "Creede, have you been guarding Dahlmar?"

"Well, of course. *Somebody* had to." The implication being that I hadn't. That'd I'd been screwing around while he did all the work. *Um, no. Time to disabuse him of that little notion.*

"Creede, before we met up at PharMart, did Dahlmar actually hire you? Sign any paperwork like, oh, I dunno, a *contract*? Give you any money?"

It took a full ten seconds for that to hit him. When it did,

Creede's face was a sight to behold. His eyes widened and he opened and shut his mouth two or three times as he tried to come up with something appropriate to say. *Poor baby.*

I let out a small chuckle. I wasn't really laughing at him, but . . . well, yeah, I guess I was. But he's been in this business a lot longer than I have. To make such a rookie mistake deserved a little teasing. "Of course not. Because he doesn't have any money. If he did, would he be running around in a frickin' Mickey Mouse T-shirt? Oh, he's probably got money stashed somewhere, but unless he goes to the U.S. government and claims asylum, he can't get to it—and the second he does, the opposition will be able to track him."

Creede just stared at me, so I continued. "I came on board your little operation for one purpose: to introduce him to the sirens. I did it as a freebie because he pulled all sorts of major strings to keep me from being locked up. Now he's here. He's met the sirens. My job's done. Don't be thinking I'm your backup or anything. You'll be disappointed."

"So you're not protecting him. He's on his own?" Creede didn't exactly sound judgmental, more curious and embarrassed.

I sighed. "Oh, I'll probably help his ass. I like him. Besides which, the people he's up against are using spawn and maybe full-out demons and are probably the same people who put a death curse on me. But he's safe enough here. He doesn't need me watching him. Queen Lopaka isn't going to let anything happen to him. I need to get what information I can and rest up while I've got the opportunity. Question is, what are you going to do?"

Creede grew thoughtful. "People think they're using demons, but it backfires and before long the demon's using them—they're an open door to our world."

"Yup."

"George Miller was my partner for years and my best friend longer than that. Somebody connected with this used him and destroyed him."

I nodded.

"I'm in."

"I figured as much. But why don't you let Bubba go back to bed?"

"I'll do that." Creede grinned. "Poor man has a helluva hangover. You should've warned him not to try to keep up with you now that you have an unfair advantage."

"I was drinking Coke and he was pretty far gone before I even got here. I'm not thinking he's loving the whole lap of luxury thing."

"Whereas you, *Princess*, seem to be doing just fine."

"Don't make me throw peanuts at you." I pointed a finger at him in warning and was rewarded with a puzzled look. I laughed it off. "Never mind. Private joke. But you need to get out of here. I've got to dress and get something to eat. I went to bed late, but it's been close to four hours—"

"Right. Wouldn't want to wind up a snack. I'll go." He rose. "But if magic isn't going to help us find our siren, how are we going to track her down?"

I sighed and stood, following him to the door. "Do you really think we'll have to? She wants me dead, wants Dahlmar dead. I figure all we've got to do is stay in one place."

"You think she'll try again."

I lifted one shoulder, mostly in defeat. "Don't you?"

We stood there staring at each other for a long moment, him in the doorway and me with one hand on the door. Tension appeared between us, fully formed, like that moment when he pulled his hand away from my leg. There was fire in the back of his eyes—real fire. The strongest mages always have a flicker of magic that you can see when you stare deep. Bruno's eyes had always sucked me inside until that flame surrounded me. Even as a human I could feel his magic, but when I was a vampire it had blown me away.

Creede's magic wasn't as powerful, but there was a weight to his gaze that had nothing to do with magic. It unnerved me. Not only because of the intensity of it but also because of the charm around his neck. He leaned closer as my hand froze on the door, my fingernails digging into the hard wood, not because I didn't want him to come closer but because I did.

He was close enough now that I could feel his breath like heat on my skin. He might not have me in a total binding spell, but something had me frozen in place.

"Yeah. I do." The words were powerful and full of meaning, but I'd forgotten the question. He closed his eyes then and I tensed. But he just took a deep, slow breath, as though smelling the air around me. A full-body shudder overcame him and he shook his head before turning without a word.

It was at least a full minute before I could move again, and when I shut the door I was shaking.

18

Dahlmar and Lopaka were in meetings again, so I had some time to kill. I spent it using the computer on my desk to catch up on stuff at home. I'd qualified for the loan. I'd need to swing by the bank when I got back. Mom was in detox. Apparently she'd gotten the DTs in jail. Gran was upset but hanging in there. The news that I'd be able to buy her house cheered her up quite a bit. Of course she wanted everything to happen now. When she found out I wasn't in town and couldn't take care of it immediately she got downright snappish. She was even madder when I told her I probably wouldn't even be back in time to take her to church Sunday. I was glad to hang up the phone.

E-mails were plentiful and informative. Warren's friend was okay. She'd had car trouble, but it was fixed. She'd invited us to come up to dinner next week. Unfortunately, the "us" referred to me and Bruno, which ripped the scab right off that wound. The next message only heaped on the salt.

Emma had arrived in New York. The apartment was amazing. The office was amazing. Irene was amazing. Everything was just . . . amazing. Emma's boss was in and out of meetings the first day, but she expected Em to jump right in. In fact, she'd be flying out this morning on the corporate jet for a business trip. She sounded excited and incredibly happy, but I could tell she felt a little guilty, too. After all, my life pretty much sucked right now. I sent her a quick note telling her not to worry and that I was happy for her. That accomplished, I shut down the computer and went to take advantage of the spa-style bathroom facilities.

There were lots of mirrors, so I was able to check out every inch of my body. Good news, it didn't look like I'd be getting any new scars from yesterday's little adventure. Yay. Considering how bad the burns had been, that was pretty remarkable. I was vain enough to be relieved.

I'd poked around in the dresser before stepping into the shower. Someone (I was guessing Hiwahiwa) had gone to the west side of the island to shop for me, so when I was clean I pulled on brand-new everything. Of course whoever it was had based her choices on what I'd been wearing the first time she saw me, so it was a little more goth than I was used to, but the clothes were clean and comfortable. She'd even done a good job of guessing the size of my bra and panties. Then again, she'd gotten to see them.

I blushed furiously and tried not to think about that too hard. I needed to get over my embarrassment about nudity. Hell, I'd been wearing as much as most people wore around the pool. But it just wasn't the same in my head. I wasn't sure quite how to cope other than to pretend it hadn't happened. Easier said than done.

Lunch killed another hour or so, but by mid-afternoon I was bored out of my mind. Creede was with Dahlmar. Bubba had gone to the west side to see what replacement boats might be available in his price range. I had nothing to do and lots of empty hours to do it in.

Salvation came in the form of Agent Baker and an invitation from Queen Lopaka's personal seer.

> *Queen Lopaka has told me of the curse you bear. I believe I can be of assistance to you in unraveling the mystery surrounding this. If you would like me to try, I will be home most of the day. My daughter, Agent Baker, will be happy to escort you here.*
>
> *Pili*

Baker drove the golf cart on a road of sparkling white gravel that wound snakelike through the manicured jungle plants of the queen's compound. A pair of guards, male this time, jogged alongside. We moved at a nice steady clip through a secluded group of buildings that had been designed in such a way that while they were actually fairly close together, they had been incorporated into the landscape so well that they were practically invisible to one another. I was told we were a couple of miles from the village where the royal staffers lived and quite a few miles from West Island and the cities. Baker suggested that, if I had time, I should head west and see the sights, maybe even go clubbing. A lovely thought, but I doubted I'd get the chance.

The grounds were amazing. The birds were spectacular, too. Some of them were as bright and colorful as the flowers. I found my depression and frustration falling away as we drove. We finally came to a stop in a little gravel parking area. Looking up,

I could barely see the outline of a small building up among the trees, on a rocky hill, almost completely hidden from view. We had to walk the last hundred yards or so straight up stairs that climbed a hill steep enough that my calves hated me for it. But there was a waterfall and the sunlight cast rainbows through the mist thrown up by the water as it hit the pool. Gorgeous. Absolutely breathtaking.

A woman was waiting for us at the top of the staircase. She was old and withered looking, with skin tanned until it was the color and texture of an unshelled Brazil nut. Her gray hair was coarse and curly, shorn close to her scalp. Her eyes, an odd, almost metallic gold with flecks of copper. She was wearing a lavalava in the rich blue-green of Caribbean waters, with a white tank top that bared the sagging flesh of her upper arms.

"Thank you, Helen. You can wait below." It was a politely worded order. Baker might be a bodyguard, but this was her *mom*. Still, she looked to me to confirm. At my nod, she started back down the path.

"My name is Pili and you are Celia. Welcome to my home." She extended her hand and I shook it. She led me around the last bend in the path and onto a paved patio that provided a glorious ocean view. The breeze that played with my hair smelled of salt water and flowers. The roar of the waterfall was background noise, as were the calls of the many birds hidden in the distant trees.

"It's beautiful."

"Thank you." She let me stare for a minute or two before she said, "We'd best get inside before you burn."

She was probably right. *Damn it.*

I walked through the door she held open, into the dim, artificial cool of an air-conditioned living room. The living area held a bamboo-framed couch with worn floral cushions plus a pair of comfortable-looking chairs, all arranged around a glass-topped bamboo coffee table. On top of the table was a silver-rimmed crystal bowl half-full of water.

She lowered herself onto the couch, gesturing toward the chair across from her. "We have some time. Our queen and your king have made their agreement. The plan is in place, but we must wait on the usurper."

My king. I didn't really think of Dahlmar that way, but technically he was. I was both an American and Ruslandic citizen legally now. Did the whole princess thing make me Serenitian? And was that even what the sirens called themselves?

"You want to know when the curse was placed on you and by whom. And since your prophet is back on the mainland, I thought I might assist."

She leaned forward and I felt a pulse of power hit the water. There was a sound like the ringing of a bell and images began to form.

I felt myself falling forward, the images passing me like mist. They rolled backward in time, moving so fast that I could only catch faded glimpses: the fight on the boat; the fight in the desert; the standoff with the demon in the parking lot at Anaheim Stadium. Each deadly event was represented.

We're looking at events the curse has created or influenced.

There were certainly a lot of them. I shuddered at the image of the vampire attack that almost had killed me and had changed my life forever. But I almost threw up when we reached the night of Ivy's death. I didn't want to see that. Wasn't sure I could bear reliving it. Fortunately, it quickly rolled past.

I was twelve, nine, six. Close calls I didn't even remember— a car running a red light and almost hitting me; being swept off my grandpa's boat in a sudden squall. The images were more solid now, and in color. Finally they slowed to normal speed.

I was playing with a ballerina Barbie on the floor of our house on Parker Street. I recognized the worn russet brown carpet and the plaid couch and matching chair made from fabric that was well nigh indestructible. I could hear Mom giving Dad a friendly lecture on taking care of my sister and me. There'd been such love between them. I remember that time, if only barely. "The baby's asleep. She *shouldn't* need anything—"

"Lana, will you relax? You're just going to the store for a few minutes. We'll be *fine.*"

Tears pricked my eyes as I looked into my past, at my parents. They looked so young, so happy. You'd never know, looking at this pleasant little domestic scene, that it would all go so horribly wrong.

"I know. I know." She went up on tiptoe to give him a kiss. "It's silly, but I worry."

"We'll be fine. I'm not a total incompetent." He shook his head with amusement. "Besides, Celia's here. She'll help me. Won't you, baby?"

I looked up from my play to nod yes.

"Well"—my mom smiled—"I guess there's nothing to worry about, then." She gathered up her purse and her shopping list from the coffee table and hurried out the door.

She hadn't been gone more than five minutes when there was a light tap on the front door. My father went to answer it. The door opened. The child me continued playing.

"You will take me to see your daughters."

It was a female voice and there was power in it. My father didn't answer, didn't hesitate. He simply stepped aside and let her in.

I should have been able to see her face. In the vision I hovered above the scene, watching everything. I *should* have seen. But I couldn't. I could see her perfect legs, the three-inch heels in a shade of blue-green that perfectly matched the color of her raw-silk suit. I could see the coil of shining dark hair in a French twist. But her face was a blur.

She knelt down beside me on the carpet, smoothing the line of her skirt with her hands.

"Hello, little one." The voice was pleasant, musical, and there was a pull to it that was almost irresistible. "Give me your hand." I looked up at my father for confirmation, but he was just staring off into space. He'd left the front door open, too, which was weird. He was always scolding me, telling me not to "let the air-conditioning out."

I set down my doll and put my hand in hers. She held it tight, too tight. She started saying something that I could not understand. Heat surged through her hand and into mine and I started to scream.

I fought. Not that it did me any good. I was a child. She was an adult, too big and too strong for me to make any headway, and my dad was useless. He just stared. I squirmed, punched, and kicked to no avail. I bit her hard enough to draw blood and she cursed. The flames of magic that had been focused on my hand spread to hers and she was forced to fling me away from her to break the spell.

I lay on the floor, curled in the fetal position, whimpering in agony. Cradling her hand, she rose. Blood dripped onto her skirt and onto the carpet in a trail leading to the nursery. A moment later, the baby began to shriek.

A dark mist began swirling into the vision, obscuring the images and making them blur. As if from a distance, I heard Pili gasp, felt her gathering her power. She was trying to break loose but to no avail. I pulled back, trying to close my eyes and break the connection. It was hard. I felt overmatched, much like the child I'd been in the vision. With growing dread, I watched a shape begin to take form as the dark mist began gathering itself into something solid and terrifyingly familiar.

A voice, thick and rich as dark chocolate and far more sinful, greeted me. A demon. The same demon we'd driven off in the parking lot of Anaheim Stadium. He chuckled, as the snake must have chuckled to Eve. "Well, if it isn't my little siren—and not a priest in sight."

Pili slid bonelessly to the ground. I could feel her life force fading as the demon bled her power to make himself corporeal. I was screaming and it made him smile, his sensuous lips twitching with amusement at my terror.

He was just as beautiful as I remembered. Glorious. A fallen angel. Lesser demons are hideous. Greater demons are breathtaking enough to make you weep.

"Will you *stop*? It's quite annoying and won't do you the least bit of good. Besides, you don't really want to be rescued, do you?" A delicate gesture of his hand and my screams cut off. I was still *trying* to scream, mind you, but no sound was coming out. I couldn't move. He smiled at me and my heart leapt for joy. Even as the sane part of me shivered in terror at the knowledge of what this ancient creature of unimaginable evil would eventually do to me, I wanted to please him, worship him, do *anything* to have him smile.

He gave a low wicked chuckle and my body responded, almost painfully. A moan escaped my lips as my nipples tightened and I grew wet with aching need. I reached out to the water, even as I struggled against my own actions. He likewise reached out, and only that thin layer of water kept our hands apart. He let my tension build, seeming to savor the whimpering sound from my throat that was equally hopeless and eager.

"Yes, I think I'll have you, siren. To toy with you physically as you slip into madness . . . yes, that would be an amusing distraction. As soon as I manifest, you'll give your body to me and your downfall will be complete. What form should I take when we join? Your wolf? The mage who rejected you, or the new one who fights his desire for you?"

Even as my mind shrieked in fear at his words, my body ached. I wanted . . . *needed* . . .

Crash! The glass of the bowl shattered and filthy water, smelling of sulfur, sprayed in an arc and poured onto the floor. I jumped back, more from instinct than intent, and managed to only get sprayed with a couple of drops. But those drops burned just like the acid sprayed by the lesser demon. I screamed in shock and pain.

I could scream.

I was free. He didn't have me. He didn't *have* me. I blinked, practically sobbing with relief.

Adriana stood over the broken bowl, holding a broom handle like a club. Smoking burn holes marred her jeans and blouse, showing scorched and blistered skin. Her hair was braided, pulled back tight away from a face that was drawn in grim lines, her eyes blazing with fury. Helen Baker was kneeling by her mother. "You"—Adriana pointed to the nearest guard—"get Ren. We need holy water and a doctor. Now."

"Yes, ma'am."

I forced myself to stop screaming, swallowed my fear along with the taste of bile. My knees were shaking. But I was upright.

"Sit down before you fall down," Adriana snapped. She dropped the broom, rushing over to join Baker where Pili was sprawled on the floor. I couldn't tell whether or not the old woman was breathing. I started to take a step forward, to see if I could help. But the world swam when I did.

One of the guards grabbed me and shoved me forcibly into a chair. Pressing on my back, he forced my head between my knees.

"Breathe. Deep and even. Just keep breathing."

I breathed. Slow and steady. When the world steadied, I lifted my head to see Adriana and a third uniformed guard giving CPR to Pili. I heard: "I have a pulse," followed by weak coughing.

"Oh, thank God." Adriana sat on the floor, looking utterly weary. I wasn't positive that she wouldn't have keeled over had her back not been propped up against the wall. CPR is hard, nerve-wracking work.

Ren appeared, priest in tow, and disappeared an instant later—no doubt in search of a doctor.

The priest stared wide-eyed at the acid water eating its way through the floorboards. Praying fervently in what sounded like Italian, he opened a black valise and pulled out a plastic gallon jug of holy water.

I didn't watch him. I was looking at Adriana. "How did you know?" My voice was still a little hoarse and breathy. I was shaking. I couldn't seem to stop. I knew it was over and my feet were as far from the smoking mess of acid as I could get them, but I couldn't seem to get warm and I couldn't stop shaking.

"Pili told us last night that she was going to do this for you. I felt it start even over at the palace. I felt when it went wrong."

Ren was back with the doctor. Pili was stirring now. She was still terribly pale and too weak to sit up. But she was breathing and moving. She was alive.

"You should have the priest look at her. Bless her. Just in case."

Ren turned to the priest, her Italian fluid and fluent. He frowned and nodded but didn't immediately move to obey. Instead, he continued praying and pouring holy water around the edges of the pool burning through the floor.

She spoke more sharply, her eyes flashing with irritation.

He didn't like that. Not one bit. He snapped out a retort. She rose and opened her mouth, but Adriana interrupted her, using her full name to get her attention.

"Eirene! Let him do his job. He knows better than we do what the lingering effects of this sort of thing can be."

"You do not give me orders," she snarled at the other princess, her beautiful face distorted with fury. Adriana stiffened and I decided to intervene. We didn't need them to get in a catfight. Now was so not the time.

"Can it. Both of you." I spoke quietly, without a whole lot of inflection. Frankly, I didn't have the energy. "He was a greater demon and he nearly manifested right here. Unless we want there to be a permanent weak spot in the realities where he can come and go at will, you need to let the priest do his job. That's more important than who outranks who."

"You—" Ren opened her mouth to say something hateful. I could see it in her eyes. They were narrowed, darkened slits.

"That is *enough*." I turned to find Queen Lopaka standing tall and regal in the doorway, flanked by Chiyoko and the dark-haired queen whose name I hadn't been given.

"Daughter, enough. Please." The dark-haired queen stepped out from behind Lopaka to meet Ren's gaze. For just a moment I thought she'd argue. She was so angry—angrier than the situation deserved. It didn't make sense.

There was a pause and if her mother said anything to her mentally, it wasn't for public consumption. Still, Ren calmed fractionally and gave a small formal bow to her mother, who reached forward to stroke her daughter's fiery hair with a withered hand.

The temperature in the room began to drop and a ghostly wind stirred. Ivy. *Not now. Please. Not now.* I was too tired to deal with one more thing, even the ghost of my baby sister.

The dark-haired queen's eyes widened, then narrowed, and she gave me a glare hot enough to blister.

Her name is Stefania, said Queen Lopaka's calm voice in my head. *It was a planned insult on their part, not giving you their names. I didn't push the issue. I pick my battles carefully. As should you.*

Good advice, no doubt. I gave a slight nod of acknowledgment. Stefania was still bitter and almost as unhappy as Ren. Then again, I got the impression that this was their normal state. The pleasant, happy Ren of my first encounter had apparently just been a really good acting job. At least the argument was over.

Now if Ivy would just settle down.

What is the matter with your spirit? Adriana's voice in my head this time, sounding almost intrigued and not at all afraid. Then again, Vicki hadn't been able to do much against her the night of the wake and she was a considerably stronger ghost than my sister.

She's not my *spirit. Her name is Ivy. It's my younger sister's ghost. She's trying to warn me to be careful.* Which was the absolute truth. But it felt like more than that. She wanted to tell me something important. Unfortunately, now was not the time or the place. I tried to form that into a thought that she would understand—while at the same time keeping that same thought from everybody else in the room. No easy task. I wasn't sure how successful I was at it. While Ivy seemed to settle, Queen Lopaka's expression grew very carefully blank. Rather than meet my gaze when she saw me watching her, she turned to the priest. They held a rapid conversation in Italian and I wondered if I was the only person in the room who wasn't multilingual. While I know a handful of Spanish words and phrases, they aren't exactly the kinds of things you say in polite company.

"He will cleanse the house and says that the two of you who were directly involved should be blessed. If this is done soon, there should be no lingering effects."

He spoke again, his words rapid and intense. Queen Lopaka translated for him, "We were most lucky. Had the process gone farther—" She gave an elegant shudder and repeated, "We were lucky."

The doctor looked up. "We need to get this woman blessed and to bed as soon as possible. She overstrained her magic badly. She shouldn't be left alone for the next few days. Someone needs to be with her at all times. After that, she'll need to take it very easy and not use her powers for the next few months. But ultimately, barring complications, she should be fine. Physically."

I felt the knot in my stomach start to unwind a little. Pili would be fine. Helping me hadn't killed her, hadn't even done permanent damage. Thank God for Adriana being nosy. If she hadn't been snooping, things would've been so very much worse.

I shivered, thinking again of the demon. He'd marked me, somehow. I needed that blessing, needed it badly. Because until I got it, any time there was a weakness in my vicinity he could exploit it to come after me. I'm not a true believer. I don't have a clean enough conscience to withstand the demonic on my own. I shivered hard, feeling as though I might never get warm again.

Baker spoke softly to one of the other guards. She lifted her mother by her armpits and her companion took Pili's feet. They carried her down the hall to the back of the house, where I assumed there must be a bedroom.

"You were the other party to the vision?" I glanced up. The doctor was standing above me. I hadn't noticed him coming. Not a good sign. I was cold. So cold. Shock. I was going into shock. Maybe my vampire healing would take care of it. I tried to remember when I'd eaten last. Lunch . . . I'd had lunch. But I had no idea how long I'd been at Pili's.

"Yes."

He bent down, shining his little penlight in my eyes. I pulled back, letting out an involuntary hiss that, unfortunately, gave him a really close-up view of my elongated canines.

"Ah, so you're the abomination."

If he was trying to make me feel better, it wasn't working. Something about being called that just pisses me off. Still that little rush of anger and adrenaline seemed to warm me up a little, make me a bit clearer headed.

"I was hoping I'd get the chance to meet you while you were on the island, but I would've preferred other circumstances." He pulled out a tongue depressor. I opened my mouth and stuck out my tongue so that he could take a good look. "You're practically a medical miracle." He smiled. It was a nice enough smile that I almost forgave him the abomination comment. Almost. "I'm Dr. Ryan."

He was good-looking in that clean-cut, middle-aged way. His dark hair was cut short, his features even, pleasant but not really remarkable. He wasn't wearing a lab coat, just khakis and a melon-colored polo. I could easily picture him out on the golf course, playing a round with Dr. Scott. Maybe they shopped at the same stores.

Dr. Ryan frowned, "You're having trouble focusing, aren't you." It wasn't really a question, but I nodded. "You're a little shocky. You need to get some rest."

"What time is it?" I interrupted him before he could finish his lecture.

He frowned but checked the practical diver's watch adorning his wrist and told me.

I panicked a little. I'd lost quite a bit of time. "Shit. I need to eat. Now. I'm overdue." Fortunately, I wasn't feeling like munching on anybody. Maybe it was the shock. Whatever the reason, I really couldn't count on it lasting.

Queen Lopaka was standing a few feet away. When she heard the tension in my voice, her eyes unfocused for a second. "My chef will have everything ready and waiting for you at the guesthouse."

"Thank you."

"You are welcome."

Stefania crossed the room, stopping a bare inch from Queen Lopaka, very deliberately invading her space. She was practically quivering with rage and just looking for a fight.

"If my daughter's *services* are no longer required, we will go." The bitterness in Stefania's voice was palpable. She glared up at Lopaka, eyes blazing with defiance. For just a second I thought the high queen would call her on it. Claim insult the way Adriana had against me. But Lopaka swallowed her anger, meeting Stefania's rage with seeming indifference. "Of course the two of you may go."

The room waited breathlessly as Stefania opened her mouth to say something. She apparently decided against it. Clamping her jaw shut with an almost audible snap, she stormed over to where her daughter stood. She slid an arm around Ren's waist and I noticed the withered hand again.

I was slow, probably from the shock. I knew that the damaged hand was important, but it took me a moment to recognize the implications. Maybe it was the way she flipped her head, making that shining braid glimmer in the light. For just a moment our eyes met and a spark of something clawed through my chest. The memory of those eyes chilled me to the bone. *Crap.*

It was her. Stefania was the one who'd cursed me . . . cursed Ivy. But *why?* It made no sense.

"Yes?" The word was almost a hiss. I couldn't know whether she was listening to my thoughts or realized I knew and expected me to confront her or was just being a bitch. It could be any of them. But Lopaka was right. Now was not the time for a confrontation. Stefania was a queen. They'd never believe me if I made the accusation and certainly not without evidence.

So I lied. "I just wanted to thank Ren and Adriana. They saved us all."

Stefania's eyes narrowed. She didn't believe me. But whatever she might have said in response was cut off by Queen Lopaka's agreement. "Yes, Eirene, Adriana, thank you. You did well."

Ren gave Queen Lopaka a stiff, unhappy bow to acknowledge the praise. With one last look at me, Ren and her mother vanished.

I hadn't accused them. Without motive and proof, I couldn't. But I could find the motive, get proof. Could and would. Because Stefania's curse had quite probably killed my baby sister. Stefania was going to pay for that. One way or another, she was going to pay.

19

Rage is almost never a good thing. Rage makes it hard to think, hard to plan. Now that I'm less than human, it brings the hunger to the surface, makes my powers manifest in ways that are obvious and terrifying. Still I could not help but feel a fine, burning rage at Stefania. She'd cursed *children*, one of them an infant. She probably had some sort of reason, but let me tell you, no reason would be good enough. What she'd done was so wrong, so *evil*, it made my skin crawl. It also made my skin glow. The only thing keeping my vampire side from fully manifesting was the shock and exhaustion of having faced down the demon.

I took the tray of food I'd found in the kitchen of the guesthouse up to my suite, settling down on the couch with the balcony doors thrown wide open to let in the fresh air. The day wasn't that hot, the air conditioner wasn't running, and I was feeling more than a little claustrophobic.

Pouring a mug of soup and another of coffee, I tried to calm down, to clear my head.

Somebody had to have called the demon onto this plane of existence. Working with demons taints a person, alters their thoughts and feelings, subtly at first, then more and more obviously. Both Stefania and Ren had been acting odd and very aggressive. Personally, I was thinking Stefania was the prime candidate. She'd been with Queen Lopaka when Pili had asked permission to work with me. A woman who would put a death curse on a six-year-old and an infant was capable of pretty much anything.

Yes, Stefania was my girl. But I was thinking that as quietly as I could. I didn't know how much, or which, thoughts the sirens could/would be listening to. They probably had some social rules about eavesdropping. But good manners weren't going to keep my enemies from rummaging around in my brain. Still, now that I could communicate telepathically, there were other people to include in the discussions.

Well, not *people*, per se.

Ivy, are you here? The overhead light flicked on and off. *Am I right? Is she the one who cursed us?* The light flickered and the temperature in the room dropped like a stone.

You're absolutely sure? A single flicker and frost began forming on my glass of fruit juice.

Ghosts are spirits of the dead tied to something or someone they've got unfinished business with. Ivy's business was with me. I'd always assumed that she wants me to forgive my mother. If that was the case, she was going to be with me for a long, long time. But maybe she was bound to earth to find her murderer. Not the men who kidnapped us but the person who had cursed her to that fate when she was only a baby.

Ghosts were once human, but it's important to remember that they aren't human anymore. They have their own powers, their own agendas, and their own limits. Ivy wasn't a terribly powerful ghost. She'd never be able to take over someone's body the way Vicki had at the Will reading. Ivy had never done any really impressive physical stuff. But she had one ability that all ghosts shared. Access to knowledge. Because the spirits of the dead . . . I don't want to say they "talk" to each other, because it's simpler than that and more profound. It's almost as if they have a shared consciousness. They're still individuals. But what one knows they all know. If Ivy was certain Stefania was the one who cursed us, it was because she had access to information I didn't.

And ghosts can't lie.

I know you want to get even with her. A single flash of the light confirmed it. *I do, too. But we've got to be careful. She's powerful and smart. Can you be patient while I handle it?*

Nothing. No signal at all. Which I suppose meant "maybe."

Do you trust me?

The answer was slow in coming, but eventually the light flickered once. *Yes.*

Will it make you happier if I promise to include you in whatever plans I make? The light flashed almost before I could finish the sentence.

All right, then.

"You should probably talk to Maintenance about that light."

Creede stood in the open door to my suite looking much spiffier than the last time I'd seen him. He was wearing gray dress slacks and a black Ralph Lauren polo shirt. A black leather belt and matching dress shoes completed the outfit. I had to admit, he certainly did clean up nice. *Really* nice.

"You went shopping."

"Yeah. I needed a few things. I picked up some items for King Dahlmar while I was at it. Thank God for credit cards." He smiled. "Mind if I come in?"

"Sure, why not?"

He strolled through the room to take the seat directly across from me. Leaning back, he crossed his legs, the perfect picture of comfort.

"So, I hear you managed to get yourself into some more trouble while the king and I were otherwise occupied. You okay?"

"Better now that I've eaten and rested." I sipped my drink, which was, thanks to Ivy, quite nicely chilled. "What have you been up to besides shopping?"

"Hey, don't knock it." Creede pointed a finger at me in mock warning. "It was hard enough on Dahlmar, begging Queen Lopaka for assistance, without making him do it in a Mickey Mouse T-shirt."

I could see where that would've been gratuitously humiliating. It would also make it harder for him to be taken seriously. Appearances matter more than most people are willing to admit.

"And how did the negotiations go?" I was going to switch from fruit juice to broth but decided against it. *Cold broth. Ick.*

"Well, we have a plan."

I thought about saying something sarcastic like, "Gee, John, you sound so excited, tell me more," but he was obviously frustrated, so I decided to opt for diplomatic silence.

"Queen Lopaka doesn't completely agree that there's a siren involved, but she's willing to give him limited assistance to help him take back his throne."

I raised an eyebrow and took a long pull on my coffee as I waited for the other shoe to drop. "How limited?"

"One plane, one pilot, and a dozen elite troops: their equivalent to the Navy Seals."

My eyes widened and my mouth opened. "She thinks that's enough to put him back in power?" *Crap.* That wasn't a plan, that was assisted suicide.

"Adriana is a clairvoyant; she saw a potential weakness in Kristoff's plan that we might be able to exploit even with limited resources."

Creede leaned forward in his seat. His expression was intent. "From what we've been able to find out, from the clairvoyants and through magical means, Kristoff is going to announce his brother's death from a 'tragic accident' this afternoon. The faux Dahlmar will immediately fly back from the peace talks in Greece. Somewhere over the Aegean the plane will go down, with all hands lost, leaving Kristoff to take the throne."

Just like Dahlmar predicted. I wondered if the king had more going for him than just a charismatic personality.

Yes, that plan would make Kristoff a mourning successor rather than an evil usurper in the minds of the people. Not a bad idea, really. Sadly, not all that hard to pull off, either. One of the reasons I hate flying is one well-placed curse and it's all over but the crying.

"If King Dahlmar takes Queen Lopaka up on her offer, we're going to fly to an island in the Aegean where the necessary modifications will be made to our plane to make a switch possible. The clairvoyants have given us a time and place *and* the identification information for the plane Kristoff is crashing—"

"They're going to try a *switch*?" I couldn't believe it. I mean, yeah, I believed it. But oh, crap, there were so many things that could go wrong.

"Princess Adriana gave it an eighty percent chance of success."

"Eighty?" She had to be being optimistic. I wouldn't even have gone as high as fifty-fifty.

"She seemed to think there was the possibility of betrayal." He said it totally deadpan, but there was a twist to his lips that spoke of wry humor. "She was more than a little concerned about it since she's going to be the pilot."

And then I put two and two together. An island in the Aegean.

"What?" Creede read my face like an open book.

"Would the island we're using just happen to be ruled by Stefania?"

Okay, there's desperate and there's stupid, and I was beginning to think this plan leaned more toward the latter than the former. I might have opened my mouth to say something, but the king himself appeared at my doorway at that moment. He was dressed in a gray suit, off the-rack but nice, with a crisp white shirt and conservative tie. But the shoulders beneath the jacket were hunched, as if the blows he'd received these past few days were finally starting to catch up with him.

"I have no choice. I have no military. I am not willing to reveal my circumstances to any other country's leaders. My hope was that the queen of the sirens would support me in order to clean her own house. This is not a perfect plan, perhaps not even a good plan. But it is the plan we have with the resources available."

He appeared calm, but I suspected the appearance was deceptive. Still, you don't go into a tricky military operation with a sense of defeat. It's too likely to become a self-fulfilling prophecy. "It would be easier to walk away. But I cannot. Whether my son is being manipulated or has betrayed all I hold dear, he is not fit to rule. I cannot leave my people to suffer at his hands." Sorrowful but determined, he continued, "I will be leaving here at seven this evening. You may choose for yourselves whether you will join me." With that, he left.

Well, hell.

"I did some research. He's a very good king," Creede said softly.

"From what I understand, his son's an idiot."

"So we go?"

I sighed. "I just wish it wasn't Stefania's island."

"Why?"

I hesitated for a long moment but finally told him: about the curse, the fact that someone had to have summoned the demon. Stefania had one hell of a motive to make sure we didn't survive the attempt.

Creede surprised me when he shook his head. "It couldn't have been Stefania who called the demon today."

"Why not?"

"She was in the meeting with Dahlmar, Lopaka, and Adriana. I was outside the doors. None of them left the room until after your meeting with the seer went south. And I checked them myself to ensure nobody was a demon in disguise."

Well, hell. That sort of messed with my theory. "So, she's responsible for the curse but not the rest of it?"

A shrug. He didn't disbelieve what I saw in the crystal bowl, which was something at least. "It's possible."

I snorted at his carefully blank expression. "You don't believe that any more than I do."

He rose with a sigh. "No, I don't. But I pray you're wrong. Because Dahlmar's determined to do this. And if you're right, everyone on that plane is going to be dead meat."

"Get some rest," I told him. "I'm going to go talk to my aunt."

20

I hate flying. Big plane, small plane, private, public, it really doesn't matter. I hate it. This time I hated it more than usual when I found out that Stefania and Ren had teleported ahead to "get things ready" and wouldn't be flying with us. I'd have felt more secure having Stefania right here where I could both keep an eye on her and have her as sort of a hostage to good behavior.

Still, I couldn't fault the jet. It was midsized and very nice. Even nicer than Creede's car, which was saying something. Adriana was rightfully proud of it. I just hoped it wasn't going to be a really nice coffin.

The plan had changed slightly. Britain is an island and the British have very old, very secret, ties to the sirens. Queen Lopaka had called in a favor from that other queen. The switch would take place on a military airstrip. No one on our side knew, other than the family: Queen Lopaka, Adriana, and me. It felt really weird, but I had to admit I was glad to be included. We would keep it that way until the last possible moment, so we could watch all parties for signs of trouble.

The head of the task force, Harry Thompson, had introduced himself and his men to those of us civilians who were coming along. While he hadn't said a word against us, his approach had somehow made it abundantly clear that he wasn't happy to be joined by a bunch of amateurs, however well armed, and that we'd damned well better stay out of his people's way. He'd then disembarked and made a nose-to-tail inspection of the aircraft. Creede had already checked for magical problems, but that didn't stop Thompson and his men from checking again.

The task force's mage was at least equal to Creede and just shy of Bruno's talent. At first the two men had watched each other with skepticism that bordered on hostility. Then they'd started crafting, and their hostility turned first to grudging acceptance of each other's talent and then to open admiration.

Everything else that could be done was being done. Still, I found myself squirming in my seat, wishing I were anywhere but here.

I didn't have to do this. I could get up, walk out, leave King Dahlmar and the others to whatever fate awaited them. Thompson would be thrilled to see me go. One less civilian to worry about. I'm a bodyguard, not a magician, and not—I repeat *not*—an elite ops soldier. I could even justify it by saying that the death curse on me put everyone in more danger. Nobody would argue, nobody would blame me.

Nobody but me.

If I walked out now and everything went to hell—literally— I'd spend the rest of my life trying to live with the guilt. I'm still dealing with two deaths like that: Ivy and Bob Johnson. Every day I wake up I still wonder—what if I'd done this, or hadn't done that. I might not be able to make this mission a success, but I could protect King Dahlmar with my life.

Somewhere in the course of gathering my courage I'd closed my eyes. I opened them at the sound of a soft cough to find Hiwahiwa standing in front of me, wearing a more casual version of the lavalava in green with a leaf pattern. Even without makeup she had an undeniable beauty. She looked excruciatingly uncomfortable and hesitant to interrupt, but frankly, I was glad for the distraction. Now that I'd made up my mind to stay, I needed something to keep me from thinking too much.

"Can I help you with something?"

She flushed and I wondered what I'd said wrong.

"There is a teenager outside named Okalani. She claims to have an appointment to meet with you."

Oh, crap. The kid. I'd said I'd talk to her. But I hadn't had time, not with everything that was going on. And now we were leaving and there was a good chance we wouldn't be coming back.

"I'm sorry, Hiwahiwa. I've been so busy. . . ."

"I realize you are leaving and there isn't much time. But this matters so much to her—"

"No, it's all right. We don't have a lot of time, but I'll do what I can."

I hadn't even finished speaking when the kid stepped out of the empty air in front of me, trying not to look scared in her very hip low-rise jeans and neon green tank top. She was prettier than I remembered, and young. So damned young that she made me feel ancient.

Everybody out of the plane now. Adriana's voice sounded in my head and everyone around me rose with an urgency just short of flat-out panic. Something had gone terribly wrong.

Before we could move toward the exits, I felt the world lurch sideways and every person on the plane was suddenly standing on the tarmac a hundred yards or so from the jet. Which gave us all a perfect view of the fireball when it exploded.

21

I don't like this, Celia." Queen Lopaka's voice was cold and harsh. Two spots of red had appeared high on her cheeks and I wouldn't have been surprised if the storm gray of her eyes would've been flashing with lightning, given her expression. "If it had not been for pure chance and Okalani's extraordinary talent, I would have lost my daughter and many of my people. We have a traitor in our midst. Proceeding further is simply too much of a risk."

We were in the palace, in the beautifully appointed office where Queen Lopaka did the work of running the siren kingdoms. The floor was covered with thick carpet the color of sand, carpet that felt the same underfoot as walking across a quiet beach. Two entire walls were windowed, looking out over manicured gardens and, in the distance, the Pacific. There were curtains, but I got the impression they were seldom closed. I would've had to close them. The view would've been too distracting. I'd never get anything done.

Now, however, I was having no trouble focusing at all. Because the queen and I were having issues. "I understand, Your Majesty." I kept my eyes down, my voice even. "But the jet had been inspected, *thoroughly* inspected, by your people and mine just minutes before. The only way someone could've planted that bomb was by teleporting."

"There are others with that capability."

And thank God for that, I thought. But I didn't say it. Gran would be so proud. She's been working with me on not mouthing off since prepuberty. Of course I was dealing with a telepath, so Queen Lopaka probably heard me anyway. Maybe she'd appreciate the effort.

"You believe that Eirene is the siren involved in Kristoff's coup."

Hell, yes! Her mother, too. And we only have one chance to defeat them. I kept my lips zipped, but I thought it loud. Gulls began to swoop outside the window as I got more agitated.

The queen paused, glaring at me. I had told her my suspicions about Ren and Stefania before. When the evidence was circumstantial, she'd been willing to take the steps of switching landing sites "just in case." Yet now that we knew we were betrayed she was reluctant, not wanting to risk any of her people on what she considered a bad bet—even if she might secure a strong European alliance and flush out a pair of dangerous and highly placed traitors.

Creede, Adriana, and I were arguing in favor of Plan B: acting as though everyone on board had died and hiding us out of sight until Kristoff's press conference, then having Okalani teleport us into the middle of it.

It was bold. It was crazy. And it just might work. If the queen would let us do it.

Adriana spoke up. "Your Majesty . . . Mother. If our enemies believe they've succeeded, they'll let their guard down. If we are going to attempt to help King Dahlmar, this could be a priceless advantage. I've seen an eighty-five percent chance of success with this new plan."

"And if we're wrong? If they are innocent?"

I thought—but quietly—*You have got to be kidding me!* She couldn't be that deep in denial. What did I have to do to make her believe me? Show her the memories?

Yes. Adriana answered my thought.

Well, shit. Of course. Who could do the deed? Pili was down for the count.

Adriana answered me. I guessed she was projecting to both of us at once given the look in Queen Lopaka's eyes. Nifty.

I can do it. I might not be strong enough to take you through all of your memories, but we know what to look for now, know when it happened. If I show you, Mother, if you can see this for yourself, will you give King Dahlmar the aid he seeks?

Queen Lopaka let out a frustrated breath and slammed a fist down on the desk, eyes flashing. She looked just like . . . me in that moment. *Why is this so important to you, Adriana? Why do you press so?*

Adriana let out a low noise that was like a refined growl. Her eyes glinted with righteous anger. *She cursed children, Mother. She brought demons onto the soil of our island. This cannot be allowed to stand. If in helping ourselves we can help an ally as well, then it is well and good.*

Queen Lopaka stared into her daughter's eyes for a long moment. When she finally answered, it was as if she'd aged a decade before my eyes. "Show me."

It took very little time. We knew the memory we needed, so there was no searching, no spooling through my life and the damage the curse had inflicted. Adriana simply took my memories and played them out as an image above the tropical fish tank against the wall.

Queen Lopaka sat, silent and still, for a long moment after the scene had played out. Neither Adriana nor I dared move.

When the queen finally spoke, it was in an intense whisper. "It's her. I recognize her, even without seeing her face. I knew she was desperate for Eirene to rule, knew she was capable of much to achieve it. But cursing our own children? Such *evil*—" She shook her head and a single tear trickled down her perfect cheek. "Dear Goddess. Stefania . . . why?"

I didn't know what to say in the face of her obvious pain. I'd expected her to be angry. God knows I was. Then again, for me it was personal.

She wiped the tear away with an impatient gesture and turned to me. "Do what you will. You have my support."

I gave a low bow and started toward the door. I'd barely gone three steps when her voice stopped me. I turned back to see an expression on the queen's face that I'd seen in the mirror more than once. Contrite, pained. "I'm sorry, Celia. I should've believed you. Know that I would've protected you had I known."

There was nothing to do but shrug. "You didn't know."

"But I should have." Something in her voice told me that this failure would haunt her for the rest of her life.

Just like me.

They put us in a large conference room with attached restrooms. Everyone who had been on the plane was there, along with a couple dozen more of the queen's Elite Guard—a special-forces unit that worked together like a well-oiled machine. Creede is one hell of a mage. His concentration and attention to detail were impressive. He, the guards, and the mage squad formed a force to be reckoned with. The minute we were all behind closed doors, the mages set up a magical perimeter so tight that even Okalani couldn't have teleported through it. Nothing was going to break that barrier: not sound or sight and certainly no magic. The power of it burned across my senses when I tried to test it, and the air in the room felt thick enough to drink. My ears actually popped two or three times, adjusting.

I wasn't part of the military end of things. The queen had given her orders; General Carson and his staff were calculating the best means of carrying them out. They went through the plan minute-by-minute, covering contingencies that might arise and what the response would be. The loss of the plane, despite their precautions, hadn't shaken them as much as made them angry and even more determined to succeed. Before, they had been content with implying that the civilians should stay back. Such subtlety had been abandoned now, with Thompson taking Creede and me aside and bluntly telling us to "stay the fuck out of our way." They didn't like that we were being brought along. But Okalani was our transport and King Dahlmar had insisted that Creede and I be his personal bodyguards.

The clairvoyant was starting to display the image of the press conference on a wall of the conference room when I felt a massive blow hit the shield. It had a pinpoint focus and two of the mages responsible for the protections nearest the doors fell in their tracks, eyes rolling back in their heads. A third staggered, only keeping himself upright by force of will—and because he had a table to lean on.

No one knew what was happening. Medics rushed to aid the fallen. Creede looked grim and rushed toward the door with me at his heels.

A second blow, followed by a sensation like maggots crawling across my skin. I smelled sulfur, tasted bile. I started swallowing convulsively to keep the contents of my stomach *in* my stomach.

Someone out there meant business. With the shields crumbling I could hear the sound of fighting in the hall. Gunshots, boomers, and screams of pain were all clear to me.

"What is it?" Okalani stared at me wide-eyed.

"Get to the other side of the room, *now!*" I ordered as I pulled the 9mm I'd been given to replace my trusty Colt.

"It's going to fall," Creede announced. "I can feel it."

"Carson, you hear that?"

"Civilians to the far side." He barked out other orders and his people moved into place with crisp efficiency.

Okalani ran to the far side of the room to join Princess Adriana, King Dahlmar, and most of the others.

Carson sidled up beside me, weapon at the ready. "You do realize that you're technically a civilian," he said coldly.

"Bite me." I flashed fangs. I felt the shield wavering. It wasn't going to last much longer.

Creede's grin flashed bright for just an instant, fading as he started counting backward. "In three, two, one—"

The shield fell and the door and a fair part of the wall were blasted into pieces—not by the demon I'd been expecting but by good old-fashioned explosives.

The ground shook and I dropped to one knee. The blast deafened me and the combination of billowing brick dust and smoke was thick enough to make me choke. Chaos reigned. I could barely see through my streaming eyes. Adrenaline kicked in and with it vampire powers. My vision shifted into hyperfocus and time seemed to slow so that it felt as though I had an eternity to take it all in.

Carson was on one knee beside me. He raised a fist in a signal to hold positions. We froze, guns ready.

Through the smoke I saw Queen Stefania, with more than a dozen of her personal guard surrounding her. They had taken out the half dozen of Queen Lopaka's Elite Guard who'd been hiding behind magic in the hall. But more than a few black-clad bodies were down as well. Stefania had to know she was almost out of time, that reinforcements were coming. But she refused to give up. Eyes blazing, she turned and pointed directly at me.

Me? Why me? What the *hell*?

I used every bit of vampire speed I had to hit my belly and crawl as fast as I could, moving toward the limited shelter offered by the nearest pile of debris as guns fired, aimed at where I'd been an instant before. Whether I'd moved too quickly or just benefited from the smoke and confusion, her men lost track of me for a second. I used that second to fire directly at Stefania. The shots should have taken out most of her chest, but they didn't even hit. She had some sort of shield, a force field protecting her. My bullets just bounced off as she laughed.

Well, wasn't that just dandy?

I ducked down again and scurried to another pile of debris as her people turned their sights on my position.

Our troops had moved forward, cutting off Stefania's soldiers, forming a wall of resistance between them and me. I was grateful for the cover and for the time. I needed to think. We needed to take down Stefania.

But a force field? That was freaking impossible. No way in hell should she be able to do that. And then it occurred to me—it was exactly that: the power of hell, the magic of a demon, protecting her.

The nine clicked empty. I slid it back into its holster. I drew a different pair of weapons and began moving carefully, keeping under cover as best I could, using the chaos to my advantage. I couldn't get too close. But with the right angle, I didn't have to be close. I adjusted my weapons, gauged the angles, and emptied both One Shots of holy water against her shield.

The invisible barrier flared like magnesium, then fell. When it did, I pounced.

The thing is, when you rely on a demon's magic for too long, you get overconfident. She'd lost her ability to fight. Taken by surprise, she went down hard. It was amazingly satisfying to punch her right in the face with every bit of my strength. Her cheek collapsed under the weight of the blow and blood rushed to the surface of her skin, instantly forming a blackish-purple bruise.

But she got her wits about her quicker than I'd anticipated. She got her legs under me and kicked me off, hard enough to send me flying at least ten feet. She stood and started to stalk forward.

Bullets began to rain on her from a dozen different directions. Blood and flesh exploded from each impact as her body did a gruesome, jerking dance before toppling face-first onto the ground.

A male voice filled my head. I recognized it as the voice of the greater demon, no longer syrupy sweet but so angry his very voice was a bludgeon. *This isn't over, Celia. I will have you.*

I retched from the force of the intrusion. If Creede hadn't caught me, I'd have fallen. He helped me to sit, shoved my head between my knees, and surrounded us both with a shield that pushed the demon away.

Those few of Stefania's troops who were still alive laid down their arms as Queen Lopaka arrived with the reinforcements. They kept her guarded behind a wall of troops until every last enemy was bound. Only then did she step out from behind her guards to walk over to where Stefania lay.

I rose, a little unsteadily, and went to join her, as did Adriana and Hiwahiwa.

"She's not dead." I was shocked. There was no way Stefania could possibly have survived her wounds; from the look of things, most of the blood had drained from her body. Yet that same body still drew ragged breaths. I felt my stomach heave again. You'd think the vampire in me would be attracted to all the blood, but it wasn't. She was just raw, bloody meat and I wanted none of it. I asked, of anyone who could answer, "Why isn't she dead?"

Queen Lopaka spoke softly. "We are immortal, for the most part. Jealousy can kill us. That, and certain special magical weapons." She knelt on the bloody ground, her trousers instantly becoming soaked with gore. Reaching beneath her jacket sleeve, she drew a knife—the knife I had given her. Thrusting her left hand into Stefania's hair, she pulled the wounded woman's head up sharply, exposing a length of pale neck. Their eyes met and Lopaka's went frighteningly cold.

"You are relieved of your throne, sister." She slashed the knife across that pale expanse of skin, but there wasn't enough blood left in Stefania's body for it to spray.

The vanquished siren gave one long, violent shudder and was still.

22

was in shock. Again. The doctor said so. They wrapped me in blankets, fed me chicken broth mixed with something. It was insanely good and I wasn't really sure I wanted to ask about the secret ingredient.

Someone herded me into the infirmary. I didn't see who. Didn't see much of anything, really. I kept slipping in and out of focus. Some kind soul had brought me a tall mug of hot coffee. Warmth, food, and caffeine were slowly beginning to work their wonders.

"This is insane!" Creede snarled. "The whole plan should be scrapped. There's no way we still have the element of surprise, and without it this is a suicide mission. You can see for yourself, she's in no shape to do anything."

Queen Lopaka sat in a chair next to the bed I was sitting on. She was listening calmly and politely as everyone around her shouted and argued.

"I have seen—" Adriana's voice was cold, hard.

"Seers have been wrong before," he interrupted her. "No offense meant." The apology was perfunctory and I wasn't positive he meant it. Apparently he and Adriana weren't hitting it off.

"I've seen it. The rest of the clairvoyants have seen it. It is necessary." She gave me an odd look. "And Celia is tougher than you think: tougher than I would've suspected."

"I don't like it," Creede growled. "It smells like a trap."

"You don't have to like it," Adriana snapped back. "What do you think, Mother?"

Everybody turned to the queen, including me, though I felt like retching when I did. Concussion, thy name is Celia. "King Dahlmar has to do this if he is to have any hope of regaining his throne. He intends to go forward with the plan, with or without Celia's participation."

"Without," Creede snapped. Adriana opened her mouth to begin the argument anew but stopped at a small gesture of the queen's hand.

"That's up to Celia."

"I'm going." I stood up and threw off the blanket. I didn't even wobble . . . much. "How much time have I lost?"

Creede answered me, his tone making it clear that he didn't think I'd be ready. His growl was almost protective enough to be sweet. "We leave in a half hour."

But I don't need protection, though I appreciated the gesture. "Good. There's time. I'm going to need some more of that broth and I need somebody to get me a phone."

Adriana passed me her BlackBerry. "Use mine."

"I'll get your food." Hiwahiwa rose. She'd been so quiet, back in the corner, that I hadn't even noticed she was there. I nodded my thanks as she hustled out the door. Sliding open the phone, I dialed a number I knew from memory.

"DeLuca residence." I didn't recognize the voice. Not really surprising. It sounded like a kid, and several of Bruno's siblings had been breeding like bunnies. I'm not sure how he can even keep track of them all.

I didn't bother with greetings. If I started in on the niceties and checking on all the family I could be talking for a week. "I need Matty's direct number. It's an emergency."

"Hang on. He's right here." By the muffled sound of what followed, the kid had put his hand over the speaker. It didn't make a difference to vampire hearing. "Uncle Matty, it's for you. She says it's an emergency."

He took the phone. "Hello?"

"Matty? It's me."

"Celia . . . look, I'm really sorry, but—"

I interrupted him before he could say more. I didn't want to talk about Bruno. I couldn't even afford to think about him right now. There was no time and I couldn't afford the distraction. "Matty, this isn't about Bruno. It's about the demon, the one you helped banish in the stadium parking lot. He's back and he's actively trying to get into this dimension."

Matty didn't swear, but I could tell he wanted to. He gave a sharp intake of breath and there was the sound of a door being firmly closed. "Tell me."

I did. Even talking as quickly as I could, it took a few minutes to cover it all. But he was a good listener and smart. He let me get it all out before he started asking questions.

"So one of the summoners is dead, but there's at least one more out there."

That pretty well summed it up. Someone was still pulling the strings and my money was on Ren. A family that summons together and all that. "Yes."

"And he's targeted you specifically? Spoke directly into your mind?"

"Yes."

"All right. When you were hurt last time, when the demon actually touched you, what did the priests at the hospital do?"

"They cleaned the wounds with holy water and blessed me. Why?"

He swore again. "They didn't do a full exorcism?"

"No. I wasn't possessed. They didn't think it was necessary."

Matteo gave out a growl that would do Kevin proud in wolf form. "Is that what they said?"

"Yes."

"So they didn't do an exorcism."

Now I let out an exasperated breath and stopped pacing around the room. "Didn't I just say that? I think I'd remember an exorcism, Matty. They're supposed to be pretty intense."

He swore some more. I was pretty sure a few of the words weren't approved by the order. "All right. I can't be sure without looking for myself, but I'm guessing that what we have here is a breach. Working with demons stains the soul. The more you do it, the more of a tie you have with them. Eventually they can and do use the summoner himself as a doorway to get into our reality. Being injured the way you were marked you—creating a link between you and the demon. Killing the first summoner closed one door."

"But—"

"But you've been marked. If there's another summoner, that person can bring him over and he can use the mark to home right in on you."

It was my turn to swear. I wasn't precisely surprised, but I'd hoped for better news. "Is there any way to *un*mark me?"

Silence dragged on for what seemed like an eternity. "Maybe," he admitted. "If you were human, I'd suggest a full exorcism. But with you being part vampire—"

He didn't have to finish. I knew the answer. "It could kill me."

"Yeah."

I didn't even hesitate. Better to die clean than risk eternity with a demon. "How long would it take you?"

"Let me get in touch with a few people. In the meantime, get to a church—"

I interrupted him. "Can't. We're going after the other summoner. Is there anything we can do for now? Some sort of 'patch'?"

"You need a priest." His voice was hard, unyielding. "You'll be slaughtered without one. And if you die now, with the demon having marked you—"

I shuddered. I couldn't help it. The problem was there weren't any priests on Serenity. Ren had fetched the one this afternoon from freaking Italy. Then again, knowing what I did now, that could've been a stalling tactic. But even if there was a local church, they certainly hadn't ever needed one of the militant orders. No monsters. Not until now.

"I'll catch the next plane."

I shook my head while everyone in the room stared at me. The sirens' expressions made me think they were eavesdropping through my own mind. Creede was probably listening in with magic. "There's not enough time."

"Make time, Celia. I'm serious. People will die, but that's nothing compared to what will happen to you."

Pale and trembling, Okalani began tugging at my sleeve. They'd brought her to the infirmary to be checked for shock. She'd come up clean, but she and her mother hadn't left yet.

"Hang on, Matty." I covered the receiver. "Yes, Okalani?"

"I can bring him here. I just need to see where he is." She was scared enough that I could see white all around the pupils of her eyes. But she was determined, too, and smart. I hadn't even thought about what she was proposing. Good kid.

Tell Matteo I'm going to be joining his thoughts, Adriana ordered. I did, then watched as she began concentrating. On the other end of the line, I heard Matty swear yet again. A moment later, Okalani gave an abrupt nod and vanished. The call cut off.

It seemed like the longest few minutes of my life, waiting for Okalani to reappear. Hiwahiwa had come back with my food.

I felt the familiar lurch and Okalani and Matty were in front of me.

A Catholic priest from the Order of St. Michael, Matty is one of God's own warriors. He'd be impressive under any circumstances—the DeLuca boys aren't small and Matty works out hard. He was even more impressive than usual at that moment, having come prepared. He was carrying a black bag that looked like a doctor's bag; a large water cannon filled with what was probably a quart of holy water; a silver tube on a sling that I knew from past experience held communion wafers; and a sawed-off shotgun whose shells were undoubtedly filled with silver shot. Even the queen raised her eyebrows before putting one hand to her chest and bowing her head in a gesture of respect.

Matty opened the black bag, pulled out a small jar of oil, and stepped in front of me.

"All right. This is a short-term solution only. As soon as this is all over, you and I are going to the nearest church and doing the full exorcism. Understood?"

He sounded so much like his uncle Sal it was uncanny. Absolute authority. *Wow. Little Matty had grown up.*

"Yes, sir."

"All right." He took a deep breath, made the sign of the cross, and began murmuring a prayer in Latin. I felt movement in the air; it coalesced into heat. He poured a tiny amount of oil onto his fingers and anointed my head with the sign of the cross.

It burned. I screamed and dropped to my knees, blinded and gasping with pain, my eyes streaming tears. Seconds later, I could see again. People began to rush to my side, but Matty held out his hand for them to stop. His cross was glowing with a white light so bright it was like a tiny dwarf star.

Everyone stood still, but it was obvious they didn't like it. He continued to chant and I screamed as fast as I could draw breath. For long seconds I thought I might die, almost hoped I would, just to end the agony. And then, as abruptly as if a switch had been hit, it was over.

"You okay?" Creede was on his knees beside me instantly. He gently smoothed my hair back from my face and looked down at me with worried eyes. I was still too shaken to speak easily, but I nodded and managed to gasp out the word, "Peachy."

Matty snorted while Okalani gave a nervous giggle. But Creede just looked at me. After a long moment when he did nothing but clench and unclench one fist, he shook his head and pulled back. "I think this is a bad idea. You should stay here, rest, and recover."

I managed to half sit up. I didn't vomit. Yay, progress! "Would you, if the situation was reversed?"

"Yeah, I would."

"Liar." I smiled when I said it, to take the sting from the words. He didn't smile, but the corner of his mouth twitched.

Queen Lopaka shifted in her seat. She was still in her ruined clothing but, to my amazement, managed to look regal despite it. *If you are going to do this, you will need to go to the staging area.*

Do you think this is a bad idea?

She paused for a long moment before responding, *I think it is foolish but necessary.*

I blinked a little. Maybe it was the shock, but that didn't make a bit of sense to me. Lopaka gave me a gentle smile and explained, *Eirene must be stopped before she sets loose great evil on the world. The prophets told us there was a tainted child of our line who would destroy all traitors among the sirens and save the world from evil. When you were a child, Stefania's prophet must have told her that the savior would be you or your sister.*

That's why she cursed us and why she was willing to run a suicide mission to take me out in the conference room.

Precisely. So, foolish or not, you must go. This must end. When the time comes, you must not hesitate.

I won't.

She rose from her chair. Then she did something that shocked all of us. She *hugged* me. She let me go very abruptly and turned to her daughter. "I would speak to you for a moment." She drew Adriana to the far side of the room. She spoke softly—aloud rather than mind-to-mind. I didn't know why. Still, no one without vampire hearing would be able to overhear. I pretended I couldn't, either, gathering up my things as noisily as I could to make it harder for everyone else to hear what they said.

"I really wish you wouldn't do this, Adriana. I don't want to risk losing you."

"I'll never rule, Mother."

Queen Lopaka gave a gusty sigh, as if her daughter was being particularly dense. "I'm not worried about losing you as a princess. I'm worried about losing my daughter. I love you. It would kill me to lose you."

Adriana smiled. "You won't die, because I'll be careful."

"I could order you to stay."

The daughter and subject acknowledged that with a nod. But then she touched her mother's cheek softly. "Please don't. I want to do this. It's important. I need to be . . . to do . . . something important."

I didn't miss the change in wording. Neither did Lopaka.

Creede checked his watch, his voice all business again. "If we're doing this we need to get going." He strode toward the door. Okalani was right behind him. I followed her, stopping to hold the door for Adriana.

She gave her mother a fierce hug. "I love you, too. Try not to worry." She hurried past me and down the hall.

Hiwahiwa looked at me for a long moment, her brows furrowed and her face intent as she looked after Okalani. *Take care of the child. I'm no prophet, but I believe she's important. More important than we know.*

I'll do my best.

"Five minutes. Take your positions." The commander's voice cut through the confusion like a razor. King Dahlmar rose from his seat at the table where a group of us had settled in to wait, moving to take up a position in the center of the group. Creede rose next and reached his hand down to me. Normally I wouldn't need the help, but I really did feel like I'd been hit by a truck. Whatever Matty had done hadn't killed me, yay. But it had done me some damage. What remained to be seen was whether or not it was worth it.

"I'm coming with you," Matty said in a tone that brooked no argument. "You need me in case she summons that demon."

Creede looked at King Dahlmar, who gave a curt nod. Matty had blessed each and every person in our group. Those who weren't Christian weren't really sure what to think about the man in black with the cross, but a holy man is a holy man in pretty much every religion. It also surprised me that Matty was able to switch between languages easily and that the prayer he offered was slightly different for each person.

Creede stood directly in front of the king, Matty and I immediately behind Dahlmar; the four of us and Adriana were surrounded by a thick ring of soldiers. I felt my stomach tighten with nerves as a deep voice in the far corner began to count down from ten. At "one" I felt the familiar lurch, as if the world were moving sideways. I barely heard the word *"now"* and we were there.

23

It's one thing to see a plan play out in a clairvoyant's bowl. It is another to have it happen in real life.

I'd half-expected Okalani to run into a magical shield like the one we'd erected earlier around the conference room. Whether Kristoff was too arrogant, didn't have mages with enough oomph, or there were too many people going in and out of the room, he hadn't bothered.

We materialized into absolute chaos. The press conference was being held in a large room, but the space was crammed with press and equipment. The only clear spots were a small area in front of the stage and another small space between the table where Kristoff sat behind the microphone and his uniformed men stood guard.

We appeared in front of the stage, weapons at the ready. Okalani disappeared immediately and the mages who'd replaced those injured by the demon attack raised a barrier, sealing the room.

There were screams and the flashing of cameras. Kristoff's guards went for their guns and curses—and froze in place when King Dahlmar stepped into view.

Kristoff staggered to his feet so abruptly that the chair clattered to the floor behind him. He didn't realize the mike was live when he gasped, "No. You're *dead*," in a tone of unmistakable horror that made it absolutely clear just how unhappy he was that his father had made it home. Kristoff reached inside his jacket, probably for a weapon, only to be knocked to the ground and subdued by one of his own guards—a man loyal to the rightful ruler of the country.

In all the confusion, I shouldn't have been able to hear Matty's horrified gasp: "*Irene? Emma?*"

I turned and stared at the familiar faces that Matty was addressing . . . *Eirene?* Eirene, Irene, Ren. How stupid could I be?

Her perfect features were twisted in rage. Emma screamed in shock and outrage as Eirene grabbed her from behind and wrapped an arm around her throat. Emma kicked and struggled, scratching at the siren's arm, but Eirene had preternatural strength and knew what she was doing. She'd cut off enough of her captive's oxygen that Emma couldn't fight for long before she passed out from lack of oxygen. Still using Emma's limp body as a shield, Eirene pulled a small ceramic disk from her pocket. "You will let me go, now. Or I will summon the demon to destroy you all."

Kristoff reached out a hand toward her, panic etched on his face. "Irene . . . beloved, *wait*! Take me with you!" *Great, just great.* The prince struggled against the guards holding him, but they shoved his face to the floor with considerable force. When the guard jammed the barrel of his 9mm against the prince's temple, Kristoff stilled.

"Tell them, Celia. They do not believe me, but they

should. I will loose the demon." She smiled and it sent chills down my spine. God help us, a part of her wanted to do it. She'd used the demonic too often. The demon was gaining the upper hand. She thought she controlled him, but she was a fool. I could see it in her eyes.

"Let Emma go and I'll tell them to let you leave."

She laughed, just like I expected her to. But hey, nothing ventured— "You don't get to give me orders, Celia. No one is ever going to give me orders again. Adriana may be satisfied with the scraps of power the others are willing to throw her. I am not."

Matty struggled against the guards on our side to reach her. He still believed he could talk sense into her. I was sorry for that. Knowing that she was tainted by a demon, that she'd been in the DeLuca home, in the heart of their family—that was going to haunt him. "Irene . . . think of the baby. You have to give yourself up. We can help you."

That's when it really struck home with me that Bruno had lain with this . . . *creature*. He'd dated her, made love to her, and given her a child. Had he just been bewitched by a siren's charms, or was it a much deeper, demonic issue? That thought scared the crap out of me.

"Baby?" She sneered and there was an unpleasant edge of hysteria to it. "Ah, you mean the *lie* I told your fool of a brother." She turned to me. "There was no baby. I merely convinced the doctor to tell him that. But *you*—" She pointed at me with a long finger that was starting to blacken from her constant brush with the demonic. "You *didn't break*. I took your man from you. That should drive a true siren insane. But it didn't. You weren't destroyed. Not by that, not by the curse, not even when we killed your prophet. You were supposed to *break*, supposed to *die*."

At last I knew who was behind Vicki's death. That she'd remained in ghost form after we jailed the doctor said something was wrong. I was both relieved that she could finally have peace and heartsick that she'd been killed just to hurt me. She deserved so much better.

A man's voice came from behind me. "You'll never get away with this." It was a cliché, of course, but somebody had to say it. I suppose Creede was as good a choice as anyone else. "Give up while you can."

"I don't think so." She turned to Dahlmar. "Order your people to drop the barrier. Let me leave, or die with the rest."

He stared at her and for a moment I thought he'd take his chances, such hate blazed in his eyes. She'd cost him both his sons, nearly cost him his throne. I was sure he'd have his men shoot her through Emma's unconscious body.

I was right. At a gesture they opened fire and hit—nothing. Over and over again. The press were screaming and stampeding each other trying to find cover where there was none. Bullet holes riddled the wall behind where Eirene stood, but there was no blood. None at all.

"Cease fire!" I bellowed, trying to be heard over the deafening sound of too much gunfire in a confined space. "You're wasting your ammo. She's phasing in and out too fast." It was a smart move and not something I'd have guessed she could do. But it made sense. She might not be able to move out of the room, but she could teleport a fraction of an inch *within* the room and be dematerialized 99 percent of the time, giving them nothing to hit.

"Cease fire," King Dahlmar repeated, and the guns fell silent.

Eirene held the ceramic disk in front of Emma's face where we could all see it. "No more of this. I leave. Now."

Dahlmar's voice was cold, hard. But he gave the order she wanted: "Let her go."

The world lurched and they vanished. Eirene and the demon had Emma.

Oh, shit.

24

S this another one of Dahlmar's plans?" It was late evening and I was sitting in a cheap motel room. There wasn't much space, the whole place was probably only twelve-by-twelve, with most of the room taken up by a double bed. There was a dresser and a battered old television, a mini-fridge, a microwave, and one of those small prefab laminate tables, its surface pocked with cigarette scars. Helen Baker had set up a scrying bowl in the center of the table and was trying to sooth my frazzled nerves by showing me what was going on.

It wasn't helping. I was in a foul mood and trying not to take it out on anyone. Of course the only person I could take it out on right now was Baker, and she wasn't exactly the type to put up with it.

I looked up from the scrying bowl to the woman using it. Baker might not be as powerful a clairvoyant as her mother but had enough talent for this. She also had the added advantage of being able to do double duty and serve as a guard.

"King Dahlmar may have been involved in the planning, I'm not sure." She gave me a puzzled look.

"It just sounds like one of his plans." I drained the last of my packaged shake and tossed the empty can into the trash. I knew I should stop grumbling, but I couldn't seem to help myself. A big part of it was that the plan had been foisted on me. I hadn't been part of the process. I'd just been told what to do. I don't obey orders well. But the people in charge of this operation were all heavy hitters and I owed more than one of them my freedom and/or my life. So I went along . . . grudgingly. It didn't help that I thought it was damned cruel, allowing most of my friends and family to believe I was dead—to the point of actually holding the visitation and funeral. Only a very choice few were privy to the truth: King Dahlmar, Matty, Bruno, Kevin, Creede, Queen Lopaka and a couple of her people, and my grandmother. Too many, really. If you want to keep a secret a secret, you don't tell *anyone.*

"They couldn't have at least picked a *high-end* hotel for this?"

Baker laughed. "High-end hotels have security cameras and staff that actually pay attention to the comings and goings. Our people wouldn't be able to stand guard unnoticed."

True enough. But still. I couldn't help but look at the grubby carpeting again, not really wanting to walk across it in *shoes,* much less barefoot.

I turned my attention back to the scene playing out in the bowl. I'd been afraid Gran wouldn't be able to pull off the whole mourning thing, but I could see she was acting up a storm. Maybe she'd missed her true calling in life.

"You did actually die, you know. During the exorcism." Baker sounded impressed. I was guessing it was because of the exorcism, not the death. Being in the military, she'd probably seen plenty of the latter. Then again, the sirens aren't exactly a military superpower, so maybe not.

"So they tell me." King Dahlmar and Matty had arranged for me to have an exorcism right at the scene. A little unusual, but Creede's spell had actually held the demon away from me and they were afraid if they waited, the demon would be able to zero in again. I'd gone along because I wanted the demon mark off of me. If we were going after Eirene to rescue Emma, none of us could afford for me to have that kind of a weakness. First, Matty had cleansed the room, moving in smaller and smaller circles until only Creede and I were left. The closer Matty got, the worse I started to feel and the more Creede had to drain his own energy to keep the gate closed.

I didn't really remember the actual exorcism. I only remember Matty starting to chant in a singsong voice and then hideous, intense pain engulfed me for what seemed like an eternity. The pain was followed by . . . nothing. Light, air, and absolute quiet. I remember standing with Ivy and Vicki and that they wouldn't let me step past them. I vaguely remember Vicki pushing me down a long flight of stairs . . . and then there was pain again as apparently my soul rushed back into my body.

When I first woke, I'd been incredibly angry with Vicki. More than I had ever been before. Later, I realized what had happened and I was grateful. In what was very likely her last act on this plane of existence she'd saved me one last time.

I shuddered, my hand automatically reaching to touch the scars from where the demon had clawed me. Weird, that. Before the exorcism there hadn't *been* scars—just an invisible mark that had served as a psychic tie he could follow to find me anywhere. The full rite had cut that tie. Thank God there was a medic ready with the heart machine. It wasn't until after they revived me that the scars had appeared. I only wish I

were confident that the demon mark was gone. But I didn't
think it would be until Eirene was dead.

I watched the image of Dottie moving slowly up the aisle
with her walker. Her expression was solemn, not sad precisely,
more worried. I wondered then, if she knew. Clairvoyant that
she was, she might just have "peeked." It was something she'd
do. She looked up and I could swear her eyes met mine, that
she could see me watching.

"I just don't see the *point*," I protested. "What makes
anyone think my dying is going to bring Eirene out of the
woodwork?"

Baker explained it to me again, with only a hint of impa-
tience. "She is obsessed with you. You ruined her plans. You
have everything she wants. She will want to be *sure* you are
dead. And failing that, the demon possessing her wants you. He
felt you die. But if he can search all of the various planes of existence for you, he will not find you. And then he will wonder."

"That doesn't mean it'll draw them out."

"The bowl says otherwise. I've seen it and so have all of the
others."

I didn't say a word, just looked at her. She knew as well or
better than I did that the future is subject to change. And
while the odds got better if more than one clairvoyant got the
same images, that didn't make it certain.

"Fine. Our profilers and those of the church agree that it is
in the nature of this particular demon to require it of her. It
is most likely that he is the one in charge by now, whether
Eirene knows it or not."

That seemed likely. "But it makes no *sense*."

She threw up her hands in a gesture of irritated surrender.

"Celia, think about what you said. She's insane. He's a demon. Of course it makes no sense to sane humans. Why would it?"

Okay, fine. I could concede that, but I still didn't like it. Something about the whole plan just felt . . . wrong. I am more of a believer in planning than hunches—probably because I never was psychic enough to get hunches. But I could understand now why people believe in them. I was even more convinced something was wrong when the temperature in the room began to plummet.

"Something's happening." Could one of the ghosts have remained behind to see this through? Whoever it was, was trying to get my attention.

"We've got people surrounding the building. If something was wrong, one of them would warn us." Kevin was on guard, along with two more of Lopaka's people. Since he'd been missing since shortly after Vicki's death, no one would expect him to make it to my funeral. As a werewolf with a background in black ops, he was a good choice for a guard. Plus he'd insisted.

After all, Emma was his sister.

Considering his skill set and metaphysical power, I should've felt safe. Instead, I felt trapped.

Baker gave me a look. Whatever she saw in my face made her uneasy. She extinguished the scene playing out in the bowl, reached for her gun, and switched off the safety. I did the same thing with my gun, then patted my pockets, making sure everything else I packed was in place.

There was a tap on the door and a familiar voice whispered, "It's Kevin. We have a change of plan."

Uh . . . a change of plan? I don't think so. I pulled my One Shot left-handed. The little gun of holy water didn't require the strength or accuracy the handgun did. All I needed it was a quick squirt to make sure Kevin *was* Kevin. Call me paranoid if you will, but it keeps me alive.

Baker started to position herself behind the door, but I shook my head. She was strong, but she wasn't going to be strong enough to hold the door closed against whatever might be impersonating Kevin. Hell, I wasn't positive I was strong enough, but I had a better shot at it. So I passed her the squirt gun and got in position.

"We need to verify you're who you say you are," I said calmly. I wasn't feeling calm. It was turning into an icebox in here and several small objects were starting to levitate.

"Damn it, Celia, we don't have time—"

That was totally unlike Kevin and I flicked a glance at Helen. She scowled and nodded. Yeah, we were going to do this. *Shit.*

"Fine, then." I yanked open the door and Helen sprayed him.

It wasn't an impostor. Maybe we'd have been better off if it was.

I heard a soft *pffut* of sound, barely audible over the sound of the water hitting Kevin. Baker staggered back, slapping at her neck. Her gun arm rose but too slow. Kevin slapped it away as he hit the door with all his strength and weight.

Crap. Kevin had been turned. Or was he ever on our side? He'd left me a note after Vicki died that said he'd "be back for me." Was I one of his "hard targets"? As a sleeper agent, he could keep tabs on me and now he was going to kill me. I couldn't decide whether I was more angry or hurt that he was doing this. Probably an equal mix of both.

I pressed on the door with everything I had.

I'd thought I was strong, but I was not as strong as a big, mo-tivated werewolf. He shoved the door back like it was nothing. I dived out of the way, throwing myself between the bed and the window, and firing as I went.

I hit him. Square in the chest and hard enough to send him back a pace. But the bullet didn't do more than piss him off. He had to be wearing a Kevlar vest.

The ghost in the room tried to help. Everything that wasn't held down flew at Kevin's face. He batted it all away as I scrambled to my feet and turned to flee out the hotel window.

I'd climbed onto the heater/AC unit when he grabbed me by the leg and threw me onto the glass-strewn carpet. I tried to turn my gun on him, but he had my hand in an instant. *My God, the* strength *of him.* He pinned me with his body and his arms and there wasn't a damned thing I could do about it. God knows I tried, squirming, fighting, and screaming for all I was worth. I bit him with the fangs, but he healed almost before I could pull them out. I was careful not to swallow, though I wanted to.

But nothing made any difference. I struggled helplessly as Warren, the man I trusted more than anyone else—even more than Bruno—strode into the room. He pulled a dart gun from his pocket and shot me. The same way he'd shot Baker.

Damn.

I couldn't move. I tried. My body simply wouldn't respond. I could feel my skin resting against smooth leather uphol-stery, could feel the movement of a car, but I couldn't even lift an eyelid. I panicked then, because even though the adrenaline rushing through my system made my heart race until I could hear my pulse pound like a kettledrum in my ears, my body remained sullenly unresponsive.

"Please don't struggle. You'll only hurt yourself." Warren's voice was a disembodied and slightly mechanical whisper in my left ear. "I combined a curse with the drug in the dart. You won't be able to move a single voluntary muscle until Kevin says the word that releases you."

I felt a wave of pure unadulterated rage fueled by the pain of complete betrayal. These were two of the people I held dearest in the world. I would have given my life to defend them and they do *this*?

Warren's voice sounded in my ear again. Now that I thought about it, I could feel the headset attached to my ear. "I'm so sorry, Celia. I can only imagine how angry you are right now. But we had no choice. Irene contacted Kevin through his employer. She swore she would feed Emma, body and soul, to the demon unless we turned you over to her." He paused. "I can't let that happen. I can't." He sighed. "But I won't turn you over to that fate, either. So we've arranged a rescue."

My mouth wasn't working thanks to the curse. But I was thinking some pretty choice things about Warren, his son, and the fact that they hadn't seen fit to include me in the planning. Did they think I wouldn't have helped save Emma? Did they really believe I'd let her not only die but also be tortured to death and for freaking eternity? Because if that's what they thought, they didn't know me at all.

"They're using magic to watch us, so Kevin doesn't dare let on you're conscious. When the car stops, he'll unstrap you from the seat and take off the Bluetooth. There isn't much time, so you have to listen carefully."

It was a simple plan. They had betrayed me, drugged me, and stuffed me in my own car. I was now being delivered, like a sacrificial lamb, to a warehouse on the desert edge of Santa Maria. Eirene would be waiting there, with the demon and about half a dozen mercenaries. Warren didn't say how he knew about the mercenaries. My guess was that he had hired a clairvoyant—or maybe some of Kevin's coworkers had done manual surveillance. I'd once met one who had the ability to practically vanish—a more extreme version of the illusion that Bruno and Ivan had used. However they'd managed it, Warren was certain of the number and was confident in their abilities.

I was the bait. Kevin would bring me in for the exchange and get back Emma. At which point the nice folks at "the firm" would swoop in. Under the cover of the resulting chaos, I would escape and get Emma the hell out of there. Kevin was bringing me in the Miata so that I would have a getaway car.

It was a desperate plan, with every chance of failure. Still, it had the advantage of being simple, elegant, with success mostly dependent upon superior firepower. Of course I wasn't getting any firepower. The assumption was that we'd all be searched when they brought me in, so I was weaponless.

Can I say how much I thought that sucked?

"What the *fuck*?" Kevin didn't bother to keep the frustration and rage from his voice. The car began to slow. *Terrific.* We hadn't even gotten out of the car yet and something was going wrong with the plan.

I felt the car come to a halt and heard the whir of the window going down.

The man's voice was a Darth Vader imitation. He was using a voice synthesizer so he couldn't be recognized. That meant it was either someone I knew or someone Kevin did. "Cut the engine and step out of the car."

"Hello, gentlemen. What's up?" Kevin was trying to keep cool, but I could sense his emotions. He was lividly angry and scared. I didn't like it. He was the person everybody else feared. After a second or two of silence he turned off the car, apparently instructed by hand motions. He spoke one more sentence before the door handle jiggled from the outside: "What's the problem?"

A wave of power hit me like a sledgehammer as soon as the word "problem" left his mouth. The magic holding me back was released so suddenly it was all I could do not to give the game away by gasping or opening my eyes.

The Darth Vader voice spoke again: "Out. Get out. Now."

I heard the car door open, felt it shift as Kevin climbed out. I wanted so badly to move, to do *something*. But my one advantage right now was the fact that they thought I was unconscious. I had to bide my time and wait for the right moment. The truth was that I wasn't positive I could move yet. My hands and feet were bound. My seat belt was on. And the drugs hadn't worked their way out of my system.

Warren's voice in my ear, sounding afraid: "Celia. What's happening? I heard Kevin release you. What's wrong?"

I cracked open my eyes a bare slit. An armed guard was watching me through the window. So I didn't dare answer. Not out loud at any rate.

"Hands against the car." I felt the car shift as Kevin put his weight on his hands against the hood. "Feet spread and back." They were frisking him and the search was apparently pretty damn fruitful.

Warren. I still wasn't very good at talking mind-to-mind, but I'd learned enough during my brief stay with the sirens to manage it. I tried to picture El Jefe's face, tried to think of my words being written on paper and stuffed in his ear canal. I just hoped Eirene wasn't listening, or things were going to go even further south than they already had. *They had a roadblock set up. They're frisking Kevin now. I'm faking still being unconscious.*

"Do you know where you are?" Warren's voice was an urgent hiss. Yay, I got through.

Faking unconsciousness, eyes closed. Even mentally it sounded bitchy. Then again, I wasn't precisely the happiest camper at the moment.

"Celia, we have reinforcements, but they're outside the warehouse. I have to know where to send them."

I was deciding how best to go about it when I heard the first male voice give another order.

"Check the girl."

Hang up Warren, now.

The door next to me opened. If I could've moved I might have used the advantage of surprise to fight. There were obviously problems with that. First, they were armed, I wasn't. Neither was Kevin. And while *I* might want to kill him, I didn't want *them* to do it. Too, even if I got away, the same basic problem remained. They had Emma. Our best chance at getting her back was to stick with Warren and Kevin's plan. *Warren, have them use magic to trace us.*

I couldn't move, at least not well enough to fight. Warren's curse might have lifted, but the drugs hadn't worn off. I let my eyes fly open, but that was the most I could manage. I had no choice but to sit there, utterly limp, as a strange man ran his hands all over my body. I fought down a wave of rage and panic. I tried to scream, I couldn't help it. Too many memories. But all that came out was a whistling squeak that wouldn't even carry outside the car. At least this wasn't personal—some sadistic treasure hunter getting his jollies. It was just business. He was thorough, too, even to the point of running his fingers through my hair checking to make sure nothing had been hidden in it. He found the earpiece.

"She's clean. She was wearing a phone, but the line is dead and she can't talk anyway."

"You sure?"

"She tried to scream when I searched her."

"Bound?"

"Duct tape, hands and feet. Can't tell whether it's spelled or not."

"Hands in front or behind the back?"

"In front." My guy sounded disgusted by that. Apparently he was a pro and knew better. There are so many things you can do, even bound, if your hands are in front of you, and there's a much better chance of escape.

Kevin's voice came next, calm and clear. "There was no point in hurting her. It was just a precaution in case the drugs wore off more quickly than they should. Her metabolism is pretty weird. Besides," he continued, "you know as well as I do that it's hard to get the body to sit right in the car seat with the arms behind the back. I didn't want to get pulled over by the cops."

The grunt from the man next to me might have been an acknowledgment. It couldn't have been exertion from lifting me out of the car. I'm not that heavy.

He threw me over his shoulder like a sack of grain. My head hung down nearly to his waist. The drugs were wearing off, but I had a horrible case of cottonmouth and my head was throbbing in time with each of his steps, to the point where I was in real danger of tossing my cookies. That would be bad with tape over my mouth. It would be easy to choke to death. Of course, I was facedown, so likely all that would happen is that the vomit would pool my sinuses and run out my nose.

Ick.

I tried to get my bearings with no success. Two men appeared from a hiding place next to the road, which was blocked by a pair of black SUVs. The first climbed into the Miata and took off, with the SUVs trailing it. The second man strolled over to our group.

"Should've put her in the trunk."

"Have you seen what passes for the trunk of a Miata? No way she'd fit." Kevin sounded disgusted. A couple of the men laughed shortly.

There were six of them. They cuffed Kevin, using handcuffs with hefty enough spells that I could feel the magic from ten feet away. Even so, they made sure that four men surrounded him, staying out of reach, weapons at the ready. A werewolf is no laughing matter. The man carrying me stayed well back and behind him. The man from the road, with his very businesslike semiauto, followed.

The scrub brush that lined both sides of the road gave way to loose rock, sand, and cactus. We were climbing. The man carrying me was breathing hard but didn't say anything. Then again, neither did anybody else. The whole march was eerily silent; even the creatures native to this place had gone still at our approach. I was thinking hard, trying to figure out who to call for help and what landmarks to give them. There weren't any. Desert covers a lot of territory in Southern California. We were far enough away from the bulk of the city that light pollution was minimal but not so far out that there weren't still a few warehouses.

There was a definite chill to the breeze and the sky overhead was a rich indigo blue. I could see more stars than you ever catch sight of in town. I tried to find the North Star to orient myself, but it was too much effort to move my head and neck even that much. Which meant I had no freaking idea where I was. None.

Kevin, where are we?

I spoke in his mind. But it was Eirene who answered me, just before I felt a wall of power cut us off from outside help. It locked us down so that no magic, not even telepathy, would be able to penetrate.

The words she spoke raised every hair on my body: *A place where no one will hear you scream.*

25

Wow, that was nicely melodramatic. Had she been watching old movies or was that just her natural bent?

Sarcasm isn't going to save you.

No. But it'll keep me occupied while I ponder ways of kicking your ass. Hollow bragging in the face of disaster? Quite possibly. Then again, maybe not. Because I might be unarmed and physically helpless, but I wasn't completely out of options.

The guy carrying me was really struggling now. It wasn't so much the uneven ground as the sand combined with loose rocks. Made getting stable footing a bitch, which put more strain on the muscles. One of the reasons I run on the soft part of the beach is that the give in the sand works your legs harder than a firm surface does.

"Is there a problem, Barnes?"

"Nah, I've got it. At least she isn't struggling. What'd you give her anyway?"

Kevin answered cheerfully, "Combination of drugs and a curse. She can be hell on wheels when she's pissed and I didn't want to deal with it."

If we both got out of this mess alive, he sure as hell *would* be dealing with it. Thinking about going toe-to-toe with him gave me another little bit of incentive. I don't trust people, but I'd trusted him. My mistake. One I wouldn't be making again.

We stopped at the top of a rocky ridge. A narrow trail snaked down the steep incline to a narrow valley. I twisted a little and craned my neck to get as much of a look around as I could. I saw a trio of tents in a semicircle, their entrances facing a large campfire that had been surrounded by a stone ring, just like they taught us to do in Girl Scouts. My eyes shifted into vampire hyperfocus and I could see Emma's body, curled in a fetal position on the ground.

Eirene was sitting on a director's chair next to Emma's head, holding a stick into the fire. She was roasting marshmallows. *Roasting marshmallows! You have got to be fucking kidding me.*

Her voice in my head was rich with amusement: *I like toasted marshmallows. And it gave me something to do while I waited.*

What have you done to Emma?

Don't take that tone with me, Celia. You're not a princess here. Just a victim.

I'm not really a princess anywhere. And I'm nobody's victim.

We'll see about that. She looked up at us and her smile was chilling. Setting aside the roasting stick, she stood. Reaching into her pocket, she pulled out a ceramic disk about the size of a quarter. There was a sigil on it.

My blood ran cold at the sight and I fought down a wave of nausea. A summoning disk. No doubt made for the sole purpose of bringing forth a certain major demon.

You'd think I'd be used to the idea. After all, I'd been facing the demonic more than most militant priests lately. But it's just not something you *get* used to. Particularly not when you know for a fact that said demon has been making specific plans just for you.

My mouth went dry and I fought not to show just how terrified that little disk made me. Fought and failed. Because Eirene was a telepath. She could hear the fear in my mind. To my shock, the look of pure anticipatory evil it brought to her face wasn't entirely hers.

The demon. She hadn't summoned him yet, but the connection between them had reached a point where soon, very soon, she wouldn't need to. She would be his permanent open door to this dimension.

She had to be stopped. Oh hell, who was I kidding? She had to be *killed.* Because killing her was the only way to seal the breach. Unfortunately, all sirens are about as hard to kill as Stefania had been.

I was thinking all this as our merry little band made its way down the treacherous trail to the camp. As I thought, I was testing my muscles. I was beginning to be able to move. The adrenaline pumping through my system at the thought of the demon was beginning to drive off the effects of the drugs. I felt a chill breeze blow gently against me, ruffling my hair. First one, then two. Both ghosts were here?

Part of me was relieved and part of me was sad. I'd actually panicked a little when I'd woken up from the exorcism. I'd been angry at Vicki, yes. But I'd been devastated that I hadn't been able to say good-bye to Ivy. I guess in my mind, she's not really dead. It's more like she's grown up and moved on with her life and sometimes comes back to visit. And then everything's just like when we were little. The same bantering, the same old jokes. In reality, she's been a ghost for a lot longer than she was a human. I know it's best for her to move on. Maybe it's me that's keeping her here rather than her staying to finish something.

I waited until we reached a sharp turn where the track was narrowest. Kevin and all of his guards were around the bend, leaving just me and Barnes on this side. He was actually panting now. I knew he was too focused on his goal to notice the ghosts or much of anything else.

I managed to croak out a bare whisper, telling them what I wanted. "Sandstorm, on my signal." Then I began carefully working my wrists back and forth, using vampire strength to try to loosen my bindings. At first I couldn't feel any progress at all. But as we neared the campfire I felt the tiniest give.

Barnes wasn't exactly gentle, dropping me to the ground next to the fire. It knocked the wind out of me with a sharp whoosh. In a blur of movement Eirene rose from her chair, rushed to where I lay, and kicked me in the gut as hard as she could. I rolled over, curling into a ball, and gasped out the word, "Now."

I wasn't curled up from the pain, although the kick had *hurt*. But this way nobody could see me tearing my hands free. It was working. I just needed a little more time. Even with both ghosts working together, it was going to take them time to do what I wanted. If they could.

"Oh no, Cousin." Eirene raised a hand and I felt a burst of magic erupt in the air like firecrackers. "I've seen too well what your guardian spirits can do. They're not invited to this little

party." A shield dropped around the group. I knew that protection against spirits existed. Many houses in Hollywood Hills
had them, where murders and suicides had been rampant in
the early days of film.

I could *feel* Ivy racing around the boundaries of the circle,
attacking it from every angle. She was wearing herself out
quickly in her panic. But Vicki was just hovering, right where
she'd been following me.

Could ghosts *plan*? Was she still clairvoyant enough to be
biding her time, waiting for a specific event to occur?

Kevin's voice found my ears. It used to be that his voice
calmed me. Now it just made me feel cold inside. "I've done
what you asked. Give me Emma and let us go."

Bastard.

Eirene curled up one lip in a sneer. I knew damned
well she hadn't planned to let Emma go. Why would she?
"Beg me."

Even as she spoke, I felt a wind starting to build and circle,
tasted the first hint of dust on my tongue. How could that be?
I could still feel the spell. It seemed odd that Eirene hadn't
noticed the light breeze, because there shouldn't be any
wind at all inside the bubble of the casting. Or had I just
imagined it?

I stared into the pitch-darkness, looking for any hint of an
entry point. When I found it, I smiled. She'd crafted the spell
wrong, or at least hadn't made herself clear to the mage who
did. She'd made certain that nothing could get in that hadn't
been here when they dropped the curtain. She'd planned for
things trying to get in, not things trying to get *out*. The low-
liest of creatures was going to be her downfall if this worked

the way I wanted it to. A little scorpion was out for its evening hunt and they're surprisingly good diggers. One minute it was inside the shield. The next minute it was out, and two sparkling phantoms slid in along the path the insect had made. The larger spirit rose high into the air and the smaller one followed, creating the breeze I'd felt. People so seldom look up that it was a perfect place to hide in plain sight.

"What the hell are you talking about? I'm not going to beg you to do what you've already agreed to. Release Emma and let me take her." Kevin always got mad when he'd been tricked. Warren was the same way. Of course, had they involved me, I could probably have mentioned all this.

Eirene's voice was silken and unpleasant. She was really enjoying herself. "I would, but there's this little problem." Eirene turned to face him. "You failed to deal in good faith. There was a trap set up at the warehouse. If I hadn't anticipated that, this whole situation could have gone very, very wrong." She shook her head in mock sorrow. "I did warn you not to try anything. But some men just can't resist playing the hero. I've no doubt my demon friend will enjoy using your sister as an appetizer prior to the main course."

It explained the fetal ball that Emma was in. If she was actually *seeing* what was going to happen if the demon got loose . . . *dear God.*

I'd been working my hands the whole time. Finally, the tape tore. The ripping noise wasn't loud, but I held my breath, waiting to see if Eirene would notice. She didn't. She was too busy toying with Kevin.

"You *bitch.*" Kevin spit the words at her and then lunged, an inhuman growl rising from his throat.

Eirene's expression darkened. I don't know why the swearing angered her. I mean, seriously, she had to have heard it before and it certainly was richly deserved. Then again, sanity wasn't her strong suit anymore—if it ever had been. She turned to Barnes. "Shoot him. But to wound, not kill. For that insult, he gets to watch them die."

A pair of gunshots. Kevin screamed. I smelled blood and worse and my stomach heaved even as the glands at the back of my mouth tightened hungrily.

That finally pissed Vicki off. Kevin wasn't her favorite person, but there was no way in heaven or hell that she was going to let Emma be tortured by a demon.

In the space of an eyeblink the temperature dropped and a pressure vacuum sucked air upward so that it was hard to breathe. The fire guttered in an instant of utter stillness before gale-force winds drove sand and debris into a swirling vortex that blotted out the night.

"*Noooo!*" Eirene screamed as she hit at the wind uselessly. Apparently she'd realized what I already had: in order to banish the spirits, she'd have to drop the spell circle. Of course, she couldn't do that and still raise the demon, so she was quite literally screwed.

Dirt and debris peppered my face and arms, slicing away most of the hair on my skin like an electric sander. I had to narrow my eyes to slits or risk being blinded. The world had become a painful, seething brown soup inside a pressure kettle. I could barely hear Eirene's scream of rage over the howl of the sand-laden winds that staggered her like a blow. Through slitted eyes I watched her reach into her pocket, knew what she intended to do.

"*No!*" I gasped as I launched myself forward. Grabbing her ankle, I pulled with every ounce of vampire, siren, and human strength I possessed. She went down and I saw the disk fly from her fingers before her body slammed against the unforgiving earth hard enough to stun her. I used that precious instant to crawl on top of her. Sand blasted against my skin as I pulled her gun from its holster. Heavy objects were being blown now, too—sticks, rocks, and chunks of cactus slammed into my body. I could barely see. Tears were streaming down my face. But I switched off the safety and pointed the gun between those startlingly beautiful eyes.

I saw her start to regain her strength, saw realization and consciousness flow back into her eyes. And as I watched her gather herself for one last desperate fight I thought of Bruno.

Of him singing in the shower. *Her* shower.

Of him in her bed, having sex, looking down at her and smiling.

I gathered every image I could imagine of the two of them together, focusing them, making them real, until jealousy filled me like water fills a cup.

It took just a second too long. She fought with the desperation of the doomed and damned. She began clawing, kicking, and biting: raining blows on my body, bucking and squirming. She screamed out nearly unpronounceable words and I felt the barrier surrounding the encampment go down. The sudden release of pressure hit me hard, the equivalent of a pocket of turbulence on a plane ride. The wind rushed out and the sand with it.

She struck.

I cursed as she knocked the gun from my grasp. In a hand-to-hand struggle, we were almost perfectly matched. I still had the advantage; I was on top, and despite her best efforts, she couldn't get out from under me. I *felt* her call in my head as she tried to summon the men to her aid. I felt them responding, trying to get to her, despite the fury of the tornadic winds that tried to kick up the storm again. Vicki was really doing herself proud. If this didn't kill her, I'd buy her something nice. There must be something that a ghost needs.

But first, I had to survive. If Eirene succeeded in taking control of the minds of every male here, it was over: for me, for Emma, and for Kevin.

Fuck that.

I gathered my will, using everything I'd learned on Serenity to throw out my own call. Yes, it was the caw of seagulls versus the sweet melody of songbirds. But there is something very compelling about gulls and I used it to my advantage. I used the energy of my rage, hurt, and fear as fuel to power it. My mind met hers in a battle for the hearts and wills of the men we could reach. The fight was every bit as desperate as the physical battle we were fighting. I didn't feel Kevin, and even angry as I was at him, I hoped he didn't feel this, that it wouldn't control him. In fact, I only felt some of her men. Were the others dead? Gone? I didn't know. I only knew I couldn't let her control those who were left.

The power of our clashing wills was too much. I felt their minds flicker like candles in the wind, felt their sanity and will snuffed out.

No! I didn't mean to—

"You're weak, Celia!" She said the words out loud, saving her mental energy for the struggle. "You actually care for these pitiful humans." She considered my guilt a weakness and tried to use it against me. That was a mistake. Yes, I would have to live with the knowledge of what we'd just done for the rest of my life. But Eirene made the mistake of putting a person who'd been a victim in a corner. Every survivor has already been faced with a life-or-death decision and chosen life. Nothing else matters once that choice has been made.

I dived off of her, reaching for the gun.

She scrambled to her feet, but I lashed out in a vicious kick of my bound feet to her knee. Even over the wind I heard the grinding wet pop as it bent backward and tore. She screamed in agony, swallowing sand as she did.

I had the gun. I turned, watching as she crawled away from me as fast as she could manage.

It was hard to see but not as hard as it had been. The winds were dying down. Vicki and Ivy had worn themselves out. I could see Eirene well enough to aim. So I did. I aimed my weapon and thought of Bruno locked in a postcoital embrace with her. I embraced my jealousy. Then I pulled the trigger.

26

I lay on the ground for long minutes, utterly exhausted. The barrier was down. Which meant I could call for help. If only I had the energy. But my mind was as exhausted as my body. My head hurt and at the same time felt strangely empty. The power I'd come to recognize and use these past few weeks was gone. Maybe forever.

I looked around the encampment. Moon- and starlight illuminated a strange and eerie scene. Everything was coated with dust and debris. The dome tents had been pulled up from the ground to roll where they would. One of them was upside down, pressed up against a rock outcropping.

One of the men was lying on his back, breathing but utterly limp, his eyes wide open and empty staring at the night sky. Another sat up, drool tracking from his mouth through the coating of dust that covered a face that was vacant of any semblance of intellect.

I felt a new wave of guilt and my stomach lurched. I did that. At least part of it. I didn't feel guilty about killing Eirene. But this, oh, God, yes.

Movement and moaning to my left. I turned to see Kevin

struggling to free himself of the enveloping sand, some of which was wet and stained dark with his blood. His motions were getting slower with each beat of his heart. Not far from him, Emma stirred. She was coated with dust but not buried, whether from a trick of the winds or by Vicki's and Ivy's deliberate action I had no clue.

I didn't have the energy to stand, even if my feet weren't still bound. But I had to try to help. Yeah, I was mad at him . . . furious, in fact. But it was his sister he'd been trying to save.

So I started dragging myself toward him. I was halfway there when I heard the sound of a helicopter approaching fast.

Help? I hoped so. I didn't have any more fight left in me.

I was digging out a very limp and barely breathing Kevin with my bare hands when the chopper landed. I shouted for a medic and was rewarded by running footsteps. Men in blackface and camo pushed me out of the way so that more men with medical equipment could get to work.

Someone knelt beside me. It took me a minute to realize it was Creede. Pulling a knife from his pocket, he sawed silently at the tape that bound my legs. How had he gotten here? Wasn't he supposed to be at the visitation?

He answered my questions before I could even voice them.

"When things went south, Warren called Bruno on his cell. We worked together with Dottie to find you. Bruno refused to come with us at first. Said he couldn't face you." His voice was flat and inflectionless, but his eyes told a different story.

"Thanks." Not for making Bruno come but for . . . oh, hell, he knew what for.

We sat and watched as Kevin was loaded onto a stretcher.

They seemed to know what they were doing. They already had a couple of IVs hooked up to him and were rushing him toward the helicopter, Warren running beside him. He was a werewolf. Bad as it was, with the right medical attention he could probably heal it. Of course he'd be outed at any regular hospital. Which would mean a life sentence in the state facility.

Another medical type was kneeling next to Emma. At a murmured word from Kevin Warren left his son and hurried to where she lay. Warren took her in his arms, holding her close, tears streaming down his face. At first she didn't react at all. Then her arms moved, snaking around his neck.

"Are you okay?" Creede was looking at me oddly. Had he been talking to me the whole time? Maybe. Probably.

"Hell, no." I sounded weak, damn it. I forced a little more energy into the next line: "But I will be." A thought occurred to me. There was something terribly important that needed to be done right now. "John, I need you to do something."

"What?"

"Eirene had a disk to summon the demon. She dropped it in our fight. Can you use your magic to find it? We need to recover it, get it to the priests. I don't trust these other guys not to take it, maybe even use it."

He started to swear. "I'm on it." He folded his knife, putting it back into his pocket, and rose. "Approximately where should I start?"

I pointed in the general direction of where I'd seen it fall. I watched his face still, taking on an expression of calm concentration. Power washed across my other senses in a surprisingly gentle wave. Then again, he wasn't trying to do anything, just sense the latent magical energy contained in the disk. I watched for a few minutes as he paced back and forth.

I was still watching when I felt Bruno approach.

He stopped a couple of feet away, squatting down so that we'd be eye-to-eye if I looked at him. He waited for me to look. Willed me to do it. And while I didn't want to, in the end I gave in.

"Are you all right?"

Stupid question. Did I *look* all right? But it's what you say. Hell, it's what Creede had said just a minute ago. So why did hearing it from Bruno make me angry? Because I was angry. So very angry.

"I will be."

"Celie . . ." Whatever he had to say, I didn't want to hear it. I just didn't. I couldn't talk to him right now. I was too hurt, too raw from everything that had happened, from everything I'd done. Maybe if he'd rushed over and taken me in his arms like they do in those stupid, romantic movies. But he hadn't. He'd gone to *Irene's* body. Maybe I wasn't supposed to notice, but I did.

I knew Bruno loved me. Loves me. But he loved her, too. It was plain in the anger and hurt in his face as he'd looked back at her and then at me. And I wasn't ready to deal with that.

"Don't, Bruno. Please. Just . . . don't."

I don't know if he would've listened if Creede's voice hadn't interrupted us. "I'm not finding it. DeLuca, get your ass over here."

Bruno rose to his feet in a smooth movement. He didn't say anything, but the look he gave me promised that we'd be having a long conversation soon. Maybe we would; then again, maybe not.

I didn't watch them any longer. Turning away, I saw Warren holding Emma, an echo of the pietà. I hoped she'd be all right. Hoped it was all worth it. Because the cost had been so hideously high. Eirene needed to die, I truly believed that. But those men . . . and I didn't even want to think about Kevin and what would happen at any hospital they might take him to. Even if they saved his life, he'd be put in the state asylum. I wouldn't wish that on my worst enemy.

I knew why Kevin and Warren did what they'd done. But that didn't make it hurt any less. What a frickin' mess. There were bound to be legal repercussions; I doubted even Kevin's "company" could sweep this much crap under the rug. If they didn't, I was so screwed.

In the distance I could hear the chopper coming back. A little bit of dust stirred and I shivered, more from memory than cold. Although, come to think on it, it was a little chilly.

One of the medics finally made it over to me. He squatted down a little ways from me, much as Bruno had done. "How you doin'?" he asked in a voice that was pure Jersey. It was even worse than Bruno's cousin Little Joey, which was saying something.

It made me smile, for no reason at all.

"You with me? Having trouble focusing?" The medic flicked a penlight in my eyes. It hurt and I found myself hissing.

He saw the fangs and jerked back his hands. "Sorry."

"S'all right."

"You're Graves, then. My name's Gaetano. We were told you've got vampire healing?" He made it a question.

"Yeah. But I do better when I've eaten and it's been a while. I need to eat more when I push myself, too."

"You had a pretty tough time here. You having any blood-lust?" He sounded so calm about it. Matter-of-fact, as if he dealt with that sort of thing all the time. How bizarre.

"Not yet."

He gave me a crooked smile. "I'd like to keep it that way. Let's get you out of here so you can get something to eat." He rose, extending his hand. I took it and he pulled me to my feet. With his help, I was able to walk to the helicopter.

27

I sat on the front porch of my grandmother's . . . no, wait, *my* house, watching the sun set. As always, Gran was in the old metal rocker. I'd brought out one of her kitchen chairs. We were drinking margaritas strong enough to knock a mule on its ass. I'd never known my gran to drink. But she hadn't needed directions to make the drinks. We'd agreed to get together and celebrate the sale of the house going through

She'd been oddly quiet for nearly an hour now. Well, maybe not so oddly. She loves this house. She and Gramps had moved here right after they got married. But it wasn't as if she were moving out. I wouldn't do that to her and I'd told her so.

"I spoke to your mother this morning." Gran took a long pull of her drink. She sounded odd. Sad. Of course she'd been like that a lot lately, as the realization sank in that Mom's case was pretty much hopeless.

"She told me she's taking the plea bargain. She doesn't want me spending any more of my money on her defense."

I stared at her. I know my jaw was hanging open. I shut it and stammered a little, trying to wrap my head around the implications of what she'd just said. "B-but . . . if you knew that, why did you sell? We could've canceled it."

She shook her head and then patted my hand like she had when I'd first asked her about dating—that little pat that said, *There's so much you don't understand, sweetie.* "You need a place to live, Celie. A solid place of your own where you can settle in and feel safe. This house isn't anything fancy, but you can hear the ocean in the mornings and its always been a safe place for you. Right now you need that."

Really, I couldn't do this to her. I couldn't. "But Gran—"

She talked over the top of me. "This old place was getting to be too much for me anyway. I can't hardly keep up with the yard work and you just can't find kids willing to mow or pick weeds like you used to. Used to be kids wanted to earn money. Now they just spend their parents'." She shook her head and took another drink.

I didn't know what to say. I couldn't think. She was leaving? Was she sick? "I was talking to some of the other church ladies and there's a real nice senior apartment complex over on Sherman Road. It's got a shuttle to church every Sunday and once a week to the grocery stores and the mall. It's right on the bus line, too, so I still can get out and about if I want to. And no, I'm not sick."

Was she telepathic? Or did she just know me that well? "You've been thinking about this for a while."

She nodded. "A bit. Since before Lana got in trouble this last time. But I didn't want to give up the house and I . . . well, I know it'll sound silly to you, but . . . I wanted her to have a home to come back to if she needed it."

It didn't sound silly. It sounded sad. Heartbreaking. My

throat got tight just hearing her say it. I couldn't talk and I blinked back tears. She saw that and gave me a sad smile.

"You haven't talked much about Bruno these past couple days. Still haven't ironed things out?"

It was my turn to stare out at the flowers for a long moment. A thousand thoughts and emotions ran through me. "I'm not sure we can."

"She lied to him, Celie. She was a siren; she befuddled his mind and she lied. That's not his fault. He was trying to do the right thing, the honorable thing."

"Yeah, Gran, I know. But that's not really the problem." I'd figured out what was really bugging me. "It's that he didn't include me in the decision. We'd been thinking of a future together, planning to give it another try. When she told him, he could have called me. It's not like I hadn't known there might be someone else in his life. We could have tried to come up with options, tried to work something out. Maybe adopting the baby, my being a stepmom. Or me moving east so he could be part of raising the kid. Oh, I know Eirene wouldn't have gone along with it, even if there had really been a baby. But I would've been part of the process. Instead, he made the decision by himself and walked away. He thinks that's okay. Maybe it is for some people. But not for me."

She sighed. "I understand. But I hate to see you hurting, punkin. I really do. Have you at least talked to Kevin and the Professor?"

It was my turn to sigh. Kevin had survived and wasn't in a cage. The men who'd rescued us were from his employer and they'd taken him to one of their private medical facilities. Emma had told me. She'd thought I'd want to know.

"No, Gran. I haven't talked to them. And I'm not going to. I'll visit Emma. None of this was her fault. But not Kevin and not Warren. That's over."

Gran didn't ask about Creede, and frankly, I wouldn't have known what to say if she had. He'd gone back to the business and thrown himself into work. Miller was gone, but Creede wanted to keep the Miller & Creede name intact. He'd probably find another partner, but he said he had to try to give his friend's torture and death some meaning. It was noble of him, I suppose. But I hadn't heard from him since that night. Maybe I never would again. And maybe that was best.

The phone rang just then. I glanced at the caller ID display. It was Alex. Was I ready to talk to her yet or was even that too much right now? I let it ring again while I decided.

I put the ringing phone on the railing and took another sip of lime and tequila. Maybe tomorrow. Right now, I was out of energy.

Another long sigh from Gran punctuated the final ring before the call went to voice mail. "Baby, you need to accept that people aren't perfect. They make mistakes. And when they do, you have to forgive them. And you need to forgive yourself, too. Maybe that most of all."

"I'm not sure I can. I did . . . things." I hadn't told her about most of what had happened in the desert. I hadn't wanted to burden her, for one thing. But I was still ashamed. What Eirene and I did to those men was horrible. I hadn't even tried to check on them. I was afraid of what I'd find out. I'm not normally that chicken, but there are some things a person is better off not knowing. Besides, my only contact to that crew was Kevin. I did find it rather ominous that I hadn't heard so much as a peep on the news. Or from the police. Another good reason not to answer phones.

I may not have told her what had happened, but my gran is no fool. She gave me a penetrating look, speaking slowly, choosing her words very carefully. "You did things. Maybe terrible things. But you are not a bad person. I know that to my very soul. You did what you had to do to survive. You defended yourself and you saved Emma Landingham. God knows there's evil in this world. I've seen it. You've seen it."

No shit, I'd seen evil. Unfortunately, I probably would again. Creede and Bruno couldn't find the summoning disk. Had someone taken it during the confusion, or had it buried itself so as not to be found until at the right time?

A shudder overtook me as Gran continued, "But *you're* not evil, Celie. Give it time. It'll get better if you let it. But you've got to forgive yourself, learn what you can from it, and let it go." She let out a deep sigh and it was enough to break my heart. "Because life doesn't stop, baby. Not for you, not for anybody. And that's a fact."